COME RACK, COME ROPE

CLUNY CLASSICS

RICCARDO BACCHELLI
The Mill on the Po: God Save You (BOOK ONE)
The Mill on the Po: Misery (BOOK TWO)
The Mill on the Po: Nothing New Under the Sun (BOOK THREE)

ROBERT HUGH BENSON
Come Rack, Come Rope
Dawn of All
The Light Invisible
None Other Gods

GEORGES BERNANOS
A Bad Dream
Joy
Under the Sun of Satan

ORESTES BROWNSON
Like a Roaring Lion

MALACHY G. CARROLL
The Stranger

G. K. CHESTERTON
A Chesterton Reader

MYLES CONNOLLY
The Bump on Brannigan's Head
Dan England and the Noonday Devil
Mr. Blue
The Reason for Ann & Other Stories
Three Who Ventured

ALICE CURTAYNE
House of Cards

GERTRUD VON LE FORT
The Pope from the Ghetto
The Veil of Veronica

JOSÉ MARÍA GIRONELLA
The Cypresses Believe in God (VOLUME ONE)
The Cypresses Believe in God (VOLUME TWO)

RUMER GODDEN
A Breath of Air
Five for Sorrow, Ten for Joy
In This House of Brede

CAROLINE GORDON
The Life and Passion of Aleck Maury
The Malefactors

NATHANIEL HAWTHORNE
The Shattered Fountain: Selected Tales

ELISABETH LANGGÄSSER
The Quest

FRANÇOIS MAURIAC
The Dark Angels
The Desert of Love
Genetrix
A Kiss for the Leper
The Lamb
The River of Fire
The Unknown Sea
Vipers' Tangle
What Was Lost

DOROTHY L. SAYERS
Whose Body?

IGNAZIO SILONE
Fontamara
Bread and Wine
The Seed Beneath the Snow

SIGRID UNDSET
The Burning Bush
The Wild Orchid
Four Stories
Images in a Mirror
Madame Dorthea

LEO L. WARD
Men in the Field: Eighteen Short Stories

COME RACK, COME ROPE

A Novel

Robert Hugh Benson

CLUNY
Providence, Rhode Island

Cluny Media edition, 2017

For information regarding this title
or any other Cluny Media publication,
please write to info@clunymedia.com, or to
Cluny Media, P.O. Box 1664, Providence, RI 02901

VISIT US ONLINE AT WWW.CLUNYMEDIA.COM

Cluny Media edition copyright © 2017 Cluny Media LLC

All rights reserved

ISBN: 978-1944418427

Cover design by Clarke & Clarke
Cover image: Caspar David Friedrich, *Walk at Dusk*,
between 1830 and 1835, oil on canvas
Courtesy of Wikimedia Commons

CONTENTS

Part One   ✣ ✣   1

Part Two   ✣ ✣   90

Part Three   ✣ ✣   184

Part Four   ✣ ✣   253

PART ONE

CHAPTER I

I

THERE should be no sight more happy than a young man riding to meet his love. His eyes should shine, his lips should sing; he should slap his mare upon her shoulder and call her his darling. The puddles upon his way should be turned to pure gold, and the stream that runs beside him should chatter her name.

Yet, as Robin rode to Marjorie none of these things were done. It was a still day of frost; the sky was arched above him, across the high hills—hard blue from horizon to horizon; the fringe of feathery birches stood like filigree-work above him on his left; on his right ran the Derwent, sucking softly among his sedges; on this side and that lay the flat bottom through which he went—meadowland broken by rushes; his mare Cecily stepped along, now cracking the thin ice of the little pools with her dainty feet, now going gently over peaty ground, blowing thin clouds from her red nostrils, yet unencouraged by word or caress from her rider, who sat, heavy and all but slouching, staring with his blue eyes under puckered eyelids, as if he went to an appointment which he would not keep.

Yet he was a very pleasant lad to look upon, smooth-faced and gallant. He wore great gauntlets on his hands; he was in his habit of green; he had his steel-buckled leather belt upon him beneath his cloak and a pair of daggers in it, with his long-sword looped up; he had his felt hat on his head, buckled again, and decked with half a pheasant's tail; he had his long boots of undressed leather, that rose above his knees; and on his left wrist sat his grim falcon Agnes, hooded and belled, not because he rode after game, but from mere custom, and to give her the air.

He was meeting his first man's trouble.

Last year he had said goodbye to Derby Grammar School. Here he had done the right and usual things; he had learned his grammar; he had fought; he had been chastised; he had robed the effigy of his pious founder in a patched doublet with a saucepan on his head (but that had been done before he had learned veneration)—and so had gone home again to Matstead, proficient in Latin, English, history, writing, good manners, and chess, to live with his father, to hunt, to hear Mass when a priest was within reasonable distance, to compose painful letters now and then on matters of the estate, and to learn how to bear himself generally as should one of Master's rank—the son of a gentleman who bore arms, and his father's father before him. He dined at twelve, he supped at six, he said his prayers, and blessed himself when no strangers were by. He was something of a herbalist, as a sheer hobby of his own; he went to feed his falcons in the morning, he rode with them after dinner (from last August he had found himself riding north more often than south, since Marjorie lived in that quarter); and now all had been crowned last Christmas Eve, when in the enclosed garden at her house he had kissed her two hands suddenly, and made her a little speech he had learned by heart; after which he kissed her on the lips as a man should, in the honest noon sunlight.

Marjorie was an only daughter as he an only son. Her father, it is true, was but a Derby lawyer, but he and his wife had a good little estate above the Hathersage valley, and a stone house in it. As for religion, that was all well too. Master Manners was as good a Catholic as Master Audrey himself; and the families met at Mass perhaps as much as four or five times in the year, either at Padley, where Sir Thomas' chapel still had priests coming and going; sometimes at Dethick in the Babingtons' barn; sometimes as far north as Harewood.

And now a man's trouble was come upon the boy. The cause of it was as follows.

Robin Audrey was no more religious than a boy of seventeen should be. His mother had taught him well, up to the time of her death ten years ago; and he had learned from her, as well as from his father, that there were two kinds of religion in the world, the true and the false—that is to say, the Catholic religion and the other one. Certainly there were shades of differences in the other one; yet these distinctions were subtle and negligible; they were all swallowed up in an unity of falsehood. Next he had learned that the Catholic religion was at present blown upon by many persons in high position; that pains and penalties lay upon all who adhered to it. Sir Thomas FitzHerbert, for instance, lay now in the Fleet in London on that very account. His own father, too, three or four times in the year, was under necessity of paying over heavy sums for the privilege of not attending Protestant worship; and, indeed, had been forced last year to sell a piece of land over on Lees Moor for this very purpose. All this was in his bones and blood. One took one's precautions, one hoped for the best; and one was quite sure that one day the happy ancient times his mother had told him of would come back, and Christ's cause be vindicated.

And now the foundations of the earth were moved and heaven reeled above him; for his father, after a month or two of brooding, had announced, on St. Stephen's Day, that he could tolerate it no longer; that God's demands were unreasonable; that, after all, the Protestant religion was the religion of her Grace, that men must learn to move with the times, and that he had paid his last fine. At Easter, he observed, he would take the bread and wine in Matstead Church, and Robin would take them too.

II

THE sun stood halfway towards his setting as Robin rode up from the valley, past Padley, over the steep ascent that led towards Booth's

Edge. The boy was brighter a little as he came up; he had counted above eighty snipe within the last mile and a half, and he was coming near to Marjorie. About him, rising higher as he rose, stood the great low-backed hills. Cecily stepped out more sharply, snuffing delicately, for she knew her way well enough by now, and looked for a feed; and the boy's perplexities stood off from him a little. Matters must surely be better so soon as Marjorie's clear eyes looked upon them.

Then the roofs of Padley disappeared behind him, and he saw the smoke going up from the little timbered Hall, standing back against its bare wind-blown trees.

A great clatter and din of barking broke out as the mare's hoofs sounded on the half-paved space before the great door; and then, in the pause, a gaggling of geese, solemn and earnest, from out of sight. Jacob led the outcry, a great mastiff, chained by the entrance. Then two harriers whipped round the corner, and a terrier's head showed itself over the wall of the herb-garden on the left, as a man, bareheaded, in his shirt and breeches, ran out suddenly with a thonged whip, in time to meet a pair of spaniels in full career. Robin sat on his horse silently till peace was restored, his right leg flung across the pommel, untwisting Agnes' leash from his fist. Then he asked for Mistress Marjorie, and dropped to the ground, leaving his mare and falcon in the man's hands.

He flicked his fingers to growling Jacob as he went past to the side entrance on the east, stepped in through the little door that was beside the great one, and passed on as he had been bidden into the little court, turned to the left, went up an outside staircase, and so down a little passage to the ladies' parlour, where he knocked upon the door. The voice he knew called to him from within; and he went in, smiling to himself. Then he took the girl who awaited him there in both his arms, and kissed her twice—first her hands and then her lips, for respect should come first and ardour second.

"My love," said Robin, and threw off his hat with the pheasant's tail, for coolness' sake.

It was a sweet room this which he already knew by heart; for it was here that he had sat with Marjorie and her mother, silent and confused, evening after evening, last autumn; it was here, too, that she had led him last Christmas Eve, scarcely ten days ago, after he had kissed her in the enclosed garden. But the low frosty sunlight lay in it now, upon the blue painted wainscot that rose half up the walls, the tall presses where the linen lay, the pieces of stuff, embroidered with pale lutes and wreaths that Mistress Manners had bought in Derby, hanging now over the plaster spaces. There was a chimney, too, newly built, that was thought a great luxury; and in it burned an armful of logs, for the girl was setting out new linen for the household, and the scents of lavender and burning wood disputed the air between them.

"I thought it would be you," she said, "when I heard the dogs."

She piled the last rolls of linen in an ordered heap, and came to sit beside him. Robin took one hand in his and sat silent.

She was of an age with him, perhaps a month the younger; and, as it ought to be, was his very contrary in all respects. Where he was fair, she was pale and dark; his eyes were blue, hers black; he was lusty and showed promise of broadness, she was slender.

"And what news do you bring with you now?" she said presently.

He evaded this.

"Mistress Manners?" he asked.

"Mother has a megrim," she said; "she is in her chamber." And she smiled at him again. For these two, as is the custom of young persons who love one another, had said not a word on either side—neither he to his father nor she to her parents. They believed, as young persons do, that parents who bring children into the world, hold it as a chief danger that these children should follow their example, and themselves be married. Besides, there is something delicious in secrecy.

"Then I will kiss you again," he said, "while there is opportunity."

Making love is a very good way to pass the time. He spoke of a hundred things that were of no importance: of the dress that she wore—russet, as it should be, for country girls, with the loose sleeves folded back above her elbows that she might handle the linen; her apron of coarse linen, her steel-buckled shoes. He told her that he loved her better in that than in her costume of state—the ruff, the brocaded petticoat, and all the rest. He talked then, of Tuesday seven-night, when they would meet for hawking in the lower chase of the Padley estates; and proceeded then to speak of Agnes, whom he had left on the fist of the man who had taken his mare, of her increasing infirmities and her crimes of crabbing; and all the while he held her left hand in both of his, and fitted her fingers between his, and kissed them again when he had no more to say on any one point; and wondered why he could not speak of the matter on which he had come, and how he should tell her. And then at last she drew it from him.

"And now, my Robin," she said, "tell me what you have in your mind. You have talked of this and that and Agnes and Jock, and Padley chase, and you have not once looked me in the eyes since you first came in."

Now it was not shame that had held him from telling her, but rather a kind of bewilderment. The affair might hold shame, indeed, or anger, or sorrow, or complacence, but he did not know; and he wished, as young men of decent birth should wish, to present the proper emotion on its right occasion. He had pondered on the matter continually since his father had spoken to him on St. Stephen's night; and at one time it seemed that his father was acting the part of a traitor and at another of a philosopher. If it were indeed true, after all, that all men were turning Protestant, and that there was not so much difference between the two religions, then it would be the act of a wise man to turn Protestant too, if only for a while. And on the other hand his pride of birth and his education by his mother and his practice ever since drew him hard the other way. He did not know what to think, and he feared what Marjorie might think.

"How did you know I had anything in my mind?" he asked. "Is it not enough reason for my coming that you should be here?"

She laughed softly, with a pleasant scornfulness.

"I read you like a printed book," she said. "What else are women's wits given them for?"

He fell to stroking her hand again at that, but she drew it away.

"Not until you have told me," she said.

So then he told her.

It was a long tale, for it began as far ago as last August, when his father had come back from giving evidence before the justices at Derby on a matter of witchcraft, and had been questioned again about his religion. It was then that Robin had seen moodiness succeed to anger, and long silence to moodiness. He told the tale with a true lover's art, for he watched her face and trained his tone and his manner as he saw her thoughts come and go in her eyes and lips, like gusts of wind across standing corn; and at last he told her outright what his father had said to him on St. Stephen's night, and how he himself had kept silence.

Marjorie's face flamed up bright and rosy as he finished.

"You kept silence!" she cried.

"I did not wish to anger him, my dear; he is my father," he said gently.

The colour died out of her face again and she nodded once or twice, and a great pensiveness came down on her. He took her hand again softly, and she did not resist.

"The only doubt," she said presently, as if she talked to herself, "is whether you had best be gone at Easter, or stay and face it out."

"Yes," said Robin, with his dismay come fully to the birth.

Then she turned on him, full of a sudden tenderness and compassion.

"Oh! my Robin," she cried, "and I have not said a word about you and your own misery. I was thinking but of Christ's honour. You must forgive me... What must it be for you!... That it should be your father! You are sure that he means it?"

"My father does not speak until he means it. He is always like that. He asks counsel from no one. He thinks and he thinks, and then he speaks; and it is finished."

She fell then to thinking again, her sweet lips compressed

together, and her eyes frightened and wondering, searching round the hanging above the chimney-breast. (It presented Icarus in the chariot of the sun; and it was said in Derby that it had come from my lord Abbot's lodging at Bolton.)

Meantime Robin thought too. He was as wax in the hands of this girl, and knew it, and loved that it should be so. Yet he could not help his dismay while he waited for her seal to come down on him and stamp him to her model. For he foresaw more clearly than ever now the hundred inconveniences that must follow, now that it was evident that to Marjorie's mind (and therefore to God Almighty's) there must be no tampering with the old religion. He had known that it must be so; yet he had thought, on the way here, of a dozen families he knew who, in his own memory, had changed from allegiance to the Pope of Rome to that of her Grace, without seeming one penny the worse. There were the Martins, down there in Derby; the Squire and his lady of Ashenden Hall; the Conways of Matlock; and the rest—these had all changed; and though he did not respect them for it, yet the truth was that they were not yet stricken by thunderbolts or eaten by the plague. He had wondered whether there were not a way to do as they had done, yet without the disgrace of it... However, this was plainly not to be so with him.

She turned to him again at last. Twice her lips opened to speak, and twice she closed them again. The third time she spoke.

"I think you must go away," she said, "for Easter. Tell your father that you cannot change your religion simply because he tells you so. I do not see what else is to be done. He will think, perhaps, that if you have a little time to think you will come over to him. Well, that is not so, but it may make it easier for him to believe it for a while... You must go somewhere where there is a priest.... Where can you go?"

Robin considered.

"I could go to Dethick," he said.

"That is not far enough away, I think."

"I could come here," he suggested artfully.

A smile lit in her eyes, shone in her mouth, and passed again into seriousness.

"That is scarcely a mile further," she said. "We must think.... Will he be very angry, Robin?"

Robin smiled grimly.

"I have never withstood him in a great affair," he said. "He is angry enough over little things."

"Poor Robin!"

"Oh! he is not unjust to me. He is a good father to me."

"That makes it all the sadder," she said.

"And there is no other way?" he asked presently.

She glanced at him.

"Unless you would withstand him to the face. Would you do that, Robin?"

"I will do anything you tell me," he said simply.

"You darling!... Well, Robin, listen to me. It is very plain that sooner or later you will have to withstand him. You cannot go away every time there is communion at Matstead, or, indeed, every Sunday. Your father would have to pay the fines for you, I have no doubt, unless you went away altogether. But I think you had better go away for this time. He will almost expect it, I think. At first he will think that you will yield to him; and then, little by little (unless God's grace brings himself back to the Faith), he will learn to understand that you will not. But it will be easier for him that way; and he will have time to think what to do with you, too.... Robin, what would you do if you went away?"

Robin considered again.

"I can read and write," he said. "I am a Latinist. I can train falcons and hounds and break horses. I do not know if there is anything else that I can do."

"You darling!" she said again.

These two were as simple as children, and as serious. How could they ever wed if Robin were to quarrel with his father? There was the religion which was in their bones and blood—the religion for which already they had suffered and their fathers before them. There was the honour and loyalty which this new and more personal suffering demanded now louder than ever; and in Marjorie at least there was a strong love of Jesus Christ and His Mother, whom she knew, from her hidden crucifix and her beads, and her Jesus Psalter—which she used every day—as well as in her own soul—to be wandering together once more among the hills of Derbyshire, sheltering, at peril of Their lives, in stables and barns and little secret chambers, because there was no room for Them in Their own places. It was this last consideration, as Robin had begun to guess, that stood strongest in the girl; it was this, too, as again he had begun to guess, that made her all that she was to him, that gave her that strange serious air of innocence and sweetness, and drew from him a love that was nine-tenths reverence and adoration.

So then they sat and considered and talked. They did not speak much of her Grace, nor of her Grace's religion, nor of her counsellors and affairs of state: these things were but toys and vanities compared with matters of love and faith; neither did they speak much of the Commissioners that had been to Derbyshire once and would come again, or of the alarms and the dangers and the priest hunters, since those things did not at present touch them very closely. It was rather of Robin's father, and whether and when the maid should tell her parents, and how this new trouble would conflict with their love. They spoke, that is to say, of their own business and of God's; and of nothing else. The frosty sunshine crept down the painted wainscot and lay at last at their feet, reddening to rosiness....

III

ROBIN rode away at last with a very clear idea of what he was to do in the immediate present, and with no idea at all of what was to be done later. Marjorie had given him three things—advice, a pair of beads that had been the property of Mr. Guthbert Maine, seminary priest, recently executed in Cornwall for his religion, and a kiss—the first deliberate, free-will kiss she had ever given him. The first he was to keep, the second he was to return, the third he was to remember; and these three things, or, rather, his consideration of them, worked upon him as he went. Her advice, besides that which has been described, was, principally, to say his Jesus Psalter more punctually, to hear Mass whenever that were possible, to trust in God, and to be patient and submissive with his father in all things that did not touch divine love and faith. The pair of beads that were once Mr. Maine's, he was to keep upon him always, day and night, and to use them for his devotions. The kiss—well, he was to remember this, and to return it to her upon their next meeting.

A great star came out as he drew near home. His path took him not through the village, but behind it, near enough for him to hear the barkings of the dogs and to smell upon the frosty air the scent of the wood fires. The house was a great one for these parts. There was a small gatehouse before it, built by his father for dignity, with a lodge on either side and an arch in the middle, and beyond this lay the short road, straight and broad, that went up to the court of the house. This court was, on three sides of it, buildings; the hall and the buttery and the living rooms in the midst, with the stables and falconry on the left, and the servants' lodgings on the right; the fourth side, that which lay opposite to the little gatehouse, was a wall, with a great double gate in it, hung on stone posts that had, each of them, a great stone dog that held a blank shield. All this, the wall with the gate, the stables and the servants' lodgings, as well as the gatehouse without, had been built by the lad's father twenty years ago, to bring home his wife to; for, until that time, the house had been but a little place, though built of stone, and solid and good enough. The house stood halfway up the rise of the hill, above the village, with woods about it and behind it; and it was above these woods behind that the great star came out; and Robin looked at it, and fell to thinking of Marjorie again, putting all other thoughts away. Then, as he rode through into the court on to the cobbled stones, a man ran out from the stable to take his mare from him.

"Master Babington is here," he said. "He came half an hour ago."

"He is in the hall?"

"Yes, sir; they are at supper."

The hall at Matstead was such as that of most esquires of means. Its dais was to the south end, and the buttery entrance and the screens to the north, through which came the servers with the meat. In the midst of the floor stood the reredos with the fire against it, and a round vent overhead in the roof through which went the smoke and came the rain. The tables stood down the hall, one on either side, with the master's table at the dais end set crossways. It was not a great hall, though that was its name; it ran perhaps forty feet by twenty. It was lighted, not only by the fire that burned there through the winter day and night, but by eight torches in cressets that hung against the walls and sadly smoked them; and the master's table was lighted by six candles, of latten on common days and of silver upon festivals.

There were but two at the master's table this evening, Mr. Audrey himself, a smallish, high-shouldered man, ruddy-faced, with bright blue eyes like his son's, and no hair upon his face (for this was the way of old men then, in the country, at least); and Mr. Anthony Babington, a young man scarcely a year older than Robin himself, of a brown complexion and a high look in his face, but a little pale, too, with study, for he was learned beyond his years and read all the books that he could lay hand to. It was said even that his own verses, and a prose-lament he had written upon the Death of a Hound, were read with pleasure in London by the lords and gentlemen. It was as long ago as '71, that his verses had first become known, when he was still serving in the school of good manners as page in my Lord Shrewsbury's household. They were considered remarkable for so young a boy. So it was to this company that Robin came, walking up between the tables after he had washed his hands at the lavatory that stood by the screens.

"You are late, lad," said his father.

"I was over to Padley, sir.... Good-day, Anthony."

Then silence fell again, for it was the custom in good houses to keep silence, or very nearly, at dinner and supper. At times music would play, if there was music to be had; or a scholar would read from a book for awhile at the beginning, from the holy gospels in devout households, or from some other grave book. But if there were neither music nor reading, all would hold their tongues.

Robin was hungry from his riding and the keen air; and he ate well. First he stayed his appetite a little with a bunch of cheat-bread, and a glass of wine, while the servant was bringing him his entry of eggs cooked with parsley. Then he ate this; and next came half a wild-duck cooked with sage and sweet potatoes; and last of all a florentine which he ate with a cup of Canarian. He ate heartily and quickly, while the two waited for him and nibbled at marzipan. Then, when the doors were flung open and the troop of servants came in to their supper, Mr. Audrey blessed himself, and for them, too; and they went out by a door behind into the wainscoted parlour, where the conserves and muscadel awaited them. For this, or like it, had been the procedure in Matstead hall ever since Robin could remember, when first he had come from the women to eat his food with the men.

"And how were all at Booth's Edge?" asked Mr. Audrey, when all had pulled off their boots in country fashion, and were sitting each with his glass beside him.

"I saw Marjorie only, sir," said the boy. "Mr. Manners was in Derby, and Mrs. Manners had a megrim."

"Mrs. Manners is ageing swifter than her husband," observed Anthony.

There seemed a constraint upon the company this evening. Robin spoke of his ride, of things which he had seen upon it, of a wood that should be thinned next year; and Anthony made a quip or two such as he was accustomed to make; but the master sat silent for the most part, speaking to the lads once or twice for civility's sake, but no more. And presently silences began to fall, that were very unusual things in Mr. Anthony's company, for he had a quick and a gay wit, and talked enough for five. Robin knew very well what was the matter; it was what lay upon his own heart as heavy as lead; but he was sorry that the signs of it should be so evident, and wondered what he should say to his friend Anthony when the time came for telling; since Anthony was as ardent for the old Faith as any in the land. It was a bitter time, this, for the old families that served God as their fathers had, and desired to serve their prince too; for, now and again, the rumour would go abroad that another house had fallen, and another name gone from the old roll. And what would Anthony Babington say, thought the lad, when he heard that Mr. Audrey, who had been so hot and persevered so long, must be added to these?

An agony seized upon Robin lest his father should say all that was in his mind. He knew it must be said; yet he feared its saying, and with a quick wit he spoke of that which he knew would divert his friend.

"And the Queen of the Scots," he said. "Have you heard more of her?"

Now Anthony Babington was one of those spirits that live largely within themselves, and therefore see that which is without through a haze or mist of their own moods. He read much in the poets; you would say that Vergil and Ovid, as well as the poets of his own day, were his friends; he lived within, surrounded by his own images, and therefore he loved and hated with ten times the ardour of a common man. He was furious for the Old Faith, furious against the new; he dreamed of wars and gallantry and splendour; you could see it even in his dress, in his furred doublet, the embroideries at his throat, his silver rapier, as well as in his port and countenance: and the burning heart of all his images, the mirror on earth of Mary in heaven, the emblem of his piety, the mistress of his dreams—she who embodied for him what the courtiers in London protested that Elizabeth embodied for them—the pearl of great price, the one among ten thousand—this, for him, was Mary Stuart, Queen of Scotland, now prisoner in her cousin's hands, going to and fro from house to house, with a guard about her, yet with all the seeming of liberty and none of its reality....

The rough bitterness died out of the boy's face, and a look came upon it as of one who sees a vision.

"Queen Mary?" he said, as if he pronounced the name of the Mother of God. "Yes; I have heard of her.... She is in Norfolk, I think."

Then he let flow out of him the stream that always ran in his heart like sorrowful music ever since the day when first, as a page, in my Lord Shrewsbury's house in Sheffield, he had set eyes on that queen of sorrows. Then, again, upon the occasion of his journey to Paris, he had met with Mr. Morgan, her servant, and the Bishop of Glasgow, her friend, whose talk had excited and inspired him. He had learned from them something more of her glories and beauties, and remembering what he had seen of her, adored her the more. He leaned back now, shading his eyes from the candles upon the table, and began to sing his love and his queen. He told of new insults that had been put upon her, new deprivations of what was left to her of liberty; he did not speak now of Elizabeth by name, since a fountain, even of talk, should not give out at once sweet water and bitter; but he spoke of the day when Mary should come herself to the throne of England, and take that which was already hers; and the Faith should come again like the flowing tide, and all things be again as they had been from the beginning. It was rank treason that he talked, such as would have brought him to Tyburn if it had been spoken in London in indiscreet company; it was that treason which her Grace herself had made possible by her faithlessness to God and man; such treason as God Himself must have mercy upon, since He reads all hearts and their intentions. The others kept silence.

At the end he stood up. Then he stooped for his boots.

"I must be riding, sir," he said.

Mr. Audrey raised his hand to the latten bell that stood beside him on the table.

"I will take Anthony to his horse," said Robin suddenly, for a thought had come to him.

"Then good night, sir," said Anthony, as he drew on his second boot and stood up.

THE sky was all ablaze with stars now as they came out into the court. On their right shone the high windows of the little hall where peace now reigned, except for the clatter of the boys who took away the dishes; and the night was very still about them in the grip of the frost, for the village went early to bed, and even the dogs were asleep.

Robin said nothing as they went over the paving, for his determination was not yet ripe, and Anthony was still aglow with his own talk. Then, as the servant who waited for his master, with the horses, showed himself in the stable-arch with a lantern, Robin's mind was made up.

"I have something to tell you," he said softly. "Tell your man to wait."

"Eh?"

"Tell your man to wait with the horses."

His heart beat hot and thick in his throat as he led the way through the screens and out beyond the hall and down the steps again into the pleasaunce. Anthony took him by the sleeve once or twice, but he said nothing, and went on across the grass, and out through the open iron gate that gave upon the woods. He dared not say what he had to say within the precincts of the house, for fear he should be overheard. Then, when they had gone a little way into the wood, into the dark out of the starlight, Robin turned; and, as he turned, saw the windows of the hall go black as the boys extinguished the torches.

"Well?" whispered Anthony sharply (for a fool could see that the news was to be weighty, and Anthony was no fool).

Robin stood still, silent, breathing so heavily that Anthony heard him.

"Tell me, Rob; tell me quickly."

Robin drew a long breath.

"You saw that my father was silent?" he said.

"Yes."

"Stay.... Will you swear to me by the Mass that you will tell no one what you will hear from me till you hear it from others?"

"I will swear it," whispered Anthony in the darkness.

Again Robin sighed in a long, shuddering breath. Anthony could hear him tremble with cold and pain.

"Well," he said, "my father will leave the Church next Easter. He is tired of paying fines, he says. And he has bidden me to come with him to Matstead Church."

There was dead silence.

"I went to tell Marjorie today," whispered Robin. "She has promised to be my wife some day; so I told her, but no one else. She has bidden me to leave Matstead before Easter, and pray to God to show me what to do afterwards. Can you help me, Anthony?"

He was seized suddenly by the arms.

"Robin... No...no! It is not possible!"

"It is certain. I have never known my father to turn from his word."

From far away in the wild woods came a cry as the two stood there. It might be a wolf or fox, if any were there, or some strange night-bird, or a woman in pain. It rose, it seemed, to a scream, melancholy and dreadful, and then died again. The two heard it, but said nothing, one to the other. No doubt it was some beast in a snare or a-hunting, but it chimed in with the desolation of their hearts so as to seem but a part of it. So the two stood in silence.... It was not until this instant that Robin understood the utter shame and the black misery of that which he had said, and the other heard.

CHAPTER II

I

THERE were excuses in plenty for Robin to ride abroad, to the north towards Hathersage or to the south towards Dethick, as the whim took him; for he was learning to manage the estate that should be his one day. At one time it was to quiet a yeoman whose domain had been ridden over and his sown fields destroyed; at another, to dispute with a miller who claimed for injury through floods for which he held his lord responsible; at a third, to see to the woodland or the fences broken by the deer. He came and went then as he willed; and on the second day, after Anthony's visit, set out before dinner to meet him, that they might speak at length of what lay now upon both their hearts.

He turned southwards through the village for the Dethick road. At the entrance to the village he passed the minister, Mr. Barton, coming out of his house, that had been the priest's lodging, a middle-aged man, made a minister under the new Prayer-Book, and therefore, no priest as were some of the ministers about, who had been made priests under Mary. He was a solid man, of no great wit or learning, but there was not an ounce of harm in him. (They were fortunate, indeed, to have such a minister; since many parishes had but laymen to read the services; and in one, not twenty miles away, the squire's falconer held the living.) Mr. Barton was in his sad-coloured cloak and round cap, and saluted Robin heartily in his loud, bellowing voice.

"Riding abroad again," he cried, "on some secret errand!"

"I will give your respects to Mr. Babington," said Robin, smiling heavily. "I am to meet him about a matter of a tithe too!"

"Ah! you Papists would starve us altogether if you could," roared the minister, who wished no better than to be at peace with his neighbours, and was all for liberty.

"You will get your tithe safe enough—one of you, at least," said Robin, "It is but a matter as to who shall pay it."

He waved good-day to the minister and set his horse to the Dethick track.

There was no going fast today along this country road. The frosts and the thaws had made of it a very way of sorrows. Here in the harder parts was a tumble of ridges and holes, with edges as hard as steel; here in the softer, the faggots laid to build it up were broken or rotted through, making it no better than a trap for horses' feet; and it was a full hour before Robin finished his four miles and turned up through the winter woodland to the yeoman's farm where he was to meet Anthony. It was true, as he had said to Mr. Barton, that they were to speak of a matter of tithe—this was to be their excuse if his father questioned him—for there was a doubt as to in which parish stood this farm, for the yeoman tilled three meadows that were in the Babington estate and two in Matstead.

As he came up the broken ground on to the crest of the hill, he saw Anthony come out of the yard-gate and the yeoman with him. Then Anthony mounted his horse and rode down towards him, bidding the man stay, over his shoulder.

"It is all plain enough," shouted Anthony loud enough for the man to hear. "It is Dethick that must pay. You need not come up, Robin; we must do the paying."

Robin checked his mare and waited till the other came near enough to speak.

"Young Thomas FitzHerbert is within. He is riding round his new estates," said the other beneath his breath. "I thought I would come out and tell you; and I do not know where we can talk or dine. I met him on the road, and he would come with me. He is eating his dinner there."

"But I must eat my dinner too," said Robin, in dismay.

"Will you tell him of what you have told me? He is safe and discreet, I think."

"Why, yes, if you think so," said Robin. "I do not know him very well."

"Oh! he is safe enough, and he has learned not to talk. Besides, all the country will know it by Easter."

So they turned their horses back again and rode up to the farm.

It was a great day for a yeoman when three gentlemen should take their dinners in his house; and the place was in a respectful uproar. From the kitchen vent went up a pillar of smoke, and through its door, in and out continually, fled maids with dishes. The yeoman himself, John Merton, a dried-looking, lean man, stood cap in hand to meet the gentlemen; and his wife, crimson-faced from the fire, peeped and smiled from the open door of the living room that gave immediately upon the yard. For these gentlemen were from three of the principal estates here about. The Babingtons had their country house at Dethick and their town house in Derby; the Audreys owned a matter of fifteen hundred acres at least all about Matstead; and the FitzHerberts, it was said, scarcely knew themselves all that they owned, or rather all that had been theirs until the Queen's Grace had begun to strip them of it little by little on account of their faith. The two Padleys, at least, were theirs, besides their principal house at Norbury; and now that Sir Thomas was in the Fleet Prison for his religion, young Mr. Thomas, his heir, was of more account than ever.

He was at his dinner when the two came in, and he rose and saluted them. He was a smallish kind of man, with a little brown beard, and his short hair, when he lifted his flapped cap to them, showed upright on his head; he smiled pleasantly enough, and made space for them to sit down, one at each side.

"We shall do very well now, Mrs. Merton," he said, "if you will bring in that goose once more for these gentlemen."

Then he made excuses for beginning his dinner before them: he was on his way home and must be off again presently.

It was a well-furnished table for a yeoman's house. There was a linen napkin for each guest. The twelve silver spoons were laid out on the smooth, elm table, and a silver salt stood before Mr. Thomas. There was, of course, an abundance to eat and drink, even though no more than two had been expected; and John Merton himself stood hatless on the further side of the table and took the dishes from the bare-armed maids to place them before the gentlemen.

They talked of this and of that and of the other, freely and easily. John Merton inquired after Sir Thomas, and openly shook his head when he heard of his sufferings; and when the room was empty for a moment of the maids, spoke of a priest who, he had been told, would say Mass in Tansley next day. Then, when the maids came in again, the battle of the tithe was fought once more, and Mr. Thomas pronounced sentence for the second time.

They blessed themselves, all four of them, openly at the end, and went out at last to their horses.

"Will you ride with us, sir?" asked Anthony; "we can go your way. Robin here has something to say to you."

"I shall be happy if you will give me your company for a little. I must be at Padley before dark, if I can, and must visit a couple of houses on the way."

He called out to his two servants, who ran out from the kitchen wiping their mouths, telling them to follow at once, and the three rode off down the hill.

Then Robin told him.

He was silent for a while after he had put a question or two, biting his lower lip a little, and putting his little beard into his mouth. Then he burst out.

"And I dare not ask you to come to me for Easter," he said. "God only knows where I shall be at Easter. I shall be married, too, by then. My father is in London now and may send for me. My uncle is in the Fleet. I am here now only to see what money I can raise for the fines and for the solace of my uncle. I cannot ask you, Mr. Audrey, though God knows that I would do anything that I could. Have you nowhere to go? Will your father hold to what he says?"

Robin told him yes; and he added that there were four or five places he could go to. He was not asking for help or harbourage, but advice only.

"And even of that I have none," cried Mr. Thomas. "I need all that I can get myself. I am distracted, Mr. Babington, with all these troubles."

Robin asked him whether the priests who came and went should be told of the blow that impended; for at those times every apostasy was of importance to priests who had to run here and there for shelter.

"I will tell one or two of the more discreet ones myself," said Mr. Thomas, "if you will give me leave. I would that they were all discreet, but they are not. We will name no names, if you please; but some of them are unreasonable altogether and think nothing of bringing us all into peril."

He began to bite his beard again.

"Do you think the Commissioners will visit us again?" asked Anthony. "Mr. Fenton was telling me—"

"It is Mr. Fenton and the like that will bring them down on us if any will," burst out Mr. FitzHerbert peevishly. "I am as good a Catholic, I hope, as any in the world; but we can surely live without the sacraments for a month or two sometimes! But it is this perpetual coming and going of priests that enrages her Grace and her counsellors. I do not believe her Grace has any great enmity against us; but she soon will, if men like Mr. Fenton and Mr. Bassett are for ever harbouring priests and encouraging them. It is the same in London, I hear; it is the same in Lancashire; it is the same everywhere. And all the world knows it, and thinks that we do contemn her Grace by such boldness. All the mischief came in with that old Bull, *Regnans in Excelsis*, in '69, and—"

"I beg your pardon, sir," came in a quiet voice from beyond him; and Robin, looking across, saw Anthony with a face as if frozen.

"Pooh! pooh!" burst out Mr. Thomas, with an uneasy air. "The Holy Father, I take it, may make mistakes, as I understand it, in such matters, as well as any man. Why, a dozen priests have said to me they thought it inopportune; and—"

"I do not permit," said Anthony with an air of dignity beyond his years, "that any man should speak so in my company."

"Well, well; you are too hot altogether, Mr. Babington. I admire such zeal indeed, as I do in the saints; but we are not bound to imitate all that we admire. Say no more, sir; and I will say no more either."

They rode in silence.

It was, indeed, one of those matters that were in dispute at that time amongst the Catholics. The Pope was not swift enough for some, and too swift for others. He had thundered too soon, said one party, if, indeed, it was right to thunder at all, and not to wait in patience till the Queen's Grace should repent herself; and he had thundered not soon enough, said the other. Whence it may at least be argued that he had been exactly opportune. Yet it could not be denied that since the day when he had declared Elizabeth cut off from the unity of the Church and her subjects absolved from their allegiance—though never, as some pretended then and have pretended ever since, that a private person might kill her and do no wrong—ever since that day her bitterness had increased yearly against her Catholic people, who desired no better than to serve both her and their God, if she would but permit that to be possible.

II

It would be an hour later that they bid goodbye to Mr. Thomas FitzHerbert, high among the hills to the east of the Derwent River; and when they had seen him ride off towards Wingerworth, rode yet a few furlongs together to speak of what had been said.

"He can do nothing, then," said Robin; "not even to give good counsel."

"I have never heard him speak so before," cried Anthony; "he must be near mad, I think. It must be his marriage, I suppose."

"He is full of his own troubles; that is plain enough, without seeking others. Well, I must bear mine as best I can."

They were just parting—Anthony to ride back to Dethick, and Robin over the moors to Matstead, when over a rise in the ground they saw the heads of three horsemen approaching. It was a wild country that they were in; there were no houses in sight; and in such circumstances it was but prudent to remain together until the character of the travellers should be plain; so the two, after a word, rode gently forward, hearing the voices of the three talking to one another, in the still air, though without catching a word. For, as they came nearer the voices ceased, as if the talkers feared to be overheard.

They were well mounted, these three, on horses known as Scottish nags, square-built, sturdy beasts, that could cover forty miles in the day. They were splashed, too, not the horses only, but the riders also, as if they had ridden far, through streams or boggy ground. The men were dressed soberly and well, like poor gentlemen or prosperous yeomen; all three were bearded, and all carried arms as could be seen from the flash of the sun on their hilts. It was plain, too, that they were not rogues or cutters, since each carried his valise on his saddle, as well as from their appearance. Our gentlemen, then, after passing them with a salute and a good-day, were once more about to say goodbye one to the other, and appoint a time and place to meet again for the hunting of which Robin had spoken to Marjorie, and, indeed, had drawn rein—when one of the three strangers was seen to turn his horse and come riding back after them, while his friends waited.

The two lads wheeled about to meet him, as was but prudent; but while he was yet twenty yards away he lifted his hat. He seemed about thirty years old; he had a pleasant, ruddy face.

"Mr. Babington, I think, sir," he said.

"That is my name," said Anthony.

"I have heard Mass in your house, sir," said the stranger. "My name is Garlick."

"Why, yes, sir, I remember—from Tideswell. How do you do, Mr. Garlick? This is Mr. Audrey, of Matstead."

They saluted one another gravely.

"Mr. Audrey is a Catholic, too, I think?"

Robin answered that he was.

"Then I have news for you, gentlemen. A priest, Mr. Simpson, is with us; and will say Mass at Tansley next Sunday. You would like to speak with his reverence?"

"It will give us great pleasure, sir," said Anthony, touching his horse with his heel.

"I am bringing Mr. Simpson on his way. He is just fresh from Rheims. And Mr. Ludlam is to carry him further on Monday," continued Mr. Garlick as they went forward.

"Mr. Ludlam?"

"He is a native of Radbourne, and has but just finished at Oxford.... Forgive me, sir; I will but just ride forward and tell them."

The two lads drew rein, seeing that he wished first to tell the others who they were, before bringing them up; and a strange little thing fell as Mr. Garlick joined the two. For it happened that by now the sun was at his setting; going down in a glory of crimson over the edge of the high moor; and that the three riders were directly in his path from where the two lads waited. Robin, therefore, looking at them, saw the three all together on their horses with the circle of the sun about them, and a great flood of blood-coloured light on every side; the priest was in the midst of the three, and the two men leaning towards him seemed to be speaking and as if encouraging him strongly. For an instant, so strange was the light, so immense the shadows on this side spread over the tumbled ground up to the lads themselves, so vast the great vault of illuminated sky, that it seemed to Robin as if he saw a vision... Then the strangeness passed, as Mr. Garlick turned away again to beckon to them; and the boy thought no more of it at that time.

They uncovered as they rode towards the priest, and bowed low to him as he lifted his hand with a few words of Latin; and the next instant they were in talk.

Mr. Simpson, like his friends, was a youngish man, with a kind face and great, innocent eyes that seemed to wonder and question. Mr. Ludlam, too, was under thirty years old, plainly not of gentleman's birth, though he was courteous and well-mannered. It seemed a great matter to these three to have fallen in with young Mr. Babington, whose family was so well-known, and whose own fame as a scholar, as well as an ardent Catholic, was all over the county.

Robin said little; he was overshadowed by his friend; but he listened and watched as the four spoke together, and learned that Mr. Simpson had been made priest scarcely a month before, and was come from Yorkshire, which was his own county, to minister in the district of the Peak at least for awhile. He heard, too, news from Douay, and that the college, it was thought, might move from there to another place under the protection of the family of De Guise, since her Grace was very hot against Douay, whence so many of her troubles proceeded, and was doing her best to persuade the Governor of the Netherlands to suppress it. However, said Mr. Simpson, it was not yet done.

Anthony, too, in his turn gave the news of the county; he spoke of Mr. Fenton, of the FitzHerberts and others that were safe and discreet persons; but he said nothing at that time of Mr. Audrey of Matstead, at which Robin was glad, since his shame deepened on him every hour, and all the more now that he had met with those three men who rode so gallantly through the country in peril of liberty or life itself. Nor did he say anything of the FitzHerberts except that they might be relied upon.

"We must be riding," said Garlick at last; "these moors are strange to me; and it will be dark in half an hour."

"Will you allow me to be your guide, sir?" asked Anthony of the priest. "It is all in my road, and you will not be troubled with questions or answers if you are in my company."

"But what of your friend, sir?"

"Oh! Robin knows the country as he knows the flat of his hand. We were about to separate as we met you."

"Then we will thankfully accept your guidance, sir," said the priest gravely.

An impulse seized upon Robin as he was about to say good-day, though he was ashamed of it five minutes later as a modest lad would be. Yet he followed it now; he leapt off his horse and, holding Cecily's rein in his arm, kneeled on the stones with both knees.

"Your blessing, sir," he said to the priest. And Anthony eyed him with astonishment.

III

ROBIN was moved, as he rode home over the high moors, and down at last upon the woods of Matstead, in a manner that was new to him, and that he could not altogether understand. It was perhaps something in the priest's face that had so affected him; for there was a look in it of a kind of surprised timidity and gentleness, as if he wondered at himself for being so foolhardy, and as if he appealed with that same wonder and surprise to all who looked on him. His voice, too, was gentle, as if tamed for the seminary and the altar; and his whole air and manner wholly unlike that of some of the priests whom Robin knew—loud-voiced, confident, burly men whom you would have sworn to be country gentlemen or yeomen living on their estates or farms and fearing to look no man in the face. It was this latter kind, thought Robin, that was best suited to such a life—to riding all day through north-country storms, to lodging hardily where they best could, to living such a desperate enterprise as a priest's life then was, with prices upon their heads and spies everywhere. It was not a life for quiet persons like Mr. Simpson, who, surely, would be better at his books in some college abroad, offering the Holy Sacrifice in peace and security, and praying for adventurers more hardy than himself.

THERE was yet more than an hour before supper-time when he rode into the court at last; and Dick Sampson, his own groom, came to take his horse from him.

"The master's not been from home today, sir," said Dick when Robin asked of his father.

"Not been from home?"

"No, sir—not out of the house, except that he was walking in the pleasaunce half an hour ago."

Robin ran up the steps and through the screens to see if his father was still there; but the little walled garden, so far as he could see it in the light from the hall windows, was empty; and, indeed, it would be strange for any man to walk in such a place at such an hour. He wondered, too, to hear that his father had not been from home; for on all days, except he were ill, he would be about the estate, here and there. As he came back to the screens he heard a step going up and down in the hall, and on looking in met his father face to face. The old man had his hat on his head, but no cloak on his shoulders, though even with the fire the place was cold. It was plain that he had been walking up and down to warm himself. Robin could not make out his face very well, as he stood with his back to a torch.

"Where have you been, my lad?"

"I went to meet Anthony at one of the Dethick farms, sir—John Merton's."

"You met no one else?"

"Yes, sir; Mr. Thomas FitzHerbert was there and dined with us. He rode with us, too, a little way." And then as he was on the point of speaking of the priest, he stopped himself; and in an instant knew that never again must he speak of a priest to his father; his father had already lost his right to that. His father looked at him a moment, standing with his hands clasped behind his back.

"Have you heard anything of a priest that is newly come to these parts—or coming?"

"Yes, sir. I hear Mass is to be said…in the district, on Sunday."

"Where is Mass to be said?"

Robin drew a long breath, lifted his eyes to his father's and then dropped them again.

"Did you hear me, sir? Where is Mass to be said?"

Again Robin lifted and again dropped his eyes.

"What is the priest's name?"

Again there was dead silence. For a son, so to behave towards his father, was an act of very defiance. Yet the father said nothing. There the two remained; Robin with his eyes on the ground, expecting a storm of words or a blow in the face. Yet he knew he could do no otherwise; the moment had come at last and he must act as he would be obliged always to act hereafter.

Then his father turned suddenly on his heel; and the son went out trembling.

CHAPTER III

I

"I will speak to you tonight, sir, after supper," said his father sharply a second day later, when Robin, meeting his father setting out before dinner, had asked him to give him an hour's talk.

Robin's mind had worked fiercely and intently since the encounter in the hall. His father had sat silent both at supper and afterwards, and the next day was the same; the old man spoke no more than was necessary, shortly and abruptly, scarcely looking his son once in the face, and the rest of the day they had not met. It was plain to the boy that something must follow his defiance, and he had prepared all his fortitude to meet it. Yet the second night had passed and no word had been spoken, and by the second morning Robin could bear it no longer; he must know what was in his father's mind. And now the appointment was made, and he would soon know all. His father was absent from dinner and the boy dined alone. He learned from Dick Sampson that his father had ridden southwards.

It was not until Robin had sat down nearly half an hour later than supper-time that the old man came in. The frost was gone; deep mud had succeeded, and the rider was splashed above his thighs. He stayed at the fire for his boots to be drawn off and to put on his soft-leather shoes, while Robin stood up dutifully to await him. Then he came forward, took his seat without a word, and called for supper. In ominous silence the meal proceeded, and with the same thunderous air, when it was over, his father said grace and made his way, followed by his son, into the parlour behind. He made no motion at first to pour out his wine; then he helped himself twice and left the jug for Robin.

Then suddenly he began without moving his head.

"I wish to know your intentions," he said, with irony so serious that it seemed gravity. "I cannot flog you or put you to school again, and I must know how we stand to one another."

Robin was silent. He had looked at his father once or twice, but now sat downcast and humble in his place. With his left hand he fumbled, out of sight, Mr. Maine's pair of beads. His father sat with his head propped on his hand, not doing enough courtesy to his son even to look at him.

"Do you hear me, sir?"

"Yes, sir. But I do not know what to say."

"I wish to know your intentions. Do you mean to thwart and disobey me in all matters, or in only those that have to do with religion?"

"I do not wish to thwart or disobey you, sir, in any matters except where my conscience is touched." (The substance of this answer had been previously rehearsed, and the latter part of it even verbally.)

"Be good enough to tell me what you mean by that."

Robin licked his lips carefully and sat up a little in his chair.

"You told me, sir, that it was your intention to leave the Church. Then how can I tell you of what priests are here, or where Mass is to be said? You would not have done so to one who was not a Catholic six months ago."

The man sneered visibly.

"There is no need," he said. "It is Mr. Simpson who is to say Mass tomorrow, and it is at Tansley that it will be said, at six o'clock in the morning. If I choose to tell the justices, you cannot prevent it." (He turned round in a flare of anger.) "Do you think I shall tell the justices?"

Robin said nothing.

"Do you think I shall tell the justices?" roared the old man insistently.

"No, sir. Now I do not."

The other growled gently and sank back.

"But if you think that I will permit my son to flout me to my face in my own hall, and not to trust his own father—why, you are immeasurably mistaken, sir. So I ask you again how far you intend to thwart and disobey me."

A kind of despair surged up in the boy's heart—despair at the fruitlessness of this ironical and furious sort of talk; and with the despair came boldness.

"Father, will you let me speak outright, without thinking that I mean to insult you? I do not; I swear I do not. Will you let me speak, sir?"

His father growled again a sort of acquiescence, and Robin gathered his forces. He had prepared a kind of defence that seemed to him reasonable, and he knew that his father was at least just. He was curt, obstinate, and even boisterous in his anger; but there was a kindliness beneath that the boy always perceived—a kindliness which permitted the son an exceptional freedom of speech, which he used always in the last resort. This, then, was plainly a legitimate occasion for it, and he had prepared himself to make the most of it. He began formally:

"Sir," he said, "you have brought me up in the Old Faith, sent me to Mass, and to the priest to learn my duty, and I have obeyed you always. You have taught me that a man's duty to God must come before all else—as our Saviour Himself said, too. And now you turn on me, and bid me forget all that, and come to church with you.... It is not for me to say anything to my father about his own conscience; I must leave that alone. But I am bound to speak of mine when occasion rises, and this is one of them.... I should be dishonouring and insulting you, sir, if I did not believe you when you said you would turn Protestant; and a man who says he will turn Protestant has done so already. It was for this reason, then, and no other, that I did not answer you the other day; not because I wish to be disobedient to you, but because I must be obedient to God. I did not lie to you, as I might have done, and say that I did not know who the priest was nor where Mass was to be said. But I would not answer, because it is not right or discreet for a Catholic to speak of these things to those who are not Catholics—"

"How dare you say I am not a Catholic, sir!"

"A Catholic, sir, to my mind," said Robin steadily, "is one who holds to the Catholic Church and to no other. I mean nothing offensive, sir; I mean what I said I meant, and no more. It is not for me to condemn—"

"I should think not!" snorted the old man.

"Well, sir, that is my reason. And further—"

He stopped, doubtful.

"Well, sir—what further?"

"Well, I cannot come to the church with you at Easter." His father wheeled round savagely in his chair.

"Father, hear me out, and then say what you will.... I say I cannot come with you to church at Easter, because I am a Catholic. But I do not wish to trouble or disobey you openly. I will go away from home for that time. Good Mr. Barton will cause no trouble; he wants nothing but peace. Father, you are not just to me. You have taught me too much, or you have not given me time enough—"

Again he broke off, knowing that he had said what he did not mean, but the old man was on him like a hawk.

"Not time enough, you say? Well, then—"

"No, sir; I did not mean that," wailed Robin suddenly. "I do not mean that I should change if I had a hundred years; I am sure I shall not. But—"

"You said, 'Not time enough,'" said the other meditatively. "Perhaps if I give you time—"

"Father, I beg of you to forget what I said; I did not mean to say it. It is not true. But Marjorie said—"

"Marjorie! What has Marjorie to do with it?"

Robin found himself suddenly in deep waters. This was the second mistake he had made in saying what he did not mean.... Again the courage of despair came to him, and he struck out further.

"I must tell you of that too, sir," he said, "Mistress Marjorie and I—"

He stopped, overwhelmed with shame. His father turned full round and stared at him.

"Go on, sir."

Robin seized his glass and emptied it.

"Well, sir. Mistress Marjorie and I love one another. We are but boy and girl, sir; we know that—"

Then his father laughed. It was laughter that was bitter. It might all have been otherwise if he had been kind, or if he had been sad or disappointed, or even if he had been merely angry; but the soreness and misery in the old man's heart—misery at his own acts and words, and at the outrage he was doing to his own conscience—turned his judgment bitter, and with that bitterness his son's heart shut tight against him.

"But boy and girl!" sneered the man. "A couple of blind puppies, I would say rather—you with your falcons and mare and your other toys, and the down on your chin, and your conscience; and she with her white face and her mother and her linen-parlour and her beads"— (his charity prevailed so far as to hinder him from more outspoken contempt)—"And you two babes have been prattling of conscience and prayers together—I make no doubt, and thinking yourselves Cecilies and Laurences and all the holy martyrs—and all this without a by-your-leave, I dare wager, from parent or father, and thinking yourselves man and wife; and you fondling her, and she too modest to be fondled, and—"

The plain truth struck him with sudden splendour, at least sufficiently strong to furnish him with a question.

"And have you told Mistress Marjorie about your sad rogue of a father?"

Robin, white with anger, held his lips grimly together and the wrath blazed in an instant up from the scornful old heart, whose very love was turned to gall.

"Tell me, sir—I will have it!" he cried.

Robin looked at him with such hard fury in his eyes that for a moment the man winced. Then he recovered himself, and again his anger rose to the brim.

"You need not look at me like that, you hound. Tell me, I say!"

"I will not!" shouted Robin, springing to his feet.

The old man was up too by now, with all the anger of his son hardened by his dignity.

"You will not?"

"No."

For a moment the fate of them both still hung in the balance. Neither would yield. There was the fierce northern obstinacy in them both. The father seized his ultimate right, and struck his son across the face.

Then the son answered by his only weapon.

For a sensible pause he stood there, his fresh face paled to chalkiness, except where the print of five fingers slowly reddened. Then he made a courteous little gesture, as if to invite his father to sit down; and as the other did so, slowly and shaking all over, struck at him by careful and calculated words, delivered with a stilted and pompous air:

"You have beaten me, sir; so, of course, I obey. Yes, I told Mistress Marjorie Manners that my father no longer counted himself a Catholic, and would publicly turn Protestant at Easter, so as to please her Grace and be in favour with the Court and with the county justices. And I have told Mr. Babington so as well, and also Mr. Thomas FitzHerbert. It will spare you the pain, sir, of making any public announcement on the matter. It is always a son's duty to spare his father pain."

Then he bowed, wheeled, and went out of the room.

II

Two hours later Robin was still lying completely dressed on his bed in the dark.

It was a plain little chamber where he lay, fireless, yet not too cold, since it was wainscoted from floor to ceiling, and looked out eastwards upon the pleasaunce, with rooms on either side of it. A couple of presses sunk in the walls held his clothes and boots; a rush-bottomed chair stood by the bed; and the bed itself was laid immediately on the ground. His bows and arrows, with a pair of dags or pistols, hung on a rack against the wall at the foot of his bed, and a little brass cross engraved with a figure of the Crucified hung over it.

A hundred thoughts had gone through his mind since he had flung himself down here shaking with passion; and these had begun already, to repeat themselves, like a turning wheel, in his head. Marjorie; his love for her; his despair of that love; his father; all that they had been, one to the other, in the past; the priest's face as he had seen it three days ago; what would be done at Easter, what later—all these things turned continually in his head, and he was too young and too simple to extricate one from the other all at once.

Well, the event was certain with such as Robin, and he was presently standing at the door of his room, his boots drawn off and laid aside, listening, with a heart beating in his ears to hinder him, for any sound from beneath. He did not know whether his father were abed or not. If not, he must ask his pardon at once.

He went downstairs at last, softly, to the parlour, and peeped in. All was dark, except for the glimmer from the stove, and his heart felt lightened. Then, as he was cold with his long vigil outside his bed, he stirred the embers into a blaze and stood warming himself.

How strange and passionless, he thought, looked this room, after the tempest that had raged in it just now. The two glasses stood there—his own not quite empty—and the jug between them. His father's chair was drawn to the table, as if he were still sitting in it; his own was flung back as he had pushed it from him in his passion. There was an old print over the stove at which he looked presently—it had been his mother's, and he remembered it as long as his life had been—it was of Christ carrying His cross.

His shame began to increase in him. How wickedly he had answered, with every word a wound! He knew that the most poisonous of them all were false; he had known it even while he spoke them; it was not to curry favour with her Grace that his father had lapsed; it was that his temper was tried beyond bearing by those continual fines and rebuffs; the old man's patience was gone—that was all. And he, his son, had not said one word of comfort or strength; he had thought of himself and his own wrongs, and being reviled he had reviled again...."

There stood against the walk between the windows a table and an oaken desk that held the estate bills and books; and beside the desk were laid clean sheets of paper, an inkpot, a pounce-box, and three or four feather pens. It was here that he wrote, being newly from school, at his father's dictation, or his father sometimes wrote himself, with pain and labour, the few notices or letters that were necessary. So he went to this and sat down at it; he pondered a little; then he wrote a single line of abject regret.

"I ask your pardon and God's, sir, for the wicked words I said before I left the parlour. R." He folded this and addressed it with the proper superscription; and left it lying there.

III

It was a strange ride that he had back from Tansley next morning after Mass.

Dick Sampson had met him with the horses in the stable-court at Matstead a little after four o'clock in the morning; and together they had ridden through the pitch darkness, each carrying a lantern fastened to his stirrup.

But the return journey was another matter; for they needed no lanterns, and the dawn rose steadily overhead, showing all that they passed in ghostly fashion, up to final solidity.

It resembled, in fact, the dawn of Faith in a soul.

First from the darkness outlines only emerged, vast and sinister, of such an appearance that it was impossible to tell their proportions or distances. No breeze stirred the twigs overhead or the undergrowth through which they rode. Once, as the two, riding a little apart, turned suddenly together, up a ravine into thicker woods, they came upon a herd of deer, who stared on them without any movement that the eye could see. Here a stag stood with two hinds beside him; behind, Robin saw the backs and heads of others that lay still. So, by little and little, cocks crew from over the hills one to the other; dogs barked far away, till the face of the world was itself again, and the smoke from Matstead rose above the trees in front.

Robin had ridden perhaps twenty times at such an hour, with his father beside him, after Mass on some such occasion. Yet it seemed to him this time that it was the Mass which he had seen, and his own solitariness, that had illuminated his eyes. Henceforward he would go alone, or with a servant only; alone he would pass upstairs through the darkened house to the shrouded room, garret or bed-chamber, where the group was assembled, all in silence; and then, alone of all that were of blood-relationship to him, he would witness the Holy Sacrifice....

One thing more, too, had moved him this morning; and that, the sight of the young priest at the altar whom he had met on the moor. Here, more than ever, was the gentle priestliness and innocency apparent. He stood there in his red vestments; he moved this way and that; he made his gestures; he spoke in undertones. Surely this man should say Mass for ever; yet surely never again ride over the moors to do it, amidst enemies. He was of the strong castle and the chamber, not of the tent and the battle.... And yet it was of such soldiers as these, as well as of the sturdy and the strong, that Christ's army was made.

It was in broad daylight, though under a weeping sky, that Robin rode into the court at Matstead. He shook the rain from his cloak within the screens, and stamped to get the mud away; and, as he lifted his hat to shake it, his father came in from the pleasaunce.

Robin glanced up at him, swift and shy, half smiling, expecting a word or a look. His father must surely have read his little letter by now, and forgiven him. But the smile died away again, as he met the old man's eyes; they were as hard as steel; his clean-shaven lips were set like a trap, and, though he looked at his son, it seemed that he did not see him. He passed through the screens and went down the steps into the court.

Then he went into the hall, and swiftly through it. There on the desk in the window lay the pen he had flung down last night, but no more; the letter was gone; and, as he turned away, he saw lying among the wood-ashes of the cold stove a little crumpled ball. He stooped and drew it out. It was his letter, tossed there after the reading; his father had not taken the pains to keep it safe, nor even to destroy it.

CHAPTER IV

I

THE company was already assembled both within and without Padley, when Robin rode up from the riverside, on a fine, windy morning, for the sport of the day. Perhaps a dozen horses stood tethered at the entrance to the little court, with a man or two to look after them, for the greater part of their riders were already within; and a continual coming and going of lads with dogs; falconers each with his cadge, or three-sided frame on which sat the hawks; a barking of hounds, a screaming of birds, a clatter of voices and footsteps in the court—all this showed that the boy was none too early. A man stepped forward to take his mare and his hawks; and Robin slipped from his saddle and went in.

Padley Hall stood upon the side of the hill, well set-up above the damps of the valley, yet protected from the northeasterly winds by the higher slopes, on the tops of which lay Burbage Moor, where the hawking was to be held. On the south, over the valley, stood out the modest hall and buttery with a door between them, well buttressed in two places upon the falling ground, in one by a chimney, in the other by a slope of masonry; and behind these buildings stood the rest of the court, the stables, the wash-house, the bake-house and such like, below; and, above, the sleeping rooms for the family and the servants.

Robin entered through the great gate on the east side and rode through into the court; and here, indeed, was the company; for out of the windows of the low hall on his left came a babble of tongues, while two or three gentlemen with pots in their hands saluted him from the passage door, telling him that Mr. Thomas FitzHerbert was within. Mr. Fenton was one of these, come over from North Lees, where he had his manor, a brisk, middle-aged man, dressed soberly and well, with a pointed beard and pleasant, dancing eyes.

"And Mr. John, too, came last night," he said; "but he will not hawk with us. He is ridden from London on private matters."

It was an exceedingly gay sight on which Robin looked as he turned into the hall. It was a low room, ceiled in oak and wainscoted halfway up, with a great fire burning in a chimney on the south side, and perhaps a dozen and a half persons sitting over their food and drink, since they were dining early today to have the longer time for sport.

A voice hailed him as he came in; and he went up to pay his respects to Mr. John FitzHerbert, a tall man, well past middle-age, who sat with his hat on his head, at the centre of the high table, with the arms of Eyre and FitzHerbert beneath the canopy, all emblazoned, to do the honours of the day.

"You are late, sir, you are late!" he cried out genially. "We are just done."

Robin saluted him. He liked this man, though he did not know him very well; for he was continually about the country, now in London, now at Norbury, now at Swinnerton, always occupied with these endless matters of fines and recusancy.

Robin saluted him then, and said a word or two; bowed to Mr. Thomas, his son, who came up to speak with him; and then looked for Marjorie. She sat there, at the corner of the table, with Mrs. Fenton at one side, and an empty seat on the other. Robin immediately sat down in it, to eat his dinner, beginning with the "gross foods," according to the English custom. There was a piece of Christmas brawn today, from a pig fattened on oats and peas, and hardened, by being lodged (while he lived) on a boarded floor; all this was told Robin across the table with particularity, while he ate it, and drank, according to etiquette, a cup of bastard. He attended to all this zealously, while never for an instant was he unaware of the girl.

They tricked their elders very well, these two innocent ones. You would have sworn that Robin looked for another place and could not see one, you would have sworn that they were shy of one another, and spoke scarcely a dozen sentences. Yet they did very well each in the company of the other; and Robin, indeed, before he had finished his partridge, had conveyed to her that there was news that he had, and must give to her before the day was out. She looked at him with enough dismay in her face for him at least to read it; for she knew by his manner that it would not be happy news.

So, too, when the fruit was done and dinner was over (for they had no opportunity to speak at any length), again you would have sworn that the last idea in his mind, as in hers, was that he should be the one to help her to her saddle. Yet he did so; and he fetched her hawk for her, and settled her reins in her hand; and presently he on one side of her, with Mr. Fenton on the other side, were riding up through Padley chase; and the talk and the laughter went up too.

II

THE sport was done in this way:

The two that rode in front selected each from the cadge one of his own falcons (it was peregrines that were used at the beginning of the day, since they were first after partridges), and so rode, each carrying his falcon on his wrist, hooded, belled, and in the leash, ready to cast off. Immediately before them went a lad with a couple of dogs to nose the game—these also in a leash until they stiffened. Then the lad released them and stepped softly back, while the riders moved on at a foot's-pace, and the spaniels behind rose on their hind legs, choked by the chain, whimpering, fifty yards in the rear. Slowly the dogs advanced, each a frozen model of craft and blood-lust, till an instant afterwards, with a whir and a chattering like a broken clock, the covey whirled from the thick growth underfoot, and flashed away northwards; and, a moment later, up went the peregrines behind them. Then, indeed, it was *sauve qui peut*, for the ground was full of holes here and there, though there were grass-stretches as well on which all rode with loose rein, the two whose falcons were sprung always in front, according to custom, and the rest in a medley behind.

Away then went the birds, pursued and pursuers, till, like a falling star, the falcon stooped, and then, maybe, the other a moment later, down upon the quarry; and a minute later there was the falcon back again shivering with pride and ecstasy, or, all ruffle-feathered with shame, back on his master's wrist, and another torn partridge, or maybe two, in the bottom of the lad's bag; and arguments went full pelt, and cries, and sometimes sharp words, and faults were found, and praise was given, and so on for another pair.

It was but natural that Robin and Marjorie should compete one against the other, for they were riding together and talked together. So presently Mr. Thomas called to them, and beckoned them to their places. Robin set aside Agnes on to the cadge and chose Magdalen, and Marjorie chose Sharpie. The array was set, and all moved forward.

It was a short chase and a merry one. Two birds rose from the heather and flew screaming, skimming low, as from behind them moved on the shadows of death, still as clouds, with great noiseless sweeps of sickle-shaped wings. Behind came the gallopers; Marjorie on her black horse, Robin on Cecily, seeming to compete, yet each content if either won, each, maybe, desiring that the other should win. And the wind screamed past them as they went.

Then came the stoops—together as if fastened by one string—faultless and exquisite; and, as the two rode up and drew rein, there, side by side on the windy turf, two fierce statues of destiny—cruel-eyed, blood-stained on the beaks, resolute and suspicious—eyed them motionless, the claws sunk deeply through back and head—awaiting recapture.

Marjorie turned swiftly to the boy as he leaped off.

"In the chapel," she said, "at Padley."

Robin stared at her. Then he understood and nodded his head, as Mr. Thomas rode up, his beard all blown about by the wind, breathless but congratulatory.

III

It fell on Robin's mind with a certain heaviness and reproach that it should have been she who should have carried in her head all day the unknown news that he was to give her, and he who should have forgotten it. He understood then a little better of all that he must be to her, since, as he turned to her, it was to her mind that the under-thought had leapt, that here was their first, and perhaps their last, chance of speaking in private.

It was indeed their last chance, for the sun already stood over Chapel-en-le-Frith far away to the south-west; and they must begin their circle to return, in which the ladies should fly their merlins after larks, and there was no hope henceforth for Robin. Henceforth she rode with Mrs. Fenton and two or three more, while the gentlemen who loved sport more than courtesy turned to the left over the broken ground to work back once more after partridges. And Robin dared no more ride with his love, for fear that his company all day with her should be marked.

It was within an hour of sunset that Robin, riding ahead, having lost a hawk and his hat, having fallen into a bog-hole, being one mask of mud from head to foot, slid from his horse into Dick's hands and demanded if the ladies were back.

"Yes, sir; they are back half an hour ago. They are in the parlour."

Robin knew better. "I shall be riding in ten minutes," he said; "give the mare a mouthful."

He limped across the court, and looking behind him to see if any saw, and finding the court at that instant empty, ran up, as well as he could, the stone staircase that rose from the outside to the chapel door. It was unlatched. He pushed it open and went in.

It was a brave thing that the FitzHerberts did in keeping such a place at all, since the greatest Protestant fool in the valley knew what the little chamber was that had the angels carved on the beam-ends, and the piscina in the south wall. Windows looked out every way; through those on the south could be seen now the darkening valley and the sunlit hills, and, yet more necessary, the road by which any travellers from the valley must surely come. Within, too, scarcely any pains were taken to disguise the place. It was wainscoted from roof to floor—ceiled, floored, and walled in oak. A great chest stood beneath the little east window of two lights, that cried "Altar" if any chest ever did so. A great press stood against the wooden screen that shut the room from the ladies' parlour next door; filled in three shelves with innocent linen, for this was the only disguise that the place stooped to put on. You could not swear that Mass was said there, but you could swear that it was a place in which Mass would very suitably be said. A couple of benches were against the press, and three or four chairs stood about the floor.

Robin saw her against the light as soon as he came in. She was still in her blue riding-dress, with the hood on her shoulders, and held her whip in her hand; but he could see no more of her head than the paleness of her face and the gleam on her black hair.

"Well, then?" she whispered sharply; and then: "Why, what a state you are in!"

"It's nothing," said Robin. "I rolled in a bog-hole."

She looked at him anxiously.

"You are not hurt? ...Sit down at least."

He sat down stiffly, and she beside him, still watching to see if he were the worse for his falling. He took her hand in his.

"I am not fit to touch you," he said.

"Tell me the news; tell me quickly."

So he told her; of the wrangle in the parlour and what had passed between his father and him; of his own bitterness; and his letter, and the way in which the old man had taken it.

"He has not spoken to me since," he said, "except in public before the servants. Both nights after supper he has sat silent and I beside him."

"And you have not spoken to him?" she asked quickly.

"I said something to him after supper on Sunday, and he made no answer. He has done all his writing himself. I think it is for him to speak now. I should only anger him more if I tried it again."

She sighed suddenly and swiftly, but said nothing. Her hand lay passive in his, but her face was turned now to the bright southerly window, and he could see her puzzled eyes and her down-turned, serious mouth. She was thinking with all her wits, and, plainly, could come to no conclusion.

She turned to him again.

"And you told him plainly that you and I...that you and I—"

"That you and I loved one another? I told him plainly. And it was his contempt that angered me."

She sighed again.

It was a troublesome situation in which these two children found themselves. Here was the father of one of them that knew, yet not the parents of the other, who should know first of all. Neither was there any promise of secrecy and no hope of obtaining it. If she should not tell her parents, then if the old man told them, deception would be charged against her; and if she should tell them, perhaps he would not have done so, and so all be brought to light too soon and without cause. And besides all this there were the other matters, heavy enough before, yet far more heavy now—matters of their hopes for the future, the complications with regard to the religion, what Robin should do, what he should not do.

So they sat there silent, she thinking and he waiting upon her thought.

She sighed again and turned to him her troubled eyes.

"My Robin," she said, "I have been thinking so much about you, and I have feared sometimes—"

She stopped herself, and he looked for her to finish. She drew her hand away and stood up.

"Oh! it is miserable!" she cried. "And all might have been so happy."

The tears suddenly filled her eyes so that they shone like flowers in dew.

He stood up, too, and put his muddy arm about her shoulders.

"It will be happy," he said. "What have you been fearing?"

She shook her head and the tears ran down.

"I cannot tell you yet.... Robin, what a holy man that travelling priest must be, who said Mass on Sunday."

The lad was bewildered at her swift change of thought, for he did not yet see the chain on which they hung. He strove to follow her.

"It seemed so to me too," he said. "I think I have never seen—"

"It seemed so to you too," she cried. "Why, what do you know of him?"

He was amazed at her vehemence. She had drawn herself clear of his arm and was looking at him full in the face.

"I met him on the moor," he said. "I had some talk with him. I got his blessing."

"You got his blessing! Why, so did I, after the Mass, when you were gone."

"Then that should join us more closely than ever," he said.

"In Heaven, perhaps, but on earth—" She checked her self again. "Tell me what you thought of him, Robin."

"I thought it was strange that such a man as that should live such a rough life. If he were in the seminary now, safe at Douay—"

She seemed a shade paler, but her eyes did not flicker.

"Yes," she said. "And you thought—?"

"I thought that it was not that kind of man who should fare so hardly. If it were a man like John Merton, who is accustomed to such things, or a man like me—"

Again he stopped; he did not know why. But it was as if she had cried out, though she neither spoke nor moved.

"You thought that, did you, Robin?" she said presently, never moving her eyes from his face. "I thought so, too."

"But I do not know why we are talking about Mr. Simpson," said the lad. "There are other affairs more pressing."

"I am not sure," said she.

"Marjorie, my love, what are you thinking about?"

She had turned her eyes and was looking out through the little window. Outside the red sunlight still lay on the crags and slopes beyond the deep valley beneath them, and her face was bright in the reflected brightness. Yet he thought he had never seen her look so serious. She turned her eyes back to him as he spoke.

"I am thinking of a great many things," she said. "I am thinking of the Faith and of sorrow and of love."

"My love, what do you mean?"

Suddenly she made a swift movement towards him and took him by the lapels. He could see her face close beneath his, yet it was in shadow again, and he could make out of it no more than the shadows of mouth and eyes.

"Robin," she said, "I cannot tell you unless God tells you Himself. I am told that I am too scrupulous some times.... I do not know what I think, nor what is right, nor what are fancies.... But...but I know that I love you with all my heart...and...and that I cannot bear—"

Then her face was on his breast in a passion of weeping, and his arms were round her, and his lips on her hair.

IV

DICK found his master a poor travelling companion as they rode home. He made a few respectful remarks as to the sport of the day, but he was answered by a wandering eye and a complete lack of enthusiasm. Mr. Robin rode loosely and heavily. Three or four times his mare stumbled (and no wonder, after all that she had gone through), and he jerked her savagely.

Then Dick tried another tack and began to speak of the company, but with no greater success. He discoursed on the riding of Mrs. Fenton, and the peregrine of Mr. Thomas, who had distinguished herself that day, and he was met by a lack-lustre eye once more.

Finally he began to speak of the religious gossip of the countryside—how it was said that another priest, a Mr. Nelson, had been taken in London, as Mr. Maine had been in Cornwall; that, it was said again, priests would have to look to their lives in future, and not only to their liberty; how the priest, Mr. Simpson, was said to be a native of Yorkshire, and how he has ridden northwards again, still with Mr.

Ludlam. And here he met a little more encouragement. Mr. Robin asked where was Mr. Simpson gone to, and Dick told him he did not know, but that he would be back again by Easter, it was thought, or, if not, another priest would be in the district. Then he began to gossip of Mr. Ludlam; how a man had told him that his cousin's wife thought that Mr. Ludlam was to go abroad to be made priest himself, and that perhaps Mr. Garlick would go too.

"That is the kind of priest we want, sir," said Dick.

"Eh?"

"That is the kind of priest we want, sir," repeated Dick solemnly. "We should do better with natives than foreigners. We want priests who know the county and the ways of the people—and men too, I think, sir, who can ride and know something of sport, and can talk of it. I told Mr. Simpson, sir, of the sport we were to have today, and he seemed to care nothing about it!"

Robin sighed aloud.

"I suppose so," he said.

"Mr. John looked well, sir," pursued Dick, and proceeded to speak at length of the FitzHerbert troubles, and the iniquities of the Queen's Grace. He was a shrewd man in his way, with the simplicity which belongs to such shrewdness; he disliked the new ways which he experienced chiefly in the towns, and put them down, not wholly without justice, to the change of which religion formed an integral part; he hated the beggars and would gladly have gone to see one flogged; and he disliked the ministers and their sermons and their "prophesyings" with all the healthy ardour of prejudice. Once in the year did Dick approach the sacraments, and a great business he made of it, being unusually morose before them and almost indecently boisterous after them. He was feudal to the very heart of him; and it was his feudality that made him faithful to his religion as well as to his masters, for either of which he would resolutely have died. And what in the world he would do when he discovered, at Easter, that the objects of his fidelity were to take opposite courses, Robin could not conceive.

As they rode in at last, Robin, who had fallen silent again after Dick's last piece of respectful vehemence, suddenly beat his own leg with his whip and uttered an inaudible word. It seemed to Dick that the young master had perceived clearly that which plainly had been worrying him all the way home, and that he did not like it.

CHAPTER V

I

MR. Manners sat in his parlour ten days after the beginning of Lent, full of perplexing thoughts. He had eaten well and heartily after his week of spare diet, and then, while in high humour with all the world, first his wife and then his daughter had laid before him such revelations that all the pleasure of digestion was gone. It was but three minutes ago that Marjorie had fled from him in a torrent of tears, for which he could not see himself responsible, since he had done nothing but make the exclamations and comments that should be expected of a father in such a case.

The following were the points for his reflection—to begin with those that touched him less closely.

First that his friend Mr. Audrey, whom he had always looked upon with reverence and a kind of terror because of his hotness in matters of politics and religion, had capitulated to the enemy and was to go to church at Easter. Mr. Manners himself had something of timidity in his nature: he was conservative certainly, and practised, when he could without bringing himself into open trouble, the old religion in which he had been brought up. He, like the younger generation, had been educated at Derby Grammar School, and in his youth had sat with his parents in the nave of the old Cluniac church of St. James to hear Mass. He had then entered his father's office in Derby, about the time that the Religious Houses had fallen, and had transferred the scene of his worship to St. Peter's. At Queen Mary's accession, he had stood, with mild but genuine enthusiasm, in his lawyer's gown, in the train of the sheriff who proclaimed her in Derby marketplace; and stood in the crowd, with corresponding dismay, six years later to shout for Queen

Elizabeth. Since that date, for the first eleven years he had gone, as did other Catholics, to his parish church secretly, thankful that there was no doubt as to the priesthood of his parson, to hear the English prayers; and then, to do him justice, though he heard with something resembling consternation the decision from Rome that compromise must cease and that, henceforth, all true Catholics must withdraw themselves from the national worship, he had obeyed without even a serious moment of consideration. He had always feared that it might be so, understanding that delay in the decision was only caused by the hope that even now the breach might not be final or complete; and so was better prepared for the blow when it came. Since that time he had heard Mass when he could, and occasionally even harboured priests, urged thereto by his wife and daughter; and, for the rest, still went into Derby for three or four days a week to carry on his lawyer's business, with Mr. Biddell his partner, and had the reputation of a sound and careful man without bigotry or passion.

It was, then, a shock to his love of peace and serenity, to hear that yet another Catholic house had fallen, and that Mr. Audrey, one of his clients, could no longer be reckoned, as one of his co-religionists.

The next point for his reflection was that Robin was refusing to follow his father's example; the third, that somebody must harbour the boy over Easter, and that, in his daughter's violently expressed opinion, and with his wife's consent, he, Thomas Manners, was the proper person to do it. Last, that it was plain that there was something between his daughter and this boy, though what that was he had been unable to understand. Marjorie had flown suddenly from the room just as he was beginning to put his questions.

It is no wonder, then, that his peace of mind was gone. Not only were large principles once more threatened—considerations of religion and loyalty, but also those small and intimate principles which, so far more than great ones, agitate the mind of the individual. He did not wish to lose a client; yet neither did he wish to be unfriendly to a young confessor for the faith. Still less did he wish to lose his daughter, above all to a young man whose prospects seemed to be vanishing.

About half an hour later the door opened once more and Marjorie came in again. She was in her fine dress today—fine, that is, according to the exigencies of the time and place, though sober enough if for a town-house—in a good blue silk, rather dark, with a little ruff, with lace ruffles at her wrists, and a quilted petticoat, and silver buckles. For she was a gentleman's daughter, quite clearly, and not a yeoman's, and she must dress to her station. Her face was very pale and quite steady. She stood opposite her father.

"Father," she said, "I am very sorry for having behaved like a goose. You were quite right to ask those questions, and I have come back to answer them."

He looked at her timidly and yet with an attempt at severity. He knew what was due from him as a father. But for the present he had forgotten what questions they were; his mind had been circling so wildly.

"You are right to come back," he said, "you should not have left me so."

"I am very sorry," she said again.

"Well, then—you tell me that Mr. Robin has nowhere else to go."

She flushed a little.

"He has ten places to go to. He has plenty of friends. But none have the right that we have. He is a neighbour; it was to me, first of all, that he told the trouble."

Then he remembered.

"Sit down," he said. "I must understand much better first. I do not understand why he came to you first. Why not, if he must come to this house at all—why not to me? I like the lad; he knows that well enough."

He spoke with an admirable dignity, and began to feel more happy in consequence.

She had sat down as he told her, on the other side of the table; but he could not see her face.

"It would have been better if he had, perhaps," she said. "But—"

"Yes? What 'But' is that?"

Then she faced him, and her eyes were swimming.

"Father, he told me first because he loves me, and because I love him."

He sat up. This was speaking outright what she had only hinted at before. She must have been gathering her resolution to say this, while she had been gone. Perhaps she had been with her mother. In that case he must be cautious....

"You mean—"

"I mean just what I say. We love one another, and I am willing to be his wife if he desires it—and with your permission. But—"

He waited for her to go on,

"Another 'But!'" he said presently, though with increasing mildness.

"I do not think he will desire it after a while. And...and I do not know what I wish. I am torn in two."

"But you are willing?"

"I pray for it every night," she cried piteously. "And every morning I pray that it may not be so."

She was staring at him as if in agony, utterly unlike what he had looked for in her. He was completely bewildered.

"I do not understand one word—"

Then she threw herself at his knees and seized his hands; her face was all torn with pain.

"And I cannot explain one word.... Father, I am in misery. You must pray for me and have patience with me.... I must wait...I must wait and see what God wishes."

"Now, now..."

"Father, you will trust me, will you not?"

"Listen to me. You must tell me this. Do you love this boy?"

"Yes, yes."

"And you have told him so? He asked you, I mean?"

"Yes."

He put her hands firmly from his knee.

"Then you must marry him, if matters can be arranged. It is what I should wish. But I do not know—"

"Father, you do not understand—you do not understand. I tell you I am willing enough, if he wishes it...if he wishes it."

Again she seized his hands and held them. And again bewilderment came down on him like a cloud.

"Father! you must trust me. I am willing to do everything that I ought." (She was speaking firmly and confidently now.) "If he wishes to marry me, I will marry him. I love him dearly.... But you must say nothing to him, not one word. My mother agrees with this. She would have told you herself; but I said that I would—that I must be brave.... I must learn to be brave.... I can tell you no more."

He lifted her hands and stood up.

"I see that I understand nothing that you say after all," he said with a fine fatherly dignity. "I must talk with your mother."

II

IT was an hour before sunset when Marjorie came out again into the walled garden that had become for her now a kind of sanctuary, and in her hand she carried a letter, sealed and inscribed. On the outside the following words were written:

To Mr. Robin Audrey. At Matstead. Haste, haste, haste.

Within, the sheet was covered from top to bottom with the neat convent-hand. It began with such words as you would expect from a maid to her lover; it continued to inform him that her parents were willing, and, indeed, desirous, that he should come to them for Easter, and that her father would write a formal letter later to invite him; it was to be written from Derby, that it might cause less comment when Mr. Audrey saw it, and was to be expressed in terms that would satisfy him. Finally, it closed as it had begun, and was subscribed by his "loving friend, M. M."

One paragraph, however, is worth attention.

I have told my father and mother that we love one another, my Robin;

and that you have asked me to marry you, and that I have consented should you wish to do so when the time comes. They have consented most willingly; and so Jesu have you in His keeping, and guide your mind aright.

It was this paragraph that had cost her half of the hour occupied in writing; for it must be expressed just so and not otherwise; and its wording had cost her agony. The love of Robin was there—that she knew; and the love of Christ was there—so she thought; and yet where the divine and the human passion mingled, she could not tell; nor whether, indeed, for certain, it were the love of Christ at all, and not a vain imagination of her own as to how Christ, in this case, would be loved. Only she knew that across her love for Robin a shadow had fallen; she could scarcely tell when it had first come to her, and whence. Yet it had so come; it had deepened rapidly and strongly during the Mass that Mr. Simpson had said, and, behold! in its very darkness there was light. And so it had continued till confusion had fallen on her which none but Robin could dissolve. It must be his word finally that must give her the answer to her doubts; and she must make it easy for him to give it. He must know, that is, that she loved him more passionately than ever, that her heart would break if she had not her desire; and yet that she would not hold him back if a love that was greater than hers could be for him or his for her called him to another wedding than that of which either had yet spoken. A broken heart and God's will done would be better than that God's will should be avoided and her own satisfied.

It was this kind of consideration, therefore, that sent her swiftly to and fro, up and down the path under the darkening sky—if they can be called considerations which beat on the mind like a clamour of shouting; and, as she went, she strove to offer all to God; she entreated Him to do His will, yet not to break her heart; to break her heart, yet not Robin's; to break both her heart and Robin's, if that will could not otherwise be served.

Her lips moved now and again as she went; but her eyes were downcast and her face untroubled....

As the bell in the court rang for supper she went to the door and looked through. The man was just saddling up in the stable-door opposite.

"Jack," she called, "here is the letter. Take it safely."

Then she went in to supper.

CHAPTER VI

I

It was a great and solemn day when the squire of Matstead went to Protestant communion for the first time. It was Easter Day, too, but this was less in the consideration of the village. There was first the minister, Mr. Barton, in a condition of excited geniality from an early hour. He was observed soon after it was light, by an old man who was up early, hurrying up the village street in his minister's cassock and gown, presumably on his way to see that all preparations were complete for the solemnity. His wife was seen to follow him a few minutes later.

By eight o'clock the inhabitants of the village were assembled at points of vantage; some openly at their doors, others at the windows; and groups from the more distant farms, decked suitably, stood at all corners; to be greeted presently by their minister hurrying back once more from the church to bring the communion vessels and the bread and wine. The four or five soldiers of the village—a couple of billmen and pikemen and a real gunner—stood apart in an official group, but did not salute him. He did not speak of that which was in the minds of all, but he waved a hand to this man, bid a happy Easter to another, and disappeared within his lodgings leaving a wake of excitement behind him.

By a quarter before nine the three bells had begun to jangle from the tower; and the crowd had increased largely, when Mr. Barton once more passed to the church in the spring sunshine, followed by the more devout who wished to pray, and the more timid who feared a disturbance.

The bells ceased at nine o'clock, and upon the moment, a group came round the churchyard wall, down from the field-path and the stile that led to the manor.

First, walking alone, came the squire, swiftly and steadily. His face was flushed a little, but set and determined. He was in his fine clothes, ruff and all; his rapier was looped at his side, and he carried a stick. Behind him came three or four farm servants; then a yeoman and his wife; and last, at a little distance, three or four onlookers.

There was dead silence as he came; the hum of talk died at the corners; the bells' clamour had even now ceased. It seemed as if each man waited for his neighbour to speak. There was only the sound of the squire's brisk footsteps on the few yards of cobbles that paved the walk up to the lych-gate. At the door of the church, seen beyond him, was a crowd of faces.

Then a man called something aloud from fifty yards away; but there was no voice to echo him. The folk just watched their lord go by, staring on him as on some strange sight, forgetting even to salute him.

As he entered he lifted his hand to his head, but dropped it again; and passed on, sturdy, and (you would have said) honest and resolute too, to his seat behind the reading desk. He was met by silence; he was escorted by silence; and in silence he sat down.

Then the waiting crowd surged in, poured this way and that, and flowed into the benches. And Mr. Barton's voice was raised in holy exhortation.

"At what time soever a sinner doth repent him of his sin from the bottom of his heart, I will put all his wickedness out of remembrance, saith the Lord."

II

Those who could best observe (for the tale was handed on with the careful accuracy of those who cannot read or write) professed themselves amazed at the assured ease of the squire. No sound came from the seat half-hidden behind the reading-desk where he sat alone; and, during the prayers when he stood or kneeled, he moved as if he understood well enough what he was at. A great bound Prayer Book, it was known, rested before him on the book-board, and he was observed to turn the pages more than once.

It was, indeed, a heavy task that Mr. Barton had to do. For first there was the morning prayer, with its psalms, its lessons, and its prayers; next the Litany, and last the communion, in the course of which was delivered one of the homilies set forth by authority, especially designed for the support of those who were not preachers—preceded and followed by a psalm.

But all was easy today to a man who had such cause for exultation. There, seen full when he sat down, and in part when he knelt and stood, was the man who hitherto had stood to them for the old order, the old faith, the old tradition—the man whose horse's footsteps had been heard, times and again, before dawn, in the village street, bearing him to the mystery of the Mass; through whose gate strangers had ridden, perhaps three or four times in the year, to find harbourage—strangers dressed indeed as plain gentlemen or yeomen, yet known, every one of them, to be under her Grace's ban, and to ride in peril of liberty if not of life.

Yet here he sat—a man feared and even loved by some—the first of his line to yield to circumstance, and to make peace with his times. Not a man of all who looked on him believed him certainly to be that which his actions professed him to be; some doubted, especially those who themselves inclined to the old ways or secretly followed them; and the hearts of these grew sick as they watched. But the crown and climax was yet to come.

THE minister finished at last the homily—it was one which inveighed more than once against the popish superstitions; and he had chosen it for that reason, to clench the bargain, so to say—all in due order; for he was a careful man and observed his instructions, unlike some of his brethren who did as they pleased; and came back again to the long north side of the linen-covered table to finish the service.

He went on to pray for the whole estate of Christ's Church militant here on earth, especially for God's "servant, Elizabeth our Queen, that under her we may be godly and quietly governed"; then came the exhortation, urging any who might think himself to be "a blasphemer of God, a hinderer or slanderer of His Word...or to be in malice or envy," to bewail his sins, and "not to come to this holy table, lest after the taking of that holy sacrament, the devil enter into him, as he entered into Judas, and fill him full of all iniquities."

So forward with the rest. He read the Comfortable Words; the English equivalent for *Sursum Corda* with the Easter Preface; then another prayer; and finally rehearsed the story of the Institution of the Most Holy Sacrament, though without any blessing of the bread and wine. Then he stood up again, holding the silver plate in his hand for an instant, before proceeding to the squire's seat to give him the communion.

Then those who still watched, and who spread the tale about afterwards, saw that the squire did not move from his seat to kneel down. He had put off his hat again after the homily, and had so sat ever since; and now that the minister came to him, still there he sat.

Now such a manner of receiving was not unknown; yet it was the sign of a Puritan; and, so far from the folk expecting such behaviour in their squire, they had looked rather for Popish gestures, knockings on the breast, signs of the cross.

For a moment the minister stood before the seat, as if doubtful what to do. He held the plate in his left hand and a fragment of bread in his fingers. Then, as he began the words he had to say, one thing at least the people saw, and that was that a great flush dyed the old man's face, though he sat quiet. Then, as the minister held out the bread, the squire seemed to recover himself; he put out his fingers quickly, took the bread sharply and put it into his mouth; and so sat again, until the minister brought the cup; and this, too, he drank of quickly, and gave it back.

Then, as the communicants, one by one, took the bread and wine and went back to their seats, man after man glanced up at the squire.

But the squire sat there, motionless and upright, like a figure cut of stone.

III

THE court of the manor seemed deserted half an hour before dinner-time. Drama was in the air—the tragedy of seeing the squire come back from church for the first time, bearing himself as he always did, resolute and sturdy, yet changed in his significance after a fashion of which none of these simple hearts had ever dreamed.

In silence he went up the court, knowing that eyes were upon him, yet showing no sign that he knew it; he went up the steps with the same assured air, and disappeared into the hall.

Then the spell broke up and the bustle began, for it was only half an hour to dinner and guests were coming.

First Dick came out and strode out to the gate. He was still in his boots, for he had ridden to Padley and back since early morning with a couple of the maids and the stable-boy. He went to the gate of the court, the group dissolving as he came, and shut it in their faces. A noise of talking came out of the kitchen windows and the clash of a saucepan: the maids' heads vanished from the upper windows.

Even as Dick shut the gate he heard the sound of horses' hoofs down by the porter's lodge. The justices were coming—the two whose names he had heard with amazement last week, as the last corroboration of the incredible rumour of his master's defection. For these were a couple of magistrates—harmless men, indeed, as regarded their hostility to the old Faith—yet Protestants who had sat more than once on the bench in Derby to hear cases of recusancy. Old Mrs. Marpleden had told him they were to come, and that provision must be made for their horses—Mrs. Marpleden, the ancient housekeeper of the manor, who had gone to school for a while with the Benedictine nuns of Derby in King Henry's days. She had shaken her head and eyed him, and then had suffered three or four tears to fall down her old cheeks.

Well, they were coming, so Dick must open the gate again, and pull the bell for the servants; and this he did, and waited, hat in hand.

Up the little straight road they came, with a servant or two behind them—the two harmless gentlemen, chattering as they rode; and Dick loathed them in his heart.

"The squire is within?"

"Yes, sir."

They dismounted, and Dick held their stirrups. "He has been to church—eh?"

Dick made no answer. He feigned to be busy with one of the saddles. The magistrate glanced at him sharply.

It was a strange dinner that day.

Outwardly, again, all was as usual—as it might have been on any other Sunday in spring. The three gentlemen sat at the high table, facing down the hall; and, since there was no reading, and since it was a festival, there was no lack of conversation. The servants came in as usual with the dishes—there was roast lamb today, according to old usage, among the rest; and three or four wines. A little fire burned against the reredos, for cheerfulness rather than warmth, and the spring sunshine flowed in through the clear-glass windows, bright and genial.

Yet the difference was profound. To the servants who came and went, it was as if their master were another man altogether, and his hall some unknown place. There was no blessing of himself before meat; he said something, indeed, before he sat down, but it was unintelligible, and he made no movement with his hand. But it was deeper than this…and his men who had served him for ten or fifteen years looked on him as upon a stranger or a changeling.

CHAPTER VII

I

THE same Easter Day at Padley was another matter altogether.

As early as five o'clock in the morning the house was astir: footsteps passed along corridors and across the court; parties began to arrive. All was done without ostentation, yet without concealment, for Padley was a solitary place, and had no fear, at this time, of a sudden descent of the authorities. For form's sake—scarcely for more—a man kept watch over the valley road, and signalled by the flashing of a lamp twice every party with which he was acquainted, and there were no others than these to signal. A second man waited by the gate into the court to admit them. They rode and walked in from all round. Altogether perhaps a hundred and twenty persons were within Padley Manor—and the gate secured—by six o'clock.

Meanwhile, within, the priest had been busy since half-past four with the hearing of confessions. He sat in the chapel beside the undecked altar, and they came to him one by one. The household and a few of the nearer neighbours had done their duty in this matter the day before, and a good number had already made their Easter duties earlier in Lent; so by six o'clock all was finished.

Then began the bustle.

A group of ladies, FitzHerberts and Fentons, entered, so soon as the priest gave the signal by tapping on the parlour wall, bearing all things necessary for the altar; so that by the time that the priest was ready to vest, the place was transformed. Stuffs and embroideries hung upon the wall about the altar, making it seem, indeed, a sanctuary; two tall silver candlesticks, used for no other purpose, stood upon the linen cloths, under which rested the slate altar-stone, taken, with the sacred vessels and the vestments, from one of the privy hiding-holes. It was rumored that half a dozen such places had been contrived within the precincts, two of which were great enough to hold two or three men at a pinch.

Soon after six o'clock, then, the altar was ready and the priest stood vested. He retired a pace from the altar, signed himself with the cross, and with Mr. John FitzHerbert and his son Thomas on either side of him, began the preparation...

It was a strange and an inspiriting sight that the young priest (for it was Mr. Simpson who was saying the Mass) looked upon as he turned round after the gospel to make his little sermon. From end to end the tiny chapel was so full, that few could kneel and none sit down. The two doors were open, and here two faces peered in; and behind, rank after rank down the steps and along the little passage, the folk stood or knelt, out of sight of both priest and altar, and almost out of sound.

His little sermon was plain enough for the most foolish there. He spoke of Christ's Resurrection; of how death had no power to hold Him, nor pains nor prison to detain Him; and he spoke, too, of that mystical life of His which He yet lived in His body, which was the Church; of how Death, too, stretched forth his hands against Him there, and yet had no more force to hold Him than in His natural life lived on earth near sixteen hundred years ago; how a Resurrection awaited Him here in England as in Jerusalem, if His friends would be constant and courageous, not faithless, but believing.

"Even here," he said, "in this upper chamber, where we are gathered for fear of the Jews, comes Jesus and stands in the midst, the doors being shut. Upon this altar He will be presently, the Lamb slain yet the Lamb victorious, to give us all that peace which the world can neither give nor take away."

And he added a few words of exhortation and encouragement, bidding them fear nothing whatever might come upon them in the future; to hold fast to the faith once delivered to the saints, and so to attain the heavenly crown. He was not eloquent, for he was but a young man newly come from college, with no great gifts. Yet not a soul there looked upon him, on his innocent, wondering eyes and his quivering lips, but was moved by what he saw and heard.

The priest signed himself with the cross, and turned again to continue the Mass.

II

"You tell me, then," said the girl quietly, "that all is as it was with you? God has told you nothing?" Robin was silent.

Mass had been done an hour or more, and for the most part the company was dispersed again, after refreshment spread in the hall, except for those who were to stay to dinner, and these two had slipped away at last to talk together in the woods; for the court was still filled with servants coming and going, and the parlours occupied.

Robin had come to Booth's Edge at the beginning of Passion week, and had been there ever since. He had refrained, at Marjorie's entreaty, from speaking of her to her parents; and they, too, ruled by their daughter, had held their tongues on the matter. Everything else, however, had been discussed—the effect of the squire's apostasy, the alternatives that presented themselves to the boy, the future behaviour of him to his father. Yet not much had come of it. If the worst came to the worst, the lawyer had offered the boy a place in his office; Anthony Babington had proposed his coming to Dethick if his father turned him out; while Robin himself inclined to a third alternative—the begging of his father to give him a sum of money and be rid of him; after which he proposed, with youthful vagueness, to set off for London and see what he could do there.

Marjorie, however, had seemed strangely uninterested in such proposals. She had listened with patience, bowing her head in assent to each, beginning once or twice a word of criticism, and stopping herself before she had well begun. But she had looked at Robin with more than interest; and her mother had found her more than once on her knees in her own chamber, in tears. Yet she had said nothing, except that she would speak her mind after Easter, perhaps.

And now, it seemed, she was doing it.

"You have had no other thought?" she said again, "besides those of which you talked with my father?"

"I have had other thoughts," said the boy slowly, "but they are so wild and foolish that I have determined to think no more of them."

"You are determined?"

He bowed his head.

"You are sure, then, that they are not from God?" asked the girl, torn between fear and hope. He was silent; and her heart sank again.

He looked, indeed, a bewildered boy, borne down by a weight that was too heavy for his years. He walked with his hands behind his back, his hatless head bowed, regarding his feet and the last year's leaves on which he walked.

"My Robin," said the girl, "the last thing I would have you do is to tell me what you would not... Will you not speak to the priest about it?"

"I have spoken to the priest."

"Yes?"

"He tells me he does not know what to think."

"Would you do this thing—whatever it may be—if the priest told you it was God's will?"

There was a pause; and then:

"I do not know," said Robin, so low she could scarcely hear him.

She drew a deep breath to reassure herself.

"Listen!" she said. "I must say a little of what I think; but not all. Our Lord must finish it to you, if it is according to His will."

He glanced at her swiftly, and down again, like a frightened child.

"You know first," she said, "that I am promised to you. I hold that promise as sacred as anything on earth can be."

Her voice shook a little. The boy bowed his head again. She went on:

"But there are some things," she said, "more sacred than anything on earth—those things that come from heaven. Now, I wish to say this—and then have done with it: that if such should be God's will, I would not hold you for a day. We are Catholics, you and I.... Your father—"

Her voice broke; and she stopped; yet without leaving go of her hold upon herself. Only she could not speak for a moment.

Then a great fury seized on the boy. It was one of those angers that for a while poison the air and turn all things sour; yet without obscuring the mind—an anger in which the angry one strikes first at that which he loves most, because he loves it most, knowing, too, that the words he speaks are false. For this, for the present, was the breaking-point in the lad. She would give him no peace; she continued to press on him from without that which already pained him within; so he turned on her.

"You wish to be rid of me!" he cried fiercely.

She looked at him with her lips parted, her eyes astonished, and her face gone white.

"What did you say?" she said.

His conscience pierced him like a sword. Yet he set his teeth.

"You wish to be rid of me. You are urging me to leave you. You talk to me of God's will and God's voice, and you have no pity on me at all. It is an excuse—a blind."

He stood raging. The very fact that he knew every word to be false made his energy the greater; for he could not have said it otherwise.

"You think that!" she whispered.

There, then, they stood, eyeing one another. Then there surged over the boy a wave of shame, and the truth prevailed. His fair face went scarlet, and his eyes filled with tears. He dropped on his knees in the leaves, seized her hand and kissed it.

"Oh! You must forgive me," he said. "But...but I cannot do it."

III

It was a great occasion in the hall that Easter Day. The three tables, which, according to custom, ran along the walls, were filled today with guests; and a second dinner was to follow, scarcely less splendid than the first, for their servants as well as for those of the household. The floor was spread with new rushes; jugs of March beer, a full month old, as it should be, were ranged down the tables; and by every plate lay a posy of flowers. From the passage outside came the sound of music.

The feast began with the reading of the Gospel; at the close, Mr. John struck with his hand upon the table as a signal for conversation; the doors opened; the servants came in, and a babble of talk broke out. At the high table the master of the house presided, with the priest on his right, Mrs. Manners and Marjorie beyond him; on his left, Mrs. Fenton and her lord. At the other two tables Mr. Thomas presided at one and Mr. Babington at the other.

The talk was, of course, within the bounds of discretion; though once and again sentences were spoken which would scarcely have pleased the minister of the parish. For they were difficult times in which they lived; and it is no wonder at all if bitterness mixed itself with charity. Hardly one of the folk there but had paid a heavy price for his conscience; and all the worship that was permitted to them, and that by circumstance, and not by law, was such as they had engaged in that morning with shuttered windows and a sentinel for fear that, too, should be silenced.

The climax of the talk came when dinner was over, and the muscadel, with the mould-jellies, had been put upon the tables. It was at this moment that Mr. John nodded to his son, who went to the door to see the servants out, and stood by it to see that none listened. Then his father struck his hands together for silence, and himself spoke.

"Mr. Simpson," he said, "has something to say to us all. It is not a matter to be spoken of lightly, as you will understand presently.... Mr. Simpson."

The priest looked up timidly, pulling out a paper from his pocket.

"You have heard of Mr. Nelson?" he said to the company.

"Well, he was a priest; and I have news of his death. He was executed in London on the third of February for his religion. And another man, a Mr. Sherwood, was executed a few days afterwards."

There was a rustle along the benches. Some there had heard of the fact, but no more; some had heard nothing of either the man or his death. Two or three faces turned a shade paler; and then the silence settled down again. For here was a matter that touched them all closely enough; since up to now scarcely a priest except Mr. Cuthbert Maine had suffered death for his religion; and even of him some of the more tolerant said that it was treason with which he was charged. They had heard, indeed, of a priest or two having been sent abroad into exile for his faith; but the most of them thought it a thing incredible that in England at this time a man should suffer death for it. Fines and imprisonment were one thing; to such they had become almost accustomed. But death was another matter altogether. And for a priest! Was it possible that the days of King Harry were coming back; and that every Catholic henceforth should go in peril of his life as well as of liberty?

The folks settled themselves then in their seats; one or two men drank off a glass of wine.

"I have heard from a good friend of mine in London," went on the priest, looking at his paper, "one who followed every step of the trial; and was present at the death. They suffered at Tyburn.... However, I will tell you what he says. He is a countryman of mine, from Yorkshire, as was Mr. Nelson, too.

"'Mr. Nelson was taken in London on the first of December last year. He was born at Shelton, and was about forty-three years old; he was the son of Sir Nicholas Nelson.'

"So much," said the priest, looking up from his paper, "I knew myself. I saw him about four years ago just before he went to Douay, and he came back to England as a priest, a year and a half after. Mr. Sherwood was not a priest; he had been at Douay, too, but as a scholar only.... Well, we will speak of Mr. Nelson first. This is what my friend says."

He spread the paper before him on the table; and Marjorie, looking past her mother, saw that his hands shook as he spread it.

"'Mr. Nelson,'" began the priest, reading aloud with some difficulty, "'was brought before my lords, and first had tendered to him the oath of the Queen's supremacy. This he refused to take, saying that no lay prince could have pre-eminence over Christ's Church; and, upon being pressed as to who then could have it, answered, Christ's Vicar only, the successor of Peter. Further, he proceeded to say, under questioning, that since the religion of England at this time is schismatic and heretical, so also is the Queen's Grace who is head of it.

"'This, then, was what was wanted; and after a delay of a few weeks, the same questions being put to him, and his answers being the same, he was sentenced to death. He was very fortunate in his imprisonment. I had speech with him two or three times and was the means, by God's blessing, of bringing another priest to him, to whom he confessed himself; and with whom he received the Body of Christ a day before he suffered.

"'On the third of February, knowing nothing of his death being so near, he was brought up to a higher part of the prison, and there told he was to suffer that day. His kinsmen were admitted to him then, to bid him farewell; and afterwards two ministers came to turn him from his faith if they could; but they prevailed nothing.'"

There was a pause in the reading; but there was no movement among any that listened. Robin, watching from his place at the right-hand table, cold at heart, ran his eyes along the faces. The priest was as white as death, with the excitement, it seemed, of having to tell such a tale. His host beside him seemed downcast and quiet, but perfectly composed. Mrs. Manners had her eyes closed; Anthony Babington was frowning to himself with tight lips; Marjorie he could not see.

With a great effort the reader resumed:

"'When he was laid on the hurdle he refused to ask pardon of the Queen's Grace; for, said he, I have never yet offended her. I was beside him, and heard it. And he added, when those who stood near stormed at him, that it was better to be hanged than to burn in hell-fire.

"'There was a great concourse of people at Tyburn, but kept back by the officers so that they could not come at him. When he was in the cart, first he commended his spirit into God's hands, saying *In manus tuas*, etc.; then he besought all Catholics that were present to pray for him; I saw a good many who signed themselves in the crowd; and then he said some prayers in Latin; with the psalms *Miserere* and *De Profundis*. And then he addressed himself to the people, telling them he died for his religion, which was the Catholic Roman one, and prayed, and desired them to pray, that God would bring all Englishmen into it. The crowd cried out at that, exclaiming against this *Catholic Romish Faith*; and so he said what he had to say, over again. Then, before the cart was drawn away from him to leave him to hang, he asked pardon of all them he had offended, and even of the Queen, if he had indeed offended her. Then one of the sheriffs called on the hangman to make an end; so Mr. Nelson prayed again in silence, and then begged all Catholics that were there once more to pray that, by the bitter passion of Christ, his soul might be received into everlasting joy. And they did so; for as the cart was drawn away a great number cried out, and I with them, *Lord, receive his soul.*

"'He was cut down, according to sentence, before he was dead, and the butchery begun on him; and when it was near over, he moved a little in his pain, and said that he forgave the Queen and all that caused or consented to his death: and so he died.'"

The priest's voice, which had shaken again and again, grew so tremulous as he ended that those that were at the end of the hall could scarcely hear him; and, as it ceased, a murmur ran along the seats.

Mr. FitzHerbert leaned over to the priest and whispered. The priest nodded, and the other held up his hand for silence.

"There is more yet," he said.

Mr. Simpson, with a hand that still shook so violently that he could hardly hold his glass, lifted and drank off a cup of muscadel. Then he cleared his throat, sat up a little in his chair, and resumed:

"'Next I went to see Mr. Sherwood, to talk to him in prison and to encourage him by telling him of the passion of the other and how bravely he bore it, Mr. Sherwood took it very well, and said that he was afraid of nothing, that he had reconciled his mind to it long ago, and had rehearsed it all two or three times, so that he would know what to say and how to bear himself.'"

Mr. FitzHerbert leaned over again to the priest at this point and whispered something. Mr. Simpson nodded, and raised his eyes.

"Mr. Sherwood," he said, "was a scholar from Douay, but not a priest. He was lodging in the house of a Catholic lady, and had procured Mass to be said there, and it was through her son that he was taken and charged with recusancy."

Again ran a rustle through the benches. This executing of the laity for religion was a new thing in their experience. The priest lifted the paper again.

"'I found that Mr. Sherwood had been racked many times in the Tower, during the six months he was in prison, to force him to tell, if they could, where he had heard Mass and who had said it. But they could prevail nothing. Further, no visitor was admitted to him all this time, and I was the first and the last that he had; and that though Mr. Roper himself had tried to get at him for his relief; for he was confined underground and lay in chains and filth not to be described. I said what I could to him, but he said he needed nothing and was content, though his pain must have been very great all this while, what with the racking repeated over and over again and the place he lay in.

"'I was present again when he suffered at Tyburn, but was too far away to hear anything that he said, and scarcely, indeed, could see him; but I learned afterwards that he died well and courageously, as a Catholic should, and made no outcry or complaint when the butchery was done on him.

"'This, then, is the news I have to send you—sorrowful, indeed, yet joyful, too; for surely we may think that they who bore such pains for Christ's sake with such constancy will intercede for us whom they leave behind. I am hoping myself to come North again before I go to Douay next year, and will see you then and tell you more.'"

The priest laid down the paper, trembling.

Mr. FitzHerbert looked up.

"It will give pleasure to the company," he said, "to know that the writer of the letter is Mr. Ludlam, from Radbourne, in this county. As you have heard, he, too, hopes by God's mercy to be made priest and to come back to England."

CHAPTER VIII

I

IN the following week Robin went home again. He thought he had come to a decision last week; he found that the decision was shattered as soon as made. He had talked to the priest; he had resisted Marjorie; and yet to neither of them had he put into formal words what it was that troubled him. He had asked questions about vocation, about the place that circumstance occupies in it, of the value of dispositions, fears, scruples, and resistance. He had, that is, fingered his wound, glanced at it and then glanced aside; yet the one thing he had not done was to probe it—not even to allow another to do so.

As he rode through Frodggatt, he saw a group of saddle-horses standing at the inn door, but thought nothing of it, till a man ran out of the door, still holding his pot, and saluted him, and he recognised him to be one of Mr. Babington's men.

"My master is within, sir," he said; "he bade me look out for you."

Robin drew rein, and as he did so, Anthony, too, came out.

"Ah!" he said. "I heard you would be coming this way. Will you come in? I have something to say to you."

Robin slipped off, leaving his mare in the hands of Anthony's man, since he himself was riding alone, with his valise strapped on behind.

It was a little room, very trim and well kept, on the first floor, to which his friend led him. Anthony shut the door carefully and came across to settle by the window-seat.

"Well," he said, "I have bad news for you, my friend. Will you forgive me? I have seen your father and had words with him."

"Eh?"

"I said nothing to you before," went on the other, sitting down beside him. "I knew you would not have it so, but I went to see for myself and to put a question or two. He is your father, but he has also been my friend. That gives me rights, you see!"

"Tell me," said Robin heavily.

It appeared that Anthony, who was a precise as well as an ardent young man, had had scruples about trusting to hearsay. Certainly it was rumoured far and wide that the squire of Matstead had done as he had said he would do, and gone to church; but Mr. Anthony was one of those spirits who will always have things, as they say, from the fountain-head; partly from instincts of justice, partly, no doubt, for the pleasure of making direct observations to the principals concerned. This was what he had done in this case. He had ridden, without a word to any, up to Matstead, and had demanded to be led to the squire; and there and then, refusing to sit down till he was answered, had put his question. There had been a scene. The squire had referred to puppies who wanted drowning, to young sparks, and to such illustrative similes; and Anthony, in spite of his youthful years, had flared out about turn-coats and lick-spittles. There had been a very pretty ending: the squire had shouted for his servants and Anthony for his, and the two parties had eyed one another, growling like dogs, until bloodshed seemed imminent. Then the visitor had himself solved the situation by stalking out of the house from which the squire was proposing to flog him, mounting his horse, and with a last compliment or two had ridden away. And here he was at Froggatt on his return journey, having eaten there that dinner which no longer would be spread for him at Matstead.

Robin sat silent till the tale was done, and at the end of it Anthony was striding about the room, aflame again with wrath, gesticulating and raging aloud.

Then Robin spoke, holding up his hand for moderation. "You will have the whole house here," he said. "Well, you have cooked my goose for me."

"Bah! that was cooked at Passiontide when you went to Booth's Edge. Do you think he'll ever have a Papist in his house again?"

"Did he say so?"

"No; but he said enough about his young cub.... Nonsense, man! Come home with me to Dethick. We'll find occupation enough."

"Did he say he would not have me home again?"

"No," bawled Anthony, "I have told you he did not say so outright. But he said enough to show he'd have no rebels, as he called them, in his Protestant house! Dick's to leave. Did you hear that?"

"Dick!"

"Why, certainly. There was a to-do on Sunday, and Dick spoke his mind. He'll come to me, he says, if you have no service for him."

Robin set his teeth. It seemed as if the pelting blows would never cease.

"Come with me to Dethick!" said Anthony again. "I tell you—"

"Well?"

"There'll be time enough to tell you when you come. But I promise you occupation enough."

He paused, as if he would say more and dared not.

"You must tell me more," said the lad slowly. "What kind of occupation?"

Then Anthony did a queer thing. He first glanced at the door, and then went to it quickly and threw it open. The little lobby was empty. He went out, leaned over the stair and called one of his men.

"Sit you there," he said, with the glorious nonchalance of a Babington, "and let no man by till I tell you."

He came back, closed the door, bolted it, and then came across and sat down by his friend.

"Do you think the rest of us are doing nothing?" he whispered. "Why, I tell you that a dozen of us in Derbyshire—" He broke off once more. "I may not tell you," he said, "I must ask leave first."

A light began to glimmer before Robin's mind; the light broadened suddenly and intensely, and his whole soul leapt to meet it.

"Do you mean—?" And then he, too, broke off, well knowing enough, though not all of, what was meant.

It was quiet here within this room, in spite of the village street outside. It was dinner-time, and all were within doors or out at their affairs; and except for the stamp of a horse now and again, and the scream of the wind in the keyhole and between the windows, there was little to hear. And in the lad's soul was a tempest.

He knew well enough now what his friend meant, though nothing of the details; and from the secrecy and excitement of the young man's manner he understood what the character of his dealings would likely be, and towards those dealings his whole nature leaped as a fish to the water. Was it possible that this way lay the escape from his own torment of conscience? Yet he must put a question first, in honesty.

"Tell me this much," he said in a low voice. "Do you mean that this…this affair will be against men's lives…or…or such as even a priest might engage in?"

Then the light of fanaticism leaped to the eyes of his friend, and his face brightened wonderfully.

"Do they observe the courtesies and forms of law?" he snarled. "Did Nelson die by God's law, or did Sherwood—those we know of? I will tell you this," he said, "and no more unless you pledge yourself to us…that we count it as warfare—in Christ's Name yes—but warfare for all that."

There then lay the choice before this lad, and surely it was as hard a choice as ever a man had to make. On the one side lay such an excitement as he had never yet known—for Anthony was no merely mad fool—a path, too, that gave him hopes of Marjorie, that gave him an escape from home without any more ado, a task besides which he could tell himself honestly was, at least, for the cause that lay so near to Marjorie's heart, and was beginning to lie near his own. And on the other there was open to him that against which he had fought now day after day, in misery—a life that had no single attraction to the natural man in him, a life that meant the loss of Marjorie for ever.

"Come," whispered Anthony again.

Robin stood up; he made as if to speak; then he silenced himself.

He could hear voices from the room beneath—Anthony's men talking there no doubt. They might be his men, too, at the lifting of a finger—they and Dick. There were the horses waiting without; he heard the jingle of a bit as one tossed his head. Those were the horses that would go back to Dethick and Derby, and, maybe, half over England.

He walked to and fro half a dozen times without speaking, and, if he had but guessed it, he might have been comforted to know that his manhood flowed in upon him, as a tide coming in over a flat beach. Yet, though he conquered then, he did not know that he conquered. He still believed, as he turned at last and faced his friend, that his mind was yet to make up, and his whisper was harsh and broken. "I do not know," he whispered. "I must go home first."

II

DICK was waiting by the porter's lodge as the boy rode in, and walked up beside him with his brown hand on the horse's shoulder. Robin could not say much, and, besides, his confidence must be tied.

"So you are going," he said softly.

The man nodded.

"I met Mr. Babington.... You cannot do better, I think, than go to him."

It was with a miserable heart that an hour or two later he came down to supper. His father was already at table, sitting grimly in his place; he made no sign of welcome or recognition as his son came in. During the meal itself this was of no great consequence, as silence was the custom; but the boy's heart sank yet further as, still without a word to him, the squire rose from table at the end and went as usual through the parlour door. He hesitated a moment before following. Then he grasped his courage and went after.

All things were as usual there—the wine set out and the sweet-meats, and his father in his usual place. Yet still there was silence.

It was this room that was associated with so much that was happy in his life—drawn-out hours after supper, when his father was in genial moods, or when company was there—company that would never come again—and laughter and gallant talk went round. There was the fire burning in the new stove: there was the table where he had written his little letter; there was "Christ carrying His Cross."

"So you have sent your friend to insult me, now!"

Robin started. The voice was quiet enough, but full of a suppressed force.

"I have not, sir. I met Mr. Babington at Froggatt on his way back. He told me. I am very sorry for it."

"And you talked with him at Padley, too, no doubt?"

"Yes, sir."

His father suddenly wheeled round on him.

"Do you think I have no sense, then? Do you think I do not know what you and your friends speak of?"

Robin was silent.

He was astonished how little afraid he was. His heart beat loud enough in his ears; yet he felt none of that helplessness that had fallen on him before when his father was angry.... Certainly he had added to his stature in the parlour at Froggatt.

The old man poured out a glass of wine and drank it. His face was flushed high, and he was using more words than usual.

"Well, sir, there are other affairs we must speak of; and then no more of them. I wish to know your meaning for the time to come. There must be no more fooling this way and that. I shall pay no fines for you—mark that! If you must stand on your own feet, stand on them.... Now then!"

"Do you mean, am I coming to church with you, sir?"

"I mean, who is to pay your fines?...Miss Marjorie?"

Robin set his teeth at the sneer.

"I have not yet been fined, sir."

"Now do you take me for a fool? D'you think they'll let you off? I was speaking—"

The old man stopped.

"Yes, sir?"

The other wheeled his face on him.

"If you will have it," he said, "I was speaking to my two good friends who dined here on Sunday. I was plain with them and they were plain with me. 'I shall not pay for my brat of a son,' I said. 'Then he must pay for himself,' said they, 'unless we lay him by the heels.' 'Not in my house, I hope,' I said; and they laughed at that. We were very merry together."

"Yes, sir?"

"Good God! have I a fool for a son? I ask you again, who is to pay?"

"When will they demand it?"

"Why, they may demand it next week, if they will! You were not at church on Sunday!"

"I was not in Matstead," said the lad.

"But—"

"And Mr. Barton will not, I think—"

The old man struck the table suddenly and violently.

"I have dropped words enough," he cried, "Where's the use of it? If you think they will let you alone, I tell you they will not. There are to be doings before Christmas, at latest; and what then?"

Then Robin drew his breath sharply between his teeth; all doors seemed closing, save that which terrified him...

"I have thought in my mind—" he began; and stopped, for the terror of what was on his tongue grew suddenly upon him.

"Eh?"

Robin stood up.

"I must have time, sir," he cried; "I must have time. Do not press me too much."

His father's eyes shone bright and wrathful. He beat on the table with his open hand; but the boy was too quick for him.

"I beg of you, sir, not to make me speak too soon. It may be that you would hate that I should speak more than my silence."

His whole person was tense and magnetic; his face was paler than ever; and it seemed as if his father understood enough, at least, to make him hesitate. The two looked at one another; and it was the man's eyes that fell first.

"You may have till Pentecost," he said.

III

IT would be at about an hour before dawn that Robin awoke for the third or fourth time that night; for the conflict still roared within his soul and would give him no peace. And, as he lay there staring up into the dark, once more weighing and balancing this and the other, swayed by enthusiasm at one moment, weighed down with melancholy the next—there came to him, distinct and clear through the still night, the sound of horses' hoofs, perhaps of three or four beasts, walking together.

Now, whether it was the ferment of his own soul, or the work of some interior influence, or indeed, the very intimation of God Himself, Robin never knew (though he inclined later to the last of these); yet it remains as a fact that when he heard that sound, so fierce was his curiosity to know who it was that rode abroad in company at such an hour, he threw off the blankets that covered him, went to his window and threw it open. Further, when he had listened there a second or two, and had heard the sound cease and then break out again clearer and nearer, signifying that the party was riding through the village, his curiosity grew so intense, that he turned from the window, snatched up and put on a few clothes, groping for them as well as he could in the dimness, and was presently speeding, barefooted, downstairs, telling himself in one breath that he was a fool, and in the next that he must reach the churchyard wall before the horses did.

It was but a short run when he had come down into the court, by the little staircase that led from the men's rooms; the ground was soaking with the rains of yesterday, but he cared nothing for that; and, as the riding party turned up the little ascent that led beneath the churchyard, Robin, on the other side of the wall, was keeping between the tombstones to see, and not be seen.

It was within an hour of dawn, at that time when the sky begins to glimmer with rifts above the two horizons, showing light enough at least to distinguish faces. It was such a light as that in which he had seen the deer looking at him motionless as he rode home with Dick. Yet the three who now rode up towards him were so muffled about the faces that he feared he would not know them. They were men, all three of them; and he could make out valises strapped to the saddle of each; but, what seemed strange, they did not speak as they came; and it appeared as if they wished to make no more noise than was necessary, since one of them, when his horse set his foot upon the cobblestones beside the lych-gate, pulled him sharply off them.

And then, just as they rounded the angle of the wall where the boy crouched peeping, the man that rode in the middle sighed as if with relief, and pulled the cloak that was about him, so that the collar fell from his face, and at the same time turned to his companion on his right, and said something in a low voice.

But the boy heard not a word; for he found himself staring at the thin-faced young priest from whom he had received Holy Communion at Padley. It was but for an instant; for the man to whom the priest spoke answered in the same low voice, and the other pulled his cloak again round his mouth.

Yet the look was enough. The sight, once more, of this servant of God, setting out again upon his perilous travels—seen at such a moment, when the boy's judgment hung in the balance (as he thought): this one single reminder of what a priest could do in these days of sorrow, and of what God called on him to do—the vision, for it was scarcely less, all things considered, of a life such as this—presented, so to say, in this single scene of a furtive and secret ride before the dawn, leaving Padley soon after midnight—this, falling on a soul that already leaned that way, finished that for which Marjorie had prayed, and against which the lad himself had fought so fiercely.

Half an hour later he stood by his father's bed, looking down on him without fear.

"Father," he said, as the old man stared up at him through sleep-ridden eyes, "I have come to give you my answer. It is that I must go to Rheims and be a priest."

Then he turned again and went out of the room, without waiting.

CHAPTER IX

I

MRS. Manners was still abed when her daughter came in to see her. She lay in the great chamber that gave upon the gallery above the hall whence, on either side, she could hear whether or no the maids were at their business—which was a comfort to her if a discomfort to them. And now that her lord was in Derby, she lay here all alone.

The first that she knew of her daughter's coming was a light in her eyes; and the next was a face, as of a stranger, looking at her with great eyes, exalted by joy and pain. The light, held below, cast shadows upwards from chin and cheek, and the eyes shone in hollows. Then, as she sat up, she saw that it was her daughter, and that the maid held a paper in her hands; she was in her night-linen, and a wrap lay over her shoulders and shrouded her hair.

"He is to be a priest," she whispered sharply. "Thank our Lord with me...and...and God have mercy on me!"

Then Marjorie was on her knees by the bedside, sobbing so that the curtains shook.

THE mother got it all out of her presently—the tale of the girl's heart torn two ways at once. On the one side there was her human love for the lad who had wooed her—as hot as fire, and as pure—and on the other that keen romance that had made her pray that he might be a priest. This second desire had come to her, as sharp as a voice that calls, when she had heard of the apostasy of his father; it had seemed to her the riposte that God made to the assault upon His honour. The father would no longer be His worshipper? Then let the son be His priest; and so the balance be restored. And so the maid had striven with the two loves that, for once, would not agree together; she had not dared to say a word to the lad of anything of this lest it should be her will and not God's that should govern him, for she knew very well what a power she had over him; but she had prayed God, and begged Robin to pray too and to listen to His voice; and now she had her way, and her heart was broken with it, she said:

"And when I think," she wailed across her mother's knees, "of what it is to be a priest; and of the life that he will lead, and of the death that he may die! ...And it is I...I...who will have sent him to it. Mother!..."

"But our Lord will take care of him, will He not? And not suffer—"

Mrs. Manners fell to patting her head.

"And who brought the message?" she asked.

Mrs. Manners was one of those experienced persons who are fully persuaded that youth is a disease that must be borne with patiently. Time, indeed, will cure it; yet until the cure is complete, elders must bear it as well as they can and not seem to pay too much attention to it. A rigorous and prudent diet; long hours of sleep, plenty of occupation—these are the remedies for the fever. So, while Marjorie first began to read the lad's letter, and then, breaking down altogether, thrust it into her mother's hand, Mrs. Manners was searching her memory as to whether any imprudence the day before, in food or behaviour, could be the cause of this crisis. Love between boys and girls was common enough; she herself twenty years ago had suffered from the sickness when young John had come wooing her; yet a love that could thrust from it that which it loved was beyond her altogether. Either Marjorie loved the lad, or she did not, and if she loved him, why did she pray that he might be a priest? That was foolishness; since priesthood was a bar to marriage. She began to conclude that Marjorie did not love him; it had been but a romantic fancy; and she was encouraged by the thought.

"Madge," she began, when she had read through the confused line or two, in the half-boyish, half-clerkly hand of Robin, scribbled and dispatched by the hands of Dick scarcely two hours ago. "Madge—"

She was about to say something sensible when the maid interrupted her again.

"And it is I who have brought it all on him!" she wailed. "If it had not been for me—"

Her mother laid a firm hand on her daughter's mouth. It was not often that she felt the superior of the two; yet here was a time, plain enough, when maturity and experience must take the reins.

"Madge," she said, "it is plain you do not love him; or you never—"

The maid started back, her eyes ablaze.

"Not love him! Why—"

"That you do not love him truly; or you would never have wished this for him.... Now listen to me, and listen carefully!"

She raised an admonitory finger, complacent at last. But her speech was not to be made at that time; for her daughter swiftly rose to her feet, controlled at last by the shock of astonishment.

"Then I do not think you know what love is," she said softly. "To love is to wish the other's highest good, as I understand it."

Mrs. Manners compressed her lips, as might a prophetess before a prediction. But her daughter was beforehand with her again.

"That is the love of a Christian, at least," she said. Then she stooped, took the letter from her mother's knees, and went out.

Mrs. Manners sat for a moment as her daughter left her. Then she understood that her hour of superiority was gone with Marjorie's hour of weakness; and she emitted a short laugh as she took her place again behind the child she had borne.

II

It was a strange time that Marjorie had until two days later when Robin came and told her all, and how it had fallen out. For now, it seemed, she walked on air; now in shoes of lead. When she was at her prayers (which was pretty often just now), and at other times, when the air lightened suddenly about her and the burdens of earth were lifted as if another hand were put to them, why, then, all was glory, and she saw Robin as transfigured and herself beneath him all but adoring. Little visions came and went before her imagination. Robin riding, like some knight on an adventure, to do Christ's work; Robin at the altar, in his vestments; Robin absolving penitents—all in a rosy light of faith and romance. She saw him even on the scaffold, undaunted and resolute, with God's light on his face, and the crowd awed beneath him; she saw his soul entering heaven, with all the harps ringing to meet him, and eternity begun.... And then, at other times, when the heaviness came down on her, as clouds upon the Derbyshire hills, she understood nothing but that she had lost him; that he was not to be hers, but Another's; that a loveless and empty life lay before her, and a womanhood that was without its fruition. And it was this latter mood that fell on her, swift and entire, when, looking out from her window a little before dinner-time, she saw suddenly his hat, and Cecily's head, jerking up the steep path that led to the house.

She fell on her knees by her bedside.

"Jesu!" she cried. "Jesu! Give me strength to meet him."

Mrs. Manners, too, hearing the horse's footsteps on the pavement a minute later, and Marjorie's steps going downstairs, also looked forth and saw him dismounting. She was a prudent woman, and did not stir a finger till she heard the bell ringing in the court for the dinner to be served. They would have time, so she thought, to arrange their attitudes.

And, indeed, she was right: for it was two quiet enough persons who met her as she came down into the hall: Robin flushed with riding, yet wholly under his own command—bright-eyed, and resolute and natural (indeed, it seemed to her that he was more of a man than she had thought him). And her daughter, too, was still and strong; a trifle paler than she should be, yet that was to be expected. At dinner, of course, nothing could be spoken of but the most ordinary affairs— in such speaking, that is, as there was. It was not till they had gone out into the walled garden and sat them down, all three of them, on the long garden-seat beside the rose-beds, that a word was said on these new matters. There was silence as they walked there, and silence as they sat down.

"Tell her, Robin," said the maid.

It appeared that matters were not yet as wholly decided as Mrs. Manners had thought. Indeed, it seemed to her that they were not decided at all. Robin had written to Dr. Allen, and had found means to convey his letter to Mr. Simpson, who, in his turn, had undertaken to forward it at least as far as to London; and there it would await a messenger to Douay. It might be a month before it would reach Douay, and it might be three or four months, or even more, before an answer could come back. Next, the squire had taken a course of action which, plainly, had disconcerted the lad, though it had its conveniences too. For, instead of increasing the old man's fury, the news his son had given him had had a contrary effect. He had seemed all shaken, said Robin; he had spoken to him quietly, holding in the anger that surely must be there, the boy thought, without difficulty. And the upshot of it was that no more had been said as to Robin's leaving Matstead for the present—not one word even about the fines. It seemed almost as if the old man had been trying how far he could push his son, and had recoiled when he had learned the effect of his pushing.

"I think he is frightened," said the lad gravely. "He had never thought that I could be a priest."

Mrs. Manners considered this in silence.

"And it may be autumn before Dr. Allen's letter comes back?" she asked presently.

Robin said that that was so.

"It may even be till winter," he said. "The talk among the priests, Mr. Simpson tells me, is all about the removal from Douay. It may be made at any time, and who knows where they will go?"

Mrs. Manners glanced across at her daughter, who sat motionless, with her hands clasped. Then she was filled with the spirit of reasonableness and sense: all this tragic to-do about what might never happen seemed to her the height of folly.

"Nay, then," she burst out, "then nothing may happen after all. Dr. Allen may say 'No,' the letter may never get to him. It may be that you will forget all this in a month or two."

Robin turned his face slowly towards her, and she saw that she had spoken at random. Again, too, it struck her attention that his manner seemed a little changed. It was graver than that to which she was accustomed.

"I shall not forget it," he said softly. "And Dr. Allen will get the letter. Or, if not he, someone else."

There was silence again, but Mrs. Manners heard her daughter draw a long breath.

III

It was an hour later that Marjorie found herself able to say that which she knew must be said.

Robin had lingered on, talking of this and that, though he had said half a dozen times that he must be getting homewards; and at last, when he rose, Mistress Manners, who was still wholly misconceiving the situation, after the manner of sensible middle-aged folk, archly and tactfully took her leave and disappeared down towards the house, advancing some domestic reason for her departure.

Robin sighed, and turned to the girl, who still sat quiet. But as he turned she lifted her eyes to him swiftly.

"Goodbye, Mr. Robin," she said.

He pulled himself up.

"You understand, do you not?" she said. "You are to be a priest. You must remember that always. You are a sort of student already."

She could see him pale a little; his lips tightened. For a moment he said nothing; he was taken wholly aback.

"Then I am not to come here again?"

Marjorie stood up. She showed no sign of the fierce self-control she was using.

"Why, yes," she said. "Come as you would come to any Catholic neighbour. But no more than that…. You are to be a priest."

The spring air was full of softness and sweetness as they stood there. The whole world, it seemed, was kindling with love and freshness. Yet these two had to stand here and be cold, one to the other.... He was to be a priest; that must not be forgotten, and they must meet no more on the old footing. That was gone. Already he stood among the Levites, at least in intention; and the Lord alone was to be the portion of his inheritance and his Cup.

It was a minute before either of them moved, and during that minute the maid felt her courage ebb from her like an outgoing tide, leaving a desolation behind. It was all that she could do not to cry out.

But when at last Robin made a movement and she had to look him in the face, what she saw there braced and strengthened her.

"You are right, Mistress Marjorie," he said both gravely and kindly. "I will bid you good-day and be getting to my horse."

He kissed her gently, as the manner was, and went down the path alone.

PART TWO

CHAPTER I

I

It was with a sudden leap of her heart that Marjorie, looking out of her window at the late autumn landscape, her mind still running on the sheet of paper that lay before her, saw a capped head, and then a horse's crest, rise over the broken edge of land up which Robin had ridden so often two and three years ago. Then she saw who was the rider, and laid her pen down again.

It was two years since the lad had gone to Rheims, and it would be five years more, she knew (since he was not overquick at his books), before he would return a priest. She had letters from him: one would come now and again, a month or two sometimes after the date of writing. It was only in September that she had had the letter which he had written her on hearing of her father's death, and Mr. Manners had died in June. She had written back to him then, a discreet and modest letter enough, telling him of how Mr. Simpson had read Mass over the body before it was taken down to Derby for the burying; and telling him, too, of her mother's rheumatics that kept her abed now three parts of the year. For the rest, the letters were dull enough reading to one who did not understand them: the news the lad had to give was of a kind that must be disguised, lest the letters should fall into other hands, since it concerned the coming and going of priests whose names must not appear. Yet, for all that, the letters were laid up in a press, and the heap grew slowly.

It was Mr. Anthony Babington who was come now to see her, and it was his third visit since the summer. But she knew well enough what he was come for, since his young wife, whom he had married last year, was no use to him in such matters: she had lately had a child, too, and lived quietly at Dethick with her women. His letters, too, would come at intervals, carried by a rider, or sometimes some farmer's man on his way home from Derby, and these letters, too, held dull reading enough for such as were not in the secret. Yet the magistrates at Derby would have given a good sum if they could have intercepted and understood them.

It was in the upper parlour now that she received him. A fire was burning there, as it had burned so long ago, when Robin found her fresh from her linen, and Anthony sat down in the same place. She sat by the window, with the paper in her hands at which she had been writing when she first saw him.

He had news for her, of two kinds, and, like a man, gave her first that which she least wished to hear. (She had first showed him the paper.)

"That was the very matter I was come about," he said. "You have only a few of the names, I see. Now the rest will be over before Christmas, and will all be in London together."

"Can you not give me the names?" she said.

"I could give you the names, certainly. And I will do so before I leave; I have them here. But—Mistress Marjorie, could you not come to London with me? It would ease the case very much."

"Why, I could not," she said. "My mother—And what good would it serve?"

"This is how the matter stands," said Anthony, crossing his legs. "We have a dozen priests coming all together—at least, they will not travel together, of course, but they will all reach London before Christmas, and there they will hold counsel as to who shall go to the districts. Eight of them, I have no doubt, will come to the north. There are as many priests in the south as are safe at the present time—or as are needed. Now if you were to come with me, mistress—with a serving-maid, and my sister would be with us—we could meet these priests, and speak with them, and make their acquaintance. That would remove a great deal of danger. We must not have that affair again which fell out last month."

Marjorie nodded slowly. (It was wonderful how her gravity had grown on her these last two years.)

She knew well enough what he meant. It was the affair of the clerk who had come from Derby on a matter connected with her father's will about the time she was looking for the arrival of a strange priest, and who had been so mistaken by her. Fortunately he had been a well-disposed man, with Catholic sympathies, or grave trouble might have followed. But this proposal of a visit to London seemed to her impossible. She had never been to London in her life; it appeared to her as might a voyage to the moon. Derby seemed oppressively large and noisy and dangerous; and Derby, she understood, was scarcely more than a village compared to London.

"I could not do it," she said presently. "I could not leave my mother."

Anthony explained further.

It was evident that Booth's Edge was becoming more and more a harbour for priests, owing largely to Mistress Marjorie's courage and piety. It was well placed; it was remote; and it had so far avoided all suspicion. Padley certainly served for many, but Padley was nearer the main road; and besides, had fallen under the misfortune of losing its master for the very crime of recusancy. It seemed to be all important, therefore, that the ruling mistress of Booth's Edge, since there was no master, should meet as many priests as possible, in order that she might both know and be known by them; and here was such an opportunity as would not easily occur again. Here were a dozen priests, all to be together at one time; and of these, at least two-thirds would be soon in the north. How convenient, therefore, it would be if their future hostess could but meet them, learn their plans, and perhaps aid them by her counsel.

But she shook her head resolutely.

"I cannot do it," she said.

Anthony made a little gesture of resignation. But, indeed, he had scarcely hoped to persuade her. He knew it was a formidable thing to ask of a country-bred maid.

"Then we must do as well as we can," he said. "In any case, I must go. There is a priest I have to meet in any case; he is returning as soon as he has bestowed the rest."

"Yes?"

"His name is Ballard. He is known as Fortescue, and passes himself off as a captain. You would never know him for a priest."

"He is returning, you say?"

A shade of embarrassment passed over the young man's face, and Marjorie saw that there was something behind which she was not to know.

"Yes," he said, "I have business with him. He is not to come over on the mission yet, but only to bring the others and see them safe—"

He broke off suddenly.

"Why, I was forgetting," he cried. "Our Robin is coming too. Just today I had a letter from him, and another for you."

He searched in the breast of his coat, and did not see the sudden rigidity that fell on the girl. For a moment she sat perfectly still; her heart had leapt to her throat, it seemed, and was hammering there.... But by the time he had found the letter she was herself again.

"Here it is," he said.

She took it; but made no movement to open it.

"But he is not to be a priest for five years yet?" she said quietly.

"No; but they send them sometimes as servants and such like, to make a party seem what it is not, as well as to learn how to avoid her Grace's servants. He will go back with Mr. Ballard, I think, after three or four weeks. You have had letters from him, you told me?"

She nodded.

"Yes; but he said nothing of it, but only how much he longed to see England again."

"He could not. It has only just been arranged. He has asked to go."

There was a silence for a moment. But Anthony did not understand what it meant. He had known nothing of the affair of his friend and this girl, and he looked upon them merely as a pair of acquaintances, above all, when he had heard of Robin's determination to go to Rheims. Even the girl saw that he knew nothing, in spite of her embarrassment, and the thought that had come to her when she had heard of Robin's coming to London grew on her every moment. But she thought she must gain time.

She stood up.

"You would like to see his letters?" she asked. "I will bring them."

And she slipped out of the room.

II

Anthony Babington sat still. It was true that he was sincere and active enough in all that he did up here in the north for the priests of his faith; indeed, he risked both property and liberty on their behalf, and was willing to continue doing so as long as these were left to him. But it seemed to him sometimes that too much was done by spiritual ways and too little by temporal. Certainly the priesthood and the Mass were instruments—and, indeed, the highest instruments in God's hand; it was necessary to pray and receive the sacraments, and to run every risk in life for these purposes. Yet it appeared to him that the highest instruments were not always the best for such rough work.

It was now over two years ago since the thought had first come to him, and since that time he had spared no effort to shape a certain other weapon, which, he thought, would do the business straight and clean. Yet how difficult it had been to raise any feeling on the point. At first he had spoken almost freely to this or that Catholic whom he could trust; he had endeavoured to win even Robin; and yet, with hardly an exception, all had drawn back and bidden him be content with a spiritual warfare. One priest, indeed, had gone so far as to tell him that he was on dangerous ground...and the one and single man who up to the present had seemed on his side was the very man, Mr. Ballard, then a layman, whom he had met by chance in London, and who had been the occasion of first suggesting any such idea. It was, in fact, for the sake of meeting Ballard again that he was going to London; and, he had almost thought from his friend's last letter, it had seemed that it was for the sake of meeting him that Mr. Ballard was coming across once more.

So the young man sat, with that moody look on his face, until Marjorie came back, wondering what news he would have from Mr. Ballard, and whether the plan, at present only half conceived, was to go forward or be dropped. He was willing enough, as has been said, to work for priests, and he had been perfectly sincere in his begging Marjorie to come with him for that very purpose; but there was another work which he thought still more urgent.... However, that was not to be Marjorie's affair.... It was work for men only.

"HERE they are," she said, holding out the packet.

He took them and thanked her.

"I may read them at my leisure? I may take them with me?"

She had not meant that, but there was no help for it now.

"Why, yes, if you wish," she said. "Stay; let me show you which they are. You may not wish to take them all."

THE letters were written on stout white paper, each occupying one side of a sheet that was folded three or four times, sealed, and inscribed to "Mistress Marjorie Manners" in the middle, with the word "Haste" in the lower corner. The first was written within a week of Robin's coming to Rheims, and told the tale of the sailing, the long rides that followed it, the pleasure the writer found at coming to a Catholic country. But names and places were scrupulously omitted. Dr. Allen was described as "my host"; and, in more than one instance, the name of a town was inscribed with a line drawn beneath it to indicate that this was a kind of alias.

The second letter gave some account of the life lived in Rheims—was a real boy's letter—and this was more difficult to treat with discretion. It related that studies occupied a certain part of the day; that "prayers" were held at such and such times, and that the sports consisted chiefly of a game called "Cat."

So with the eight or nine that followed. The third and fourth were bolder, and spoke of certain definitely Catholic practices—of prayers for the conversion of England, and of Mass said on certain days for the same intention. It seemed as if the writer had grown confident in his place of security. But later, again, his caution returned to him, and he spoke in terms so veiled that even Marjorie could scarcely understand him. Yet, on the whole, the letters, if they had fallen into hostile hands, would have done no irreparable injury; they would only have indicated that a Catholic living abroad, in some unnamed university or college, was writing an account of his life to a Catholic named Mistress Marjorie Manners, living in England.

When the girl had finished her explaining, it was evident that there was no longer any need for Anthony to take them with him. He said so.

"Ah! but take them, if you will," cried the girl.

"It would be better not. You have them safe here. And—"

Marjorie flushed. She felt that her ruse had been too plain.

"I would sooner you took them," she said. "You can read them at your leisure."

So he accepted, and slipped them into his breast with what seemed to the girl a lamentable carelessness. Then he stood up.

"I must go," he said. "And I have never asked after Mistress Manners."

"She is abed," said the girl. "She has been there this past month now."

She went with him to the door, for it was not until then that she was courageous enough to speak as she had determined.

"Mr. Babington," she said suddenly.

He turned.

"I have been thinking while we talked," she said. "You think my coming to London would be of real service?"

"I think so. It would be good for you to meet these priests before they—"

"Then I will come, if my mother gives me leave. When will you go?"

"We should be riding in not less than a week from now. But, mistress—"

"No, I have thought of it. I will come—if my mother gives me leave."

He nodded briskly and brightly. He loved courage, and he understood that this decision of hers had required courage.

"Then my sister shall come for you, and—"

"No, Mr. Babington, there is no need. We shall start from Derby?"

"Why, yes."

"Then my maid and I will ride down there and sleep at the inn, and be ready for you on the day that you appoint."

When he was gone at last she went back again to the parlour. She was in an agony lest she had been unmaidenly in determining to go so soon as she heard that Robin was to be there.

CHAPTER II

I

Anthony lifted his whip and pointed.

"London," he said.

Marjorie nodded; she was too tired to speak.

The journey had taken them some ten days, by easy stages; each night they had slept at an inn, except once, when they stayed with friends of the Babingtons and had heard Mass. They had had the small and usual adventures: a horse had fallen lame; a baggage-horse had bolted; they had passed two or three hunting-parties; they had been stared at in villages and saluted, and stared at and not saluted.

They were a small party for so long a journey—the three with four servants—two men and two maids: the men had ridden armed, as the custom was; one rode in front, then came the two ladies with Anthony; then the two maids, and behind them the second man. In towns and villages they closed up together lest they should be separated, and then spread out once more as the long, straight track lengthened before them. Anthony and the two men-servants carried each a case of dags or pistols at the saddle-bow, for fear of highwaymen. But none had troubled them.

A strange dreamlike mood had come down on Marjorie. At times it seemed to her in her fatigue as if she had done nothing all her life but ride; at times, as she sat rocking, she was living still at home, sitting in the parlour, watching her mother; the illusion was so clear and continuous that its departure, when her horse stumbled or a companion spoke, was as an awaking from a dream. At other times she looked about her; talked; asked questions.

She found Mistress Alice Babington a pleasant friend, some ten years older than herself, who knew London well, and had plenty to tell her. She was a fair woman, well built and active; very fond of her brother, whom she treated almost as a mother treats a son; but she seemed not to be in his confidence, and even not to wish to be; she thought more of his comfort than of his ideals. She was a Catholic, of course, but of the quiet, assured kind, and seemed unable to believe that anyone could seriously be anything else; she seemed completely confident that the present distress was a passing one, and that when politics had run their course, it would presently disappear.

Though Marjorie had nodded only when the spires of London shone up suddenly in the evening light, a sharp internal interest awakened in her. It was as astonishing as a miracle that the end should be in sight; the past ten days had made it seem to her as if all things which she desired must eternally recede.... She touched her horse unconsciously, and stared out between his ears, sitting upright and alert again.

It was not a great deal that met the eye, but it was so disposed as to suggest a great deal more. Far away to the right lay a faint haze, and in it appeared towers and spires, with gleams of sharp white here and there, where some tall building rose above the dark roofs. To the left again appeared similar signs of another town—the same haze, towers and spires—linked to the first. She knew what they were; she had heard half a dozen times already of the two towns that made London—running continuously in one long line, however, which grew thin by St. Mary's Hospital and St. Martin's, she was told—the two troops of houses and churches that had grown up about the two centres of Court and City, Westminster and the City itself. But it was none the less startling to see these with her proper eyes.

Presently, in spite of herself, as she saw the spire of St. Clement Danes, where she was told they must turn city-wards, she began to talk, and Anthony to answer.

II

The Red Bull was like other inns. A curved archway opened on the narrow street; and beneath this they rode, to find themselves in a paved court, already lighted, surrounded by window-pierced walls, and high galleries to right and left. The stamping of horses from the further end; and, almost immediately, the appearance of a couple of hostlers, showed where the stables lay. Beside it Marjorie could see through the door of the brightly lit bake-house.

She was terribly stiff, as she limped up the three or four stairs that led up to the door of the living-part of the inn; and she was glad enough to sit down in a wide, low parlour with her friend as Mr. Babington went in search of the host. The room was lighted only by a fire leaping in the chimney; and she could make out little, except that pieces of stuff hung upon the walls, and a long row of metal vessels and plates were ranged in a rack between the windows.

"It is a quiet inn," said Alice. Marjorie nodded again. She was too tired to speak; and almost immediately Anthony came back, with a tall, clean-shaven, middle-aged man, in an apron, following behind.

"It is all well," he said. "We can have our rooms and the parlour complete. These are the ladies," he added.

The landlord bowed a little, with a dignity beyond that of his dress.

"Supper shall be served immediately, madam," he said, with a tactful impartiality towards them both.

They were indeed very pleasant rooms; and, as Anthony had described them to her, were situated towards the back of the long, low house, on the first floor, with a private staircase leading straight up from the yard to the parlour itself. The sleeping-rooms, too, opened upon the parlour; that which the two ladies were to occupy was furthest from the yard, for quietness' sake; that in which Anthony and his man would sleep, upon the other side. The windows of all three looked straight out upon a little walled garden that appeared to be the property of some other house. The rooms were plainly furnished, but had a sort of dignity about them, especially in the carved woodwork about the doors and windows. There was a fireplace in the parlour, plainly a recent addition; and a maid rose from kindling the logs and turf, as the two ladies came back after washing and changing.

A table was already laid, lit by a couple of candles: it was laid with fine napery, and the cutlery was clean and solid. Marjorie looked round the room once more; and, as she sat down, Anthony came in, still in his mud-splashed dress, carrying three or four letters in his hands.

"News," he said.... "I will be with you immediately," and vanished into his room.

WHEN Anthony came back, the supper was all laid out. He had given orders that no waiting was to be done; his own servants would do what was necessary. He had a bright and interested face, Marjorie thought; and the instant they were sat down, she knew the reason of it.

"We are just in time," he said. "These letters have been lying here for me the last week. They will be here, they tell me, by tomorrow night. But that is not all—"

He glanced round the dusky room; then he laid down the knife with which he was carving; and spoke in a yet lower voice.

"Father Campion is in the house," he said.

His sister started.

"In the house? ...Do you mean—"

He nodded mysteriously, as he took up the knife again.

"He has been here three or four days. And I have spoken with him; he is coming here after supper. He had already supped."

Marjorie leaned back in her chair; but she said nothing. From beneath in the house came the sound of singing, from the tavern parlour where boys were performing madrigals.

It seemed to her incredible that she should presently be speaking with the man whose name was already affecting England as perhaps no priest's name had ever affected it. He had been in England, she knew, a comparatively short time; yet in that time, his name had run like fire from mouth to mouth. To the minds of Protestants there was something almost diabolical about the man; he was here, he was there, he was everywhere, and yet, when the search was up, he was nowhere. Tales were told of his eloquence that increased the impression that he made a thousandfold; it was said that he could wile birds off their branches and the beasts from their lairs; and this eloquence, it was known, could be heard only by initiates, in far-off country houses, or in quiet, unsuspected places in the cities. He preached in some shrouded and locked room in London one day; and the next, thirty miles off, in a cow-shed to rustics. And his learning and his subtlety were equal to his eloquence: her Grace had heard him at Oxford years ago, before his conversion; and, it was said, would refuse him nothing, even now, if he would but be reasonable in his religion; even Canterbury, it was reported, might be his. And if he would not be reasonable—then, as was fully in accordance with what was known of her Grace, nothing was too bad for him.

Such feeling then, on the part of Protestants, found its fellow in that of the Catholics. He was their champion, as no other man could be. Had he not issued his famous "challenge" to any and all of the Protestant divines, to meet them in any argument on religion that they cared to select, in any place and at any time, if only his own safe conduct were secure? And was it not notorious that none would meet him? He was, indeed, a fire, a smoke in the nostrils of his adversaries, a flame in the hearts of his friends. Everywhere he ranged, he and his comrade, Father Persons; sometimes in company, sometimes apart; and wherever they went the Faith blazed up anew from its dying embers, in the lives of rustic knave and squire.

And she was to see him!

"HE is here for four or five days only," went on Anthony presently, still in a low, cautious voice. "The hunt is very hot, they say. Not even the host knows who he is; or, at least, makes that he does not. He is under another name, of course; it is Mr. Edmonds, this time. He was in Essex, he tells me; but comes to the wolves' den for safety. It is safer, he says, to sit secure in the midst of the trap, than to wander about its doors; for when the doors are opened he can run out again, if no one knows he is there...."

III

When supper was finished at last, and the maids had borne away the dishes, there came almost immediately a tap upon the door; and before any could answer, there walked in a man, smiling.

He was of middle size, dressed in a dark, gentleman's suit, carrying his feathered hat in his hand, with his sword. He appeared far younger than Marjorie had expected—scarcely more than thirty years old, of a dark and yet clear complexion, large-eyed, with a look of humour; his hair was long and brushed back; and a soft, pointed beard and moustache covered the lower part of his face. He moved briskly and assuredly, as one wholly at his ease.

"I am come to the right room?" he said. "That is as well."

His voice, too, had a ring of gaiety in it; it was low, quite clear and very sympathetic; and his manners, as Marjorie observed, were those of a cultivated gentleman, without even a trace of the priest. She would not have been astonished if she had been told that the man was of the court, or some great personage of the country. There was no trace of furtive hurry or of alarm about him; he moved deftly and confidently; and when he sat down, after the proper greetings, crossed one leg over the other, so that he could nurse his foot. It seemed more incredible even than she had thought, that this was Father Campion!

"You have pleasant rooms here, and music to cheer you, too," he said. "I understand that you are often here, Mr. Babington."

Anthony explained that he found them convenient and very secure.

"Roberts is a prudent landlord," he said.

Father Campion nodded.

"He knows his own business, which is what few landlords do, in these degenerate days; and he knows nothing at all of his guests'. In that he is even more of an exception. And so, God blesses him in those who use his house."

They talked for a few minutes in this manner. Father Campion spoke of the high duty that lay on all country ladies to make themselves acquainted with the sights of the town; and spoke of three or four of these. Her Grace, of course, must be seen; that was the greatest sight of all. They must make an opportunity for that; and there would surely be no difficulty, since her Grace liked nothing better than to be looked at. And they must go up the river by water, if the weather allowed, from the Tower to Westminster; not from Westminster to the Tower, since that was the way that traitors came, and no good Catholic could, even in appearance, be a traitor. And, if they pleased, he would himself be their guide for a part of their adventures. He was to lie hid, he told them; and he knew no better way to do that than to flaunt as boldly as possible in the open ways.

"If I lay in my room," said he, "with a bolt drawn, I would soon have some busy fellow knocking on the door to know what I did there. But if I could but dine with her Grace, or take an hour with Mr. Topcliffe, I should be secure for ever."

Marjorie glanced shyly towards Alice, as if to ask a question. (She was listening, it seemed to her, with every nerve in her tired body.) The priest saw the glance.

"Mr. Topcliffe, madam? Well, let us say he is a dear friend of the Lieutenant of the Tower, and has, I think, lodgings there just now. And he is even a friend of Catholics, too—to such, at least, as desire a heavenly crown."

"He is an informer and a tormentor!" broke in Anthony harshly.

"Well, sir; let us say that he is very loyal to the letter of the law; and that he presides over our Protestant bed of Procrustes."

"The—" began Marjorie, emboldened by the kindness of the priest's voice.

"The bed of Procrustes, madam, was a bed to which all who lay upon it had to be conformed. Those that were too long were made short; and those that were too short were made long. It is a pleasant classical name for the rack."

Marjorie caught her breath. But Father Campion went on smoothly.

"We shall have a clear day tomorrow, I think," he said. "If you are at liberty, sir, and these ladies are not too wearied—I have a little business in Westminster; and—"

"Why, yes," said Anthony, "for tomorrow night we expect friends. From Rheims, sir."

The priest dropped his foot and leaned forward.

"From Rheims?" he said sharply.

The other nodded.

"Eight or ten at least will arrive. Not all are priests. One is a friend of our own from Derbyshire, who will not be made priest for five years yet."

"I had not heard they were to come so soon," said Father Campion. "And what a company of them!"

"There are a few of them who have been here before. Mr. Ballard is one of them."

The priest was silent an instant.

"Mr. Ballard," he said. "Ballard! Yes; he has been here before. He travels as Captain Fortescue, does he not? You are a friend of his?"

"Yes, sir."

Father Campion made as if he would speak; but interrupted himself and was silent; and it seemed to Marjorie as if another mood was fallen on him. And presently they were talking again of London and its sights.

IV

In spite of her weariness, Marjorie could not sleep for an hour or two after she had gone to bed. It was an extraordinary experience to her to have fallen in, on the very night of her coming to London, with the one man whose name stood to her for all that was gallant in her faith. As she lay there, listening to the steady breathing of Alice, who knew no such tremors of romance, to the occasional stamp of a horse across the yard, and, once or twice, to voices and footsteps passing on some paved way between the houses, she rehearsed again and again to herself the tales she had heard of him.

Now and again she thought of Robin. She wondered whether he, too, one day (and not of necessity a far-distant day, since promotion came quickly in this war of faith), would occupy some post like that which this man held so gaily and so courageously; and for the first time, perhaps, she understood not in vision merely, but in sober thought, what the life of a priest in those days signified. Certainly she had met man after man before—she had entertained them often enough in her mother's place, and had provided by her own wits for their security— men who went in peril of liberty and even of life; but here, within the walls of London, in this "wolves' den" as Father Campion had called it, where men brushed against one another continually, and looked into a thousand faces a day, where patrols went noisily with lights and weapons, where the great Tower stood, where her Grace, the mistress of the wolves, had her dwelling—here, peril assumed another aspect, and pain and death another reality, from that which they presented on the wind-swept hills and the secret valleys of the country from which they came.... And it was with Father Campion himself, in his very flesh, that she had talked this evening—it was Father Campion who had given her that swift, kindly look of commendation, as Mr. Babington had spoken of her reason for coming to London, and of her hospitality to wandering priests—Father Campion, the Angel of the Church, was in England. And tomorrow Robin, too, would be here.

THEN, as sleep began to come down on her tired and excited brain, and to form, as so often under such conditions, little visible images, even before the reason itself is lulled, there began to pass before her, first tiny and delicate pictures of what she had seen today—the low hills to the north of London, dull and dark below the heavy sky, but light immediately above the horizon as the sun sank down; the appearance of her horse's ears—those ears and that tuft of wayward mane between them of which she had grown so weary; the lighted walls of the London streets; the monstrous shadows of the eaves; the flare of lights; the moving figures—these came first; and then faces— Father Campion's, smiling, with white teeth and narrowed eyes, bright against the dark chimney-breast; Alice's serene features, framed in flaxen hair; and then, as sleep had all but conquered her, the imagination sent up one last idea, and a face came into being before her, so formless yet so full, so sinister, so fierce and so distorted, that she drew a sudden breath and sat up, trembling...

Why had they spoken to her of Topcliffe?

CHAPTER III

I

It was a soft winter's morning as the party came down the little slope towards the entrance gate of the Tower next day. The rain last night had cleared the air, and the sun shone as through thin veils of haze, kindly and sweet. The river on the right was at high tide, and up from the water's edge came the cries of the boatmen, pleasant and invigorating.

Here and there some personage had been pointed out to her by the trim, merry gentleman who walked by her side with his sword swinging (Anthony went with his sister just behind, as they threaded their way through the crowded streets, and the two men-servants followed.) She saw a couple of city dignitaries in their furs, with slavemen to clear their road; a little troop of the Queen's horse, blazing with colour, under the command of a young officer who might have come straight from Romance. But she was more absorbed—or, rather, she returned every instant to the man who walked beside her with such an air and talked so loudly and cheerfully. Certainly, it seemed to her, his disguise was perfect, and himself the best part of it. She compared him in her mind with a couple of ministers, splendid and awful in their gowns and ruffs, whom they had met turning into one of the churches just now, and smiled at the comparison; and yet perhaps these were preachers too, and eloquent in their own fashion.

And now, here was the Tower—the end of all things, so far as London was concerned. Beyond it she saw the wide rolling hills, the bright reaches of the river, and the sparkle of Placentia, far away.

"Her Grace is at Westminster these days," exclaimed the priest; "she is moving to Hampton Court in a day or two; so I doubt not we shall be able to go in and see a little. We shall see, at least, the outside of the Paradise where so many holy ones have lived and died. There are three or four of them here now; but the most of them are in the Fleet or the Marshalsea."

Marjorie glanced at him. She did not understand.

"I mean Catholic prisoners, mistress. There are several of them in ward here, but we had better speak no names."

He wheeled suddenly as they came out into the open and moved to the left.

"There is Tower Hill, mistress; where my lord Cardinal Fisher died, and Thomas More."

Marjorie stopped short. But there was nothing great to see—only a rising ground, empty and bare, with a few trimmed trees; the ground was without grass; a few cobbled paths crossed this way and that.

"And here is the gateway," he said, "whence they come out to glory.... And there on the right" (he swept his arm towards the river) "you may see, if you are fortunate, other criminals called pirates, hung there till they be covered by three tides."

Still standing there, with Mr. Babington and his sister come up from behind, he began to relate the names of this tower and of that, in the great tumbled mass of buildings surmounted by the high keep. But Marjorie paid no great attention except with an effort: she was brooding rather on the amazing significance of all that she saw. It was under this gateway that the martyrs came; it was from those windows in that tower which the priest had named just now, that they had looked.... And this was Father Campion. She turned and watched him as he talked. He was dressed as he had been dressed last night, but with a small cloak thrown over his shoulders; he gesticulated freely and easily, pointing out this and that; now and again his eyes met hers, and there was nothing but a grave merriment in them.... Only once or twice his voice softened, as he spoke of those great ones that had shown Catholics how both to die and live.

"And now," he said, "with your permission I will go and speak to the guard, and see if we may have entrance."

It was almost with terror that she saw him go—a solitary man, with a price on his head, straight up to those whose business it was to catch him—armed men, as she could see—she could even see the quilted jacks they wore—who, it may be, had talked of him in the guard-room only last night. But his air was so assured and so magnificent that even she began to understand how complete such a disguise might be; and she watched him speaking with the officer with a touch even of his own humour in her heart. Indeed, there was some truth in the charge of Jesuitry after all!

Then the figure turned and beckoned, and they went forward.

II

A certain horror, in spite of herself and her company, fell on her as she passed beneath the solid stone vaulting, passed along beneath the towering wall, turned up from the water-gate, and came out into the wide court round which the Lieutenant's lodgings, the little church, and the enormous White Tower itself are grouped. There was a space, not enclosed in any way, but situated within a web of paths, not far from the church, that caught her attention. She stood looking at it.

"Yes, mistress," said the priest behind her. "That is the place of execution for those who die within the Tower—those usually of royal blood. My Lady Salisbury died there, and my Lady Jane Grey, and others."

He laid his hand gently on her arm,

"You must not look so grave," he said, "you must gape more. You are a country-cousin, madam."

And she smiled in spite of herself, as she met his eyes.

"Tell me everything," she said.

They went together nearer to the church, and faced about.

"We can see better from here," he said.

Then he began.

First there was the Lieutenant's lodging on the right. They must look well at that. Interviews had taken place there that had made history. (He mentioned a few names.) Then, further down on the right, beyond that corner round which they had come just now, was the famous water-gate, called "Traitors' Gate," through which passed those convicted of treason at Westminster, or, at least, those who were under grave suspicion. Such as these came, of course, by water, as prisoners on whose behalf a demonstration might perhaps be made if they came by land. So, at least, he understood was the reason of the custom.

"Her Grace herself once came that way," he said with a twinkle. "Now she sends other folks in her stead."

Then he pointed out more clearly the White Tower. It was there that the Council sat on affairs of importance.

"And it is there—" began Anthony harshly.

The priest turned to him, suddenly grave, as if in reproof.

"Yes," he said softly. "It is there that the passion of the martyrs begins."

Marjorie turned sharply.

"You mean—"

"Well," he said, "it is there that the Council sits to examine prisoners both before and after the Question. They are taken downstairs to the Question, and brought back again after it. It was there that—"

He broke off.

"Who is this?" he said.

The court had been empty while they talked except that on the far side, beneath the towering cliff of the keep, a sentry went to and fro. But now another man had come into view, walking up from the way they themselves had come; and it would appear from the direction he took that he would pass within twenty or thirty yards of them. He was a tall man, dressed in sad-coloured clothes, with a felt hat on his head and the usual sword by his side. He was plainly something of a personage, for he walked easily and confidently. He was still some distance off; but it was possible to make out that he was sallowish in complexion, wore a trimmed beard, and had something of a long throat.

Father Campion stared at him a moment, and, as he stared, Marjorie heard Mr. Babington utter a sudden exclamation. Then the priest, with one quick glance at him, murmured something which Marjorie could not hear, and walked briskly off to meet the stranger.

"Come," Anthony said in a sharp, low voice, "we must see the church."

"Who is it?" whispered Mistress Alice, with even her serene face a little troubled.

For the first moment, as they walked towards the entrance of the church, Anthony said nothing. Then as they reached it, he said, in a tone quite low and yet full of suppressed passion of some kind, a name that Marjorie could not catch.

She turned before they went in, and looked again.

The priest was talking to the stranger, and was making gestures, as if asking for direction.

"Who is it, Mr. Babington?" she asked again as they went in. "I did not—"

"Topcliffe," said Anthony.

III

"It appeared to me best to speak with him openly," said the priest quietly, as they had waited ten minutes later on the wharf outside the Tower, while the men ran to make ready their boat. "I do not know why, but I suppose I am one of those who better like their danger in front than behind. I knew him at once; I have had him pointed out to me two or three times before. So I looked him in the eyes, and asked him whether some ladies from the country might be permitted to see the White Tower, and to whom we had best apply. He told me that was not his affair, and looked me up and down as he said it. And then he went his way to...the White Tower, where I doubt not he had business."

"He said no more?" asked Anthony.

"No, he said no more. But I shall know him again better next time, and he me."

As they drew nearer Westminster, it was with Marjorie as it had been when they came to the Tower. The priest was busy pointing out this or that building—the Palace towers, the Hall, the Abbey behind, and St. Margaret's Church, as well as the smaller buildings of the

Court, and the little town that lay round about. But she listened as she listened to the noise that came from the streets clear across the water, attending to it, yet scarcely distinguishing one thing from another, and forgetting each as soon as she heard it. She was thinking all the while of Robin, and of the man whose face she had seen, of his beard and his long throat. Well, at least, Robin was not yet a priest...

THE boat was already nearing the King's Stairs at Westminster, when a new event happened that for a while distracted her.

The first they saw of it was the sight of a number of men and women running in a disorderly mob, calling out as they ran along the river-bank in the direction from Charing Old Cross towards Palace Yard. They appeared excited, but not by fear; and it was plain that something was taking place of which they wished to have a sight. As the priest stood up in the boat in order to have a clearer sight of what lay above the bank, three or four trumpet-calls of a peculiar melody rang out clear and distinct, echoed back by the walls round about, plainly audible above the rising noise of a crowd that, it seemed, must be gathering out of sight. The priest sat down again and his face was merry.

"You have come on a fortunate day, mistress," he said to Marjorie. "First Topcliffe, and now her Grace; if we make haste we may see her pass by."

"Her Grace?"

"She will be going to dinner in Whitehall, after having taken the air by the river. They will be passing the Abbey now. But she will not be in her supreme state; I am sorry for that."

As they rowed in quickly over the last hundred yards that lay between them and the stairs, Marjorie listened to the priest as he described something of what the "supreme state" signified. He spoke of the long lines of carriages, filled with the ladies and the infirm, preceded by the pike-men, and the gentlemen pensioners carrying wands, and the knights followed by the heralds. Behind these, he said, came the officers of State immediately before the Queen's carriage, and after her the guards of her person.

"But this will be but a tame affair," he said. "I wish you could have seen a Progress, with the arches and the speeches and the declamations, and the heathen gods and goddesses that reign round our Eliza, when she will go to Ashridge or Havering. I have heard it said—"

And then the prow of the boat, turned deftly at the last instant, grated along the lowest stair, and the waterman was out to steady his craft.

IV

IT was the very crown and summit of new sensation that Marjorie attained as she stood in an open gallery that looked on to the road from Westminster to Whitehall. Father Campion, speaking of a "good friend" of his that had his lodgings there, led them by a short turning or two, that avoided the crowd, straight to the door of what appeared to Marjorie a mere warren of rooms, stairs and passages. A grave little man, with a pen behind his ear, ran out upon their knocking at one of these doors, and led them straight through, smiling and talking, out into this very gallery where they now stood; and then vanished again.

The gallery was such as those which Marjorie had noted on the way to the Tower; a high-hung, airy place, running the length of the house, contrived on the level of the second floor, with the first floor roof beneath and overhanging attics above. It was supported on massive oak beams, and protected from the street by a low balustrade of a height to lean the elbows upon it. It was on this balustrade that Marjorie leaned, looking down into the street.

To the left the narrow roadway curved off out of sight in the direction of Palace Yard; on the right she could make out, a hundred yards away, some kind of a gateway, that strode across the street, and gave access, she supposed, to the Palace. Opposite, the windows were filled with faces, and an enthusiastic loyalist was leaning, red-faced and vociferous, calling to a friend in the crowd beneath, from a gallery corresponding to that from which the girl was looking.

Of the procession nothing was at present to be seen. They had caught a glimpse of colour somewhere to the east of the Abbey as they turned off opposite Westminster Hall; and already the cry of the trumpets and the increasing noise of a crowd out of sight told the listeners that they would not have long to wait.

Beneath, the crowd was arranging itself with admirable discipline, dispersing in long lines two or three deep against the walls, so as to leave a good space, and laughing good-humoredly at a couple of officious persons in livery who had suddenly made their appearance. And then, as the country girl herself smiled down, an exclamation from Alice made her turn.

At first, it was difficult to discern anything clearly in the stream whose head began to discharge itself round the curve from the left. A row of brightly-coloured uniforms, moving four abreast, came first, visible above the tossing heads of horses. Then followed a group of guards, whose steel caps passed suddenly into the sunlight that caught them from between the houses, and went again into shadow.

And then at last, she caught a glimpse of the carriage, followed by ladies on grey horses; and forgot all the rest.

This way and that she craned her head, gripping the oak post by which she leaned, unconscious of all except that she was to see her in whom England itself seemed to have been incarnated. Then on a sudden, as Elizabeth lifted her head this side and that, the girl saw her.

She was sitting in a low carriage, raised on cushions, alone. Four tall horses drew her at a slow trot: the wheels of the carriage were deep in mud, since she had driven for an hour over the deep December roads; but this added rather to the splendour within. But of this Marjorie remembered no more than an uncertain glimpse. The air was thick with cries; from window after window waved hands; and, more than all, the loyalty was real, and filled the air like brave music.

There, then, she sat, smiling.

She was dressed in some splendid stuff; jewels sparkled beneath her throat. Once a hand in an embroidered glove rose to wave an answer to the roar of salute; and, as the carriage came beneath, she raised her face.

It was a thin face, sharply pear-shaped, ending in a pointed chin; a tight mouth smiled at the corners; above her narrow eyes and high brows rose a high forehead, surmounted by strands of auburn hair drawn back tightly beneath the little head-dress. It was a strangely peaked face, very clear-skinned, and resembled in some manner a mask. But the look of it was as sharp as steel; like a slender rapier, fragile and thin, yet keen enough to run a man through. The power of it, in a word, was out of all measure with the slightness of the face... Then the face dropped; and Marjorie watched the back of the head bending this way and that, till the nodding heads that followed hid it from sight.

Marjorie drew a deep breath and turned. The faces of her friends were as pale and intent as her own. Only the priest was as easy as ever.

"So that is our Eliza," he said. Then he did a strange thing.

He lifted his cap once more with grave seriousness. "God save her Grace!" he said.

CHAPTER IV

I

ROBIN bowed to her very carefully, and stood upright again.

She had seen in an instant how changed he was, in that swift instant in which her eyes had singled him out from the little crowd of men that had come into the room with Anthony at their head. It was a change which she could scarcely have put into words, unless she had said that it was the conception of the Levite within his soul. He was dressed soberly and richly, with a sword at his side, in great riding-boots splashed to the knees with mud, with his cloak thrown back; and he carried his great brimmed hat in his hand. All this was as it might have been in Derby, though, perhaps, his dress was a shade more dignified than that in which she had ever seen him. But the change was in his face and bearing; he bore himself like a man, and a restrained man; and there was besides that subtle air which her woman's eyes could see, but which even her woman's wit could not properly describe.

She made room for him to sit beside her; and then Father Campion's voice spoke:

"These are the gentlemen, then," he said. "And two more are not yet come. Gentlemen—" he bowed. "And which is Captain Fortescue?"

A big man, distinguished from the rest by a slightly military air, and by a certain vividness of costume and a bristling feather in his hat, bowed back to him.

"We have met once before, Mr.—Mr. Edmonds," he said. "At Valladolid."

Father Campion smiled.

"Yes, sir; for five or ten minutes; and I was in the same room with your honour once at the Duke of Guise's.... And now, sir, who are the rest of your company?"

The others were named one by one; and Marjorie eyed each of them carefully. It was her business to know them again if ever they should meet in the north; and for a few minutes the company moved here and there, bowing and saluting, and taking their seats. There were still a couple of men who were not yet come; but these two arrived a few minutes later; and it was not until she had said a word or two to them all, and Father Campion had named her and her good works, to them, that she found herself back again with Robin in a seat a little apart.

"You look very well," she said, with an admirable composure.

His eyes twinkled.

"I am as weary as a man can be," he said. "We have ridden since before dawn.... And you, and your good works?"

Marjorie explained, describing to him something of the system by which priests were safeguarded now in the north—the districts into which the county was divided, and the apportioning of the responsibilities among the faithful houses. It was her business, she said, to receive messages and to pass them on; she had entertained perhaps a dozen priests since the summer; perhaps she would entertain him, too, one day, she said.

THE ordeal was far lighter than she had feared it would be. There was a strong undercurrent of excitement in her heart, flushing her cheeks and sparkling in her eyes; yet never for one moment was she even tempted to forget that he was now vowed to God. It seemed to her as if she talked with him in the spirit of that place where there is neither marrying nor giving in marriage. Those two years of quiet in the north, occupied, even more than she recognised, in the rearranging of her relations with the memory of this young man, had done their work. She still kindled at his presence; but it was at the presence of one who had undertaken an adventure that destroyed altogether her old relations with him.... She was enkindled even more by the sense of her own security; and, as she looked at him, by the sense of his security too. Robin was gone; here, instead, was young Mr. Audrey, seminary student, who even in a court of law could swear before God that he was not a priest, nor had been "ordained beyond the seas."

So they sat and exchanged news. She told him of the rumours of his father that had come to her from time to time; he would be a magistrate yet, it was said, so hot was his loyalty. Even her Grace, it was reported, had vowed she wished she had a thousand such country gentlemen on whose faithfulness she could depend. And Robin gave her news of the seminary, of the hours of rising and sleeping, of the sports there; of the confessors for the faith who came and went; of Dr. Allen. He told her, too, of Mr. Garlick and Mr. Ludlam; he often had talked with them of Derbyshire, he said. It was very peaceful and very stirring, too, to sit here in the lighted parlour, and hear and give the news; while the company, gathered round Anthony and Father Campion, talked in low voices, and Mistress Babington, placid, watched them and listened. He showed her, too, Mr. Maine's beads which she had given him so long ago, hung in a little packet round his neck.

MORE than once, as they talked, Marjorie found herself looking at Mr. Ballard, or, as he was called here, Captain Fortescue. It was he who seemed the leader of the troop; and, indeed, as Robin told her in a whisper, that was what he was. He came and went frequently, he said; his manner and his carriage were reassuring to the suspicious; he appeared, perhaps, the last man in the world to be a priest. He was a big man, as has been said; and he had a frank assured way with him; he was leaning forward, even now, as she looked at him, and seemed laying down the law, though in what was almost a whisper. Father Campion was watching him, too, she noticed; and, what she had learned of Father Campion in the last few hours led her to wonder whether there was not something of doubtfulness in his opinion of him.

Father Campion suddenly shook his head sharply.

"I am not of that view at all," he said. "I—"

And once more his voice sank so low as to be inaudible; as the rest leaned closer about him.

II

Mr. Anthony Babington seemed silent and even a little displeased when, half an hour later, the visitors were all gone downstairs to supper. Three or four of them were to sleep in the house; the rest, of whom Robin was one, had Captain Fortescue's instructions as to where lodgings were prepared. But the whole company was tired out with the long ride from the coast, and would be seen no more that night.

Marjorie knew enough of the divisions of opinion among Catholics, and of Mr. Babington in particular, to have a general view as to why her companion was displeased; but more than that she did not know, nor what point in particular it was on which the argument had run. The one party—of Mr. Babington's kind—held that Catholics were, morally, in a state of war. War had been declared upon them, without justification, by the secular authorities, and physical instruments, including pursuivants and the rack, were employed against them. Then why should not they, too, employ the same kind of instruments, if they could, in return? The second party held that a religious persecution could not be held to constitute a state of war; the Apostles Peter and Paul, for example, not only did not employ the arm of flesh against the Roman Empire, but actually repudiated it. And this party further held that even the Pope's bull, relieving Elizabeth's subjects from their allegiance, did so only in an interior sense—in such a manner that while they must still regard her personal and individual rights—such rights as any human being possessed—they were not bound to render interior loyalty to her as their Queen, and need not, for example (though they were not forbidden to do so), regard it as a duty to fight for her, in the event, let us say, of an armed invasion from Spain.

There, then, was the situation; and Mr. Anthony had, plainly, crossed swords this evening on the point.

"The Jesuit is too simple," he said suddenly, as he strode about. "I think—" He broke off.

His sister smiled upon him placidly.

"You are too hot, Anthony," she said.

The man turned sharply towards her.

"All the praying in the world," he said, "has not saved us so far. It seems to me time—"

"Perhaps our Lord would not have us saved," she said; "as you mean it."

III

IT was not until Christmas Eve that Marjorie went to St. Paul's, for all that it was so close. But the days were taken up with the visitors; a hundred matters had to be arranged; for it was decided that before the New Year all were to be dispersed. Captain Fortescue and Robin were to leave again for the Continent on the day following Christmas Day itself.

Marjorie made acquaintance during these days with more than one meeting-place of the Catholics in London. One was a quiet little house near St. Bartholomew's-the-Great, where a widow had three or four sets of lodgings, occupied frequently by priests and by other Catholics, who were best out of sight; and it was here that mass was to be said on Christmas Day. Another was in the Spanish Embassy; and here, to her joy, she looked openly upon a chapel of her faith, and from the gallery adored her Lord in the tabernacle. But even this was accomplished with an air of uneasiness in those round her; the Spanish priest who took them in walked quickly and interrupted them before they were done, and seemed glad to see the last of them. It was explained to Marjorie that the ambassador did not wish to give causeless offence to the Protestant court.

And now, on Christmas Eve, Robin, Anthony and the two ladies entered the Cathedral as dusk was falling—first passing through the burial-ground, over the wall of which leaned the rows of houses in whose windows lights were beginning to burn.

The very dimness of the air made the enormous heights of the great church more impressive. Before them stretched the long nave, over seven hundred feet from end to end; from floor to roof the eye travelled up the bunches of slender pillars to the dark ceiling, newly restored after the fire, a hundred and fifty feet. The tall windows on either side, and the clerestory lights above, glimmered faintly in the darkening light.

But to the Catholic eyes that looked on it the desolation was more apparent than the splendour. There were plenty of people here, indeed: groups moved up and down, talking, directing themselves more and more towards the exits, as the night was coming on and the church would be closed presently; in one aisle a man was talking aloud, as if lecturing, with a crowd of heads about him. In another a number of soberly dressed men were putting up their papers and ink on the little tables that stood in a row—this was Scriveners' Corner, she was told; from a third half a dozen persons were dejectedly moving away— these were servants that had waited to be hired. But the soul of the place was gone. When they came out into the transepts, Anthony stopped them with a gesture, while a couple of porters, carrying boxes on their heads, pushed by, on their short cut through the cathedral.

"It was there," he said, "that the altars stood."

He pointed between the pillars on either side, and there, up little raised steps, lay the floors of the chapels. But within all was empty, except for a tomb or two, some tattered colours and the *piscinæ* still in place. Where the altars had stood there were blank spaces of wall; piled up in one such place were rows of wooden seats set there for want of room.

Opposite the entrance to the choir, where once overhead had hung the great Rood, the four stood and looked in, through a gap which the masons were mending in the high wall that had bricked off the chancel from the nave. On either side, as of old, still rose up the towering carven stalls; the splendid pavement still shone beneath, refracting back from its surface the glimmer of light from the stained windows above; but the head of the body was gone. Somewhere, beneath the deep shadowed altar screen, they could make out an erection that might have been an altar, only they knew that it was not. It was no longer the Stone of Sacrifice, whence the smoke of the mystical Calvary ascended day by day: it was the table, and no more, where bread and wine were eaten and drunk in memory of an event whose deathless energy had ceased, in this place, at least, to operate. Yet it was here, thought Marjorie, that only forty years ago, scarcely more than twenty years before she was born, on this very Night, the great church had hummed and vibrated with life. Round all the walls had sat priests, each in his place; and beside each kneeled a penitent, making ready for the joy of Bethlehem once again—wise and simple—Shepherds and Magi—yet all simple before the baffling and entrancing Mystery. There had been footsteps and voices there too—yet of men who were busy upon their Father's affairs in their Father's house, and not upon their own. They were going from altar to altar, speaking with their Friends at Court; and here, opposite where she stood and peeped in the empty cold darkness, there had burned lights before the Throne of Him Who had made Heaven and earth, and did His Father's Will on earth as it was done in Heaven.... Forty years ago the life of this church was rising on this very night, with a hum as of an approaching multitude, from hour to hour, brightening and quickening as it came, up to the glory of the Midnight Mass, the crowded church, alight from end to end, the smell of bog and bay in the air, soon to be met and crowned by the savour of incense-smoke; and the world of spirit, too, quickened about them; and the angels (she thought) came down from Heaven, as men up from the City round about, to greet Him who is King of both angels and men.

And now, in this new England, the church, empty of the Divine Presence, was emptying, too, of its human visitors. She could hear great doors somewhere crash together, and the reverberation roll beneath the stone vaulting. It would empty soon, desolate and dark; and so it would be all night.... Why did not the very stones cry out?

Mistress Alice touched her on the arm.

"We must be going," she said. "They are closing the church."

IV

SHE had a long talk with Robin on Christmas night.

The day had passed, making strange impressions on her, which she could not understand. Partly it was the contrast between the homely associations of the Feast, begun, as it was for her, with the mass before dawn—the room at the top of the widow's house was crowded all the while she was there—between these associations and the unfamiliarity of the place. She had felt curiously apart from all that she saw that day in the streets—the patrolling groups, the singers, the monstrous-headed mummers (of whom companies went about all day), two or three glimpses of important City festivities, the garlands that decorated many of the houses. It seemed to her as a shadow-show without sense or meaning, since the heart of Christmas was gone. Partly, too, no doubt, it was the memory of a former Christmas, three years ago, when she had begun to understand that Robin loved her. And he was with her again; yet all that he had stood for, to her, was gone, and another significance had taken its place. He was nearer to her heart, in one manner, though utterly removed, in another. It was as when a friend was dead: his familiar presence is gone; but now that one physical barrier is vanished, his presence is there, closer than ever, though in another fashion....

ROBIN had come in to sup. Captain Fortescue would fetch him about nine o'clock, and the two were to ride for the coast before dawn.

The four sat quiet after supper, speaking in subdued voices, of hopes for the future, when England should be besieged, indeed, by the spiritual forces that were gathering overseas; but they slipped gradually into talk of the past and of Derbyshire, and of rides they remembered. Then, after a while, Anthony was called away; Mistress Alice moved back to the table to see her needlework the better, and Robin and Marjorie sat together by the fire.

HE told her again of the journey from Rheims, of the inns where they lodged, of the extraordinary care that was taken, even in that Catholic land, that no rumour of the nature of the party should slip out, lest some gossip precede them or even follow them to the coast of England. They carried themselves even there, he said, as ordinary gentlemen travelling together; two of them were supposed to be lawyers; he himself passed as Mr. Ballard's servant. They heard mass when they could in the larger towns, but even then not all together.

The landing in England had been easier, he said, than he had thought, though he had learned afterwards that a helpful young man, who had offered to show him to an inn in Folkestone, and in whose presence Mr. Ballard had taken care to give him a good rating for dropping a bag—with loud oaths—was a well-known informer. However, no harm was done: Mr. Ballard's admirable bearing, and his oaths in particular, had seemed to satisfy the young man, and he had troubled them no more.

Marjorie did not say much. She listened with a fierce attention, so much interested that she was scarcely aware of her own interest; she looked up, half betrayed into annoyance, when a placid laugh from Mistress Alice at the table showed that another was listening too.

She too, then, had to give her news, and to receive messages for the Derbyshire folk whom Robin wished to greet; and it was not until Mistress Alice slipped out of the room that she uttered a word of what she had been hoping all day she might have an opportunity to say.

"Mr. Audrey," she said (for she was careful to use this form of address), "I wish you to pray for me. I do not know what to do."

He was silent.

"At present," she said, gathering courage, "my duty is clear. I must be at home, for my mother's sake, if for nothing else. And, as I told you, I think I shall be able to do something for priests. But if my mother died—"

"Yes?" he said, as she stopped again.

She glanced up at his serious, deep-eyed face, half in shadow and half in light, so familiar, and yet so utterly apart from the boy she had known.

"Well," she said, "I think of you as a priest already, and I can speak to you freely.... Well, I am not sure whether I, too, shall not go overseas, to serve God better."

"You mean—"

"Yes. A dozen or more are gone from Derbyshire, whose names I know. Some are gone to Bruges; two or three to Rome; two or three more to Spain. We women cannot do what priests can, but, at least, we can serve God in Religion."

She looked at him again, expecting an answer. She saw him move his head, as if to answer. Then he smiled suddenly.

"Well, however you look at me, I am not a priest.... You had best speak to one—Father Campion or another."

"But—"

"And I will pray for you," he said with an air of finality.

Then Mistress Alice came back.

SHE never forgot, all her life long, the little scene that took place when Captain Fortescue came in with Mr. Babington, to fetch Robin away. Yet the whole of its vividness rose from its interior significance. Externally here was a quiet parlour; two ladies—for the girl afterwards seemed to see herself in the picture—stood by the fireplace; Mistress Alice still held her needlework gathered up in one hand, and her spools of thread and a pin-cushion lay on the polished table. And the two gentlemen—for Captain Fortescue would not sit down, and Robin had risen at his entrance—the two gentlemen stood by it. They were not in their boots, for they were not to ride till morning; they appeared two ordinary gentlemen, each hat-in-hand, and Robin had his cloak across his arm. Anthony Babington stood in the shadow by the door, and, beyond him, the girl could see the face of Dick, who had come up to say good-bye again to his old master.

That was all—four men and two ladies. None raised his voice, none made a gesture. The home party spoke of the journey, and of their hopes that all would go well; the travellers, or rather the leader (for Robin spoke not one word, good or bad), said that he was sure it would be so; there was not one-tenth of the difficulty in getting out of England as of getting into it. Then, again, he said that it was late; that he had still one or two matters to arrange; that they must be out of London as soon as the gates opened. And the scene ended.

Robin bowed to the two ladies, precisely and courteously; making no difference between them, and wheeled and went out, and she saw Dick's face, too, vanish from the door, and heard the voices of the two on the stairs. Marjorie returned the salute of Mr. Ballard, longing to entreat him to take good care of the boy, yet knowing that she must not and could not.

Then he, too, was gone, with Anthony to see him downstairs; and Marjorie, without a word, went straight through to her room, fearing to trust her own voice, for she felt that her heart was gone with them. Yet, not for one moment did even her sensitive soul distrust any more the nature of the love that she bore to the lad.

But Mistress Alice sat down again to her sewing.

CHAPTER NUMBER

I

MARJORIE was sitting in her mother's room, while her mother slept. It seemed incredible that nearly a year had passed since her visit to London, and that Christmas was upon them again. Yet in this remote country place there was little to make time run slowly. Priests came and went again unobserved; Marjorie went to the sacraments when she could, and said her prayers always. But letters came more frequently than ever to the little remote manor, carried now by some farm-servant, now left by strangers, now presented as credentials; and Booth's Edge became known in that underworld of the north as a safe place for folks in trouble for their faith.

Marjorie had had more news from London from time to time, sent on to her chiefly by Mr. Babington, though none had come to her since the summer, and she had singled out in particular all that bore upon Father Campion. There was no doubt that the hunt was hotter every month; yet he seemed to bear a charmed life. Once he had escaped, she had heard, through the quick wit of a servant-maid, who had pushed him suddenly into a horse-pond, as the officers actually came in sight, so that he came out all mud and water-weed; and had been jeered at for a clumsy lover by the very men who were on his trail.... Marjorie smiled to herself as she nursed her knee over the fire, and remembered his gaiety and sharpness.

Robin, too, was never very far from her thoughts. In some manner she put the two together in her mind. She wondered whether they would ever travel together. It was her hope that her old friend might become another Campion himself some day.

A log rolled from its place in the fire, scattering sparks. She stooped to put it back, glancing first at the bed to see if her mother were disturbed; and, as she sat back again, she heard the blowing of a horse and a man's voice, fierce and low, from beyond the windows, bidding the beast hold himself up.

She was accustomed now to such arrivals. They came and went like this, often without warning; it was her business to look at any credentials they bore with them, and then, if all were well, to do what she could—whether to set them on their way, or to give them shelter. A room was set aside now, in the further wing, and called openly and freely the "priest's room,"—so great was their security.

She got up from her seat and went out quickly on tiptoe as she heard a door open and close beneath her in the house, running over in her mind any preparations that she would have to make if the rider were one that needed shelter.

As she looked down the staircase, she saw a maid there, who had run out from the buttery, talking to a man whom she thought she knew. Then he lifted his face, and she saw that she was right: and that it was Mr. Babington.

She came down, reassured and smiling; but her breath caught in her throat as she saw his face.... She told the maid to be off and get supper ready, but he jerked his head in refusal. She saw that he could hardly speak. Then she led him into the hall, taking down the lantern that hung in the passage, and placing it on the table. But her hand shook in spite of herself.

"Tell me," she whispered.

He sat down heavily on a bench.

"It is all over," he said. "The bloody murderers!...They were gibbeted three days ago."

The girl drew a long, steady breath. All her heart cried "Robin."

"Who are they, Mr. Babington?"

"Why, Campion and Sherwine and Brian. They were taken a month or two ago.... I had heard not a word of it, and...and it ended three days ago."

"I...I do not understand."

The man struck his hand heavily on the long table against which he leaned. He appeared one flame of fury; courtesy and gentleness were all gone from him.

"They were hanged for treason, I tell you.... Treason!... Campion! ...By God! we will give them treason if they will have it so!"

All seemed gone from Marjorie except the white, splashed face that stared at her, lighted up by the lantern beside him, glaring from the background of darkness. It was not Robin...not Robin...yet—

The shocking agony of her face broke through the man's heart-broken fury, and he stood up quickly.

"Mistress Marjorie," he said, "forgive me.... I am like a madman. I am on my way from Derby, where the news came to me this afternoon. I turned aside to tell you. I came to warn you. You must be careful. I am riding for London. My men are in the valley. Mistress Marjorie—"

She waved him aside. The blood was beginning again to beat swiftly and deafeningly in her ears, and the word came back.

"I...I was shocked," she said; you must pardon me.... Is it certain?"

He tore out a bundle of papers from behind his cloak, detached one with shaking hands and thrust it before her.

She sat down and spread it on the table. But his voice broke in and interrupted her all the while.

"They were all three taken together, in the summer.... I...have been in France; my letters never reached me.... They were racked continually.... They died all together; praying for the Queen...at Tyburn.... Campion died the first..."

She pushed the paper from her; the close handwriting was no more to her than black marks on the paper. She passed her hands over her forehead and eyes.

"Mistress Marjorie, you look like death. See, I will leave the paper with you. It is from one of my friends who was there...."

The door was pushed open, and the servant came in, bearing a tray.

"Set it down," said Marjorie, as coolly as if death and horror were as far from her as an hour ago.

She nodded sharply to the maid, who went out again; then she rose and spread the food within the man's reach. He began to eat and drink, talking all the time.

As she sat and watched him and listened, remembering afterwards, as if mechanically, all that he said, she was contemplating something else. She seemed to see Campion, not as he had been three days ago, not as he was now...but as she had seen him in London—alert, brisk, quick. Even the tones of his voice were with her, and the swift merry look in his eyes.... Somewhere on the outskirts of her thought there hung other presences: the darkness, the blood, the smoking cauldron.... Oh! she would have to face these presently; she would go through this night, she knew, looking at all their terror. But just now let her remember him as he had been; let her keep off all other thoughts so long as she could....

II

When she had heard the horse's footsteps scramble down the little steep ascent in the dark, and then pass into silence on the turf beyond, she closed the outer door, barred it once more, and then went back straight into the hall, where the lantern still burned among the plates. She dared not face her mother yet; she must learn how far she still held control of herself; for her mother must not hear the news: the apothecary from Derby who had ridden up to see her this week had been very emphatic. So the girl must be as usual. There must be no sign of discomposure. Tonight, at least, she would keep her face in the shadow. But her voice? Could she control that too?

After she had sat motionless in the cold hall a minute or two, she tested herself.

"He is dead," she said softly. "He is quite dead, and so are the others. They—"

But she could not go on. Great shuddering seized on her; she shook from head to foot....

Later that night Mrs. Manners awoke. She tried to move her head, but the pain was shocking, and still half asleep, she moaned aloud.

Then the curtains moved softly, and she could see that a face was looking at her.

"Margy! Is that you?"

"Yes, Mother."

"Move my head; move my head. I cannot bear—"

She felt herself lifted gently and strongly. The struggle and the pain exhausted her for a minute, and she lay breathing deeply. Then the ease of the shifted position soothed her.

"I cannot see your face," she said. "Where is the light?"

The face disappeared, and immediately, through the curtains, the mother saw the light. But still she could not see the girl's face. She said so peevishly.

"It will weary your eyes. Lie still, Mother, and go to sleep again."

"What time is it?"

"I do not know."

"Are you not in bed?"

"Not yet, Mother."

The sick woman moaned again once or twice, but thought no more of it. And presently the deep sleep of sickness came down on her again.

They rose early in those days in England; and soon after six o'clock, as Janet had seen nothing of her young mistress, she opened the door of the sleeping-room and peeped in.... A minute later Marjorie's mind rose up out of black gulfs of sleep, in which, since her falling asleep an hour or two ago, she had wandered, bearing an intolerable burden, which she could neither see nor let fall, to find the rosy-streaked face of Janet, all pinched with cold, peering into her own. She sat up, wide awake, yet with all her world still swaying about her, and stared into her maid's eyes.

"What is it? What time is it?"

"It is after six, mistress. And the mistress seems uneasy. I—"

Marjorie sprang up and went to the bed.

III

On the evening of that day her mother died. There was no priest within reach. A couple of men had ridden out early, dispatched by Marjorie within half an hour of her awaking—to Dethick, to Hathersage, and to every spot within twenty miles where a priest might be found, with orders not to return without one. But the long day had dragged out: and when dusk was falling, still neither had come back. The country was rain-soaked and all but impassable, she learned later, across valley after valley, where the streams had risen. And nowhere could news be gained that any priest was near; for, as a further difficulty, open inquiry was not always possible, in view of the news that had come to Booth's Edge last night. The girl had understood that the embers were rising again to flame in the south; and who could tell but that a careless word might kindle the fire here, too. She had been urged by Anthony to hold herself more careful than ever, and she had been compelled to warn her messengers.

It was soon after dusk had fallen—the heavy dusk of a December day—that her mother had come back again to consciousness. She opened her eyes wearily, coming back, as Marjorie had herself that morning, from that strange realm of heavy and deathly sleep, to the pale phantom world called "life"; and agonising pain about the heart stabbed her wide awake.

"O Jesu!" she screamed.

Then she heard her daughter's voice, very steady and plain, in her ear.

"There is no priest, Mother dear. Listen to me."

"I cannot! I cannot! ...Jesu!"

Her eyes closed again for torment, and the sweat ran down her face. The slow poison that had weighted and soaked her limbs so gradually these many months past was closing in at last upon her heart, and her pain was gathering to its last assault. The silent, humorous woman was changed into one twitching, uncontrolled incarnation of torture.

Then again the voice began:

"Jesu, Who didst die for love of me—upon the Cross—let me die—for love of Thee."

"Christ!" moaned the woman more softly.

"Say it in your heart, after me. There is no priest. So God will accept your sorrow instead. Now then—"

Then the old words began—the old acts of sorrow and love and faith and hope, that mother and daughter had said together, night after night, for so many years. Over and over again they came, whispered clear and sharp by the voice in her ear; and she strove to follow them. Now and again the pain closed its sharp hands upon her heart so cruelly that all that on which she strove to fix her mind, fled from her like a mist, and she moaned or screamed, or was silent with her teeth clenched upon her lip.

"My God—I am very sorry—that I have offended Thee."

"Why is there no priest? …Where is the priest?"

"Mother, dear, listen. I have sent for a priest…but none has come. You remember now? You remember that priests are forbidden now—"

"Where is the priest?"

"Mother, dear. Three priests were put to death only three days ago in London—for…for being priests. Ask them to pray for you.… Say, Edmund Campion pray for me. Perhaps…perhaps—"

The girl's voice died away.

For a full minute, an extraordinary sensation rested on her. It began with a sudden shiver of the flesh, as sharp and tingling as water, dying away in long thrills amid her hair—that strange advertisement that tells the flesh that more than flesh is there, and that the world of spirit is not only present, but alive and energetic. Then, as it passed, the whole world, too, passed into silence. The curtains that shook just now hung rigid as sheets of steel; the woman in the bed lay suddenly still, then smiled with closed eyes. The pair of maids, kneeling out of sight beyond the bed, ceased to sob; and, while the seconds went by, as real as any knowledge can be in which the senses have no part, the certain knowledge deepened upon the girl who knelt, arrested in spite of herself, that a priestly presence was here indeed.…

Very slowly, as if lifting great weights, she raised her eyes, knowing that there, across the tumbled bed, where the darkness of the room showed between the parted curtains, the Presence was poised. Yet there was nothing there to see—no tortured, smoke-stained, throttling face—ah! that could not be—but neither was there the merry, kindly face, with large cheerful eyes and tender mouth smiling; no hand held the curtains that the face might peer in. Neither then nor at any time in all her life did Marjorie believe that she saw him; yet neither then nor in all her life did she doubt he had been there while her mother died.

Again her mother smiled—and this time she opened her eyes to the full, and there was no dismay in them, nor fear, nor disappointment; and she looked a little to her left, where the parted curtains showed the darkness of the room....

Then Marjorie closed her eyes, and laid her head on the bed where her mother's body sank back and down into the pillows. Then the girl slipped heavily to the floor, and the maids sprang up screaming.

IV

It was not till two hours later that Mr. Simpson arrived. He had been found at last at Hathersage, only a few miles away, as one of the men, on his return ride, had made one last inquiry before coming home; and there he ran into the priest himself in the middle of the street. The priest had taken the man's horse and pushed on as well as he could through the dark, in the hopes he might yet be in time.

Marjorie came to him in the parlour downstairs. She nodded her head slowly and gravely.

"It is over," she said; and sat down.

"And there was no priest?"

She said nothing.

She was in her house-dress, with the hood drawn over her head as it was a cold night. He was amazed at her look of self-control; he had thought to find her either collapsed or strainedly tragic: he had wondered as he came how he would speak to her, how he would soothe her, and he saw there was no need.

She told him presently of the sudden turn for the worse early that morning as she herself fell asleep by the bedside; and a little of what had passed during the day. Then she stopped short as she approached the end.

"Have you heard the news from London?" she said. "I mean, of our priests there?"

His young face grew troubled, and he knit his forehead.

"They are in ward," he said; "I heard a week ago.... They will banish them from England—they dare not do more!"

"It is all finished," she said quietly.

"What!"

"They were hanged at Tyburn three days ago—the three of them together."

He drew a hissing breath, and felt the skin of his face tingle.

"You have heard that?"

"Mr. Babington came to tell me last night. He left a paper with me: I have not read it yet."

He watched her as she drew it out and put it before him. The terror was on him, as once or twice before in his journeyings, or as when the news of Mr. Nelson's death had reached him—a terror which shamed him to the heart, and which he loathed yet could not overcome. He still stared into her pale face. Then he took the paper and began to read it. Presently he laid it down again. The sick terror was beginning to pass; or, rather, he was able to grip it; and he said a conventional word or two; he could do no more. There was no exultation in his heart; nothing but misery. And then, in despair, he left the subject.

"And you, mistress," he said, "what will you do now? Have you no aunt or friend—"

"Mistress Alice Babington once said she would come and live with me—if...when I needed it. I shall write to her. I do not know what else to do."

"And you will live here?"

"Why, more than ever!" she said, smiling suddenly, "I can work in earnest now."

CHAPTER VI

I

It was on a bright evening in the summer that Marjorie, with her maid Janet, came riding down to Padley, and about the same time a young man came walking up the track that led from Derby. In fact, the young man saw the two against the skyline and wondered who they were. Further, there was a group of four or five walking on the terrace below the house, that saw both the approaching parties, and commented upon their coming.

To be precise, there were four persons in the group on the terrace, and a man-servant who hung near. The four were Mr. John FitzHerbert, his son Thomas, his son's wife, and, in the midst, leaning on Mrs. FitzHerbert's arm, was old Sir Thomas himself, and it was for his sake that the servant was within call, for he was still very sickly after his long imprisonment, in spite of his occasional releases.

Mr. John saw the visitors first.

"Why, here is the company all arrived together," he said. "Now, if anything hung on that—" his son broke in, uneasily.

"You are sure of young Owen?" he said. "Our lives will all hang on him after this."

His father clapped him gently on the shoulder.

"Now, now!" he said. "I know him well enough, from my lord. He has made a dozen such places in this county alone."

Mr. Thomas glanced swiftly at his uncle.

"And you have spoken with him, too, uncle?"

The old man turned his melancholy eyes on him.

"Yes; I have spoken with him," he said.

Five minutes later Marjorie was dismounted, and was with him. She greeted old Sir Thomas with particular respect; she had talked with him a year ago when he was first released that he might raise his fines; and she knew well enough that his liberty was coming to an end. In fact, he was technically a prisoner even now; and had only been allowed to come for a week or two from Sir Walter Aston's house before going back again to the Fleet.

"You are come in good time," said Sir John, smiling.

"That is young Owen himself coming up the path."

There was nothing particularly noticeable about the young man who a minute later was standing before them with his cap in his hand. He was plainly of the working class; and he had over his shoulder a bag of tools. He was dusty up to the knees with his long tramp. Mr. John gave him a word of welcome; and then the whole group went slowly together back to the house, with the two men following. Sir Thomas stumbled a little going up the two or three steps into the hall. Then they all sat down together; the servant put a big flagon and a horn tumbler beside the traveller, and went out, closing the doors.

"Now, my man," said Mr. John. "Do you eat and drink while I do the talking. I understand you are a man of your hands, and that you have business elsewhere."

"I must be in Lancashire by the end of the week, sir."

"Very well, then. We have business enough for you, God knows! This is Mistress Manners, whom you may have heard of. And after you have looked at the places we have here—you understand me?—Mistress Manners wants you at her house at Booth's Edge.... You have any papers?"

Owen leaned back and drew out a paper from his bag of tools.

"This is from Mr. Fenton, sir."

Mr. John glanced at the address; then he turned it over and broke the seal. He stared for a moment at the open sheet.

"Why, it is blank!" he said.

Owen smiled. He was a grave-looking lad of eighteen or nineteen years old; and his face lighted up very pleasantly.

"I have had that trick played on me before, sir, in my travels. I understand that Catholic gentlemen do so sometimes to try the fidelity of the messenger."

The other laughed out loud, throwing back his head.

"Why, that is a poor compliment!" he said. "You shall have a better one from us, I have no doubt."

Mr. Thomas leaned over the table and took the paper. He examined it very carefully; then he handed it back. His father laughed again as he took it.

"You are very cautious, my son," he said. "But it is wise enough.... Well, then," he went on to the carpenter, "you are willing to do this work for us? And as for payment—"

"I ask only my food and lodging," said the lad quietly; "and enough to carry me on to the next place."

"Why—" began the other in a protest.

"No, sir; no more than that...." He paused an instant. "I hope to be admitted to the Society of Jesus this year or next."

There was a pause of astonishment. And then old Sir Thomas' deep voice broke in.

"You do very well, sir. I heartily congratulate you. And I would I were twenty years younger myself...."

II

AFTER supper that night the entire party went upstairs to the chapel.

Hugh Owen already was beginning to be known among Catholics, for his extraordinary skill in constructing hiding-holes. To the present not much more had been attempted than little secret recesses where the altar vessels and the vestments might be concealed. But the carpenter had been ingenious enough in two or three houses to which he had been called, to enlarge these so considerably that even two or three men might be sheltered in them; and, now that it seemed as if the persecution of recusants was to break out again, the idea began to spread. Mr. John FitzHerbert while in London had heard of his skill, and had taken means to get at the young man, for his own house at Padley.

Owen was already at work when the party came upstairs. He had supped alone, and, with a servant to guide him, had made the round of the house, taking measurements in every possible place. He was seated on the floor as they came in; three or four panels lay on the ground beside him, and a heap of plaster and stones.

He looked up as they came in.

"This will take me all night, sir. And the fire must be put out below."

He explained his plan. The old hiding-place was but a poor affair; it consisted of a space large enough for only one man, and was contrived by a section of the wall having been removed, all but the outer row of stones made thin for the purpose; the entrance to it was through a tall sliding panel on the inside of the chapel. Its extreme weakness as a hiding-hole lay in the fact that anyone striking on the panel could not fail to hear how hollow it rang. This he proposed to do away with, unless, indeed, he left a small space for the altar vessels; and to construct instead a little chamber in the chimney of the hall that was built against this wall; he would contrive it so that an entrance was still from the chapel, as well as one that he would make over the hearth below; and that the smoke should be conducted round the little enclosed space, passing afterwards up the usual vent. The chamber would be large enough, he thought, for at least two men. He explained, too, his method of deadening the hollowness of the sound if the panel were knocked upon, by placing pads of felt on struts of wood that would be set against the panel-door.

"Why, that is very shrewd!" cried Mr. John. He looked round the faces for approval.

For an hour or so, the party sat and watched him at his work. They talked in low voices; for the shadow was on all their hearts. It had been possible almost to this very year to hope that the misery would be a passing one; but the time for hope was gone. It remained only to bear what came, to multiply priests, and, if necessary, martyrs, and meantime to take such pains for protection as they could.

"He will be a clever pursuivant who finds this one out," said Mr. John.

The carpenter looked up from his work.

"But a clever one will find it," he said.

Mr. Thomas was heard to sigh.

III

It was on the afternoon of the following day that Marjorie rode up to her house with Janet beside her, and Hugh Owen walking by her horse.

He had finished his work at Padley an hour or two after dawn— for he worked at night when he could, and had then gone to rest. But he had been waiting for her when her horses were brought, and asked if he might walk with her; he had asked it simply and easily, saying that it might save his losing his way, and time was precious to him.

Marjorie felt very much interested by this lad, for he was no more than that. In appearance he was like any of his kind, with a countryman's face, in a working-dress; she might have seen him by chance a hundred times and not known him again. But his manner was remarkable, so wholly simple and well-bred: he was courteous always; as suited his degree; but he had something of the same assurance that she had noticed so plainly in Father Campion. (He talked with a plain, Northern dialect.)

Presently she opened, on that very point; for she could talk freely before Janet.

"Did you ever know Father Campion?" she asked.

"I have never spoken with him, mistress. I have heard him preach. It was that which put it in my heart to join the company."

"You heard him preach?"

"Yes, mistress; three or four times in Essex and Hertfordshire. I heard him preach upon the young man who came to our Saviour."

"Tell me," she said, looking down at what she could see of his face.

"It was liker an angel than a man," he said quietly. "I could not take my eyes off him from his first word to the last. And all were the same that were there."

"Was he eloquent?"

"Aye; you might call it that. But I thought it to be the Spirit of God."

"And it was then you made up your mind to join the Society?"

"There was no rest for me till I did. 'And Christ also went away sorrowful,' were his last words. And I could not bear to think that."

Marjorie was silent through pure sympathy. This young man spoke a language she understood better than that which some of her friends used—Mr. Babington, for instance. It was the Person of Jesus Christ that was all her religion to her; it was for this that she was devout, that she went to Mass and the sacraments when she could. And, above all, it was for this that she had sacrificed Robin: she could not bear that he should not serve Him as a priest, if he might. But the other talk that she had heard sometimes—of the place of religion in politics, and the justification of this or that course of public action— well, she knew that these things must be so; yet it was not the manner of her own most intimate thought, and the language of it was not hers.

The two went together so a few paces, without speaking. Then she had a sudden impulse.

"And do you ever think of what may come upon you?" she asked. "Do you ever think of the end?"

"Aye," he said.

"And what do you think the end will be?"

She saw him raise his eyes to her an instant.

"I think," he said, "that I shall die for my faith some day."

That same strange shiver that passed over her at her mother's bedside, passed over her again, as if material things grew thin about her. There was a tone in his voice that made it absolutely clear to her that he was not speaking of a fancy, but of some certain knowledge that he had. Yet she dared not ask him, and she was a middle-aged woman before the news came to her of his death upon the rack.

IV

IT was a sleepy-eyed young man who came into the kitchen early next morning, where the ladies and the maids were hard at work all together upon the business of baking. Marjorie turned to him, with her arms floured to the elbow.

"Well?" she said, smiling.

"I have done, mistress. Will it please you to see it before I go and sleep?"

They had examined the house carefully last night, measuring and sounding in the deep and thin walls alike, for there was at present no convenience at all for a hunted man. Owen had obtained her consent to two or three alternative proposals, and she had then left him to himself. From her bed, that she had had prepared, with Alice Babington's, in a loft—turning out for the night the farm-men who had usually slept there, she had heard more than once the sound of distant hammering from the main front of the house where her own room lay, that had been once her mother's as well.

He took her first into the parlour, where years ago Robin had talked with her in the wintry sunshine. The open chimney was on the right as they entered, and though she knew that somewhere on that same side would be one of the two entrances that had been arranged, all the difference she could see was that a piece of the wall-hanging that had been between the window and the fire was gone, and that there hung in its place an old picture painted on a panel. She looked at this without speaking: the wall was wainscoted in oak, as it had always been, six feet up from the floor. Then an idea came to her: she tilted the picture on one side. But there was no more to be seen than a cracked panel, which, it seemed to her, had once been nearer the door. She rapped upon this, but it gave back the dull sound as of wood against stone.

She turned to the young man, smiling. He smiled back.

"Come into the bedroom, mistress."

He led her in there, through the passage outside into which the two doors opened at the head of the outside stairs; but here, too, all that she could see was that a tall press that had once stood between the windows now stood against the wall immediately opposite to the painted panel on the other side of the wall. She opened the doors of the press, but it was as it had always been: there even hung there the three or four dresses that she had taken from it last night and laid on the bed.

She laughed outright, and, turning, saw Mistress Alice Babington beaming tranquilly from the door of the room. "Come in, Alice," she said, "and see this miracle."

THEN he began to explain it.

The back of the press had been removed, and then replaced, in such a manner that it would slide out about eighteen inches towards the window, but only when the doors of the press were closed; when they were opened, they drew out simultaneously a slip of wood on either side that pulled the sliding door tight and immovable. Behind the back of the press, thus removed, a corresponding part of the wainscot slid in the same way, giving a narrow doorway into the cell which he had excavated between the double beams of the thick wall. Next, when the person that had taken refuge was inside, with the two sliding doors closed behind him, it was possible for him, by an extremely simple device, to turn a wooden button and thus release a little wooden machinery which controlled a further opening into the parlour, and which, at the same time, as braced against the hollow panelling and one of the higher beams in such a manner as to give it, when knocked upon, the dullness of sound the girl had noticed just now. But this door could only be opened from within. Neither a fugitive nor a pursuer could make any entrance from the parlour side, unless the wainscoting itself were torn off. Lastly, the crack in the woodwork, corresponding with two minute holes bored in the painted panel, afforded, when the picture was hung exactly straight, a view of the parlour that commanded nearly all the room.

"I do not pretend that it is a fortress," said the young man, smiling gravely. "But it may serve to keep out a country constable. And, indeed, it is the best I can contrive in this house."

CHAPTER VII

I

MARJORIE found it curious, even to herself, how the press that faced the foot of the two beds where she and Alice slept side by side became associated in her mind with the thought of Robin; and she began to perceive that it was largely with the thought of him in her intention that the idea had first presented itself of having the cell constructed at all. It was not that in her deliberate mind she conceived that he would be hunted, that he would fly here, that she would save him; but rather in that strange realm of consciousness which is called sometimes the Imagination, and sometimes by other names—that inner shadow-show on which move figures cast by the two worlds—she perceived him in this place....

It was in the following winter that she was reminded of him by other means than those of his letters.

She and Alice, with Janet and a man riding behind, were on their way back from Derby, where they had gone for their monthly shopping. They had slept at Dethick, and had had news there of Mr. Anthony, who was again in the south on one of his mysterious missions, and started again soon after dawn next day to reach home, if they could, for dinner.

She knew Alice now for what she was—a woman of astounding dullness, of sterling character, and of a complete inability to understand any shades or tones of character or thought that were not her own, and yet a friend in a thousand, of an immovable stability and loyalty, one of no words at all, who dwelt in the midst of a steady kind of light which knew no dawn nor sunset. The girl entertained herself sometimes with conceiving of her friend confronted with the rack, let us say, or the gallows; and perceived that she knew with exactness what her behaviour would be; she would do all that was required of her without speeches or protest; she would place herself in the required positions, with a faint smile, unwavering; she would surfer or die with the same tranquil steadiness as that in which she lived; and, best of all, she would not be aware, even for an instant, that anything in her behaviour was in the least admirable or exceptional.

As they came towards Matstead, and, at last, rode up the street, naturally enough Marjorie again began to think of Robin. Near the churchyard wall, where once Robin had watched, himself unseen, the three riders go by, she had to attend to her horse, who slipped once or twice on the paved causeway. Then as she lifted her head again, she saw, not three yards from her, and on a level with her own face, the face of the squire looking at her from over the wall.

She had not seen him, except once in Derby, a year or two before, and that at a distance, since Robin had left England; and at the sight she started so violently, in some manner jerking the reins that she held, that her horse, tired with the long ride of the day before, slipped once again, and came down all asprawl on the stones, fortunately throwing her clear of his struggling feet. She was up in a moment, but again sank down, aware that her foot was in some way bruised or twisted.

There was a clatter of hoofs behind her as the servants rode up; a child or two ran up the street, and when, at last, on Janet's arm, she rose again to her feet, it was to see the squire staring at her, with his hands clasped behind his back.

"Bring the ladies up to the house," he said abruptly to the man; and then, taking the rein of the girl's horse that had struggled up again, he led the way, without another word, without even turning his head, round to the way that ran up to his gates.

II

It was not with any want of emotion that Marjorie found herself presently meekly seated upon Alice's horse, and riding up at a foot's-pace beneath the gatehouse of the Hall. Rather it was the balance of emotions that made her so meek and so obedient to her friend's tranquil assumption that she must come in as the squire said. She was aware of a strong resentment to his brusque order, as well as to the thought that it was to the house of an apostate that she was going; yet there was a no less strong emotion within her that he had a sort of right to command her. These feelings, working upon her, dazed as she was by the sudden sharpness of her fall, and the pain in her foot, combined to drive her along in a kind of resignation in the wake of the squire.

Still confused, yet with a rapid series of these same emotions running before her mind, she limped up the steps, supported by Alice and her maid, and sat down on a bench at the end of the hall. The squire, who had shouted an order or two to a peeping domestic, as he passed up the court, came to her immediately with a cup in his hand.

"You must drink this at once, mistress."

She took it at once, drank and set it down, aware of the keen, angry-looking face that watched her.

"You will dine here, too, mistress—" he began, still with a sharp kindness.... And then, on a sudden, all grew dark about her; there was a roaring in her ears, and she fainted.

THE three women dined together. There was no escape from the pressure of circumstance. It was unfortunate that such an accident should have fallen out here, in the one place in all the world where it should not; but the fact was a fact. Meanwhile, it was not only resentment that Marjorie felt: it was a strange sort of terror as well—a terror of sitting in the house of an apostate—of one who had freely and deliberately renounced that faith for which she herself lived so completely; and that it was the father of one whom she knew as she knew Robin—with whose fate, indeed, her own had been so intimately entwined—this combined to increase that indefinable fear that rested on her as she stared round the walls, and sat over the food and drink that this man provided.

The climax came as they were finishing dinner: for the door from the hall opened abruptly, and the squire came in. He bowed to the ladies, as the manner was, straightening his trim, tight figure again defiantly; asked a civil question or two; directed a servant behind him to bring the horses to the parlour door in half an hour's time; and then snapped out the sentence which he was, plainly, impatient to speak.

"Mistress Manners," he said, "I wish to have a word with you privately."

Marjorie, trembling at his presence, turned a wavering face to her friend; and Alice, before the other could speak, rose up, and went out, with Janet following.

"Janet—" cried the girl.

"If you please," said the old man, with such a decisive air that she hesitated. Then she nodded at her maid; and a moment later the door closed.

III

"I have two matters to speak of," said the squire abruptly, sitting down in the chair that Alice had left; "the first concerns you closely; and the other less closely."

She looked at him, summoning all her power to appear at her ease.

He seemed far older than when she had last spoken with him, perhaps five years ago; and had grown a little pointed beard; his hair, too, seemed thinner—such of it as she could see beneath the house-cap that he wore; his face, especially about his blue, angry-looking eyes, was covered with fine wrinkles, and his hands were clearly the hands of an old man, at once delicate and sinewy. He was in a dark suit, still with his cloak upon him; and in low boots. He sat still as upright as ever, turned a little in his chair, so as to clasp its back with one strong hand.

"Yes, sir?" she said.

"I will begin with the second first. It is of my son Robin: I wish to know what news you have of him. He has not written to me this six months back. And I hear that letters sometimes come to you from him."

Marjorie hesitated.

"He is very well, so far as I know," she said.

"And when is he to be made priest?" he demanded sharply.

Marjorie drew a breath to give herself time; she knew that she must not answer this; and did not know how to say so with civility.

"If he has not told you himself, sir," she said, "I cannot."

The old man's face twitched; but he kept his manners.

"I understand you, mistress...." But then his wrath overcame him. "But he must understand he will have no mercy from me, if he comes my way. I am a magistrate, now, mistress, and—"

A thought like an inspiration came to the girl; and she interrupted; for she longed to penetrate this man's armour.

"Perhaps that was why he did not tell you when he was to be made priest," she said.

The other seemed taken aback.

"Why, but—"

"He did not wish to think that his father would be untrue to his new commission," she said, trembling at her boldness and yet exultant too; and taking no pains to keep the irony out of her voice.

Again that fierce twitch of the features went over the other's face; and he stared straight at her with narrowed eyes. Then a change again came over him; and he laughed, like barking, yet not all unkindly.

"You are very shrewd, mistress. But I wonder what you will think of me when I tell you the second matter, since you will tell me no more of the first."

He shifted his position in his chair, this time clasping both his hands together over the back.

"Well, it is this in a word," he said: "It is that you had best look to yourself, mistress. My lord Shrewsbury even knows of it."

"Of what, if you please?" asked the girl, hoping she had not turned white.

"Why, of the priests that come and go hereabouts! It is all known; and her Grace has sent a message from the Council—"

"What has this to do with me?"

He laughed again.

"Well, let us take your neighbours at Padley. They will be in trouble if they do not look to their goings. Mr. FitzHerbert—"

But again she interrupted him. She was determined to know how much he knew. She had thought that she had been discreet enough, and that no news had leaked out of her own entertaining of priests; it was chiefly that discretion might be preserved that she had set her hands to the work at all. With Padley so near it was thought that less suspicion would be aroused. Her name had never yet come before the authorities, so far as she knew.

"But what has all this to do with me, sir?" she asked sharply. "It is true that I do not go to church, and that I pay my fines when they are demanded. Are there new laws, then, against the old faith?"

She spoke with something of real bitterness. It was genuine enough; her only art lay in her not concealing it; for she was determined to press her question home. And, in his shrewd, compelling face, she read, her answer even before his words gave it.

"Well, mistress; it was not of you that I meant to speak—so much as of your friends. They are your friends, not mine. And as your friends, I thought it to be a kindly action to send them an advertisement. If they are not careful, there will be trouble."

"At Padley?"

"At Padley, or elsewhere. It is the persons that fall under the law, not places!"

"But, sir, you are a magistrate; and—"

He sprang up, his face aflame with real wrath.

"Yes, mistress; I am a magistrate: the commission has come at last, after six months' waiting. But I was friend to the FitzHerberts before ever I was a magistrate and—"

Then she understood; and her heart went out to him. She, too, stood up, catching at the table with a hiss of pain as she threw her weight on the bruised foot. He made a movement towards her; but she waved him aside.

"I beg your pardon, Mr. Audrey, with all my heart. I had thought that you meant harm, perhaps, to my friends and me. But now I see—"

"Not a word more! not a word more!" he cried harshly, with a desperate kind of gesture. "I shall do my duty none the less when the time comes—"

"Sir!" she cried out suddenly. "For God's sake do not speak of duty—there is another duty greater than that. Mr. Audrey—"

He wheeled away from her, with a movement she could not interpret. It might be uncontrolled anger or misery, equally. And her heart went out to him in one great flood.

"Mr. Audrey. It is not too late. Your son Robin—"

Then he wheeled again; and his face was distorted with emotion.

"Yes, my son Robin! my son Robin! ...How dare you speak of him to me? ...Yes; that is it—my son Robin—my son Robin!"

He dropped into the chair again, and his face fell upon his clasped hands.

SHE was pondering deeply all the way as she rode home. Mistress Alice was one of those folks who so long as they are answered in words are content; and Marjorie so answered her. And all the while she thought upon Robin, and his passionate old father, and attempted to understand the emotions that fought in the heart that had so disclosed itself to her—its aged obstinacy, its loyalty and its confused honourableness. She knew very well that he would do what he conceived to be his duty with all the more zeal if it were an unpleasant duty; and she thanked God that it was not for a good while yet that the lad would come home a priest.

CHAPTER VIII

I

The news came to her as she sat in the garden over her needlework on a hot evening in June. There it was as cool as anywhere in the countryside. She sat at the top of the garden, where her mother and she had sat with Robin so long before; the breeze that came over the moor bore with it the scent of the heather; and the bees were busy in the garden flowers about her.

It was first the gallop of a horse that she heard; and even at that sound she laid down her work and stood up. But the house below her blocked the most of her view; and she sat down again when she heard the dull rattle of the hoofs die away again. When she next looked up a man was running towards her from the bottom of the garden, and Janet was peeping behind him from the gate into the court. As she again stood up, she saw that it was Dick Sampson.

He was so out of breath, first with his ride and next with his run up the steep path, that for a moment or two he could not speak. He was dusty, too, from foot to knee; his cap was awry and his collar unbuttoned.

"It is Mr. Thomas, mistress," he gasped presently. "I was in Derby and saw him being taken to the gaol.... I could not get speech with him.... I rode straight up to Padley, and found none there but the servants, and them knowing nothing of the matter. And so I rode on here, mistress."

He was plainly all aghast at the blow. Hitherto it had been enough that Sir Thomas was in ward for his religion; and to this they had become accustomed. But that the heir should be taken, too, and that without a hint of what was to happen, was wholly unexpected. She made him sit down, and presently drew from him the whole tale.

Mr. Anthony Babington, his master, was away to London again, leaving the house in Derby in the hands of the servants. He then—Dick Sampson—was riding out early to take a horse to be shod, and had come back, through the town-square, when he saw the group ride up to the gaol door near the Friar Gate. He, too, had ridden up to ask what was forward, and had been just in time to see Mr. Thomas taken in. He had caught his eye, but had feigned not to know him. Then the man had attempted to get at what had happened from one of the fellows at the door, but could get no more from him than that the prisoner was a known and confessed recusant, and had been laid by the heels according to orders, it was believed, sent down by the Council. Then Dick had ridden slowly away till he had turned the corner, and then, hot foot for Padley.

"And I heard the fellow say to one of his company that an informer was coming down from London on purpose to Meal with Mr. Thomas."

Marjorie felt a sudden pang; for she had never forgotten the one she had set eyes on in the Tower.

"His name?" she said breathlessly. "Did you hear his name?"

"It was Topcliffe, mistress," said Dick indifferently. "The other called it out."

Marjorie sat silent. Not only had the blow fallen more swiftly than she would have thought possible, but it was coupled with a second of which she had never dreamed. That it was this man, above all others, that should have come; this man, who stood to her mind, by a mere chance, for all that was most dreadful in the sinister forces arrayed against her—this brought misery down on her indeed. For, besides her own personal reasons for terror, there was, besides, the knowledge that the bringing of such a man at all from London on such business meant that the movement beginning here in her own county was not a mere caprice.

II

SHE sent Dick off after a couple of hours' rest, during which once more he had told his story to Mistress Alice, with a letter to Mr. Thomas' wife, who, no doubt, would have followed her lord to Derby. She had gone apart with Alice, while Dick ate and drank, to talk the affair out, and had told her of Topcliffe's presence, at which news even the placid face of her friend looked troubled; but they had said nothing more on the point, and had decided that a letter should be written in Mistress Babington's name, offering Mrs. FitzHerbert the hospitality of Babington House, and any other services she might wish. Further, they had decided that the best thing to do was to go themselves to Derby next day, in order to be at hand; since Mr. John was in London, and the sooner Mrs. Thomas had friends with her, the better.

"They may keep him in ward a long time," said Mistress Alice, "before they bring him into open court—to try his courage. That is the way they do. The charge, no doubt, will be that he has harboured and assisted priests."

MARJORIE lay awake that night, staring through the summer dusk at the tall press which hid so much beside her dresses. Ever since she had first offered her lover to God and let him go from her, it appeared as if God had taken her at her word, and accepted in an instant that which she offered so tremblingly. There was no drawing back now, even had she wished it. And she wished it indeed, though she did not will it; she knew that she must stand in her place, now more than ever, when the blow had fallen so near. Now more than ever must she be discreet and resolute, since Padley itself was fallen, in effect, if not in fact; and Booth's Edge, in this valley at least, was the one hope of hunted men. She must stand, then, in her place; she must govern her face and her manner more perfectly than ever, for the sake of that tremendous cause.

III

DERBY was, indeed, astir as they rode in, with the servants and the baggage following behind, on the late afternoon of the next day. They had ridden by easy stages, halting at Dethick for dinner, where the Babingtons' house already hummed with dismay at the news that had come from Derby last night. Mr. Anthony was away, and all seemed distracted.

They rode in by the North road, seeing for the last mile or two of their ride the towering spire of All Saints' Church high above the smoke of the houses; they passed the old bridge half a mile from the marketplace, near the ancient camp; and even here overheard a sentence or two from a couple of fellows that were leaning on the parapet, that told them what was the talk of the town. It was plain that others besides the Catholics understood the taking of Mr. Thomas FitzHerbert to be a very significant matter.

Babington House stood on the further side of the marketplace from that on which they entered, and Alice was for going there through side streets.

"They will take notice if we go straight through," she said. "It is cheese-market today."

"They will take notice in any case," said Marjorie. "It will be over the town tomorrow that Mistress Babington is here, and it is best, therefore, to come openly, as if without fear."

And she turned to beckon the servants to draw up closer behind.

THE square was indeed crowded as they came in. From all the country round, and especially from Dovedale, the farmers came in on this day, or sent their wives, for the selling of cheeses; and the small oblong of the market—the smaller from its great Conduit and Cross—was full with rows of stalls and carts, with four lanes only left along the edges by which the traffic might pass; and even here the streams of passengers forced the horses to go in single file.

Mistress Babington rode first, preceded by one of the Dethick men whom they had taken up on their way, and who had pushed forward when they came into the town to clear the road; and Mistress Manners rode after her. The men stood aside as the cavalcade began to go between the booths, and the most of them saluted Mistress Babington.

But as they were almost out of the market they came abreast one of the inns from whose wide-open doors came a roar of voices from those that were drinking within, and a group that was gathered on the step stopped talking as the party came up. Marjorie glanced at them, and noticed there was an air about two or three of the men that was plainly town-bred; there was a certain difference in the cut of their clothes and the way they wore them. Then she saw two or three whispering together, and the next moment came a brutal shout. She could not catch the sentence, but she heard the word "Papist" with an adjective, and caught the unmistakable bullying tone of the man. The next instant there broke out a confusion: a man dashed up the step from the crowd beneath, and she caught a glimpse of Dick Sampson's furious face. Then the group bore back, fighting, into the inn door; the Dethick servant leapt off his horse, leaving it in some fellow's hands, and vanished up the step; there was a rush of the crowd after him, and then the way was clear in front, over the little bridge that spanned Bramble brook.

When she drew level with Alice, she saw her friend's face, pale and agitated.

"It is the first time I have ever been cried at," she said. "Come; we are nearly home. There is St. Peter's spire."

"Shall we not—" began Marjorie.

"No, no" (and the pale face tightened suddenly). "My fellows will give them a lesson. The crowd is on our side as yet."

IV

As they rode in under the archway that led in beside the great doors of Babington House, three or four grooms ran forward at once. It was plain that their coming was looked for with some eagerness.

Alice's manner seemed curiously different from that of the quiet woman who had sat so patiently beside Marjorie in the manor among the hills: a certain air of authority and dignity sat on her now that she was back in her own place.

"Is Mrs. FitzHerbert here?" she asked from the groom who helped her to the ground.

"Yes, mistress; she came from the inn this morning, and—"

"Well?"

"She is in a great taking, mistress. She would eat nothing, they said."

Alice nodded.

"You had best be off to the inn," she said, with a jerk of her head. "A London fellow insulted us just now, and Sampson and Mallow—"

She said no more. The man who held her horse slipped the reins into the hands of the younger groom who stood by him, and was away and out of the court in an instant. Marjorie smiled a little, astonished at her own sense of exultation. The blows were not to be all one side, she perceived. Then she followed Alice into the house.

As they came through into the hall by the side-door that led through from the court where they had dismounted, a figure was plainly visible in the dusky light, going to and fro at the further end, with a quick, nervous movement. The figure stopped as they advanced, and then darted forward, crying out piteously:

"Ah! you have come, thank God! thank God! They will not let me see him."

"Hush! hush!" said Alice, as she caught her in her arms.

"Mr. Bassett has been here," moaned the figure, "and he says it is Topcliffe himself who has come down on the matter.... He says he is the greatest devil of them all; and Thomas—"

Then she burst out crying again.

It was an hour before they could get the full tale out of her. They took her upstairs and made her sit down, for already a couple of faces peeped from the buttery, and the servants would have gathered in another five minutes; and together they forced her to eat and drink something, for she had not tasted food since her arrival at the inn yesterday; and so, little by little, they drew the story out.

Mr. Thomas and his wife were actually on their way from Norbury when the arrest had been made. Mr. Thomas had intended to pass a couple of nights in Derby on various matters of the estates; and although, his wife said, he had been somewhat silent and quiet since the warning had come to him from Mr. Audrey, even he had thought it no danger to ride through Derby on his way to Padley. He had sent a servant ahead to order rooms at the inn for those two nights, and it was through that, it appeared, that the news of his coming had reached the ears of the authorities. However that was, and whether the stroke had been actually determined upon long before, or had been suddenly decided upon at the news of his coming, it fell out that, as the husband and wife were actually within sight of Derby, on turning a corner they had found themselves surrounded by men on horses, plainly gathered there for the purpose, with a magistrate in the midst. Their names had been demanded, and, upon Mr. Thomas' hesitation, they had been told that their names were well known, and a warrant was produced, on a charge of recusancy and of aiding her Grace's enemies, drawn out against Thomas FitzHerbert, and he had been placed under arrest. Further, Mrs. FitzHerbert had been told she must not enter the town with the party, but must go either before them or after them, which she pleased. She had chosen to go first, and had been at the windows of the inn in time to see her husband go by. There had been no confusion, she said; the townsfolk appeared to know nothing of what was happening until Mr. Thomas was safely lodged in the ward.

Then she burst out crying again, lamenting the horrible state of the prison, as it had been described to her, and demanding to know where God's justice was in allowing His faithful servants to be so tormented and harried....

Marjorie watched her closely. She had met her once at Babington House, when she was still Elizabeth Westley, but had thought little or nothing of her since. She was a pale little creature, fair-haired and timorous, and had now a haunted look of misery in her eyes that was very piteous to see. It was plain they had done right in coming: this woman would be of little service to her husband.

Then when Alice had said a word or two, Marjorie began her questions.

"Tell me," she said gently, "had you no warning of this?"

The girl shook her head,

"Not beyond that which came from yourself," she said; "and we never thought—"

"Hath Mr. Thomas had any priests with him lately?"

"We have not had one at Norbury for the last six months, whilst we were there, at least. My husband said it was better not to, and that there was a plenty of places for them to go to."

"And you have not heard Mass during that time?"

The girl looked at her with tear-stained eyes.

"No," she said. "But why do you ask that? My husband says—"

"And when was the first you heard of Topcliffe? And what have you heard of him?"

The other's face fell into lines of misery.

"I have heard he is the greatest devil her Grace uses. He has authority to question priests and others in his own house. He has a rack there that he boasts makes all others as Christmas toys. My husband—"

Marjorie patted her arm gently.

"There! there!" she said kindly. "Your husband is not in Topcliffe's house. There will be no question of that. He is here in his own county, and—"

"But that will not save him!" cried the girl. "Why—"

"Tell me," interrupted Marjorie, "was Topcliffe with the men that took Mr. Thomas?"

The other shook her head.

"No; I heard he was not. He was come from London yesterday morning. That was the first I heard of him."

Then Alice began again to soothe her gently, to tell her that her husband was in no great danger as yet, that he was well known for his loyalty, and to do her best to answer the girl's pitiful questions.

She stood up presently, grave with her thoughts. Mistress Alice glanced up.

"I am going out for a little," said Marjorie.

"But—"

"May two of your men follow me at a little distance? But I shall be safe enough. I am going to a friend's house."

Marjorie knew Derby well enough from the old days when she rode in sometimes with her father and slept at Mr. Biddell's; and, above all, she knew all that Derby had once been. In one place, outside the town, was St. Mary-in-Pratis, where the Benedictine nuns had lived; St. Leonard's had had a hospital for lepers; St. Helen's had had the Augustinian hospital for poor brothers and sisters; all this she knew by heart; and it was bitter now to be here on such business. But she went briskly out from the hall, and ten minutes later she was knocking at the door of a little attorney, the old partner of her father whose house faced the Guildhall across the little market-square. It was opened by an old woman who smiled at the sight of her.

"Eh! come in, mistress. The master saw you ride into town. He is in the upstairs parlour, with Mr. Bassett."

The girl nodded to her bodyguard, and followed the old woman in. She bowed as she passed the lawyer's confidential clerk and servant, Mr. George Beaton, in the passage—a big man, with whom she had had communications more than once on Popish affairs.

Mr. John Biddell, like Marjorie's own father and his partner, was one of those quiet folks who live through storms without attracting attention from the elements, yet without the sacrifice of principle. He was a Catholic, and never pretended to be anything else; but he was so little and so harmless that no man ever troubled him. He pleaded before the magistrates unobtrusively and deftly; and would have appeared before her Grace herself or the Lord of Hell with the same timid and respectful air, in his iron-rimmed spectacles, his speckless dark suit, and his little black cap drawn down to his ears. He had communicated with Marjorie again and again in the last two or three years on the subject of wandering priests, calling them "gentlemen," with the greatest care, and allowing no indiscreet word ever to appear in his letters. He remembered King Harry, whom he had seen once in a visit of his to London; he had assisted the legal authorities considerably in the restoration under Queen Mary; and he had soundlessly acquiesced in the changes again under Elizabeth—so far, at least, as mere law was concerned.

Mr. William Bassett was a very different man. First he was the brother-in-law of Sir Thomas FitzHerbert himself; and was entirely of the proper spirit to mate with that fearless family. He had considerable estates, both at Langley and Blore, in both of which places he cheerfully evaded the new laws, maintaining and helping priests in all directions; a man, in fact, of an ardent and boisterous faith which he extended (so the report ran) even to magic and astrology; a man of means, too, in spite of his frequent fines for recusancy, and aged about fifty years old at this time, with a high colour in his face and bright, merry eyes. Marjorie had spoken with him once or twice only.

These two men, then, first turned round in their chairs, and then stood up to salute Marjorie, as she came into the upstairs parlour. It was a somewhat dark room, panelled where there was space for it between the books, and with two windows looking out on to the square.

"I thought we should see you soon," said the attorney.

"We saw you come, mistress; and the fellows that cried out on you."

"They had their deserts," said Marjorie, smiling.

Mr. Bassett laughed aloud.

"Indeed they did," he said in his deep, pleasant voice. "There were two of them with bloody noses before all was done.... You have come for the news, I suppose, mistress?"

He eyed her genially and approvingly. He had heard a great deal of this young lady in the last three or four years; and wished there were more of her kind.

"That is what I have come for," said Marjorie. "We have Mrs. Thomas over at Babington House."

"She'll be of no great service to her husband," said the other. "She cries and laments too much. Now—"

He stopped himself from paying his compliments. It seemed to him that this woman, with her fearless, resolute face, would do very well without them.

Then he set himself to relate the tale.

It seemed that little Mrs. Thomas had given a true enough report. It was true that Topcliffe had arrived from London on the morning of the arrest; and Mistress Manners was perfectly right in her opinion that this signified a good deal. But, it seemed to Mr. Bassett, the Council had made a great mistake in striking at the FitzHerberts. The quarry was too strong, he said, for such birds as the Government used—too strong and too many. For, first, no FitzHerbert had ever yet yielded in his allegiance either to the Church or to the Queen's Grace; and it was not likely that Mr. Thomas would begin: and, next, if one yielded (*suadente diabolo,* and *Deus avertat!*) a dozen more would spring up. But the position was serious for all that, said Mr. Bassett (and Mr. Biddell nodded assent), for who would deal with the estates and make suitable arrangements if the heir, who already largely controlled them, were laid by the heels? But that the largeness of the undertaking was recognised by the Council was plain enough, in that no less a man than Topcliffe (Mr. Bassett spat on the floor as he named him), Topcliffe, "the devil possessed by worse devils," was sent down to take charge of the matter.

Marjorie listened carefully.

"You have no fear for yourself, sir?" she asked presently, as the man sat back in his chair.

Mr. Bassett smiled broadly, showing his strong white teeth between the iron-grey hair that fringed his lips.

"No; I have no fear," he said. "I have a score of my men quartered in the town."

"And the trial? When will that—"

"The trial! Why, I shall praise God if the trial falls this year. They will harry him before magistrates, no doubt; and they will squeeze him in private. But the trial!…Why, they have not a word of treason against him; and that is what they are after, no doubt."

"Treason?"

"Why, surely. That is what they seek to fasten upon us all. It would not sound well that Christian should shed Christian's blood for Christianity; but that her Grace should sorrowfully arraign her subjects whom she loves and cossets so much, for treason—Why, that is as sound a cause as any in the law-books!"

He smiled in a manner that was almost a snarl, and his eyes grew narrow with ironic merriment.

"And Mr. Thomas—" began Marjorie hesitatingly.

He whisked his glance on her like lightning.

"Mr. Thomas will laugh at them all," he cried. "He is as staunch as any of his blood. I know he has been careful of late; but, then, you must remember how all the estates hang on him. But when he has his back to the wall—or on the rack for that matter—he will be as stiff as iron. They will have their work to bend him by a hair's breadth."

Marjorie drew a breath of relief. She did not question Mr. Bassett's judgment. But she had had an uneasy discomfort in her heart till he had spoken so plainly.

"Well, sir," she said, "that is what I chiefly came for. I wished to know if I could do aught for Mr. Thomas or his wife; and—"

"You can do a great deal for his wife," said he. "You can keep her quiet and comfort her. She needs it, poor soul! I have told her for her comfort that we shall have Thomas out again in a month—God forgive me for the lie!"

Marjorie stood up; and the men rose with her.

"Why, what is that?" she said; and went swiftly to the window; for the noise of the crying of the cheeses and the murmur of voices had ceased all on a sudden.

Straight opposite the window where she stood was the tiled flight of stairs that ran up from the marketplace to the first floor of the Guildhall, a great building where the business of the town was largely done, and where the magistrates sat when there was need; and a lane that was clear of booths and carts had been left leading from that door straight across the square, so that she could see the two little brobonets—or iron guns—that guarded the door on either side. It was up this lane that she looked, and down it that there advanced a little procession, the very sight of which, it seemed, had stricken the square to silence. Already the crowd was dividing from end to end, ranging itself on either side—farmers' men shambled out of the way and turned to see; women clambered on the carts holding up their children to see, and from across the square came country-folk running, that they too might see. The steps of the Cross were already crowded with sight-seers.

Yet, to outward sight, the little procession was ordinary enough. First came three or four of the town-guard in livery, carrying their staves; then half a dozen sturdy fellows; then a couple of dignified gentlemen—one of them she knew: Mr. Roger Columbell, magistrate of the town—and then, walking all alone, the figure of a man, tall and thin, a little rustily, but very cleanly dressed in a dark suit, who carried his head stooping forward as if he were looking on the ground for something, or as if he deprecated so much notice.

Marjorie saw no more than this clearly. She did not notice the group of men that followed in case protection were needed for the agent of the Council, nor the crowd that swirled behind. For, as the solitary figure came beneath the windows she recognised the man whom she had seen once in the Tower of London.

"God smite the man!" growled a voice in her ear. "That is Topcliffe, going to the prison, I daresay."

And as Marjorie turned her pale face back, she saw the face of kindly Mr. Bassett, suffused and convulsed with fury.

CHAPTER IX

I

"Marjorie! Marjorie! Wake up! The order has come. It is for tonight."

Very slowly Marjorie rose out of the glimmering depths of sleep into which she had fallen on the hot August afternoon, sunk down upon the arm of the great chair that stood by the parlour window, and saw Mrs. Thomas radiant before her, waving a scrap of paper in her hand.

Nearly two months were passed; and as yet no opportunity had been given to the prisoner's wife to visit him, and during that time it had been impossible to go back into the hills and leave the girl alone. The heat of the summer had been stifling, down here in the valley; a huge plague of grasshoppers had ravaged all England; and there were times when even in the grass-country outside Derby their chirping had become intolerable. The heat, and the necessary seclusion, and the anxiety had told cruelly upon the country girl; Marjorie's face had perceptibly thinned; her eyes had shadows above and beneath; yet she knew she must not go; since the young wife had attached herself to her altogether, finding Alice (she said) too dull for her spirits. Mr. Bassett was gone again. There was no word of a trial; although there had been a hearing or two before the magistrates; and it was known that Topcliffe continually visited the prison.

One piece of news only had there been to comfort her during this time, and that, that Mr. John's prediction had been fulfilled with regard to the captured priest, Mr. Garlick, who, back from Rheims only a few months, had been deported from England, since it was his first offence. But he would soon be over again, no doubt, and next time with death as the stake in the game.

Marjorie drew a long breath, passed her hands over her forehead.

"The order?" she said. "What order?"

The girl explained, torrentially. A man had come just now from the Guildhall; he had asked for Mrs. FitzHerbert; she had gone down into the hall to see him; and all the rest of the useless details. But the effect was that leave had been given at last to visit the prisoner—for two persons, of which Mrs. FitzHerbert must be one; and that they must present the order to the gaoler before seven o'clock, when they would be admitted. She looked—such was the constitution of her mind—as happy as if it were an order for his release. Marjorie drove away the last shreds of sleep; and kissed her.

"That is very good news," she said. "Now we will begin to do something."

As they stood before the door and waited, after beating the great iron knocker on the iron plate, a kind of despair came down on Marjorie. They had advanced just so far in two months as to be allowed to speak with the prisoner; and, from her talkings with Mr. Biddell, had understood how little that was. Indeed, he had hinted to her plainly enough that even in this it might be that they were no more than pawns in the enemy's hand; and that, under a show of mercy, it was often allowed for a prisoner's friends to have free access to him in order to shake his resolution. If there was any cause for congratulation then, it lay solely in the thought that other means had so far failed. One thing at least they knew, for their comfort, that there had been no talk of torture....

It was a full couple of minutes before the door opened to show them a thin, brown-faced man, with his sleeves rolled up, dressed over his shirt and hose in a kind of leathern apron. He nodded as he saw the ladies, with an air of respect, however, and stood aside to let them come in. Then, with the same civility, he asked for the order, and read it, holding it up to the light that came through the little barred window over the door.

It was an unspeakably dreary little entrance passage in which they stood, wainscoted solidly from floor to ceiling with wood that looked damp and black from age; the ceiling itself was indistinguishable in the twilight; the floor seemed composed of packed earth, three or four doors showed in the woodwork; that opposite to the one by which they had entered stood slightly ajar, and a smoky light shone from beyond it. The air was heavy and hot and damp, and smelled of mildew.

The man gave the order back when he had read it, made a little gesture that resembled a bow, and led the way straight forward.

They found themselves, when they had passed through the half-open door in another passage running at right-angles to the entrance, with windows, heavily barred, so as to exclude all but the faintest twilight, even though the sun was not yet set; there appeared to be foliage of some kind, too, pressing against them from outside, as if a little central yard lay there; and the light, by which alone they could see their way along the uneven earth floor, came from a flambeau which hung by the door, evidently put there just now by the man who had opened to them; he led them down this passage to the left, down a couple of steps; unlocked another door of enormous weight and thickness and closed this behind them. They found themselves in complete darkness.

"I'll be with you in a moment, mistress," said his voice; and they heard his steps go on into the dark and cease.

Marjorie stood passive; she could feel the girl's hands clasp her arm, and could hear her breath come like sobs. But before she could speak, a light shone somewhere on the roof; and almost immediately the man came back carrying another flambeau. He called to them civilly; they followed. Marjorie once trod on some soft, damp thing that crackled beneath her foot. They groped round one more corner; waited, while they heard a key turning in a lock.

Then the man stood aside, and they went past into the room. A figure was standing there; but for the first moment they could see no more. Great shadows fled this way and that as the gaoler hung up the flambeau. Then the door closed again behind them; and Elizabeth flung herself into her husband's arms.

II

WHEN Marjorie could see him, as at last he put his wife into the single chair that stood in the cell and gave her the stool, himself sitting upon the table, she was shocked by the change in his face. It was true that she had only the wavering light of the flambeau to see him by, yet even that shadowy illumination could not account for his paleness and his fallen face. He was dressed miserably, too; his clothes were disordered and rusty-looking; and his features looked out, at once pinched and elongated. He blinked a little from time to time; his lips twitched beneath his ill-cut moustache and beard; and little spasms passed, as he talked, across his whole face. It was pitiful to see him; and yet more pitiful to hear him talk; for he assumed a kind of courtesy, mixed with bitterness. Now and again he fell silent, glancing with a swift and furtive movement of his eyes from one to the other of his visitors and back again. He attempted to apologise for the miserableness of the surroundings in which he received them—saying that her Grace his hostess could not be everywhere at once; and that her guests must do the best that they could. And all this was mixed with sudden wails from his wife, sudden graspings of his hands by hers. It all seemed to the quiet girl, who sat ill-at-ease on the little three-legged stool, that this was not the way to meet adversity. Then she drove down her criticism; and told herself that she ought rather to admire one of Christ's confessors.

"And you bring me no hope, then, Mistress Manners?" he said presently (for she had told him that there was no talk yet of any formal trial)—"no hope that I may meet my accusers face to face? I had thought perhaps—"

He lifted his eyes swiftly to hers, and dropped them again. She shook her head.

"And yet that is all that I ask now—only to meet my accusers. They can prove nothing against me—except, indeed, my recusancy; and that they have known this long time back. They can prove nothing as to the harbouring of any priests—not within the last year, at any rate, for I have not done so. It seemed to me—"

He stopped again, passed his shaking hand over his mouth, eyed the two women with momentary glances, then looked down once more.

"Yes?" said Marjorie.

He slipped off from the table, and began to move about restlessly.

"I have done nothing—nothing at all," he said. "Indeed, I thought—" And once more he was silent.

He began to talk presently of the Derbyshire hills—of Padley and of Norbury. He asked his wife of news from home, and she gave it him, interrupting herself with laments. Yet all the while his eyes strayed to Marjorie as if there was something he would ask of her, but could not. He seemed completely unnerved, and for the first time in her life the girl began to understand something of what gaol-life must signify. Yet she had never before imagined what that life of confinement might be, until she had watched this man, whom she had known in the world as a curt and almost masterful gentleman, careful of his dress, particular of the deference that was due to him, now become this worn prisoner, careless of his appearance, who stroked his mouth continually, once or twice gnawing his nails, who paced about in this abominable hole, where a tumbled heap of straw and blankets represented a bed, and a rickety table with a chair and a stool his sole furniture. It seemed as if a husk had been stripped from him, and a shrinking creature had come out of it which at present she could not recognise.

Then he suddenly wheeled on her, and for the first time some kind of forcefulness appeared in his manner.

"And my Uncle Bassett?" he cried abruptly. "What is he doing all this while?"

Marjorie said that Mr. Bassett had been most active on his behalf with the lawyers, but, for the present, was gone back again to his estates. Mr. Thomas snorted impatiently.

"Yes, he is gone back again," he cried, "and he leaves me to rot here! He thinks that I can bear it for ever, it seems!"

"Mr. Bassett has done his utmost, sir," said Marjorie. "He exposed himself here daily."

"Yes, with twenty fellows to guard him, I suppose. I know my Uncle Bassett's ways.... Tell me, if you please, how matters stand."

Marjorie explained again. There was nothing in the world to be done until the order came for his trial—or, rather, everything had been done already. His lawyers were to rely exactly on the defence that had been spoken of just now; it was to be shown that the prisoner had harboured no priests; and the witnesses had already been spoken with—men from Norbury and Padley, who would swear that to their certain knowledge no priest had been received by Mr. FitzHerbert at least during the previous year or eighteen months. There was, therefore, no kind of reason why Mr. Bassett or Mr. John FitzHerbert should remain any longer in Derby. Mr. John had been there, but had gone again, under advice from the lawyers; but he was in constant communication with Mr. Biddell, who had all the papers ready and the names of the witnesses, and had made more than one application already for the trial to come on.

"And why has neither my father nor my Uncle Bassett come to see me?" snapped the man.

"They have tried again and again, sir," said Marjorie. "But permission was refused. They will no doubt try again, now that Mrs. FitzHerbert has been admitted."

He paced up and down again for a few steps without speaking. Then again he turned on her, and she could see his face working uncontrolledly.

"And they will enjoy the estates, they think, while I rot here!"

"Oh, my Thomas!" moaned his wife, reaching out to him. But he paid no attention to her.

"While I rot here!" he cried again. "But I will not! I tell you I will not!"

"Yes, sir?" said Marjorie gently, suddenly aware that her heart had begun to beat swiftly.

He glanced at her, and his face changed a little.

"I will not," he murmured, "I must break out of my prison. Only their accursed—"

Again he interrupted himself, biting sharply on his lip.

For an instant the girl had thought that all her old distrust of him was justified, and that he contemplated in some way the making of terms that would be disgraceful to a Catholic. But what terms could these be? He was a FitzHerbert; there was no evading his own blood; and he was the victim chosen by the Council to answer for the rest. Nothing, then, except the denial of his faith—a formal and deliberate apostasy—could serve him; and to think that of the nephew of old Sir Thomas, and the son of John, was inconceivable. There seemed no way out; the torment of this prison must be borne. She only wished he could have borne it more manfully.

Then he resumed his pacing; and, three or four times as he turned, the girl caught his eyes fixed on hers for one instant. She wondered what was in his mind to say.

Even as she wondered there came a single loud rap upon the door, and then she heard the key turning. He wheeled round, and seemed to come to a determination.

"My dearest," he said to his wife, "here is the gaoler come to turn you out again. I will ask him—" He broke off as the man stepped in.

"Mr. Gaoler," he said, "my wife would speak alone with you a moment." (He nodded and winked at his wife, as if to tell her that this was the time to give him the money.)

"Will you leave Mistress Manners here for a minute or two while my wife speaks with you in the passage?"

Then Marjorie understood that she had been right.

The man who held the keys nodded without speaking.

"Then, my dearest wife," said Thomas, embracing her suddenly, and simultaneously drawing her towards the door, "we will leave you to speak with the man. He will come back for Mistress Manners directly."

"Oh! my Thomas!" wailed the girl, clinging to him.

"There, there, my dearest. And you will come and see me again as soon as you can get the order."

The instant the door was closed he came up to Marjorie and his face looked ghastly.

"Mistress Manners," he said, "I dare not speak to my wife. But... but, for Jesu's sake, get me out of here. I...I cannot bear it.... Topcliffe comes to see me every day.... He...he speaks to me continually of—O Christ! Christ! I cannot bear it!"

He dropped suddenly on to his knees by the table and hid his face.

III

At Babington House Marjorie slept, as was often the custom, in the same room with her maid—a large, low room, hung all round with painted cloths above the low wainscoting.

On the night after the visit to the prison, Janet noticed that her mistress was restless; and that while she would say nothing of what was troubling her, and only bade her go to bed and to sleep, she herself would not go to bed. At last, in sheer weariness, the maid slept.

She awakened later, at what time she did not know, and, in her uneasiness, sat up and looked about her; and there, still before the crucifix, where she had seen her before she slept, kneeled her mistress. She cried out in a loud whisper; "Come to bed, mistress; come to bed."

And, at the word, Marjorie started; then she rose, turned, and in the twilight of the summer night began to prepare herself for bed, without speaking. Far away across the roofs of Derby came the crowing of a cock to greet the dawn.

CHAPTER X

I

It was a fortnight later that there came suddenly to Babington House old Mr. Biddell himself. He appeared in the great hall an hour before dinner-time, as the tables were being set, and sent a servant for Mistress Manners.

"Hark you!" he said; "you need not rouse the whole house. It is with Mistress Manners alone that my business lies."

He broke off, as Mrs. FitzHerbert looked over the gallery.

"Mr. Biddell!" she cried.

He shook his head, but he seemed to speak with some difficulty.

"It is just a rumour," he said, "such as there has been before. I beg you—"

"That...there will be no trial at all?"

"It is just a rumour," he repeated. "I did not even come to trouble you with it. It is with Mistress Manners that—"

"I am coming down," cried Mrs. Thomas, and vanished from the gallery.

Mr. Biddell acted with decision. He whisked out again into the passage from the court; and there ran straight into Marjorie, who was coming in from the little enclosed garden at the back of the house.

"Quick!" he said. "Quick! Mrs. Thomas is coming, and I do not wish—"

She led the way without a word back into the court, along a few steps, and up again to the house into a little back parlour that the steward used when the house was full. She locked the door when he had entered, and came and sat down out of sight of any that might be passing.

"Sit here," she said; and then: "Well?" she asked.

He looked at her gravely and sadly, shaking his head once or twice. Then he drew out a paper or two from a little lawyer's valise that he carried, and, as he did so, heard a hand try the door outside.

"That is Mrs. Thomas," whispered the girl. "She will not find us."

He waited till the steps moved away again. Then he began. He looked anxious and dejected.

"I fear it is precisely as you thought," he said. "I have followed up every rumour in the place. And the first thing that is certain is that Topcliffe leaves Derby in two days from now. I had it as positive information that his men have orders to prepare for it. The second thing is that Topcliffe is greatly elated; and the third is that Mr. FitzHerbert will be released as soon as Topcliffe is gone."

"You are sure this time, sir?"

He assented by a movement of his head.

"I dared not tell Mrs. Thomas just now. She would give me no peace. I said it was but a rumour, and so it is; but it is a rumour that has truth behind it. He has been moved, too, these three days back, to another cell, and has every comfort."

He shook his head again.

"But he has made no promise—" began Marjorie breathlessly.

"It is exactly that which I am most afraid of," said the lawyer. "If he had yielded, and consented to go to church, it would have been in every man's mouth by now. But he has not, and I should fear it less if he had. That's the very worst part of my news."

"I do not understand—"

Mr. Biddell tapped his papers on the table.

"If he were an open and confessed enemy, I should fear it less," he repeated. "It is not that. But he must have given some promise to Topcliffe that pleases the fellow more. And what can that be but that—"

Marjorie turned yet whiter. She sighed once as if to steady herself. She could not speak, but she nodded.

"Yes, Mistress Manners," said the old man. "I make no doubt at all that he has promised to assist him against them all—against Mr.

John his father, it may be, or Mr. Bassett, or God knows whom! And yet still feigning to be true! And that is not all."

She looked at him. She could not conceive worse than this, if indeed it were true.

"And do you think," he continued, "that Mr. Topcliffe will do all this for love, or rather, for mere malice? I have heard more of the fellow since he has been in Derby than in all my life before; and, I tell you, he is for feathering his own nest if he can." He stopped.

"Mistress, did you know that he had been out to Padley three or four times since he came to Derby?…Well, I tell you now that he has. Mr. John was away, praise God; but the fellow went all round the place and greatly admired it."

"He went out to see what he could find?" asked the girl, still whispering.

The other shook his head.

"No, mistress; he searched nothing. I had it all from one of his fellows through one of mine. He searched nothing; he sat a great while in the garden, and ate some of the fruit; he went through the hall and the rooms, and admired all that was to be seen there. He went up into the chapel-room, too, though there was nothing there to tell him what it was; and he talked a great while to one of the men about the farms, and the grazing, and such-like, but he meddled with nothing." (The old man's face suddenly wrinkled into fury.) "The devil went through it all like that, and admired it; and he came out to it again two or three times and did the like."

He stopped to examine the notes he had made, and Marjorie sat still, staring on him.

It was worse than anything she could have conceived possible. That a FitzHerbert should apostatise was incredible enough; but that one should sell his family—it was impossible.

"Mr. Biddell," she whispered piteously, "it cannot be. It is some—"

He shook his head suddenly and fiercely.

"Mistress Manners, it is as plain as daylight to me. I tell you Topcliffe has cast his foul eyes on Padley and coveted it; and he has demanded it as a price for Mr. Thomas' liberty. That is why he is so elated. He has visited Mr. FitzHerbert nigh every day; he has cajoled him, he has threatened him; he has worn out his spirit by the gaol and the stinking food and the loneliness; and he has prevailed, as he has prevailed with many another. And the end of it all is that Mr. FitzHerbert has yielded—yet not openly. Maybe that is part of the bargain upon the other side, that he should keep his name before the world. And on this side he has promised Padley, if that he may but keep the rest of the estates, and have his liberty. I tell you that alone cuts all the knots of this tangle.... Can you cut them in any other manner?"

There was a long silence. From the direction of the kitchen came the sound of cheerful voices, and the clatter of lids, and from the walled garden outside the chatter of birds....

At last the girl spoke.

"I cannot believe it without evidence," she said. "It may be so. God knows! But I do not.... Mr. Biddell?"

"Well, mistress?"

The lawyer's head was sunk, on his breast; he spoke listlessly.

"He will have given some writing to Mr. Topcliffe, will he not, if this be true? Mr. Topcliffe is not the man—"

The old man lifted his head sharply; then he nodded.

"That is the shrewd truth, mistress. Mr. Topcliffe will not trust to another's honour; he has none of his own!"

"Well," said Marjorie, "if all this be true, Mr. Topcliffe will already have that writing in his possession."

She paused.

"Eh?" said the lawyer.

They looked at one another again in silence. It would have seemed to another that the two minds talked swiftly and wordlessly together, the trained thought of the lawyer and the quick wit of the woman; for when the man spoke again, it was as if they had spoken at length.

"But we must not destroy the paper," he said, "or the fat will be in the fire. We must not let Mr. FitzHerbert know that he is found out."

"No," said the girl. "But to get a view of it.... And a copy of it, to send to his family."

Again the two looked each at the other in silence—as if they were equals—the old man and the girl.

II

IT was the last night before the Londoners were to return.

They had lived royally these last three months. The agent of the Council had had a couple of the best rooms in the inn that looked on to the market-square, where he entertained his friends, and now and then a magistrate or two. Even Mr. Audrey, of Matstead, had come to him once there, with another, but had refused to stay to supper, and had ridden away again alone.

Downstairs, too, his men had fared very well indeed. They knew how to make themselves respected, for they carried arms always now, since the unfortunate affair a day after the arrival, when two of them had been gravely battered about by two rustic servants, who, they learned, were members of a Popish household in the town. But all the provincial fellows were not like this. There was a big man, half clerk and half man-servant to a poor little lawyer, who lived across the square—a man of no wit indeed, but, at any rate, one of means and of generosity, too, as they had lately found out—means and generosity, they understood, that were made possible by the unknowing assistance of his master. In a word it was believed among Mr. Topcliffe's men that all the refreshment which they had lately enjoyed, beyond that provided by their master, was at old Mr. Biddell's expense, though he did not know it, and that George Beaton, fool though he was, was a cleverer man than his employer. Lately, too, they had come to learn that although George Beaton was half clerk, half man-servant, to a Papist, he was yet at heart as stout a Protestant as themselves, though he dared not declare it for fear of losing his place.

On this last night they made very merry indeed, and once or twice the landlord pushed his head through the doorway. The baggage was packed, and all was in readiness for a start soon after dawn.

There came a time when George Beaton said that he was stifling with the heat; and, indeed, in this low-ceilinged room after supper, with the little windows looking on to the court, the heat was surprising. The men sat in their shirts and trunks. So that it was as natural as possible that George should rise from his place and sit down again close to the door where the cool air from the passage came in; and from there, once more, he led the talk, in his character of rustic and open-handed boor; he even beat the sullen man who was next him genially over the head to make him give more room, and then he proposed a toast to Mr. Topcliffe.

It was about half an hour later, when George was becoming a little anxious, that he drew out at last a statement that Mr. Topcliffe had a great valise upstairs, full of papers that had to do with his law business. (He had tried for this piece of information last night and the night before, but had failed to obtain it.) Ten minutes later again, then, when the talk had moved to affairs of the journey, and the valise had been forgotten, it was an entirely unsuspicious circumstance that George and the man who sat next him should slip out to take the air in the stable-court. The Londoner was so fuddled with drink as to think that he had gone out at his own deliberate wish; and there, in the fresh air, the inevitable result followed; his head swam, and he leaned on big George for support. And here, by the one stroke of luck that visited poor George this evening, it fell that he was just in time to see Mr. Topcliffe himself pass the archway in the direction of Friar's Gate, in company with a magistrate, who had supped with him upstairs.

Up to this point George had moved blindly, step by step. He had had his instructions from his master, yet all that he had been able to determine was the general plan to find out where the papers were kept, to remain in the inn till the last possible moment, and to watch for any chance that might open to him. Truly, he had no more than that, except, indeed, a vague idea that it might be necessary to bribe one of the men to rob his master. Yet there was everything against this, and it was, indeed, a last resort. It seemed now, however, that another way was open. It was exceedingly probable that Mr. Topcliffe was off for his last visit to the prisoner, and, since a magistrate was with him, it was exceedingly improbable that he would take the paper with him. It was not the kind of paper—if, indeed, it existed at all—that more persons would be allowed to see than were parties to the very discreditable affair.

And now George spoke earnestly and convincingly. He desired to see the baggage of so great a man as Mr. Topcliffe; he had heard so much of him. His friend was a good fellow who trusted him (here George embraced him warmly). Surely such a little thing would be allowed as for him, George, to step in and view Mr. Topcliffe's baggage, while the faithful servant kept watch in the passage! Perhaps another glass of ale—

III

"YES, sir," said George, an hour later, still a little flushed with the amount of drink he had been forced to consume. "I had some trouble to get it. But I think this is what your honour wanted."

He began to search in his deep breast-pocket.

"Tell me," said Mr. Biddell.

"I got the fellow to watch in the passage, sir; him that I had made drunk, while I was inside. There were great bundles of papers in the valise.... No, sir, it was strapped up only.... The most of the papers were docketed very legally, sir; so I did not have to search long. There were three or four papers in a little packet by themselves; besides a great packet that was endorsed with Mr. FitzHerbert's name, as well as Mr. Topcliffe's and my lord Shrewsbury's; and I think I should not have had time to look that through. But, by God's mercy, it was one of the three or four by themselves."

He had the paper in his hand by now. The lawyer made a movement to take it. Then he restrained himself.

"Tell me, first," he said.

"Well, sir," said George, with a pardonable satisfaction in spinning the matter out, "one was all covered with notes, and was headed

'Padley.' I read that through, sir. It had to do with the buildings and the acres, and so forth. The second paper I could make nothing out of; it was in cypher, I think. The third paper was the same; and the fourth, sir, was that which I have here."

The lawyer started.

"But I told you—"

"Yes, sir; I should have said that this is the copy—or, at least, an abstract. I made the abstract by the window, sir, crouching down so that none should see me. Then I put all back as before, and came out again; the fellow was fast asleep against the door."

"And Topcliffe—"

"Mr. Topcliffe, sir, returned half an hour afterwards in company again with Mr. Hamilton. I waited a few minutes to see that all was well, and then I came to you, sir."

There was silence in the little room for a moment. It was the small back office of Mr. Biddell, where he did his more intimate business, looking out on to a paved court. The town was for the most part asleep, and hardly a sound came through the closed windows.

Then the lawyer turned and put out his hand for the paper without a word. He nodded to George, who went out, bidding him good night.

TEN minutes later Mr. Biddell walked quietly through the passengers' gate by the side of the great doors that led to the court beside Babington House, closing it behind him. He knew that it would be left unbarred till eleven o'clock that night. He passed on through the court, past the house door, to the steward's office, where through heavy curtains a light glimmered. As he put his hand on the door it opened, and Marjorie was there. He said nothing, nor did she. Her face was pale and steady, and there was a question in her eyes. For answer he put the paper into her hands, and sat down while she read it. The stillness was as deep here as in the office he had just left.

IV

It was a minute or two before either spoke. The girl read the paper twice through, holding it close to the little hand-lamp that stood on the table.

"You see, mistress," he said, "it is as bad as it can be."

She handed back the paper to him; he slid out his spectacles, put them on, and held the writing to the light.

"Here are the points, you see…" he went on. "I have annotated them in the margin. First, that Thomas FitzHerbert be released from Derby gaol within three days from the leaving of Topcliffe for London, and that he be no more troubled, neither in fines nor imprisonment; next, that he have secured to him, so far as the laws shall permit, all his inheritance from Sir Thomas, from his father, and from any other bequests whether of his blood-relations or no; thirdly, that Topcliffe do 'persecute to the death'"—(the lawyer paused, cast a glance at the downcast face of the girl) "'—do persecute to the death' his uncle Sir Thomas, his father John, and William Bassett his kinsman; and, in return for all this, Thomas FitzHerbert shall become her Grace's sworn servant—that is, Mistress Manners, her Grace's spy, pursuivant, informer and what-not—and that he shall grant and secure to Richard Topcliffe, Esquire, and to his heirs for ever, 'the manors of Over Padley and Nether Padley, on the Derwent, with six messuages, two cottages, ten gardens, ten orchards, a thousand acres of land, five hundred acres of meadow-land, six hundred acres of pasture, three hundred acres of wood, a thousand acres of furze and heath, in Padley, Grindleford, and Lyham, in the parish of Hathersage, in consideration of eight hundred marks of silver, to be paid to Thomas FitzHerbert, Esquire, etc.'"

The lawyer put the paper down, and pushed his spectacles on to his forehead.

"That is a legal instrument?" asked the girl quietly, still with downcast eyes.

"It is not yet fully completed, but it is signed and witnessed. It can become a legal instrument by Topcliffe's act; and it would pass muster—"

"It is signed by Mr. Thomas?"

He nodded.

She was silent again. He began to tell her of how he had obtained it, and of George's subtlety and good fortune; but she seemed to pay no attention. She sat perfectly still. When he had ended, she spoke again.

"A sworn servant of her Grace—" she began.

"Topcliffe is a sworn servant of her Grace," he said bitterly; "you may judge by that what Thomas FitzHerbert has become."

"We shall have his hand, too, against us all, then?"

"Yes, mistress; and, what is worse, this paper I take it—" (he tapped it) "this paper is to be a secret for the present. Mr. Thomas will still feign himself to be a Catholic, with Catholics, until he comes into all his inheritances. And, meantime, he will supply information to his new masters."

"Why cannot we expose him?"

"Where is the proof? He will deny it."

She paused.

"We can at least tell his family. You will draw up the informations?"

"I will do so."

"And send them to Sir Thomas and Mr. Bassett?"

"I will do so."

"That may perhaps prevent his inheritance coming to him as quickly as he thinks."

The lawyer's eyes gleamed.

"And what of Mrs. Thomas, mistress?"

Marjorie lifted her eyes.

"I do not think a great deal of Mrs. Thomas," she said. "She is honest, I think; but she could not be trusted with a secret. But I will tell Mistress Babington, and I will warn what priests I can."

"And if it leaks out?"

"It must leak out."

"And yourself? Can you meet Mr. Thomas again just now? He will be out in three days."

Marjorie drew a long breath.

"No, sir; I cannot meet him. I should betray what I felt. I shall make excuses to Mrs. Thomas, and go home tomorrow."

✣ PART THREE ✣

CHAPTER I

I

THE Red Bull in Cheapside was all alight; a party had arrived there from the coast not an hour ago, and the rooms that had been bespoken by courier occupied the greater part of the second floor; the rest of the house was already filled by another large company, spoken for by Mr. Babington, although he himself was not one of them. And it seemed to the shrewd landlord that these two parties were not wholly unknown to one another, although, as a discreet man, he said nothing.

The latest arrived party had plainly come from the coast. They had arrived a little after sunset on this stormy August day, splashed to the shoulders by the summer-mud, and drenched to the skin by the heavy thunder-showers. Their baggage had a battered and sea-going air about it, and the landlord thought he would not be far away if he conjectured Rheims as their starting-point; there were three gentlemen in the party, and four servants apparently; but he knew better than to ask questions or to overhear what seemed rather over-familiar conversation between the men and their masters. There was only one, however, whom he remembered to have lodged before, over five years ago. The name of this one was Mr. Alban. But all this was not his business. His duty was to be hearty and deferential and entirely stupid; and certainly this course of behaviour brought him a quantity of guests.

Mr. Alban, about half-past nine o'clock, had finished unstrapping his luggage. It was of the most innocent description, and contained nothing that all the world might not see. He had made arrangements that articles of another kind should come over from Rheims under the care of one of the "servants," whose baggage would be less suspected. The distribution would take place in a day or two. These articles comprised five sets of altar vessels, five sets of Mass vestments, made of a stuff woven of all the liturgical colours together, a dozen books, a box of medals, another of Agnus Deis—little wax medallions stamped with the figure of a Lamb supporting a banner—a bunch of beads, and a heavy little square package of very thin altar-stones.

As he laid out the suit of clothes that he proposed to wear next day, there was a rapping on his door.

"Mr. Babington is come—sir." (The last word was added as an obvious afterthought, in case of listeners.)

Robin sprang up; the door was opened by his "servant," and Anthony came in, smiling.

Mr. Anthony Babington had broadened and aged considerably during the last five years. He was still youthful-looking, but he was plainly a man and no longer a boy. And he presently said as much for his friend.

"You are a man, Robin," he said. "Why, it slipped my mind!"

He knelt down promptly on the strip of carpet and kissed the palms of the hands held out to him, as is the custom to do with newly-ordained priests, and Robin murmured a blessing.

Then the two sat down again.

"And now for the news," said Robin.

Anthony's face grew grave.

"Yours first," he said.

So Robin told him. He had been ordained priest a month ago, at Chalons-sur-Marne.... The college was as full as it could hold.... They had had an unadventurous journey.

Anthony put a question or two, and was answered.

"And now," said Robin, "what of Derbyshire; and of the country; and of my father? And is it true that Ballard is taken?"

Anthony threw an arm over the back of his chair, and tried to seem at his ease.

"Well," he said, "Derbyshire is as it ever was. You heard of Thomas FitzHerbert's defection?"

"Mistress Manners wrote to me of it, more than two years ago."

"Well, he does what he can: he comes and goes with his wife or without her. But he comes no more to Padley. And he scarcely makes a feint even before strangers of being a Catholic, though he has not declared himself, nor gone to church, at any rate in his own county. Here in London I have seen him more than once in Topcliffe's company. But I think that every Catholic in the country knows of it by now. That is Mistress Manners' doing. My sister says there has never been a woman like her."

Robin's eyes twinkled.

"I always said so," he said. "But none would believe me. She has the wit and courage of twenty men. What has she been doing?"

"What has she not done?" cried Anthony. "She keeps herself for the most part in her house; and my sister spends a great deal of time with her; but her men, who would die for her, I think, go everywhere; and half the hog-herds and shepherds of the Peak are her sworn men. I have given your Dick to her; he was mad to do what he could in that cause. So her men go this way and that bearing her letters or her messages to priests who are on their way through the county; and she gets news—God knows how!—of what is a-stirring against us. She has saved Mr. Ludlam twice, and Mr. Garlick once, as well as Mr. Simpson once, by getting the news to them of the pursuivants' coming, and having them away into the Peak. And yet with all this, she has never been laid by the heels."

"Have they been after her, then?" asked Robin eagerly.

"They have had a spy in her house twice to my knowledge, but never openly; and never a shred of a priest's gown to be seen, though Mass had been said there that day. But they have never searched it by force. And I think they do not truly suspect her at all."

"Did I not say so?" cried Robin. "And what of my father? He wrote to me that he was to be made magistrate; and I have never written to him since."

"He has been made magistrate," said Anthony drily; "and he sits on the bench with the rest of them."

"Then he is all of the same mind?"

"I know nothing of his mind. I have never spoken with him this six years back. I know his acts only. His name was in the 'Bond of Association,' too!"

"I have heard of that."

"Why, it is two years old now. Half the gentry of England have joined it," said Anthony bitterly. "It is to persecute to the death any pretender to the Crown other than our Eliza."

There was a pause. Robin understood the bitterness.

"And what of Mr. Ballard?" asked Robin.

"Yes; he is taken," said Anthony slowly, watching him. "He was taken a week ago."

"Will they banish him, then?"

"I think they will banish him."

"Why, yes—it is the first time he has been taken. And there is nothing great against him?"

"I think there is not," said Anthony, still with that strange deliberateness.

"Why do you look at me like that?"

Anthony stood up without answering. Then he began to pace about. As he passed the door he looked to the bolt carefully. Then he turned again to his friend.

"Robin," he said, "would you sooner know a truth that will make you unhappy, or be ignorant of it?"

"Does it concern myself or my business?" asked Robin promptly.

"It concerns you and every priest and every Catholic in England. It is what I have hinted to you before."

"Then I will hear it."

"It is as if I told it in confession?"

Robin paused.

"You may make it so," he said, "if you choose."

Anthony looked at him an instant. "Well," he said, "I will not make a confession, because there is no use in that now—but—Well, listen!" he said, and sat down.

II

When he ceased, Robin lifted his head. He was as white as a sheet.

"You have been refused absolution before for this?"

"I was refused absolution by two priests; but I was granted it by a third."

"Let me see that I have the tale right.

"Yourself, with a number of others, have bound yourselves by an oath to kill her Grace, and to set Mary on the throne. This has taken shape now since the beginning of the summer. You yourself are now living in Mr. Walsingham's house, in Seething Lane; under the patronage of her Grace, and you show yourself freely at court. You have proceeded so far, under fear of Mr. Ballard's arrest, as to provide one of your company with clothes and necessaries that can enable him to go to court; and it was your intention, as well as his, that he should take opportunity to kill her Grace. But today only you have become persuaded that the old design was the better; and you wish first to arrange matters with the Queen of the Scots, so that when all is ready, you may be the more sure of a rising when that her Grace is killed, and that the Duke of Parma may be in readiness to bring an army into England. It is still your intention to kill her Grace?"

"By God! it is!" said Anthony, between clenched teeth.

"Then I could not absolve you, even if you came to confession. You may be absolved from your allegiance, as we all are; but you are not absolved from charity and justice towards Elizabeth as a woman, I have consulted theologians on the very point; and—"

Then Anthony sprang up.

"See here, Robin; we must talk this out." He flicked his fingers sharply. "See—we will talk of it as two friends."

"You had better take back those words," said the priest gravely.

"Why?"

"It would be my duty to relay any information! I understood you spoke to me as to a priest, though not in confession."

"You would!" blazed the other.

"I should do so in conscience," said the priest. "But you have not yet told me as a friend, and—"

"You mean—"

"I mean that so long as you choose to speak to me of it, now and here, it remains that I choose to regard it as *sub sigillo* in effect. But you must not come to me tomorrow, as if I knew it all in a plain way. I do not. I know it as a priest only."

There was silence for a moment. Then Anthony stood up.

"I understand," he said. "But you would refuse me absolution in any case?"

"I could not give you absolution so long as you intended to kill her Grace."

Anthony made an impatient gesture.

"See here," he said. "Let me tell you the whole matter from the beginning. Now listen."

He settled himself again in his chair, and began.

"ROBIN," he said, "you remember when I spoke to you in the inn on the way to Matstead; it must be seven or eight years gone now? Well, that was when the beginning was. There was no design then, such as we have today; but the general purpose was there. I had spoken with man after man; I had been to France, and seen Mr. Morgan there, Queen Mary's man, and my lord of Glasgow; and all that I spoke with seemed of one mind—except my lord of Glasgow, who did not say much to me on the matter. But all at least were agreed that there would be no peace in England so long as Elizabeth sat on the throne.

"Well, it was after that that I fell in with Ballard, who was over here on some other affair; and I found him a man of the same mind as myself; he was all agog for Mary, and seemed afraid of nothing. Well, nothing was done for a great while. He wrote to me from France; I wrote back to him again, telling him the names of some of my friends. I went to see him in France two or three times; and I saw him here, when you yourself came over with him. But we did not know whom to trust. Neither had we any special design. Her Grace of the Scots went hither and thither under strong guards; and what I had done for her before—"

Robin looked up. He was still quite pale and quite quiet.

"What was that?" he said.

Anthony again made his impatient gesture. He was fiercely excited; but kept himself under tolerable control.

"Why, I have been her agent for a great while back, getting her letters through to her, and such like. But last year, when that damned Sir Amyas Paulet became her gaoler, I could do nothing. Two or three times my messenger was stopped, and the letters taken from him. Well, after that time I could do no more. There her Grace was, back again at Tutbury, and none could get near her. She might no more give alms, even to the poor; and all her letters must go through Walsingham's hands. And then God helped us; she was taken last autumn to Chartley, near by which is the house of the Giffords; and since that time we have been almost merry. Do you know Gilbert Gifford?"

"He has been with the Jesuits, has he not?"

"That is the man. Well, Mr. Gilbert Gifford has been God's angel to us. A quiet, still kind of a man—you have seen him?"

"I have spoken with him at Rheims," said Robin. "I know nothing of him."

"Well, he contrived the plan. He has devised a beer-barrel that has the beer all roundabout, so that when they push their rods in, there seems all beer within. But in the heart of the beer there is secured a little iron case; and within the iron case there is space for papers. Well, this barrel goes to and fro to Chartley and to a brewer that is a good

Catholic; and within the case there are the letters. And in this way, all has been prepared—"

Robin looked up again. He remained quiet through all the story; and lifted no more than his eyes. His fingers played continually with a button on his doublet.

"You mean that Queen Mary has consented to this?"

"Why, yes!"

"To her sister's death?"

"Why, yes!"

"I do not believe it," said the priest quietly, "On whose word does that stand?"

"Why, on her own! Whose else's?" snapped Anthony.

"You mean, you have it in her own hand, signed by her name?"

"It is in Gifford's hand! Is not that enough? And there is her seal to it. It is in cypher, of course. What would you have?"

"Where is she now?" asked Robin, paying no attention to the question.

"She has just now been moved again to Tixall."

"For what?"

"I do not know. What has that to do with the matter? She will be back soon again. I tell you all is arranged."

"Tell me the rest of the story," said the priest.

"There is not much more. So it stands at present. I tell you her Grace has been tossed to and fro like a ball at play. She was at Chatsworth, as you know; she has been shut up in Chartley like a criminal; she was at Babington House even. God! if I had but known it in time!"

"In Babington House! Why, when was that?"

"Last year, early—with Sir Ralph Sadler, who was her gaoler then!" cried Anthony bitterly; "but for a night only... I have sold the house."

"Sold it!"

"I do not keep prisons," snapped Anthony. "I will have none of it!"

"Well?"

"Well," resumed the other man quietly. "I must say that when Ballard was taken—"

"When was that?"

"Last week only. Well, when he was taken I thought perhaps all was known. But I find Mr. Walsingham's conversation very comforting, though little he knows it, poor man. He knows that I am a Catholic; and he was lamenting to me only three days ago of the zeal of these informers. He said he could not save Ballard, so hot was the pursuit after him; that he would lose favour with her Grace if he did."

"What comfort is there in that?"

"Why; it shows plain enough that nothing is known of the true facts. If they were after him for this design of ours do you think that Walsingham would speak like that? He would clap us all in ward—long ago."

The young priest was silent. His head still whirled with the tale, and his heart was sick at the misery of it all. This was scarcely the home-coming he had looked for! He turned abruptly to the other.

"Anthony, lad," he said, "I beseech you to give it up."

Anthony smiled at him frankly. His excitement was sunk down again.

"You were always a little soft," he said. "I remember you would have nought to do with us before. Why, we are at war, I tell you; and it is not we who declared it! They have made war on us now for the last twenty years and more. What of all the Catholics—priests and others—who have died on the gibbet, or rotted in prison? If her Grace makes war upon us, why should we not make war upon her Grace? Tell me that, then!"

"Anthony, I beseech you to give it up. I hate the whole matter, and fear it, too."

"Fear it! Why, tell me what there is to fear? What hole can you find anywhere?"

"I do not know. I hardly know the tale yet. But it seems to me there might be a hundred."

"Tell me one of them, then."

Anthony threw himself back with an indulgent smile on his face.

"Why, if you will have it," said Robin, roused by the contempt, "there is one great hole in this. All hangs upon Gifford's word, as it seems to me. You have not spoken with Mary; you have not even her own hand on it."

"Bah! Why, her Grace of the Scots cannot write in cypher, do you think?"

"I do not know how that may be. It may be so. But I say that all hangs upon Gifford."

"And you think Gifford can be a liar and a knave!" sneered Anthony.

"I have not one word against him," said the priest. "But neither had I against Thomas FitzHerbert; and you know what has befallen—"

Anthony snorted with disdain.

"Put your finger through another hole," he said.

"Well—I like not the comfort that Mr. Secretary Walsingham has given you. You told me a while ago that Ballard was on the eve of going to France. Now Walsingham is no fool. I would to God he were! He has laid enough of our men by the heels already."

"By God!" cried Anthony, roused again. "I would not willingly call you a fool either, my man! But do you not understand that Walsingham believes me as loyal as himself? Here have I been at court for the last year, bowing before her Grace, and never a word said to me on my religion. And here Walsingham has bidden me to lodge in his house, in the midst of all his spider's webs. Do you think he would do that if—"

"I think he might have done so," said Robin slowly.

Anthony sprang to his feet.

"My Robin," he said, "you were right enough when you said you would not join with us. You were not made for this work. You would see an enemy in your own father—"

He stopped confounded.

Robin smiled drearily.

"I have seen one in him," he said.

Anthony clapped him on the shoulder, not unkindly.

"Forgive me, my Robin. I did not think what I said. Well, we will leave it at that. And you would not give me absolution?"

The priest shook his head.

"Then give me your blessing," said Anthony, dropping on his knees. "And so we will close up the *quasi-sigillum confessionis.*"

III

It was a heavy-hearted priest that presently, downstairs, stood with Anthony in one of the guest-rooms, and was made known to half a dozen strangers. Every word that he had heard upstairs must be as if it had never been spoken, from the instant at which Anthony had first sat down to the instant in which he had kneeled down to receive his blessing. So much he knew from his studies at Rheims. He must be to each man that he met, that which he would have been to him an hour ago. Yet, though as a man he must know nothing, his priest's heart was heavy in his breast. It was a strange home-coming—to pass from the ordered piety of the college: to the whirl of politics and plots in which good and evil span round together—honest and fiery zeal for God's cause, mingled with what he was persuaded was crime and abomination. He had thought that a priest's life would be a simple thing, but it seemed otherwise now.

He spoke with those half-dozen men—those who knew him well enough for a priest; and presently, when some of his own party came, drew aside again with Anthony, who began to tell him in a low voice of the personages there.

"These are all my private friends," he said, "and some of them be men of substance in their own place. There is Mr. Charnoc, of Lancashire, he with the gilt sword. He is of the Court of her Grace, and comes and goes as he pleases. He is lodged in Whitehall, and comes here but to see his friends. And there is Mr. Savage, in the new clothes, with his beard cut short. He is a very honest fellow, but of a small substance though of good family enough."

"Her Grace has some of her ladies, too, that are Catholics, has she not?" asked Robin.

"There are two or three at least, and no trouble made. They hear Mass when they can at the Embassies. Mendoza is a very good friend of ours."

Mr. Charnoc came up presently to the two. He was a cheerful-looking man, of northern descent, very particular in his clothes, with large gold earrings; he wore a short, pointed beard above his stiff ruff, and his eyes were bright and fanatical.

"You are from Rheims, I understand, Mr. Alban."

He sat down with something of an air next to Robin.

"And your county—?" he asked.

"I am from Derbyshire, sir," said Robin.

"From Derbyshire. Then you will have heard of Mistress Marjorie Manners, no doubt."

"She is an old friend of mine," said Robin, smiling. (The man had a great personal charm about him.)

"You are very happy in your friends, then," said the other. "I have never spoken with her myself; but I hear of her continually as assisting our people—sending them now up into the Peak country, now into the towns, as the case may be—and never a mistake."

It was delightful to Robin to hear her praised, and he talked of her keenly and volubly. Exactly that had happened which five years ago he would have thought impossible; for every trace of his old feeling towards her was gone, leaving behind, and that only in the very deepest intimacies of his thought, a sweet and pleasant romance, like the glow in the sky when the sun is gone down. Little by little that had come about which, in Marjorie, had transformed her when she first sent him to Rheims. It was not that reaction had followed; there was no contempt, either of her or of himself, for what he had once thought of her; but another great passion had risen above it—a passion of which the human lover cannot even guess, kindled for one that is greater than man; a passion fed, trained, and pruned by those six years of studious peace at Rheims. There he had seen what Love could do when it could rise higher than its human channels; he had seen young men, scarcely older than himself, set out for England, as for their bridals, exultant and on fire; and back to Rheims had come again the news of their martyrdom: this one died, crying to Jesu as a home-coming child cries to his mother at the garden-gate; this one had said nothing upon the scaffold, but his face (they said who brought the news) had been as the face of Stephen at his stoning; and others had come back themselves, banished, with pain of death on their returning, yet back once more these had gone. And, last, more than once, there had crept back to Rheims, borne on a litter all the way from the coast, the phantom of a man who a year or two ago had played "cat" and shouted at the play—now a bent man, grey-haired, with great scars on wrists and ankles.... *Te Deums* had been sung in the college chapel when the news of the deaths had come: there were no *requiems* for such as these; and the place of the martyr in the refectory was decked with flowers.... Robin had seen these things, and wondered whether his place, too, would some day be so decked.

For Marjorie, then, he felt nothing but a happy friendliness, and a real delight when he thought of seeing her again. It was glorious, he thought, that she had done so much; that her name was in all men's mouths. And he had thought, when he had first gone to Rheims, that he would do all and she nothing! He had written to her then, freely and happily. He had told her that she must give him shelter some day, as she was doing for so many.

Meanwhile it was pleasant to hear her praises.

"Eve would be Eve," quoted Mr. Charnoc presently, in speaking of pious women's obstinacy, "though Adam would say Nay."

THEN, at last, when Mr. Charnoc said that he must be leaving for his own lodgings and stood up; once more upon Robin's heart there fell the horrible memory of all that he had heard upstairs.

CHAPTER II

I

It was strange to Robin to walk about the city, and to view all that he saw from his new interior position. Now, his very presence was an offence: he had broken every law framed expressly against such cases as his; he had studied abroad, he had been "ordained beyond the seas"; he had read his Mass in his own bedchamber; he had, practically, received a confession; and it was his fixed and firm intention to "reconcile" as many of "her Grace's subjects" as possible to the "Roman See." And, to tell the truth, he found pleasure in the sheer adventure of it, as would every young man of spirit; and he wore his fine clothes, clinked his sword, and cocked his secular hat with delight.

The burden of what he had heard still was heavy on him. It was true that in a manner inconceivable to any but a priest it lay apart altogether from his common consciousness: he had talked freely enough to Mr. Charnoc and the rest; he could not, even by a momentary lapse, allow what he knew to colour even the thoughts by which he dealt with men in ordinary life; for though it was true that no confession had been made, yet it was in virtue of his priesthood that he had been told so much. Yet there were moments when he walked alone, with nothing else to distract him, when the cloud came down again; and there were moments, too, in spite of himself, when his heart beat with another emotion, when he pictured what might not be five years hence, if Elizabeth were taken out of the way and Mary reigned in her stead. He knew from his father how swiftly and enthusiastically the old Faith had come back with Mary Tudor after the winter of Edward's reign. And if, as some estimated, a third of England were still convincedly Catholic, and perhaps not more than one twentieth convincedly Protestant, might not Mary Stuart, with her charm, accomplish more even than Mary Tudor with her lack of it?

He saw many fine sights during the three or four days after his coming to London; for he had to wait there at least that time, until a party that was expected from the north should arrive with news of where he was to go. These were the instructions he had had from Rheims. So he walked freely abroad during these days to see the sights; and even ventured to pay a visit to Fathers Garnett and Southwell, two Jesuits who arrived a month ago, and were for the present lodging in my Lord Vaux's house in Hackney.

He was astonished at Father Southwell's youthfulness.

This priest had landed but a short while before, and, for the present, was remaining quietly in the edge of London with the older man; for himself was scarcely twenty-five years old, and looked twenty at the most. He was very quiet and sedate, with a face of almost feminine delicacy, and passed a good deal of his leisure, as the old lord told Robin, in writing verses. He appeared a strangely fine instrument for such heavy work as was a priest's.

On another day Robin saw the Archbishop land at Westminster Stairs. He looked at him carefully as he came up the stairs, and was surprised at the kindly face of him, thin-lipped, however, though with pleasant, searching eyes. His coach was waiting outside Old Palace Yard, and Robin, following with the rest of the little crowd, saluted him respectfully as he climbed into it, followed by a couple of chaplains.

He came back to the city across the fields, half a mile away from the river, and, indeed, it was a glorious sight he had before him. Here, about him, was open ground on either side of the road on which he walked; and there, in front, rose up on the slope of the hill the long line of great old houses, beyond the stream that ran down into the Thames—old Religious Houses, for the most part, now disguised and pulled about beyond recognition, ranging right and left from the Ludgate itself; behind these rose again towers and roofs, and high above all the tall spire of the Cathedral, as if to gather all into one culminant aspiration.... The light from the west lay on every surface that looked to his left, golden and rosy; elsewhere lay blue and dusky shadows.

II

"THERE is a letter for you, sir," said the landlord, who had an uneasy look on his face, as the priest came through the entrance of the inn.

Robin took it. Its superscription ran shortly:

To Mr. Alban, at the Red Bull Inn in Cheapside. Haste. Haste. Haste.

He turned it over; it was sealed plainly on the back without arms or any device; it was a thick package, and appeared as if it might hold an enclosure or two.

Robin had learned caution in a good school, and what is yet more vital in true caution, an appearance of carelessness. He weighed the packet easily in his hand, as if it were of no value, though he knew it might contain very questionable stuff from one of his friends, and glanced at a quantity of baggage that lay heaped beside the wall.

"What is all this?" he said. "Another party arrived?"

"No, sir; the party is leaving. Rather, it is left already; and the gentlemen bade me have the baggage ready here. They would send for it later, they told me."

This was unusually voluble from this man. Robin looked at him quickly, and away again.

"What party?" he said.

"The gentlemen you were with this two nights past, sir," said the landlord keenly.

Robin was aware of a feeling as if a finger had been laid on his heart; but not a muscle of his face moved.

"Indeed!" he said. "They told me nothing of it."

Then he moved on easily, feeling the landlord's eyes in every inch of his back, and went leisurely upstairs.

He reached his room, bolted the door softly behind him, and sat down. His heart was going now like a hammer. Then he opened the packet; an enclosure fell out of it, also sealed, but without direction of any kind. Then he saw that the sheet in which the packet had come was itself covered with writing, rather large and sprawling, as if written in haste. He put the packet aside, and then lifted the paper to read it.

When he had finished, he sat quite still. Then he read the paper again. It ran as follows:

"It is all found out, we think. I find myself watched at every point, and I can get no speech with B. I cannot go forth from the house without a fellow to follow me, and two of my friends have found the same. Mr. G., too, has been with Mr. W. this three hours back. By chance I saw him come in, and he has not yet left again. Mr. Ch. is watching for me while I write this, and will see that this letter is bestowed on a trusty man who will bring it to your inn, and, with it, another letter to bid our party save themselves while they can. I do not know how we shall fare, but we shall meet at a point that is fixed, and after that evade or die together. You were right, you see. Mr. G. has acted the traitor throughout, with Mr. W.'s connivance and assistance. I beg of you, then, to carry this letter, which I send in this, to Her for whom we have forfeited our lives, or, at least, our country; or, if you cannot take it with safety, master the contents of it by note and deliver it to her with your own mouth. She has been taken back to C. again, whither you must go, and all her effects searched."

There was no signature, but there followed a dash of the pen, and then a scrawled "A. B.," as if an interruption had come, or as if the man who was with the writer would wait no longer.

A third time Robin read it through. It was terribly easy of interpretation. "B." was Ballard; "G." was Gifford; "W." was Walsingham; "Ch." was Charnoc; "Her" was Mary Stuart; "C." was Chartley. It fitted and made sense like a child's puzzle. And, if the faintest doubt could remain in the most incredulous mind as to the horrible reality of it all, there was the piled luggage downstairs, that would never be "sent for" (and never, indeed, needed again by its owners in this world).

Then he took up the second sealed packet, and held it unbroken, while his mind flew like a bird, and in less than a minute he decided, and opened it.

It was a piteous letter, signed again merely "A. B.," and might have been written by any broken-hearted reverent lover to his beloved. It spoke an eternal goodbye; the writer said that he would lay down his life gladly again in such a cause if it were called for, and would lay down a thousand if he had them; he entreated her to look to herself, for that no doubt every attempt would now be made to entrap her; and it warned her to put no longer any confidence in a "detestable knave, G. G." Finally, he begged that "Jesu would have her in His holy keeping," and that if matters fell out as he thought they would, she would pray for his soul, and the souls of all that had been with him in the enterprise.

He read it through three or four times; every line and letter burned itself into his brain. Then he tore it across and across; then he tore the letter addressed to himself in the same manner; then he went through all the fragments, piece by piece, tearing each into smaller fragments, till there remained in his hands just a bunch of tiny scraps, smaller than snowflakes, and these he scattered out of the window.

Then he went to his door, unbolted it, and walked downstairs to find the landlord.

III

IT was not until ten days later, soon after dawn, that Robin set out on his melancholy errand. He rode out north-ward as soon as the gates were opened, with young "Mr. Arnold," a priest ordained with him in Rheims, and one of his party, disguised as a servant, following him on a pack-horse with the luggage. It was a misty morning, white and cheerless, with the early fog that had drifted up from the river. Last night the news had come in that Anthony and at least one other had been taken near Harrow, in disguise, and the streets had been full of riotous rejoicing over the capture.

He had thought it more prudent to wait till after receiving the news, which he so much dreaded, lest haste should bring suspicion on himself, and the message that he carried; since for him, too, to disappear at once would have meant an almost inevitable association of him with the party of plotters; but it had been a hard time to pass through. Early in the morning, after Anthony's flight, he had awakened to hear a rapping upon the inn door, and, peeping from his window, had seen a couple of plainly dressed men waiting for admittance; but after that he had seen no more of them. He had deliberately refrained from speaking with the landlord, except to remark again upon the luggage of which he caught a sight, piled no longer in the entrance, but in the little room that the man himself used. The landlord had said shortly that it had not yet been sent for. And the greater part of the day—after he had told the companions that had come with him from Rheims that he had had a letter, which seemed to show that the party with whom they had made friends had disappeared, and were probably under suspicion, and had made the necessary arrangements for his own departure with young Mr. Arnold—he spent in walking abroad as usual. The days that followed had been bitter and heavy. He had liked neither to stop within doors nor to go abroad, since the one course might arouse inquiry and the second lead to his identification. He had gone to my Lord Vaux's house again and again, with his friend and without him; he had learned of the details of Anthony's capture, though he had not dared even to attempt to get speech with him; and, further, that unless the rest of the men were caught, it would not be easy to prove anything against him. One thing, therefore, he prayed for with all his heart—that the rest might yet escape. He told his party something of the course of events, but not too much. On the Sunday that intervened he went to hear Mass in Fetter Lane, where numbers of Catholics resorted; and there, piece by piece, learned more of the plot than even Anthony had told him.

Mr. Arnold was a Lancashire man and a young convert of Oxford—one of that steady small stream that poured over to the Continent—a sufficiently well-born and intelligent man to enjoy acting as a servant, which he did with considerable skill. It was common enough for gentlemen to ride side by side with their servants when they had left the town; and by the time that the two were clear of the few scattered houses outside the city gates, Mr. Arnold urged on his horse, and they rode together.

The roads, such as they were, were in a terrible state still with the heavy rain of a few days ago, and the further showers that had fallen in the night. They made very poor progress, and by dinner-time were not yet in sight of Watford. But they pushed on, coming at last about one o'clock to that little town, all gathered together in the trench of the low hills. There was a modest inn in the main street, with a little garden behind it; and while Mr. Arnold took the horses off for watering, Robin went through to the garden, sat down, and ordered food to be served for himself and his man together. The day was warmer, and the sun came out as they sat over their meal. When they had done, Robin sent his friend off again for the horses. They must not delay longer than was necessary, if they wished to sleep at Leighton, and give the horses their proper rest.

When he was left alone, he fell a-thinking once more; and, what with the morning's ride and the air and the sunshine, and the sense of liberty, he was inclined to be more cheerful. Surely England was large enough to hide the rest of the plotters for a time, until they could get out of it. Anthony was taken, indeed, yet, without the rest, he might very well escape conviction. Robin had not been challenged in any way; the gatekeepers had looked at him, indeed, as he came out of the city; but so they always did, and the landlady here had run her eyes over him; but that was the way of landladies who wished to know how much should be charged to travellers. And if he had come out so easily, why should not his friends? All turned now, to his mind, on whether the rest of the conspirators could evade the pursuivants or not.

He stood up presently to stretch his legs before mounting again, and as he stood up he heard running footsteps somewhere beyond the house: they died away; but then came the sound of another runner, and of another, and he heard voices calling. Then a window was flung up beyond the house; steps came rattling down the stairs within and passed out into the street. It was probably a bull that had escaped, or a mad dog, he thought, or some rustic excitement of that kind, and he thought he would go and see it for himself; so he passed out through the house, just in time to meet Mr. Arnold coming round with the horses.

"What was the noise about?" he asked.

The other looked at him.

"I heard none, sir," he said. "I was in the stable."

Robin looked up and down the street. It seemed as empty as it should be on a summer's day; two or three women were at the doors of their houses, and an old dog was asleep in the sun. There was no sign of any disturbance.

"Where is the woman of the house?" asked Robin.

"I do not know, sir."

They could not go without paying; but Robin marvelled at the simplicity of these folks, to leave a couple of guests free to ride away; he went within again and called out, but there was no one to be seen.

"This is laughable," he said, coming out again. "Shall we leave a mark behind us and be off?"

"Are they all gone, sir?" asked the other, staring at him.

"I heard some running and calling out just now," said Robin. "I suppose a message must have been brought to the house."

Then, as he stood still, hesitating, a noise of voices arose suddenly round the corner of the street, and a group of men with pitchforks ran out from a gateway on the other side, fifty yards away, crossed the road, and disappeared again. Behind them ran a woman or two, a barking dog, and a string of children. But Robin thought he had caught a glimpse of some kind of officer's uniform at the head of the running men, and his heart stood still.

IV

NEITHER of the two spoke for a moment.

"Wait here with the horses," said Robin, "I must see what all this is about."

Mr. Arnold was scarcely more than a boy still, and he had had all the desire of a boy, if he saw an excited crowd, to join himself to it. But he was being a servant just now, and must do what he was told. So he waited patiently with the two horses that tossed their jingling heads and stamped and attempted to kick flies off impossibly remote parts of their bodies. Certainly, the excitement was growing. After he had seen his friend walk quickly down the road and turn off where the group of rustically-armed men had disappeared in the direction where newly-made haystacks shaded their gables beyond the roofs of the houses, several other figures appeared through the opposite gateway in hot pursuit. One was certainly a guard of some kind, a stout, important-looking fellow, who ran and wheezed as he ran loud enough to be heard at the inn door. The women standing before the houses, too, presently were after the rest—all except one old dame, who put her head forth, and peered this way and that with a vindictive anger at having been left all alone. More yet showed themselves—children dragging puppies after them, an old man with a large rusty sword, a couple of lads each with a pike—these appeared, like figures in a pantomime play, whisking into sight from between the houses, and all disappearing again immediately.

And then, all on a sudden, a great clamour of voices began, all shouting together, as if some quarry had been sighted: it grew louder, sharp cries of command rang above the roar. Then there burst out of the side, where all had gone in, a ball of children, which exploded into fragments and faced about, still with a couple of puppies that barked shrilly; and then, walking very fast and upright, came Mr. Robin Audrey, white-faced and stern, straight up to where the lad waited with the horses.

Robin jerked his head.

"Quick!" he said. "We must be off, or we shall be here all night." He gathered up his reins for mounting.

"What is it, sir?" asked the other, unable to be silent.

"They have caught some fellows," he said.

"And the inn-account, sir?"

Robin pulled out a couple of coins from his pouch.

"Put that on the table within," he said. "We can wait no longer. Give me your reins!"

His manner was so dreadful that the young man dared ask no more. He ran in, laid the coins down, (they were more than double what could have been asked for their entertainment), came out again, and mounted his own horse that his friend held. As they rode down the street, he could not refrain from looking back, as a great roar of voices broke out again; but he could see no more than a crowd of men, with the pitchforks moving like spears on the outskirt, as if they guarded prisoners within, come out between the houses and turn up towards the inn they themselves had just left.

As they came clear of the village and out again upon the open road, Robin turned to him, and his face was still pale and stern.

"Mr. Arnold," he said, "those were the last of my friends that I told you of. Now they have them all, and there is no longer any hope. They found them behind the haystacks next to the garden where we dined. They must have been there all night."

CHAPTER III

I

IT had been a melancholy ride, since news had come to them, in more than one place, of the fortunes of the Babington party. A courier, riding fast, had passed them as they sighted Buckingham; and by the time they came in, he was gone again, on Government business (it was said), and the little town hummed with rumours, out of which emerged, at any rate, the certainty that the whole company had been captured. At Coventry, again, the tidings had travelled faster than themselves; for here it was reported that Mr. Babington and Mr. Charnoc had been racked; and in Lichfield, last of all, the tale was complete, and (as they learned later) tolerably accurate too.

It was from a clerk in the inn there that the story came, who declared that there was no secrecy about the matter any longer, and that he himself had seen the tale in writing. It ran as follows:

The entire plot had been known from the beginning. Gilbert Gifford had been an emissary of Walsingham throughout; and every letter that passed to and from the various personages had passed through the Secretary's hands and been deciphered in his house. There never had been one instant in which Mr. Walsingham had been at fault, or in the dark: he had gone so far, it was reported, as to insert in one of the letters that was to go to Mr. Babington a request for the names of all the conspirators, and in return there had come from him, not only a list of the names, but a pictured group of them, with Mr. Babington himself in the midst. This picture had actually been shown to her Grace in order that she might guard herself against private assassination, since two or three of the group were in her own household.

"It is like to go hard with the Scots Queen!" said the clerk bitterly. "She has gone too far this time."

Robin said nothing to commit himself, for he did not know on which side the man ranged himself; but he drew him aside after dinner, and asked whether it might be possible to get a sight of the Queen.

"I am riding to Derby," he said, "with my man. But if to turn aside at Chartley would give us a chance of seeing her, I would do so. A queen in captivity is worth seeing. And I can see you are a man of influence."

The clerk looked at him shrewdly; he was a man plainly in love with his own importance, and the priest's last words were balm to him.

"It might be done," he said. "I do not know."

Robin saw the impression he had made, and that the butter could not be too thick.

"I am sure you could do it for me," he said, "if any man could. But I understand that a man of your position may be unwilling—"

The clerk solemnly laid a hand on the priest's arm.

"Well, I will tell you this," he said. "Get speech with Mr. Bourgoign, her apothecary. He alone has access to her now, besides her own women. It might be he could put you in some private place to see her go by."

This was not much use, thought Robin; but, at least, it gave him something to begin at: so he thanked the clerk solemnly and reverentially, and was rewarded by another discreet pat on the arm.

The sight of the Chartley woods, tall and splendid in the light of the setting sun, and already tinged here and there with the first marks of autumn, brought his indecision to a point; and he realized that he had no plan. He had heard that Mary occasionally rode abroad, and he hoped perhaps to get speech with her that way; but what he had heard from the clerk and others showed him that this small degree of liberty was now denied to the Queen. In some way or another he must get news of Mr. Bourgoign. Beyond that he knew nothing.

The great gates of Chartley were closed as the two came up to them. There was a lodge beside them, and a sentry stood there. A bell was ringing from the great house within the woods, no doubt for supper-time, but there was no other human being besides the sentry to be seen. So Robin did not even check his weary horse; but turned only, with a deliberately curious air, as he went past and rode straight on. Then, as he rounded a corner he saw smoke going up from houses, it seemed, outside the park.

"What is that?" asked Arnold suddenly. "Do you hear—"

A sound of a galloping horse grew louder behind them, and a moment afterwards the sound of another. The two priests were still in view of the sentry; and knowing that Chartley was guarded now as if it had all the treasures of the earth within, Robin reflected that to show too little interest might arouse as sharp suspicion as too much. So he wheeled his horse round and stopped to look.

They heard the challenge of the sentry within, and then the unbarring of the gates. An instant later a courier dashed out and wheeled to the right, while at the same time the second galloper came to view—another courier on a jaded horse; and the two passed—the one plainly riding to London, the second arriving from it. The gates were yet open; but the second was challenged once more before he was allowed to pass and his hoofs sounded on the road that led to the house. Then the gates clashed together again.

Robin turned his horse's head once more towards the houses, conscious more than ever how near he was to the nerves of England's life, and what tragic ties they were between the two royal cousins, that demanded such a furious and frequent exchange of messages.

"We must do our best here," he said, nodding towards the little hamlet.

II

It was plainly a newly-grown little group of houses that bordered the side of the road away from the enclosed park—sprung up as a kind of overflow lodging for the dependants necessary to such a suddenly increased household; for the houses were no more than wooden dwellings, ill-roofed and ill-built, with the sap scarcely yet finished oozing from the ends of the beams and the planks. Smoke was issuing, in most cases, from rough holes cut in the roofs, and in the last rays of sunshine two or three men were sitting on stools set out before the houses.

Robin checked his horse before a man whose face seemed kindly, and who saluted courteously the fine gentleman who looked about with such an air.

"My horse is dead-spent," he said curtly, "Is there an inn here where my man and I can find lodging?"

The man shook his head, looking at the horse compassionately. He had the air of a groom about him.

"I fear not, sir, not within five miles; at least, not with a room to spare."

"This is Chartley, is it not?" asked the priest, noticing that the next man, too, was listening.

"Aye, sir."

"Can you tell me if my friend Mr. Bourgoign lodges in the house, or without the gates?"

"Mr. Bourgoign, sir? A friend of yours?"

"I hope so," said Robin, smiling, and keeping at least within the letter of truth.

The man mused a moment.

"It is possible he might help you, sir. He lodges in the house; but he comes sometimes to see a woman that is sick here."

Robin demanded where she lived.

"At the last house, sir—a little beyond the rest. She is one of her Grace's kitchen-women. They moved her out here, thinking it might be the fever she had."

This was plainly a communicative fellow; but the priest thought it wiser not to take too much interest. He tossed the man a coin and rode on.

THE last house was a little better built than the others, and stood further back from the road. Robin dismounted here, and, with a nod to Mr. Arnold, who was keeping his countenance admirably, walked up to the door and knocked on it. It was opened instantly, as if he were expected, but the woman's face fell when she saw him.

"Is Mr. Bourgoign within?" asked the priest.

The woman glanced over him before answering, and then out to where the horses waited.

"No, sir," she said at last. "We were looking for him just now…" (She broke off.) "He is coming now," she said.

Robin turned, and there, walking down the road, was an old man, leaning on a stick, richly and soberly dressed in black, wearing a black beaver hat on his head. A man-servant followed him at a little distance.

The priest saw that here was an opportunity ready-made; but there was one more point on which he must satisfy himself first, and what seemed to him an inspiration came to his mind.

"He looks like a minister," he said carelessly.

A curious veiled look came over the woman's face. Robin made a bold venture. He smiled full in her face.

"You need not fear," he said. "I quarrel with no man's religion"; and, at the look in her face at this, he added: "You are a Catholic, I suppose? Well, I am one too. And so, I suppose, is Mr. Bourgoign."

The woman smiled tremulously, and the fear left her eyes.

"Yes, sir," she said. "All the friends of her Grace are Catholics, I think."

He nodded to her again genially. Then, turning, he went to meet the apothecary, who was now not thirty yards away.

It was a pathetic old figure that was hobbling towards him. He seemed a man of near seventy years old, with a close-cropped beard and spectacles on his nose, and he carried himself heavily and ploddingly. Robin argued to himself that it must be a kindly man who would come out at this hour—perhaps the one hour he had to himself—to visit a poor dependant. Yet all this was sheer conjecture; and, as the old man came near, he saw there was something besides kindliness in the eyes that met his own.

He saluted boldly and deferentially.

"Mr. Bourgoign," he said in a low voice, "I must speak five minutes with you. And I ask you to make as if you were my friend."

The old man stiffened like a watch-dog. It was plain that he was on his guard.

"I do not know you, sir."

"I entreat you to do as I ask. I am a priest, sir. I entreat you to take my hand as if we were friends."

A look of surprise went over the physician's face.

"You can send me packing in ten minutes," went on Robin rapidly, at the same time holding out his hand. "And we will talk here in the road, if you will."

There was still a moment's hesitation. Then he took the priest's hand.

"I am come straight from London," went on Robin, still speaking clearly, yet with his lips scarcely moving. "A fortnight ago I talked with Mr. Babington."

The old man drew his arm close within his own.

"You have said enough, or too much, at present, sir. You shall walk with me a hundred yards up this road, and justify what you have said."

"We have had a weary ride of it, Mr. Bourgoign.... I am on the road to Derby," went on Robin, talking loudly enough now to be overheard, as he hoped, by any listeners. "And my horse is spent.... I will tell you my business," he added in a lower tone, "as soon as you bid me."

Fifty yards up the road the old man pressed his arm again.

"You can tell me now, sir," he said. "But we will walk, if you please, while you do so."

"First," said Robin, after a moment's consideration as to his best beginning, "I will tell you the name I go by. It is Mr. Alban. I am a newly-made priest, as I told you just now; I came from Rheims scarcely a fortnight ago. I am from Derbyshire; and I will tell you my proper name at the end, if you wish it."

"Repeat the blessing of the deacon by the priest at Mass," murmured Mr. Bourgoign to the amazement of the other, without the change of an inflection in his voice or a movement of his hand.

"*Dominus sit in corde tuo et in labiis—*" began the priest.

"That is enough, sir, for the present. Well?"

"Next," said Robin, hardly yet recovered from the extraordinary promptness of the challenge—"Next, I was speaking with Mr. Babington a fortnight ago."

"In what place?"

"In the inn called the 'Red Bull,' in Cheapside."

"Good. I have lodged there myself," said the other. "And you are one—"

"No, sir," said Robin, "I do not deny that I spoke with them all—with Mr. Charnoc and—"

"That is enough of those names, sir," said the other, with a small and fearful lift of his white eyebrows, as if he dreaded the very trees that nearly met overhead in this place. "And what is your business?"

"I have satisfied you, then—" began Robin.

"Not at all, sir. You have answered sufficiently so far; that is all. I wish to know your business."

"The night following the day on which the men fled, of whom I have just spoken, I had a letter from—from their leader. He told me that all was lost, and he gave me a letter to her Grace here—"

He felt the thin old sinews under his hand contract suddenly, and paused.

"Go on, sir," whispered the old voice.

"A letter to her Grace, sir. I was to use my discretion whether I carried it with me, or learned it by rote. I have other interests at stake besides this, and I used my discretion, and destroyed the letter."

"But you have some writing, no doubt—"

"I have none," said Robin. "I have my word only."

There was a pause.

"Was the message private?"

"Private only to her Grace's enemies. I will tell you the substance of it now, if you will."

The old man, without answering, steered his companion nearer to the wall; then he relinquished the supporting arm, and leaned himself against the stones, fixing his eyes full upon the priest, and searching, as it seemed, every feature of his face and every detail of his dress.

"Was the message important, sir?"

"Important only to those who value love and fidelity."

"I could deliver it myself, then?"

"Certainly, sir. If you will give me your word to deliver it to her Grace, as I deliver it to you, and to none else, I will ride on and trouble you no more."

"That is enough," said the physician decidedly. "I am completely satisfied, Mr. Alban. All that remains is to consider how I can get you to her Grace."

"But if you yourself will deliver—" began Robin.

An extraordinary spasm passed over the other's face, that might denote any fierce emotion, either of anger or grief.

"Do you think it is that?" he hissed. "Why, man, where is your priesthood? Do you think the poor dame within would not give her soul for a priest?...Why, I have prayed God night and day to send us a priest. She is half mad with sorrow; and who knows whether ever again in this world—"

He broke off, his face all distorted with pain; and Robin felt a strange thrill of glory at the thought that he bore with him, in virtue of his priesthood only, so much consolation. He faced for the first time that tremendous call of which he had heard so much in Rheims—that desolate cry of souls that longed and longed in vain for those gifts which a priest of Christ could alone bestow....

"...The question is," the old man was saying more quietly, "how to get you in to her Grace. Why, Sir Amyas opens her letters even, and reseals them again! He thinks me a fool, and that I do not know what he does.... Do you know aught of medicine?" he asked abruptly.

"I know only what country folks know of herbs."

"And their names—their Latin names, man?" pursued the other, leaning forward.

Robin half smiled.

"Now you speak of it," he said, "I have learned a good many, as a pastime, when I was a boy. I was something of a herbalist, even. But I have forgotten—"

"Bah! that would be enough for Sir Amyas—"

He turned and spat venomously at the name.

"Sir Amyas knows nothing save his own vile trade. He is a lout—no more. He is as grim as a goose, always. And you have a town air about you," he went on, running his eyes critically over the young man's dress. "Those are French clothes?"

"They were bought in France."

The two stood silent. Robin's excitement beat in all his veins, in spite of his weariness. He had come to bear a human message only to a bereaved Queen; and it seemed as if his work were to be rather the bearing of a Divine message to a lonely soul. He watched the old man's face eagerly. It was sunk in thought.... Then Mr. Bourgoign took him abruptly by the arm.

"Give me your arm again," he said. "I am an old man. We must be going back again. It seems as if God heard our prayers after all. I will see you disposed for tonight—you and your man and the horses, and I will send for you myself in the morning. Could you say Mass, think you, if I found you a secure place—and bring our Lord's Body with you in the morning?"

He checked the young man, to hear his answer.

"Why, yes," said Robin. "I have all things that are needed."

"Then you shall say Mass in any case...and reserve our Lord's Body in a pyx.... Now listen to me. If my plan falls as I hope, you must be a physician tomorrow, and have practised your trade in Paris. You have been in Paris?"

"No, sir."

"Bah!...Well, no more has Sir Amyas!...You have practised your trade in Paris, and God has given you great skill in the matter of herbs. And, upon hearing that I was in Chartley, you inquired for your old friend, whose acquaintance you had made in Paris, five years ago. And I, upon hearing you were come, secured your willingness to see my patient, if you would but consent. Your reputation has reached me even here; you have attended His Majesty in Paris on three occasions; you restored Mademoiselle Elise, of the family of Guise, from the very point of death. You are but a young man still; yet—Bah! It is arranged. You understand? Now come with me."

CHAPTER IV

I

IN spite of his plans and his hopes and his dreams, it was with an amazement beyond all telling, that Mr. Robert Alban found himself, at nine o'clock next morning, conducted by two men through the hall at Chartley to the little parlour where he was to await Sir Amyas Paulet and the Queen's apothecary.

Matters had been arranged last night with that promptness which alone could make the tale possible. He had walked back with the old man in full view of the little hamlet, to all appearances, the best of old friends; and after providing for a room in the sick woman's house for Robin himself, another in another house for Mr. Arnold, and stabling for the horses in a shed where occasionally the spent horses of the couriers were housed when Chartley stables were overflowing—after all this had been arranged by Mr. Bourgoign in person, the two walked on to the great gates of the park, where they took an affectionate farewell within hearing of the sentry, the apothecary promising to see Sir Amyas that night and to communicate with his friend in the morning. Robin had learned previously how strict was the watch set about the Queen's person, particularly since the news of the Babington plot had first reached the authorities, and of the extraordinary difficulty to the approach of any stranger to her presence. Nau and Curle, her two secretaries, had been arrested and perhaps racked a week or ten days before; all the Queen's papers had been taken from her, and even her jewellery and pictures sent off to Elizabeth; and the only persons ordinarily allowed to speak with her, besides her gaoler, were two of her women, and Mr. Bourgoign himself.

That morning then, before six o'clock, Robin had said Mass in the sick woman's room and given her communion, with her companion, who answered his Mass, as it was thought more prudent that the other priest should not even be present; and, at the close of the Mass he had reserved in a little pyx, hidden beneath his clothes, a consecrated particle. Mr. Bourgoign had said that he would see to it that the Queen should be fasting up to ten o'clock that day.

And now the last miracle had been accomplished. A servant had come down late the night before, with a discreet letter from the apothecary, saying that Sir Amyas had consented to receive and examine for himself the travelling physician from Paris; and here now went Robin, striving to remember the old Latin names he had learned as a boy, and to carry a medical air with him.

He had enough to occupy his mind; for not only had he the thought of the character he was to sustain presently under the scrutiny of a suspicious man; but he had the prospect, as he hoped, of coming into the presence of the most-talked-of woman in Europe and of ministering to her as a priest alone could do, in her sorest need. His hand went to his breast as he considered it, and remembered what he bore...and he felt the tiny flat circular case press upon his heart....

For his imagination was all aflame at the thought of Mary. Not only had he been kindled again and again in the old days by poor Anthony's talk, until the woman seemed to him half-deified already; but man after man had repeated the same tale, that she was, in truth, that which her lean cousin of England desired to be thought—a very paragon of women, innocent, holy, undefiled, yet of charm to drive men to their knees before her presence. More marvellous than all was that those who knew her best and longest loved her most; her servants wept or groaned themselves into fevers if they were excluded from her too long; of her as of the Wisdom of old might it be said that, "They who ate her hungered yet, and they who drank her thirsted yet." It was to this miracle of humanity, then, that this priest was to come....

He sat up suddenly, once more pressing his hand to his breast, where his Treasure lay hidden, as he heard steps crossing the paved hall outside. Then he rose to his feet and bowed as a tall man came swiftly in, followed by the apothecary.

II

It was a lean, harsh-faced man that he saw, long-moustached and melancholy-eyed—"grim as a goose," as the physician had said—wearing, even in this guarded household, a half-breast and cap of steel. A long sword jingled beside him on the stone floor and clashed with his spurred boots. He appeared the last man in the world to be the companion of a sorrowing Queen; and it was precisely for this reason that he had been chosen to replace the courtly Lord Shrewsbury and the gentle Sir Ralph Sadler. (Her Grace of England said that she had had enough of nurses for gaolers.) His voice, too, resembled the bitter clash of a key in a lock.

"Well, sir," he said abruptly, "Mr. Bourgoign tells me you are a friend of his."

"I have that honour, sir."

"You met in Paris, eh? ...And you profess a knowledge of herbs beyond the ordinary?"

"Mr. Bourgoign is good enough to say so."

"And you are after her Grace of Scotland, as they call her, like all the rest of them, eh?"

"I shall be happy to put what art I possess at her Grace of Scotland's service."

"Traitors say as much as that, sir."

"In the cause of treachery, no doubt, sir."

Sir Amyas barked a kind of laugh.

"*Vous avez raison*," he said with a deplorable accent. "As her Grace would say. And you come purely by chance to Chartley, no doubt!"

The sneer was unmistakable. Robin met it full.

"Not for one moment, sir. I was on my way to Derby. I could have saved a few miles if I had struck north long ago. But Chartley is interesting in these days."

(He saw Mr. Bourgoign's eyes gleam with satisfaction.)

"That is honest at least, sir. And why is Chartley interesting?"

"Because her Grace is here," answered Robin with sublime simplicity.

Sir Amyas barked again. It seemed he liked this way of talk. For a moment or two his eyes searched Robin—hard, narrow eyes like a dog's; he looked him up and down.

"Where are your drugs, sir?"

Robin smiled.

"A herbalist does not need to carry drugs," he said. "They grow in every hedgerow if a man has eyes to see what God has given him."

"That is true enough. I would we had more talk about God His Majesty in this household, and less of Popish trinkets and fiddle-faddle.... Well, sir; do you think you can cure her ladyship?"

"I have no opinion on the point at all, sir. I do not know what is the matter with her—beyond what Mr. Bourgoign has told me," he added hastily, remembering the supposed situation.

The soldier paid no attention. Like all slow-witted men, he was following up an irrelevant train of thought from his own last sentence but one.

"Fiddle-faddle!" he said again. "I am sick of her megrims and her vapours and her humours. Has she not blood and bones like the rest of us? And yet she cannot take her food nor her drink, nor sleep like an honest woman. And I do not wonder at it; for that is what she is not. They will say she is poisoned, I dare say.... Well, sir; I suppose you had best see her; but in my presence, remember, sir; in my presence."

Robin's spirits sank like a stone.... Moreover, he would be instantly detected as a knave (though that honestly seemed a lesser matter to him), if he attempted to talk medically in Sir Amyas' presence; unless that warrior was truly as great a clod as he seemed. He determined to risk it. He bowed.

"I can at least try my poor skill, sir," he said.

Sir Amyas instantly turned with a jerk of his head to beckon them, and clanked out again into the hall. There was not a moment's opportunity for the two conspirators to exchange even a word; for there, in the hall, stood the two men who had brought Robin in, to keep guard; and as the party passed through to the foot of the great staircase, he saw on each landing that was in sight another sentry, and, at a door at the end of the overhead gallery, against which hung a heavy velvet curtain, stood the last, a stern figure to keep guard on the rooms of a Queen, with his body-armour complete, a steel hat on his head and a pike in his hand.

It was to this door that Sir Amyas went. He pulled aside the curtain and rapped imperiously on the door. It was opened after a moment's delay by a frightened-faced woman.

"Her Grace?" demanded the officer sharply. "Is she still abed?"

"Her Grace is risen, sir," said the woman tremulously; "she is in the inner room."

Sir Amyas strode straight on, pulled aside a second curtain hanging over the further door, rapped upon that, too, and without even waiting for an answer this time, beyond the shrill barking of dogs within, opened it and passed in. Mr. Bourgoign followed; and Robin came last. The door closed softly behind him.

III

MARY was past her prime long ago; she was worn with sorrow and slanders and miseries; yet she appeared to the priest's eyes, even then, like a figure of a dream. It was partly, no doubt, the faintness of the light that came in through the half-shrouded windows that obliterated the lines and fallen patches that her face was beginning to bear; and she lay, too, with her back even to such light as there was. Yet for all that, and even if he had not known who she was, Robin could not have taken his eyes from her face. She lay there more beautiful in her downfall and disgrace, a thousand times, than when she had come first to Holyrood, or danced in the Courts of France.

Her face was almost waxen now, blue shadowed beneath the two waves of pale hair; she had a small mouth, a delicate nose, and large, searching hazel eyes. Her hands, clasped as if in prayer, emerged out of deep lace-fringed sleeves, and were covered with rings. When she spoke, a tone of assured decision revealed her quiet consciousness of royalty. It was an extraordinary mingling of fragility and power, of which this feminine and royal room was the proper frame.

Sir Amyas knelt perfunctorily, as if impatient of it; and rose up again at once without waiting for the signal. Mary lifted her fingers a little as a sign to the other two.

"I have brought the French doctor, madam," said the soldier abruptly. "But he must see your Grace in my presence."

"Then you might as well have spared him, and yourself, the pains, sir," came the quiet, dignified voice. "I do not choose to be examined in your presence."

Robin lifted his eyes to her face; but although he thought he caught an air of intense desire towards him and that which he bore, there was no faltering in the tone of her voice.

"This is absurd, madam. I am responsible for your Grace's security and good health. But there are lengths—"

"You have spoken the very word," said the Queen. "There are lengths to which none of us should go, even to preserve our health."

"I tell you, madam—"

"There is no more to be said, sir," said the Queen, closing her eyes again.

"But what do I know of this fellow? How can I tell he is what he professes to be?" barked Sir Amyas.

"Then you should never have admitted him at all," said the Queen, opening her eyes again. "And I will do the best that I can—"

"But, madam, your health is my care; and Mr. Bourgoign here tells me—"

"The subject does not interest me," murmured the Queen, apparently half asleep.

"But I will retire to the corner and turn my back, if that is necessary," growled the soldier.

There was no answer. She lay with closed eyes, and her woman began again to fan her gently.

Robin began to understand the situation a little better. It was plain that Sir Amyas was a great deal more anxious for the Queen's health than he pretended to be. There had been rumours that Elizabeth had actually caused it to be suggested to Sir Amyas that he should poison his prisoner decently and privately, and thereby save a great deal of trouble and scandal; and that Sir Amyas had refused with indignation. He remembered that Sir Amyas had referred just now to a suspicion of poison.... He determined on the bold line.

"Her Grace has spoken, sir," he said modestly. "And I think I should have a word to say. It is plain to me, by looking at her Grace, that her health is very far from what it should be—" (he paused significantly)—"I should have to make a thorough examination, if I prescribed at all; and, even should her Grace consent to this being done publicly, for my part I would not consent. I should be happy to have her women here, but—"

Sir Amyas turned on him wrathfully.

"Why, sir, you said downstairs—"

"I had not then seen her Grace. But there is no more to be said—" He kneeled again as if to take his leave, stood up, and began to retire to the door. Mr. Bourgoign stood helpless.

Then Sir Amyas yielded.

"You shall have fifteen minutes, sir. No more," he cried harshly. "And I shall remain in the next room."

He made a perfunctory salute and strode out.

The Queen opened her eyes, waited for one tense instant till the door closed; then she slipped swiftly off the couch.

"The door!" she whispered.

The woman was across the room in an instant, on tiptoe, and drew the single slender bolt. The Queen made a sharp gesture; the woman fled back again on one side, and out through the further door, and the old man hobbled after her. It was as if every detail had been rehearsed. The door closed noiselessly.

Then the Queen rose up, as Robin, understanding, began to fumble with his breast. And, as he drew out the pyx, and placed it on the handkerchief, apparently so carelessly laid by the crucifix, Mary sank down in adoration of her Lord.

"Now, *mon père*," she whispered, still kneeling, but lifting her star-bright eyes. And the priest went across to the couch where the Queen had lain, and sat down on it.

"*In nomine Patris et Filii et Spiritus Sancti—*" began Mary.

IV

WHEN the confession was finished, Robin went across, at the Queen's order, and tapped with his fingernail upon the door, while she herself remained on her knees. The door opened instantly, and the two came in, the woman first, bearing two lighted tapers. She set these down one on either side of the crucifix, and herself knelt with the old physician.

Then Robin gave holy communion to the Queen of the Scots....

V

SHE was back again on her couch now, once more as drowsy-looking as ever. The candlesticks were gone again; the handkerchief still in its place, and the woman back again behind the couch. The two men knelt close beside her, near enough to hear every whisper.

"Listen, gentlemen," she said softly, "I cannot tell you what you have done for my soul today—both of you, since I could never have had the priest without my friend.... I cannot reward you, but our Lord will do so abundantly... Listen, I know that I am going to my death, and I thank God that I have made my peace with Him. I do not know if they will allow me to see a priest again. But I wish to say this to both of you—as I said just now in my confession, to you, *mon père*—that I am wholly and utterly guiltless of the plot laid to my charge; that I had neither part nor wish nor consent in it. I desired only to escape from my captivity.... I would have made war, if I could, yes, but as for accomplishing or assisting in her Grace's death, the thought was never near me. Those whom I thought my friends have entrapped me, and have given colour to the tale. I pray our Saviour to forgive them as I do; and with that Saviour now in my breast I tell you—and you may tell all the world if you will—that I am guiltless of what they impute to me. I shall die for my religion, and nothing but that. And I thank you again, *mon père, et vous, mon ami, que vous avez...*"

Her voice died away in inaudible French, and her eyes closed.

Robin's eyes were raining tears, but he leaned forward and kissed her hand as it lay on the edge of the couch. He felt himself touched on the shoulder, and he stood up. The old man's eyes, too, were brimming with tears.

"I must let Sir Amyas in," he whispered. "You must be ready."

"What shall I say?"

"Say that you will prescribe privately, to me: and that her Grace's health is indeed delicate, but not gravely impaired.... You understand?"

Robin nodded, passing his sleeve over his eyes. The woman touched the Queen's shoulder to rouse her, and Mr. Bourgoign opened the door.

VI

"And now, sir," said Mr. Bourgoign, as the two passed out from the house half an hour later, "I have one more word to say to you. Listen carefully, if you please, for there is not much time."

He glanced behind him, but the tall figure was gone from the door; there remained only the two pikemen who kept ward over the great house on the steps.

"Come this way," said the physician, and led the priest through into the little walled garden on the south. "He will think we are finishing our consultation."

"I cannot tell you," he said presently, "all that I think of your courage and your wit. You made a bold stroke when you told him you would begone again, unless you could see her Grace alone, and again when you said you had come to Chartley because she was here. And you may go again now, knowing you have comforted a woman in her greatest need. They sent her chaplain from her when she left here for Tixall in July, and she has not had him again yet. She is watched at every point. They have taken all her papers from her, and have seduced M. Nau, I fear. Did you hear anything of him in town?"

"No," said the priest. "I know nothing of him."

"He is a Frenchman, and has been with her Grace more than ten years. He has written her letters for her, and been privy to all her counsels. And I fear he has been seduced from her at last. It was said that Mr. Walsingham was to take him into his house.... Well, but we have not time for this. What I have to ask you is whether you could come again to us?"

He peered at the priest almost timorously. Robin was startled.

"Come again?" he said. "Why—"

"You see you have already won to her presence, and Sir Amyas is committed to it that you are a safe man. I shall tell her Grace too, that she must eat and drink well, and get better, if she would see you again, for that will establish you in Sir Amyas' eyes."

Robin was silent.

The greatness of the affair terrified him; yet its melancholy drew him. He had seen her on whom all England bent its thoughts at this time, who was a crowned Queen, with broad lands and wealth, who called Elizabeth "sister"; yet who was more of a prisoner than any in the Fleet or Westminster Gatehouse, since those at least could have their friends to come to them. Her hidden fires, too, had warmed him—that passion for God that had burst from her when her gaoler left her, and she had flung herself on her knees before her hidden Saviour. It may be he had doubted her before (he did not know); but there was no more doubt in him after her protestation of her innocence. He began to see now that she stood for more than her kingdom or her son or the plots attributed to her, that she was more than a mere great woman, for whose sake men could both live and die; he began to see in her that which poor Anthony had seen—a champion for the Faith of them all, an incarnate suffering symbol, in flesh and blood, of that religion for which he, too, was in peril—that religion, which, in spite of all clamour to the contrary, was the real storm-centre of England's life.

He turned then to the old man with a suddenly flushed face.

"A message will always reach me at Mistress Manners' house, at

Booth's Edge, near Hathersage, in Derbyshire. And I will come from there, or from the world's end, to serve her Grace."

VII

"FIRST give me your blessing, Mr. Alban," said Marjorie, kneeling down before him in the hall in front of them all. She was as pale as a ghost, but her eyes shone like stars.

It was a couple of months after his leaving Chartley before he came at last to Booth's Edge. First he had had to bestow Mr. Arnold in Lancashire. He had slowly travelled north; then, coming round about from the north, after leaving his friend, saying Mass here and there where he could, crossing into Yorkshire even as far west as Wakefield, he had come at last, through this wet November day, along the Derwent valley and up to Booth's Edge, where he arrived after sunset, to find the hall filled with folks to greet him.

He was smiling, though his eyes were full of tears, by the time that he had done giving his blessings. Mr. John FitzHerbert was come up from Padley, where he lived now for short times together, greyer than ever, but with the same resolute face. Mistress Alice Babington was there, still serene looking, but with a new sorrow in her eyes; and, clinging to her, a thin, pale girl all in black, who only two months before had lost both daughter and husband; for the child had died scarcely a week or two before her father, Anthony Babington, had died miserably on the gallows near St. Giles' Fields, where he had so often met his friends after dark. It was a ghastly tale, told in fragments to Robin here and there during his journeyings by men in taverns, before whom he must keep a brave face. And a few farmers were there, old Mr. Merton among them, come in to welcome the son of the Squire of Matstead, returned under a feigned name, unknown even to his father, and there, too, was honest Dick Sampson, come up from Dethick to see his old master. So here, in the hall he knew so well, himself splashed with red marl from ankle to shoulder, still cloaked and spurred, one by one these knelt before him, beginning with Marjorie herself, and ending with the youngest farm-boy, who breathed heavily as he knelt down and got up round-eyed and staring.

"And his Reverence will hear confessions," proclaimed Marjorie to the multitude, "at eight o'clock tonight; and he will say Mass and give Holy Communion at six o'clock tomorrow morning."

VIII

He had to hear that night, after supper, and before he went to keep his engagement in the chapel-room, the entire news of the county; and, in his turn, to tell his own adventures.

Robin was no story-teller; but for half an hour he was forced to become one, until his hearers were satisfied. Even here, in the distant hills, Mary's name was a key to a treasure-house of mysteries. It was through this country, too, that she had passed again and again. It was at old Chatsworth that she had passed part of her captivity; it was in Derby that she had halted for a night last year; it was near Burton that she had slept two months ago on her road to Fotheringay, whither she had been moved last September, and to hear now of her, from one who had spoken to her that very autumn, was as a revelation. So Robin told it as well as he could.

"And it may be," he said, "that I shall have to go again. Mr. Bourgoign said that he would send to me if he could. But I have heard no word from him." (He glanced round the watching faces.) "And I need not say that I shall hear no word at all, if the tale I have told you leak out."

"Perhaps she has a chaplain again," said Mr. John, after a pause.

"I do not think so," said the priest. "If she had none at Chartley, she would all the less have one at Fotheringay."

"And it may be you will be sent for again?" asked Marjorie's voice gently from the darkness.

"It may be so," said the priest.

"The letter is to be sent here?" she asked.

"I told Mr. Bourgoign so."

"Does any other know you are here?"

"No, Mistress Marjorie."

There was a pause.

"It is growing late," said Mr. John. "Will your Reverence go upstairs with me; and these ladies will come after, I think."

IF it had been a great day for Robin that he should come back to his own country after six years, and be received in this house of strange memories; that he should sit upstairs as a priest, and hear confessions in that very parlour where nearly seven years ago he had sat with Marjorie as her accepted lover—if all this had been charged, to him, with emotions and memories which, however he had outgrown them, yet echoed somewhere wonderfully in his mind; it was no less a kind of climax and consummation to the girl whose house this was, and who had waited so long to receive back a lover who came now in so different a guise.

Yet her memories of him that remained in her had, of course, a place in her heart; and, though she knelt before him presently in the little parlour where once he had kneeled before her, as simply as a child before her father, and told her sins, and received Christ's pardon, and went away to make room for the next—though all this was without a reproach in her eyes; yet, as she went she knew that she must face a fresh struggle, and a temptation that would not have been one-tenth so fierce if it had been some other priest that was in peril. That peril was Fotheringay, and that temptation lay in the knowledge that when that letter should come (as she knew in her heart it would come), it would be through her hands that it would pass—if it passed indeed.

While the others went to the priest one by one, Marjorie kneeled in her room, fighting with a devil that was not yet come to her, as is the way with sensitive consciences.

CHAPTER V

I

THE suspense at Fotheringay grew deeper with every day that passed.

Christmas was come and gone, and no sign was made from London, so far, at least, as the little town was concerned. There came almost daily from the castle new tales of slights put upon the Queen, and now and again of new favours granted to her. Her chaplain, withdrawn for a while, had been admitted to her again a week before Christmas; a crowd had collected to see the Popish priest ride in, and had remarked on his timorous air; and about the same time a courier had been watched as he rode off to London, bearing, it was rumoured, one last appeal from one Queen to the other.

But all this had happened before Christmas, and now a month had gone by, and nothing was truly known the one way or the other. It had been proclaimed, by trumpet, in every town in England, that sentence of death was passed; yet this was two or three months ago, and the knowledge that the warrant had not yet been signed seemed an argument to some that now it never would be.

A group was waiting (as a group usually did wait) at the village entrance to the new bridge lately built by her Grace of England, towards sunset on an evening late in January. This situation commanded, so far as was possible, every point of interest. It was the beginning of the London road, up which so many couriers had passed; it was over this bridge that her Grace of Scotland herself had come from her cross-country journey from Chartley. On the left, looking northwards, rose the great old collegiate church, with its graceful lantern tower, above the low thatched stone houses of the village; on the right, adjoining the village beyond the big inn, rose the huge keep of the castle and its walls, within its double moats, ranged in form of a fetterlock of which the river itself was its straight side. Beyond, the low rolling hills and meadows met the chilly January sky.

A little more material had been supplied for conversation by the events of today. It had positively been reported, by a fellow who had been to see about a room for himself in the village, that he had been turned out of the castle to make space for her Grace's chaplain. This was puzzling. Had not the Popish priest already been in the castle five or six weeks? Then why should he now require another chamber?

The argument waxed hot by the bridge. One said that it was another priest that was come in disguise; another, that once a Popish priest got a foothold in a place he was never content till he got the whole for himself; a third, that the fellow had simply lied, and that he was turned out because he had been caught by Sir Amyas making love to one of the maids.

To this barren war of the schools came a fact at last, and its bearer was a gorgeous figure of a man-at-arms (who, later, got into trouble by talking too much), who came swaggering down the road from the New Inn, with his hat on one side, and his breast-piece loose; and declared in that strange clipped London-English of his that he had been on guard at the door of Sir Amyas' room, and had heard him tell Melville the steward and De Preau the priest that they must no longer have access to her Grace, but must move their lodgings elsewhere within the castle.

This, then, had to be discussed once more from the beginning. One said that this was an evident sign that the end was to come and that Madam was to die; another that, on the contrary, it was plain that this was not so, but that rather she was to be compelled by greater strictness to acknowledge her guilt; a third that Madam was turning Protestant at last in order to save her life, and had devised this manner of ridding herself of the priest. And the soldier damned them all round as blockfools, who knew nothing and talked all the more for it.

The dark was beginning to fall before the group broke up, and none of them took much notice of a young man on a fresh horse, who rode quietly out of the yard of the New Inn as the saunterers came up. One of them, three minutes later, however, heard suddenly from across the bridge the sound of a horse breaking into a gallop and presently dying away westwards beyond Perry Lane.

II

Within the castle that evening nothing happened that was of any note to its more careless occupants. All was as usual.

The guard at the towers that controlled the drawbridge across the outer moat was changed at four o'clock; six men came out, under an officer, from the inner court; the words were exchanged, and the six that went off duty marched into the armoury to lay by their pikes and presently dispersed, four to their rooms in the east side of the quadrangle, two to their quarters in the village. From the kitchen came the clash of dishes. Sir Amyas came out from the direction of the keep, where he had been conferring with Mr. FitzWilliam, the castellan, and passed across to his lodging on the south. A butcher hurried in, under escort of a couple of men from the gate, with a covered basket and disappeared into the kitchen entry. All these things were observed idly by the dozen guards who stood two at each of the five doors that gave upon the courtyard. Presently, too, hardly ten minutes after the guard was changed, three figures came out at the staircase foot where Sir Amyas had just gone in, and stood there apparently talking in low voices. Then one of them, Mr. Melville, the Queen's steward, came across the court with Mr. Bourgoign towards the outer entrance, passed under it, and presently Mr. Bourgoign came back and wheeled sharply in to the right by the entry that led up to the Queen's lodging. Meanwhile the third figure, whom one of the men had thought to be M. de Préau, had gone back again towards Mr. Melville's rooms.

That was all that was to be seen, until half an hour later, a few minutes before the drawbridge was raised for the night, the steward came back, crossed the court once more and vanished into the entry opposite.

It was about this time that the young man had ridden out from the New Inn.

Then the sun went down; the flambeaux were lighted beneath the two great entrances. The man at Sir Amyas' staircase looked across the court and idly wondered what was passing in the rooms opposite on the first floor where the Queen was lodged. He had heard that the priest had been forced to change his room, and was to sleep in Mr. Melville's for the present; so her Grace would have to get on without him as well as she could. There would be no Popish Mass tomorrow, then, in the oratory that he had heard was made upstairs.... He marvelled at the superstition that made this a burden....

At a quarter before six a trumpet blew, and presently the tall windows of the hall across the court from him began to kindle. That was for her Grace's supper to be served. At five minutes to six another trumpet sounded. Finally, through the ground-floor window at the foot of the Queen's stair, the man caught a glimpse of moving figures passing towards the hall. That would be her Grace going in state to her supper with her women; but, for the first time, without either priest to say grace or steward to escort her.

Meanwhile, ten miles away, along the Uppingham and Leicester track, rode a young man through the dark.

III

Sunday, too, passed as usual.

At half-past eight the bells of the church pealed out for the morning service, and the village street was thronged with worshippers and a few soldiers. At nine o'clock they ceased, and the street was empty. At eleven o'clock the trumpets sounded to announce change of guard, and to tell the kitchen folk that dishing-time was come. Half an hour later once more the little procession glinted a moment through the ground-floor window of the Queen's stair as her Grace went to dinner. At twelve o'clock she came out again and went upstairs, and at the same time, in Leicester, a young man, splashed from head to foot, slipped off a draggled and exhausted horse and went into an inn, ordering a fresh horse to be ready for him at three o'clock.

And so once more the sun went down, and the little rituals were performed, and the guards were changed, and Sir Amyas walked in from the orchard, and the drawbridge was raised. And, at the time that the drawbridge was raised, a young man on a horse was wondering when he should see the lights of Burton....

IV

THE first that Mistress Manners knew of his coming in the early hours of Monday morning was when she was awakened by Janet in the pitch darkness shaking her shoulder.

"It is a young man," she said, "on foot. His horse fell five miles off. He is come with a letter from Derby."

Sleep fell from Marjorie like a cloak. This kind of thing had happened to her before. Now and then such a letter would come from a priest who lacked money or desired a guide or information. She sprang out of bed and began to put on her outer dress and her hooded cloak, as the night was cold.

"Bring him into the hall," she said. "Get beer and some food, and blow the fire up."

Janet vanished.

When the mistress came down five minutes later, all had been done as she had ordered. The turf and wood fire leaped in the chimney; a young man, still with his hat on his head and drawn down a little over his face, was sitting over the hearth.

"I am Mistress Manners," she said. "You have a letter for me?"

The young man stood up.

"I know you well enough, mistress," he said. "I am John Merton's son."

Marjorie's heart leaped with relief. In spite of her determination that this must be a letter from a priest, there had still thrust itself before her mind the possibility that it might be that other letter whose coming she had feared. She had told herself fiercely as she came downstairs just now that it could not be. No news was come from Fotheringay all the winter; it was common knowledge that her Grace had a priest of her own. And now that this was John Merton's son. She smiled.

"Give me the letter," she said. "I should have known you, too, if it were not for the dark."

"Well, mistress," he said, "the letter was to be delivered to you, Mr. Melville said; but—"

"Who?"

"Mr. Melville, mistress: her Grace's steward at Fotheringay."

He talked on a moment or two, beginning to say that Mr. Melville himself had come out to the inn; that he, as Melville's own servant, had been lodging there, and had been bidden to hold himself in readiness, since he knew Derbyshire.... But she was not listening. She only knew that that had fallen which she feared.

"Give me the letter," she said again.

He sat down, excusing himself, and fumbled with his boot; and by the time that he held it out to her, she was in the thick of the conflict... And it was to her own house here in Derbyshire that her friend had come for shelter; it was here that he had said Mass yesterday; and it must be from this house that he must ride, on one of her horses; and it must be her hand that gave him the summons. Last of all, it was she, Marjorie Manners, that had sent him to this life, six years ago.

Then, as she took the letter, the shrewd woman in her spoke. It was irresistible, and she seemed to listen to a voice that was not hers.

"Does any here know that you are come?"

"No, mistress."

"If I bade you, and said that I had reasons for it, you would ride away again alone, without a word to any?"

"Why, yes, mistress!"

(Oh! the plan was irresistible and complete. She would send this messenger away again on one of her own horses as far as Derby; he could leave the horse there, and she would send a man for it tomorrow.

He would go back to Fotheringay and would wait, he and those that had sent him. And the priest they expected would not come. He, too, himself, had ceased to expect any word from Mr. Bourgoign; he had said a month ago that surely none would come now. He had been away from Booth's Edge, in fact, for nearly a month, and had scarcely even asked on his return last Saturday to Padley whether any message had come. Why, it was complete—complete and irresistible! She would burn the letter here in this hall fire when the man was gone again; and say to Janet that the letter had been from a travelling priest that was in trouble, and that she had sent the answer. And Robin would presently cease to look for news, and the end would come, and there would be no more trouble.)

"Do you know what is in the letter?" she whispered sharply.

"Yes, mistress," he said. "The priest was taken from her on Saturday. Mr. Bourgoign had arranged all in readiness for that."

"You said Mr. Melville."

"Mr. Melville is a Protestant, mistress; but he is very well devoted to her Grace, and has done as Mr. Bourgoign wished."

"Why must her Grace have a priest at once? Surely for a few days—"

He glanced up at her, and she, conscious of her own falseness, thought he looked astonished.

"I mean that they will surely give her her priest back again presently; and—(her voice faltered)—and Mr. Alban is spent with his travelling."

"They mean to kill her, mistress. There is no doubt of it amongst those of us that are Catholics. And it is that she may have a priest before she dies, that—"

He paused.

"Yes?" she said.

"Her Grace had a fit of crying, it is said, when her priest was taken from her, Mr. Melville was crying himself, even though—"

He stopped, himself plainly affected.

Then, in a great surge, her own heart rose up, and she understood what she was doing. As in a vision, she saw her own mother crying out for the priest that never came; and she understood that horror of darkness that falls on one who, knowing what the priest can do, knowing the infinite consolations which Christ gives, is deprived, when physical death approaches, of that tremendous strength and comfort. Indeed, she recognised to the full that when a priest cannot be had, God will save and forgive without him; yet what would be the heartlessness, to say nothing of the guilt, of one that would keep him away? For what, except that this strength and comfort might be at the service of Christ's flock, had her own life been spent? It was expressly for this that she had lived on in England when peace and the cloister might be hers elsewhere; and now that her own life was touched, should she fail?... The blindness passed like a dream, and her soul rose up again on a wave of pain and exaltation....

"Wait," she said. "I will go and awaken him, and bid him come down."

V

An hour later, as the first streaks of dawn slit the sky to the eastwards over the moors, she stood with Janet and Mistress Alice and Robin by the hall fire.

She had said not a word to any of the struggle she had passed through. She had gone upstairs resolutely and knocked on his door till he had answered, and then whispered, "The letter is come.... I will have food ready"; slipping the letter beneath the door.

Then she had sent Janet to awaken a couple of men who slept over the stables, and bid them saddle two horses at once; and herself had gone to the buttery to make ready a meal. Then Mistress Alice had awakened and come downstairs, and the three women had waited on the priest, as, in boots and cloak, he had taken some food.

Then, as the sound of the horses' feet coming round from the stables at the back had reached them, she had determined to tell Robin before he went of how she had played the coward.

She went out with him to the entry between the hall and the buttery, holding the others back with a glance.

"I near destroyed the letter," she said simply, with downcast eyes, "and sent the man away again. I was afraid of what might fall at Fotheringay.... May Christ protect you!"

She said no more than that, but turned and called the others before he could speak.

As he gathered up the reins a moment later before mounting, the three women kneeled down in the lighted entry and the two farm-men by the horses' heads, and the priest gave them his blessing.

CHAPTER VI

I

It was not until after dawn on Wednesday, the twenty-fifth of January, as the bells were ringing in the parish church for the Conversion of St. Paul, that the two draggled travellers rode in over the bridge of Fotheringay, seeing the castle-keep rise grim and grey out of the river-mists on the right; and, passing on, dismounted in the yard of the New Inn. They had had one or two small misadventures by the way, and young Merton, through sheer sleepiness, had so reeled in his saddle on the afternoon of Monday, that the priest had insisted that they should both have at least one good night's rest. But they had ridden all Tuesday night without drawing rein, and Robin, going up to the room that he was to share with the young man, fell upon the bed, and asleep, all in one act.

He was awakened by the trumpets sounding for dinner in the castle-yard, and sat up to find young John looking at him. The news that he brought drove the last shreds of sleep from his brain.

"I have seen Mr. Melville, my master, sir. He bids me say it is useless for Mr. Bourgoign, or anyone else, to attempt anything with Sir Amyas for the present. Mr. Melville has spoken to Sir Amyas as to his separation from her Grace, and could get no reason for it. But the same day—it was of Monday—her Grace's butler was forbidden any more to carry the white rod before her dishes. This is as much as to signify, Mr. Melville says, that her Grace's royalty shall no longer protect her. It is their intention, he says, to degrade her first, before they execute her. And we may look for the warrant any day, my master says."

The young man stared at him mournfully.

"And M. de Préau?"

"M. de Préau goes about as a ghost. He will come and speak with your Reverence before the day is out. Meanwhile, Mr. Melville says you may walk abroad freely. Sir Amyas never goes forth of the castle now, and none will notice. But they might take notice, Mr. Melville says, if you were to lie all day in your chamber."

It was after dinner, as Robin rose from the table in a parlour, where he had dined with two or three lawyers and an officer of Mr. FitzWilliam, that John Merton came to him and told him that a gentleman was waiting. He went upstairs and found the priest, a little timorous-looking man, dressed like a minister, pacing quickly to and fro in the tiny room at the top of the house where John and he were to sleep. The Frenchman seized his two hands and began to pour out in an agitated whisper a torrent of French and English. Robin disengaged himself.

"You must sit down, M. de Préau," he said, "and speak slowly, or I shall not understand one word. Tell me precisely what I must do. I am here to obey orders—no more. I have no design in my head at all. I will do what Mr. Bourgoign and yourself decide."

It was pathetic to watch the little priest. He interrupted himself by a thousand apostrophes; he lifted hands and eyes to the ceiling repeatedly; he named his poor mistress saint and martyr; he cried out against the barbarian land in which he found himself, and the bloodthirsty tigers with whom, like a second Daniel, he himself had to consort; he expatiated on the horrible risk that he ran in venturing forth from the castle on such an errand, saying that Sir Amyas would wring his neck like a hen's if he so much as suspected the nature of his business. He denounced, with feeble venom, the wickedness of these murderers, who would not only slay his mistress' body, but her soul as well, if they could, by depriving her of a priest. Incidentally, however, he disclosed that at present there was no plan at all for Robin's admission. Mr. Bourgoign had sent for him, hoping that he might be able to reintroduce him once more on the same pretext as at Chartley; but the incident of Monday, when the white rod had been forbidden, and the conversation of Sir Amyas to Mr. Melville had made it evident that an attempt at present would be worse than useless.

"You must yourself choose!" he cried, with an abominable accent. "If you will imperil your life by remaining, our Lord will no doubt reward you in eternity; but, if not, and you flee, not a man will blame you—least of all myself, who would, no doubt, flee too, if I but dared."

This was frank and humble, at any rate. Robin smiled.

"I will remain," he said.

The Frenchman seized his hands and kissed them.

"You are a hero and a martyr, monsieur! We will perish together, therefore."

AFTER the Frenchman's departure, and an hour's sleep in that profundity of unconsciousness that follows prolonged effort, Robin put on his sword and hat and cloak, having dressed himself with care, and went slowly out of the inn to inspect the battlefield. He carried himself deliberately, with a kind of assured insolence, as if he had supreme rights in this place, and were one of that crowd of persons—great lords, lawyers, agents of the court—to whom for the last few months Fotheringay had become accustomed. He turned first to the right towards the castle, and presently was passing down its long length.

He came back to the inn an hour later. There was but one thing to be done, and that the hardest of all—to wait. Perhaps in a few days he might get speech with Mr. Bourgoign; yet for the present that, too, as the priest had told him, was out of the question.

II

FIVE days were gone by, Sunday had come and gone, and yet there had been no news, except a letter conveyed to him by Merton, written by Mr. Bourgoign himself, telling him that he had news that Mr. Beale, the Clerk of the Council, was to arrive some time that week, and that this presaged the approach of the end. He would, therefore, do his utmost within the next few days to approach Sir Amyas and ask for the admission of the young herbalist who had done her Grace so much good at Chartley. He added that if any question were to be raised as to why he had been so long in the place, and why, indeed, he had come at all, he was to answer fearlessly that Mr. Bourgoign had sent for him.

On the Sunday night Robin could not sleep. Little by little the hideous suspense was acting upon him, and the knowledge that not a hundred yards away from him the wonderful woman whom he had seen at Chartley, the loving and humble Catholic, who had knelt so ardently before her Lord, the Queen who had received from him the sacraments for which she thirsted—the knowledge that she was breaking her heart, so near, for the consolation which a priest only could give, and that he, a priest, was free to go through all England, except through that towered gateway past which he walked every day—this increased his misery and his longing.

About midnight he could lie there no longer. He got out of bed noiselessly, went to the window-seat and sat down there, staring out, with eyes well accustomed to the darkness, towards the vast outline against the sky which he knew was the keep of the castle.... Then he drew out Mr. Maine's rosary and began to recite the "Sorrowful Mysteries."

He supposed afterwards that he had begun to doze; but he started, wide-awake, at a sudden glare of light in his eyes, as if a beacon had flared for an instant somewhere within the castle enclosure. It was gone again, however; there remained the steady monstrous mass of building and the heavy sky. Then, as he watched, it came again, without warning and without sound—that same brilliant flare of light, against which the towers and walls stood out pitch-black. A third time it came, and all was dark once more.

IN the morning, as he sat over his ale in the tavern below, he listened, without lifting his eyes, engrossed, it seemed, in a little book he was reading, to the excited talk of a group of soldiers. One of them, he said, had been on guard beneath the Queen's windows last night, and between midnight and one o'clock had seen three times a brilliant light explode itself, like soundless gunpowder, immediately over the room where she slept. And this he asserted, over and over again.

III

ON the following Saturday John Merton came up into the room where the priest was sleeping after dinner and awakened him.

"If you will come at once with me, sir, you can have speech with Mr. Bourgoign. My master has sent me to tell you so; Mr. Bourgoign has leave to go out."

Robin said nothing. It was the kind of opportunity that must not be imperilled by a single word that might be overheard. He threw on his great cloak, buckled his sword on, and followed with every nerve awake. They went up the street leading towards the church, and turned down a little passage-way between two of the larger houses; the young man pushed on a door in the wall; and Robin went through, to find himself in a little enclosed garden with Mr. Bourgoign gathering herbs from the border, not a yard from him. The physician said nothing; he glanced sharply up and pointed to a seat set under the shelter of the wall that hid the greater part of the garden from the house to which it belonged; and as Robin reached it, Mr. Bourgoign, still gathering his herbs, began to speak in an undertone.

"Do not speak except very softly, if you must," he said. "The Queen is sick again; and I have leave to gather herbs for her in two or three gardens. It was refused to me at first and then granted afterwards. From that I look for the worst.... Beale will come tomorrow, I hear.... Paulet refused me leave the first time, I make no doubt, knowing, that all was to end within a day or two: then he granted it me, for fear I should suspect his reason. Can you hear me, sir?"

Robin nodded. His heart thumped within him.

"Well, sir; I shall tell Sir Amyas tomorrow that my herbs do no good—that I do not know what to give her Grace. I have seen her Grace continually, but with a man in the room always.... Her Grace knows that you are here, and bids me thank you with all her heart.... I shall speak to Sir Amyas, and shall tell him that you are here: and that I sent for you, but did not dare to ask leave for you until now. If he refuses I shall know that all is finished, and that Beale has brought the warrant with him.... If he consents I shall think that it is put off for a little...."

He was very near to Robin now, still with a critical air pushing the herbs this way and that, selecting one now and again.

"Have you anything to say to me, sir? Do not speak loud. The fellow that conducted me from the castle is drinking ale in the house behind. He did not know of this door on the side.... Have you anything to say?"

"Yes," said Robin.

"What is it?"

"Two things. The first is that I think one of the fellows in the inn is doubtful of me. Merton tells me he has asked a great number of questions about me. What had I best do?"

"Who is he?"

"He is a servant of my lord Shrewsbury's who is in the neighbourhood."

The doctor was silent.

"Am I in danger?" asked the priest quietly. "Shall I endanger her Grace?"

"You cannot endanger her Grace. She is near her end in any case. But for yourself—"

"Yes."

"You are endangering yourself every instant by remaining," said the doctor dryly.

"The second matter—" began Robin.

"But what of yourself—"

"Myself must be endangered," said Robin softly. "The second matter is whether you cannot get me near her Grace in the event of her execution. I could at least give her absolution *sub conditione*."

Mr. Bourgoign shot a glance at him which he could not interpret.

"Sir," he said; "God will reward you.... As regards the second matter it will be exceedingly difficult. If it is to be in the open court,

I may perhaps contrive it. If it is to be in the hall, none but known persons would be admitted.... Have you anything more, sir?"

"No."

"Then you had best be gone again at once.... Her Grace prays for you.... She had a fit of weeping last night to know that a priest was here and she not able to have him.... Do you pray for her...."

IV

Sunday morning dawned; the bells pealed out; the crowds went by the church and came back to dinner; and yet no word had come to the inn. Robin scarcely stirred out all that day for fear a summons should come and he miss it. He feigned a little illness and sat wrapped up in the corner window of the parlour upstairs, whence he could command both roads—that which led to the Castle, and that which led to the bridge over which Mr. Beale must come. He considered it prudent also to do this, because of the fellow of whom Merton had told him—a man that looked like a groom, and who was lent, he heard, with one or two others by his master to do service at the Castle.

It was growing towards dark when Robin saw the group gathering as usual at the entrance to the bridge to watch the arrivals from London, who, if there were any, generally came about this time.

Then, as he looked, he saw two horsemen mount the further slope of the bridge, and come full into view.

Now there was nothing whatever about these two persons, in outward appearance, to explain the strange effect they had upon the priest. They could not possibly be the party for which he was watching. Mr. Beale would certainly come with a great company. They were, besides, plainly no more than serving-men: one wore some kind of a livery; the other, a strongly-built man who sat his horse awkwardly, was in new clothes that did not fit him. They rode ordinary hackneys; and each had luggage strapped behind his saddle. All this the priest saw as they came up the narrow street and halted before the inn door. They might, perhaps, be servants of Mr. Beale; yet that did not seem probable as there was no sign of a following party. The landlord came out onto the steps beneath; and after a word or two, they slipped off their horses wearily, and led them round into the court of the inn.

All this was usual enough; the priest had seen such arrivals a dozen times at this very door; yet he felt sick as he looked at them. There appeared to him something terrible and sinister about them. He had seen the face of the liveried servant; but not of the other: this one had carried his head low, with his great hat drawn down on his head. The priest wondered, too, what they carried in their trunks.

When he went down to supper in the great room of the inn, he could not forbear looking round for them. But only one was to be seen—the liveried servant who had done the talking.

Robin turned to his neighbour—a lawyer with whom he had spoken a few times.

"That is a new livery to me," he said, nodding towards the stranger.

"That?" said the lawyer. "That? Why, that is the livery of Mr. Walsingham. I have seen it in London."

Towards the end of supper a stir broke out among the servants who sat at the lower end of the room near the windows that looked out upon the streets. Two or three sprung up from the tables and went to look out.

"What is that?" cried the lawyer.

"It is Mr. Beale going past, sir," answered a voice.

Robin lifted his eyes with an effort and looked. Even as he did so there came a trampling of horses' hoofs; and then, in the light that streamed from the windows, there appeared a company on horseback. They were too far away from where he sat, and the lights were too confusing, for him to see more than the general crowd that went by—perhaps from a dozen to twenty all told. But by them ran the heads of men who had waited at the bridge to see them go by; and a murmuring of voices came even through the closed windows. It was plain that others besides those who were close to her Grace saw a sinister significance in Mr. Beale's arrival.

V

Robin had hardly reached his room after supper before Merton came in. He drew his hand out of his breast as he entered, and, with a strange look, gave the priest a folded letter. Robin took it without a word and read it through.

After a pause he said to the other:

"Who were those two men that came before supper? I saw them ride up."

"There is only one, sir. He is one of Mr. Walsingham's men."

"There were two," said the priest.

"I will inquire, sir," said the young man, looking anxiously from the priest's face to the note and back again.

Robin noticed it.

"It is bad news," he said shortly. "I must say no more.... Will you inquire for me; and come and tell me at once."

When the young man had gone Robin read the note again before destroying it.

"I spoke to Sir A. today. He will have none of it. He seemed highly suspicious when I spoke to him of you. If you value your safety more than her Grace's possible comfort, you had best leave at once. In any case, use great caution."

Then, in a swift, hurried hand there followed a postscript:

"Mr. B, is just now arrived, and is closeted with Sir A. All is over, I think."

Ten minutes later Merton came back and found the priest still in the same attitude, sitting on the bed.

"They will have none of it, sir," he said. "They say that one only came, in advance of Mr. Beale."

He came a little closer, and Robin could see that he was excited.

"But you are right, sir, for all their lies, I saw supper plates and an empty flagon come down from the stair that leads to the little chamber above the kitchen."

CHAPTER VII

I

SINCE soon after midnight the folks had been gathering. Many had not slept all night, ever since the report had run like fire through the little town last evening, that the sentence had been delivered to the prisoner. From that time onwards the road that led down past the Castle had never been empty. It was now moving on to dawn, the late dawn of February; and every instant the scene grew more distinct.

It was possible for those pushed against the wall, or against the chains of the bridge that had been let down an hour ago, to look down into the chilly water of the moat; to see not the silhouette only of the huge fortress, but the battlements of the wall, and now and again a steel cap and a pike-point pass beyond it as the sentry went to and fro. Noises within the Castle grew more frequent. The voice of an officer was heard half a dozen times; the rattle of pike-butts, the clash of steel. Still there was no movement of the great doors across the bridge. The men on guard there shifted their positions; nodded a word or two across to one another; changed their pikes from one hand to the other....

Then, without warning, the doors wheeled back on their hinges, disclosing a line of pikemen drawn up under the vaulted entrance; a sharp command was uttered by an officer at their head, causing the two sentries to advance across the bridge; a great roaring howl rose from the surging crowd; and in an instant the whole lane was in confusion. Robin felt himself pushed this way and that; he struggled violently, driving his elbows right and left; was lifted for a moment clean from his feet by the pressure about him; slipped down again; gained a yard or two; lost them; gained three or four in a sudden swirl;

and immediately found his feet on wood instead of earth; and himself racing desperately in a loose group of runners, across the bridge; and beneath the arch of the castle-gate.

When he was able to take breath again, he found himself tramping in a kind of stream of men into what appeared an impenetrably packed crowd. He was going between ropes, however, which formed a lane up which it was possible to move. This lane, after crossing half the court, wheeled suddenly to one side and doubled on itself, conducting the newcomers behind the crowd of privileged persons that had come into the castle overnight, or had been admitted three or four hours ago. These persons were all people of quality; many of them, out of a kind of sympathy for what was to happen, were in black. They stood there in rows, scarcely moving, scarcely speaking, some even bare-headed, filling up now, so far as the priest could see, the entire court, except in that quarter in which he presently found himself—the furthest corner away from where rose up the tall carved and traceried windows of the banqueting-hall. Yet, though no man spoke above an undertone, a steady low murmur filled the court from side to side, like the sound of a wagon rolling over a paved road.

He reached his place at last, actually against the wall of the soldiers' lodgings, and found, presently, that a low row of projecting stones enabled him to raise himself a few inches, and see, at any rate, a little better than his neighbours. He had perceived one thing instantly—namely, that his dream of getting near enough to the Queen to give her absolution before her death was an impossible one. He had known since yesterday that the execution was to take place in the hall, and here was he, within the court certainly, yet as far as possible away from where he most desired to be.

THE last two days had gone by in a horror that there is no describing. All the hours of them he had passed at his parlour window, waiting hopelessly for the summons which never came.

All in Fotheringay had been as convinced as men could be, who had not seen the warrant nor heard it read, that Mr. Beale had brought it with him on Sunday night; the priest, above all, from his communications with Mr. Bourgoign, was morally certain that the terror was come at last.... It was not until the last night of Mary's life on earth was beginning to close in that John Merton came up to the parlour, white and terrified, to tell him that he had been in his master's room half an hour ago, and that Mr. Melville had come in to them, his face all slobbered with tears, and had told him that he had but just come from her Grace's rooms, and had heard with his own ears the sentence read to her, and her gallant and noble answer.... He had bidden him to go straight off to the priest, with a message from Mr. Bourgoign and himself, to the effect that the execution was appointed for eight o'clock next morning; and that he was to be at the gate of the castle not later than three o'clock, if, by good fortune, he might be admitted when the gates were opened at seven.

II

And now that the priest was in his place, he began again to think over that answer of the Queen. The very words of it, indeed, he did not know for a month or two later, when Mr. Bourgoign wrote to him at length; but this, at least, he knew, that her Grace had said (and no man contradicted her at that time) that she would shed her blood tomorrow with all the happiness in the world, since it was for the cause of the Catholic and Roman Church that she died. It was not for any plot that she was to die: she professed again, kissing her Bible as she did so, that she was utterly guiltless of any plot against her sister. She died because she was of that Faith in which she had been born, and which Elizabeth had repudiated. As for death, she did not fear it; she had looked for it during all the eighteen years of her imprisonment.

It was at a martyrdom, then, that he was to assist.... He had known that, without a doubt, ever since the day that Mary had declared her innocence at Chartley. There had been no possibility of thinking otherwise; and, as he reflected on this, he remembered that he, too, was guilty of the same crime;...and he wondered whether he, too, would die as manfully, if the need for it ever came.

THEN, in an instant, he was called back, by the sudden crash of horns and drums playing all together. He saw again the ranks of heads before him: the great arched windows of the hall on the other side of the court, the grim dominating keep, and the merciless February morning sky over all.

It was impossible to tell what was going on.

On all sides of him men jostled and murmured aloud. One said, "She is coming down"; another, "It is all over"; another, "They have awakened her." "What is it? what is it?" whispered Robin to the air, watching waves of movement pass over the serried heads before him. The lights were still burning here and there in the windows, and the tall panes of the hall were all aglow, as if a great fire burned within. Overhead the sky had turned to daylight at last, but they were grey clouds that filled the heavens so far as he could see. Meanwhile, the horns brayed in unison, a rough melody like the notes of bugles, and the drums beat out the time.

Again there was a long pause—in which the lapse of time was incalculable. Time had no meaning here: men waited from incident to incident only—the moving of a line of steel caps, a pause in the music, a head thrust out from a closed window and drawn back again.... Again the music broke out, and this time it was an air that they played—a lilting melancholy melody, that the priest recognised, yet could not identify. Men laughed subduedly near him; he saw a face wrinkled with bitter mirth turned back, and he heard what was said. It was "Jumping Joan" that was being played—the march consecrated to the burning of witches. He had heard it long ago, as a boy....

Then the rumour ran through the crowd, and spent itself at last in the corner where the priest stood trembling with wrath and pity.

"She is in the hall."

It was impossible to know whether this were true, or whether she had not been there half an hour already. The horror was that all might be over, or not yet begun, or in the very act of doing. He had thought that there would be some pause or warning—that a signal would be given, perhaps, that all might bare their heads or pray, at this violent passing of a Queen. But there was none. The heads surged and quieted; murmurs burst out and died again; and all the while the hateful, insolent melody rose and fell; the horns bellowed; the drums crashed. It sounded like some shocking dance-measure; a riot of desperate spirits moved in it, trampling up and down, as if in one last fling of devilish gaiety....

Then suddenly the heads grew still; a wave of motionlessness passed over them, as if some strange sympathy were communicated from within those tall windows. The moments passed and passed. It was impossible to hear those murmurs, through the blare of the instruments; there was one sound only that could penetrate them; and this, rising from what seemed at first the wailing of a child, grew and grew into the shrill cries of a dog in agony. At the noise once more a roar of low questioning surged up and fell. Simultaneously the music came to an abrupt close; and, as if at a signal, there sounded a great roar of voices, all shouting together within the hall. It rose yet louder, broke out of doors, and was taken up by those outside. The court was now one sea of tossing heads and open mouths shouting—as if in exultation or in anger. Robin fought for his place on the projecting stones, clung to the rough wall, gripped a window-bar and drew himself yet higher.

Then, as he clenched himself tight and stared out again towards the tall windows that shone in bloody flakes of fire from the roaring logs within, a sudden and profound silence fell once more before being shattered again by a thousand roaring throats....

For there, in full view beyond the clear glass, stood a tall, black figure, masked to the mouth, who held in his outstretched hands a wide silver dish, in which lay something white and round and slashed with crimson....

PART FOUR

CHAPTER I

I

"THERE is no more to be said, then," said Marjorie, and leaned back with a white, exhausted face. "We can do no more."

IT was a little council of Papists that was gathered—a year after the Queen's death at Fotheringay—in Mistress Manners' parlour. Mr. John FitzHerbert was there; he had ridden up an hour before with heavy news from Padley and its messenger. Mistress Alice was there, quiet as ever, yet paler and thinner than in former years (Mistress Babington herself had gone back to her family last year). And, last, Robin himself was there, having himself borne the news from Derby.

The news was of the worst. He had heard from Catholics in Derby that Mr. Simpson, returned again after his banishment, recaptured a month or two ago, and awaiting trial at the Lent Assizes, was beginning to falter. Death was a certainty for him this time, and it appeared that he had seemed very timorous before two or three friends who had visited him in gaol, declaring that he had done all that a man could do, that he was being worn out by suffering and privation, and that there was some limit, after all, to what God Almighty should demand.

Marjorie had cried out just now, driven beyond herself at the thought of what all this must mean for the Catholics of the countryside, many of whom already had fallen away during the last year or two beneath the pitiless storm of fines, suspicions, and threats—had cried out that it was impossible that such a man as Mr. Simpson could fall; that the ruin it would bring upon the Faith must be proportionate to the influence he already had won throughout the country by his years of labour; entreating, finally, when the trustworthiness of the report had been forced upon her at last, that she herself might be allowed to go and see him and speak with him in prison.

This, however, had been strongly refused by her counsellors just now. They had declared that her help was invaluable; that the amazing manner in which her little retired house on the moors had so far evaded grave suspicion rendered it one of the greatest safeguards that the hunted Catholics possessed; that the work she was doing by her organization of messengers and letters must not be risked, even for the sake of a matter like this....

She had given in at last. But her spirit seemed broken altogether.

II

"There is one more matter," said Robin presently, uncrossing one splashed leg from over the other. "I had not thought to speak of it; but I think it best now to do so. It concerns myself a little; and, therefore, if I may flatter myself, it concerns my friends, too."

He smiled genially upon the company; for if there was one thing more than another he had learned in his travels, it was that the tragic air never yet helped any man.

Marjorie lifted her eyes a moment.

"Mistress Manners," he said, "you remember my speaking to you after Fotheringay, of a fellow of my lord Shrewsbury's who honoured me with his suspicions?"

She nodded.

"I have never set eyes on him from that day to this—to this," he added. "And this morning in the open street in Derby whom should I meet with but young Merton and his father. Well, I stopped to speak with these two. The young man has left Mr. Melville's service a while back, it seems; and is to try his fortune in France. We were speaking of this and that, when who should come by but a party of men and my lord Shrewsbury in the midst, riding with Mr. Roger Columbell; and immediately behind them my friend of the "New Inn" of Fotheringay. It was all the ill-fortune in the world that it should be at such moment; if he had seen me alone he would have thought no more of me; but seeing me with young Jack Merton, he looked from one to the other. And I will stake my hat he knew me again."

Marjorie was looking full at him now.

"What was my lord Shrewsbury doing in Derby with Mr. Columbell?" mused Mr. John, biting his moustache.

"It was the very question I put to myself," said Robin. "And I took the liberty of seeing where they went. They went to Mr. Columbell's own house, and indoors of it. The serving-men held the horses at the door. I watched them awhile from Mr. Biddell's window; but they were still there when I came away at last."

"What hour was that?" asked the old man.

"That would be after dinner-time. I had dined early; and I met them afterwards. My lord would surely be dining with Mr. Columbell. But that is no answer to my question. It rather pierces down to the further point, why was my lord Shrewsbury dining with Mr. Columbell? Shrewsbury is a great lord; Mr. Columbell is a little magistrate. My lord has his own house in the country, and there be good inns in Derby."

He stopped short.

"What is the matter, Mistress Manners?" he asked.

"What of yourself?" she said sharply; "you were speaking of yourself."

Robin laughed.

"I had forgotten myself for once!...Why, yes; I intended to ask the company what I had best do. What with this news of Mr. Simpson, and the report Mistress Manners gives us of the country-folk, a poor priest must look to himself in these days; and not for his own sake only. Now, my lord Shrewsbury's man knows nothing of me except that I had strange business at Fotheringay a year ago. But to have had strange business at Fotheringay a year ago is a suspicious circumstance; and—"

"Mr. Alban," broke in the old man, "you had best do nothing at all. You were not followed from Derby; you are as safe in Padley or here as you could be anywhere in England. All that you had best do is to remain here a week or two and not go down to Derby again for the present. I think that showing of yourself openly in towns has its dangers as well as its safeguards."

Mr. John glanced round. Marjorie bowed her head in assent.

"I will do precisely as you say," said Robin easily.

III

THEY had all risen to their feet when a knocking came on the door, and Janet looked in. She seemed a little perturbed.

"If you please, sir," she said to Mr. John, "one of your men is come up from Padley and wishes to speak to you alone."

Mr. John gave a quick glance at the others.

"If you will allow me," he said, "I will go down and speak with him in the hall."

The rest sat down again. It was the kind of interruption that might be wholly innocent; yet, coming when it did, it affected them a little. There seemed to be nothing but bad news everywhere.

The minutes passed, yet no one returned. Once Marjorie went to the door and listened, but there was only the faint wail of the winter wind up the stairs to be heard. Then, five minutes later, there were steps and Mr. John came in. His face looked a little stern, but he smiled with his mouth.

"We poor Papists are in trouble again," he said. "Mistress Manners, you must let us stay here all night, if you will; and we will be off early in the morning. There is a party coming to us from Derby—tomorrow or next day: it is not known which."

"Why, yes! and what party?" said Marjorie, quietly enough, though she must have guessed its character. The smile left his mouth.

"It is my son that is behind it," he said. "I had wondered we had not had news of him! There is to be a general search for seminarists in the High Peak" (he glanced at Robin), "by order of my lord Shrewsbury. Your namesake, mistress, Mr. John Manners, and our friend Mr. Columbell, are commissioned to search; and Mr. Fenton and myself are singled out to be apprehended immediately. Thomas knows that I am at Padley, and that Mr. Eyre will come in there for Candlemas, the day after tomorrow; in that I recognize my son's knowledge. Well, I will dispatch my man who brought the news to Mr. Eyre to bid him to avoid the place; and we two, Mr. Alban and myself, will make our way across the border into Stafford."

"There are none others coming to Padley tomorrow?" asked Marjorie.

"None that I know of. They will come in sometimes without warning; but I cannot help that. Mr. Fenton will be at Tansley: he told me so."

"How did the news come?" asked Robin.

"It seems that the preacher Walton, in Derby, has been warned that we shall be delivered to him two days hence. It was his servant that told one of mine. I fear he will be a-preparing his sermons to us, all for nothing."

He smiled bitterly again. Robin could see the misery in this man's heart at the thought that it was his own son who had contrived this. Mr. Thomas had been quiet for many months, no doubt in order to strike the more surely in his new function as "sworn man" of her Grace. Yet he would seem to have failed.

"We shall not get our candles then, this year either," smiled Mr. Thomas. "Lanterns are all that we shall have."

THERE was not much time to be lost. Luggage had to be packed, since it would not be safe for the three to return until at least two or three weeks had passed; and Marjorie, besides, had to prepare a list of places and names that must be dealt with on their way—places where word must be left that the hunt was up again, and names of particular persons that were to be warned. Mr. Garlick and Mr. Ludlam were in the county, and these must be specially informed, since they were known, and Mr. Garlick in particular had already suffered banishment and returned again, so that there would be no hope for him if he were once more captured.

The four sat late that night; and Robin wondered more than ever, not only at the self-command of the girl, but at her extraordinary knowledge of Catholic affairs in the county. She calculated, almost without mistake, as was afterwards shown, not only which priests were in Derbyshire, but within a very few miles of where they would be and at what time: she showed, half-smiling, a kind of chart which she had drawn up, of the movements of the persons concerned, explaining the plan by which each priest (if he desired) might go on his own circuit where he would be most needed. She lamented, however, the fewness of the priests, and attributed to this the growing laxity of many families—living, it might be, in upland farms or in inaccessible places, where they could but very seldom have the visits of the priest and the strength of the sacraments.

Before midnight, therefore, the two travellers had complete directions for their journey, as well as papers to help their memories, as to where the news was to be left. And at last Mr. John stood up and stretched himself.

"We must go to bed," he said. "We must be booted by five."

Marjorie nodded to Alice, who stood up, saying she would show him where his bed had been prepared.

Robin lingered for a moment to finish his last notes.

"Mr. Alban," said Marjorie suddenly, without lifting her eyes from the paper on which she wrote.

"Yes?"

"You will take care tomorrow, will you not?" she said. "Mr. John is a little hot-headed. You must keep him to his route."

"I will do my best," said Robin, smiling.

She lifted her clear eyes to his without tremor or shame.

"My heart would be broken altogether if aught happened to you. I look to you as our Lord's chief soldier in this county."

"But—"

"That is so," she said. "I do not know any man who has been made perfect in so short a time. You hold us all in your hands."

CHAPTER II

I

It was in Mr. Bassett's house at Langley that the news of the attack on Padley reached the two travellers a month later, and it bore news in it that they little expected.

For it seemed that, entirely unexpectedly, there had arrived at Padley the following night no less than three of the FitzHerbert family, Mr. Anthony the seventh son, with two of his sisters, as well as Thomas FitzHerbert's wife, who rode with them, whether as a spy or not was never known. Further, Mr. Fenton himself, hearing of their coming, had ridden up from Tansley, and missed the messenger that Marjorie had sent out. They had not arrived till late, missing again, by a series of mischances, the scouts Marjorie had posted; and, on discovering their danger, had further discovered the house to be already watched. They judged it better, therefore, as Marjorie said in her letter, to feign unconsciousness of any charge against them, since there was no priest in the house who could incriminate them.

All this the travellers learned for the first time at Langley.

They had gone through into Staffordshire, as had been arranged, and there had moved about from house to house of Catholic friends without any trouble. It was when at last they thought it safe to be moving homewards, and had arrived at Langley, that they found Marjorie's letter awaiting them. It was addressed to Mr. John FitzHerbert and was brought by Robin's old servant, Dick Sampson.

"The assault was made," wrote Marjorie, "according to the arrangement. Mr. Columbell himself came with a score of men and surrounded the house very early, having set watchers all in place the evening before: they had made certain they should catch the master and at least a priest or two. But I have very heavy news, for all that; for there had come to the house after dark Mr. Anthony FitzHerbert, with two of his sisters, Mrs. Thomas FitzHerbert and Mr. Fenton himself, and they have carried the two gentlemen to the Derby gaol. I have had no word from Mr. Anthony, but I hear that he said that he was glad that his father was not taken, and that his own taking he puts down to his brother's account, as yourself, sir, also did. The men did no great harm in Padley beyond breaking a panel or two: they were too careful, I suppose, of what they think will be Mr. Topcliffe's property some day! And they found none of the hiding-holes, which is good news. The rest of the party they let go free again for the present.

"I have another piece of bad news, too—which is no more than what we had looked for: that Mr. Simpson at the Assizes was condemned to death, but has promised to go to church, so that his life is spared if he will do so. He is still in the gaol, however, where I pray God that Mr. Anthony may meet with him and bring him to a better mind; so that he has not yet denied our Lord, even though he has promised to do so.

"May God comfort and console you, Mr. FitzHerbert, for this news of Mr. Anthony that I send."

The letter ended with messages to the party, with instructions for their way of return if they should come within the next week; and with the explanation, given above, of the series of misfortunes by which any came to be at Padley that night, and how it was that they did not attempt to break out again.

The capture of Mr. Anthony was, indeed, one more blow to his father; but Robin was astonished how cheerfully he bore it; and said as much when they were alone in the garden.

The grey old man smiled, while his eyelids twitched a little.

"They say that when a man is whipped he feels no more after awhile. The former blows prepare him and dull his nerves for the later, which, I take it, is part of God's mercy. Well, Mr. Alban, my father has been in prison a great while now; my son Thomas is a traitor, and a sworn man of her Grace; I myself have been fined and persecuted till

I have had to sell land to pay the fines with. I have seen family after family fall from their faith and deny it. So I take it that I feel the joy that I have a son who is ready to suffer for it, more than the pain I have in thinking on his sufferings. The one may perhaps atone for the sins of the other, and yet help him to repentance."

LIFE here at Langley was more encouraging than the furtive existence necessary in the north of Derbyshire.

Mr. Bassett had a confident way with him that was like wine to fainting hearts, and he had every reason to be confident; since up to the present, beyond being forced to pay the usual fines for recusancy, he had scarcely been troubled at all, and lived in considerable prosperity, having even been sheriff of Stafford in virtue of his other estates at Blore. His house at Langley was a great one, standing in a park, and showing no signs of poverty; his servants were largely Catholic; he entertained priests and refugees of all kinds freely, although discreetly; and he laughed at the notion that the persecution could be of long endurance.

The very first night the travellers had come he had spoken with considerable freedom after supper.

"Look more hearty!" he cried. "The Spanish fleet will be here before summer to relieve us of all troubles, as of all heretics, too. Her Grace will have to turn her coat once more, I think, when that comes to pass."

Mr. John glanced at him doubtfully.

"First," he said, "no man knows whether it will come. And, next, I for one am not sure if I even wish for it."

Mr. Bassett laughed loudly.

"You will dance for joy!" he said. "And why do you not know whether you wish it to come?"

"I have no taste to be a Spanish subject."

"Why, nor have I! But the King of Spain will but sail away again when he has made terms against the privateers, whether they be those that ply on the high seas against men's bodies, or here in England against their souls. There will be no subjection of England beyond that."

Mr. John was silent.

"Why, I heard from Sir Thomas but a week ago, to ask for a little money to pay his fines with. He said that repayment should follow so soon as the fleet should come. Those were his very words."

"You sent the money, then?"

"Why, yes; I made sure that a servant should throw down a bag with ten pounds in it, into a bush, and that Brittle-bank—your brother's man—should see him do it! And lo! when we looked again, the bag was gone!"

He laughed again with open mouth. Certainly he was an inspiriting man with a loud bark of his own; but Robin imagined that he would not bite too cruelly for all that. But he saw another side of him presently.

"What was that matter of Mr. Sutton, the priest who was executed in Stafford last year?" asked Mr. John suddenly.

The face of the other changed as abruptly. His eyes became pinpoints under his grey eyebrows and his mouth tightened.

"What of him?" he said.

"It was reported that you might have stayed the execution, and would not. I did not believe a word of it."

"It is true," said Mr. Bassett sharply—"at least a portion of it."

"True?"

"Listen," cried the other suddenly, "and tell me what you would have done. Mr. Sutton was taken, and was banished, and came back again, as any worthy priest would do. Then he was taken again, and condemned. I did my utmost to save him, but I could not. Then, as I would never have any part in the death of a priest for his religion, another was appointed to carry the execution through. Three days before news was brought to me by a private hand that Mr. Sutton had promised to give the names of priests whom he knew, and of houses where he had said Mass, and I know not what else; and it was said to me that I might on this account stay the execution until he had told all that he could. Now I knew that I could not save his life altogether; that was forfeited and there could be no forgiveness. All that I might do was to respite him for a little—and for what? That he might damn his own soul eternally and bring a great number of good men into trouble and peril of death for themselves. I sent the messenger away again, and said that I would listen to no such tales. And Mr. Sutton died like a good priest three days after, repenting, I doubt not, bitterly, of the weakness into which he had fallen. Now, sir, what would you have done in my place?"

He wagged his head fiercely from side to side.

Mr. John put his hand over his eyes and nodded without speaking. Robin sat silent; it was not only for priests, it seemed, that life presented a tangle.

II

THE evening before the two left for the north again, Mr. Bassett took them both into his own study. It was a little room opening out of his bedroom, and was more full of books than Robin had ever seen, except in the library at Rheims, in any room in the world. A shelf ran round the room, high on the wall, and was piled with manuscripts to the ceiling. Beneath, the book-shelves that ran nearly round the room were packed with volumes, and a number more lay on the table and even in the corners.

"This is my own privy chamber," said Mr. Bassett to the priest. "My other friends have seen it many a time, but I thought I would show it to your Reverence, too."

Robin looked round him in wonder: he had no idea that his host was a man of such learning.

"All the books are ranged in their proper places," went on the other. "I could put my finger on any of them blindfold. But this is the shelf I wished you to see."

He took him to one that was behind the door, holding up the candle that he might see. The shelf had a box or two on it, besides books, and these he opened and set on the table. Robin looked in, as he was told, but could understand nothing that he saw: in one was a round ball of crystal on a little gold stand, wrapped round in velvet; in another some kind of a machine with wheels; in a third, some dried substances, as of herbs, tied together with silk. He inspected them gravely, but was not invited to touch them. Then his host touched him on the breast with one finger, and recoiled, smiling.

"This is my magic," he said. "John here does not like it; neither did poor Mr. Fenton when he was here; but I hold there is no harm in such things if one does but observe caution."

"What do you do with them, sir?" inquired the priest curiously, for he was not sure whether the man was serious.

"Well, sir, I hold that God has written His will in the stars, and in the burning of herbs, and in the shining of the sun, and such things. There is no black magic here. But, just as we read in the sky at morning, if it be red or yellow, whether it will be foul or fair, so I hold that God has written other secrets of His in other things; and that by observing them and judging rightly we may guess what He has in store. I knew that a prince was to die last year before ever it happened, I knew that a fleet of ships will come to England this year, before ever an anchor is weighed. And I would have you notice that here are Mr. FitzHerbert and your Reverence, too, fleeing for your lives; and here sit I safe at home; and all, as I hold, because I have been able to observe by my magic what is to come to pass." Then, suddenly, an intense curiosity overcame Robin.

His life was a strange and perilous one; he carried it in his hand every day. In the morning he could not be sure but that he would be fleeing before evening. As he fell asleep, he could not be sure that he would not be awakened, to a new dream. He had long ago conquered those moods of terror which, in spite of his courage, had come down on him sometimes, in some lonely farm, perhaps, where flight would be impossible—or, in what was far more dangerous, in some crowded inn where every movement was known—these had passed, he thought, never to come back.

But in that little book-lined room, with these curious things in boxes on the table, and his merry host peering at him gravely, and the still evening outside; with the knowledge that tomorrow he was to ride back to his own country, whence he had fled for fear of his life, six weeks ago; leaving the security of this ex-sheriff's house for the perils of the Peak and all that suspected region from which even now, probably, the pursuit had not altogether died away—here a sudden intense desire to know what the future might hold overcame him.

"Tell me, sir," he said. "You have told Mr. FitzHerbert's fortune, you say, as well as others. Have you told mine since I have been here?"

There was a moment's silence. Mr. John was silent, with his back turned. Robin looked up at his host, wondering why he did not answer. Then Mr. Bassett took up the candle.

"Come," he said, "we have been here long enough."

CHAPTER III

I

"THERE will be a company of us tonight," said Mr. John to the two priests, as he helped them to dismount. "Mr. Alban has sent his man forward from Derby to say that he will be here before night."

"Mr. Ludlam and I are together for once," said Mr. Gar-lick. "We must separate again tomorrow, he is for the north again, he tells me. There has been no more trouble?"

"Not a word of it. They were beaten last time and will not try again, I think, for the present. You heard of the attempt at Candlemas, then?"

IT had been a quiet time enough ever since Lent, throughout the whole county; and it seemed as if the heat of the assault had cooled for want of success. And, indeed, it was time that the Catholics should have a little breathing-space. Things had been very bad with them—the growing luke-warmness of families that seldom saw a priest; the blows struck at the FitzHerbert family; and, above all, the defection of Mr. Thomas—all these things had brought the hearts of the faithful very low. Mr. John himself had had an untroubled time since his return a little before Easter; but he had taken the precaution not to remain too long at Padley at one time.

It was only last night, indeed, that the master had returned, in time to meet the two priests who had asked for shelter for a day or two. There were a couple of rooms kept vacant always for "men of God"; and all priests who came were instructed, of course (in case of necessity), as to the hiding-holes that Mr. Owen had contrived a few years before. Never, however, had there been any use made of them.

It was a hot July afternoon when the two priests were met today by Mr. John outside the arched gate that ran between the hall and the buttery.

They were plain men, these two; though Mr. Garlick had been educated at Oxford. In appearance he was a breezy sunburnt man, with very little of the clerk about him, and devoted to outdoor sports. He spoke in a loud voice with a strong Derbyshire accent, which he had never lost and now deliberately used. Mr. Ludlam looked far more of the priest: he was a clean-shaven man, of middle-age, with hair turning to grey on his temples, and with a very pleasant disarming smile; he spoke very little, but listened with an interested and attentive air. Both were, of course, dressed in the usual riding costume of gentlemen, and used good horses.

"I am more at peace, gentlemen," said Mr. John, "than I have been for the past five years. My son is in gaol yet; and I am proud that he should be there, since my eldest son—" (he broke off a moment). "And I think the worst of the storm is over. Her Grace is busying herself with other matters."

"You mean the Spanish fleet, sir?" said Mr. Garlick.

He nodded.

"It is not that I look for final deliverance from Spain," he said. "I have no wish to be aught but an Englishman, as I said to Mr. Bassett a while ago. But I think the fleet will distract her Grace for a while; and it may very well mean that we have better treatment hereafter."

"What news is there, sir?"

"I hear that the Londoners buzz continually with false alarms. It was thought that the fleet might arrive on any day; but I understand that the fishing-boats say that nothing has yet been seen. By the end of the month, I daresay, we shall have news."

So they talked pleasantly in the shade till the shadows began to lengthen. They were far enough here from the sea-coast to feel somewhat detached from the excitement that was beginning to seethe in the south. A beacon or two had been piled on the hills, by order of the authorities, to pass on the news when it should come;

a few lads had disappeared from the countryside to drill in Derby marketplace; but except for these things, all was very much as it had been from the beginning. The expected catastrophe meant little more to such folk than the coming of the Judgment Day—certain, but infinitely remote from the grasp of the imagination.

THE three were talking of Robin as they came down towards the house for supper, and, as they turned the corner, he himself was at that moment dismounting.

He looked surprisingly cool and well-trimmed, considering his ride up the hot valley. He had taken his journey easily, he said, as he had had a long day yesterday.

"And I made a round to pay a visit to Mistress Manners," he said. "I found her a-bed when I got there; and Mrs. Alice says she will not be at Mass tomorrow. She stood too long in the sun yesterday, at the carrying of the hay; it is no more than that."

"Mistress Manners is a marvel to me," said Garlick, as they went towards the house. "Neither wife nor nun. And she rules her house like a man; and she knows if a priest lift his little finger in Derby. She sent me my whole itinerary for this last circuit of mine; and every point fell out as she said."

ROBIN thought that he had seldom had so pleasant a supper as on that night. The windows of the low hall where he had dined so often as a boy were flung wide to catch the scented evening air. The evening was as still as night, except for the faint peaceful country sounds that came up from the valley below—the song of a lad riding home; the barking of a dog; the bleat of sheep—all minute and delicate, as unperceived, yet as effective, as a rich fabric on which a design is woven. It seemed to him as he listened to the talk and he ate the plain, good food and drank the country drink, that, in spite of all, his lot was cast in very sweet places. He found himself in one of those moods that visit all men sometimes, when the world appears, after all, a homely and a genial place; when the simplest things are the best; when no excitement can compare with the gentle happiness of a tired body that is in the act of refreshment, or of a driven mind that is finding its relaxation. At least, he said to himself, he would enjoy this night and the next day and the night after, with all his heart.

The four found themselves so much at ease here, that the dessert was brought in to them where they sat; and it was then that the first unhappy word was spoken.

"Mr. Simpson!" said Garlick suddenly. "Is there any more news of him?"

Mr. John shook his head.

"He has not yet been to church, thank God!" he said. "So much I know for certain. But he has promised to go."

"Why is he not yet gone? He promised a great while ago."

"I hear he has been sick. Derby gaol is a pestiferous place. They are waiting, I suppose, till he is well enough to go publicly, that all the world may be advertised of it!"

Mr. Garlick gave a bursting sigh.

"I cannot understand it at all," he said. "There has never been so zealous a priest. I have ridden with him again and again before I was a priest. He was always quiet; but I took him to be one of those stout-hearted souls that need never brag. Why, it was here that we heard him tell of Mr. Nelson's death!"

Mr. John threw out his hands.

"These prisons are devilish," he said; "they wear a man out as the rack can never do. Why, see my son!" he cried. "Oh! I can speak of him if I am but moved enough! It was that same Derby gaol that wore him out too! It is the darkness, and the ill food, and the stenches and the misery; A man's heart fails him there, who could face a thousand deaths in the sunlight. Man after man has fallen there—both in Derby, and in London and in all the prisons. If it were the rack and the rope only, England would be Catholic yet, I think."

The old man's face blazed with indignation; it was not often that he so spoke out his mind. It was very easy to see that he had thought continually of his son's fall.

"Mistress Manners has told me the very same thing," said Robin. "She visited Mr. Thomas in gaol once at least. She said that her heart failed her altogether there."

Mr. Ludlam smiled.

"I suppose it is so," he said gently, "since you say so. But I think it would not be so with me. The rack and the rope, rather, are what would shake me to the roots, unless God His Grace prevailed more than it ever yet has with me."

He smiled again.

Robin shook his head sharply.

"As for me—" he said grimly, with tight lips.

II

It was within an hour of dawn that the first Mass was said next morning by Mr. Robert Alban.

The chapel was decked out as they seldom dared to deck it in those days; but the failure of the last attempt on this place, and the peace that had followed, made them bold.

An extraordinary sweetness and peace seemed in the place both to the senses and the soul of the young priest as he went up to the altar to vest. Confessions had been heard last night; and, as he turned, in the absolute stillness of the morning, and saw, beneath those carved angels that still today lean from the beams of the roof, the whole little space already filled with farm-lads, many of whom were to approach the altar presently, and the grey head of their master kneeling on the floor to answer the Mass, it appeared to him as if the promise of last night were reversed, and that it was, after all, earth rather than heaven that proclaimed the peace and the glory of God....

Robin served the second Mass himself, said by Mr. Garlick, and made his thanksgiving as well as he could meanwhile; but he found what appeared to him at the time many distractions, in watching the tanned face and hands of the man who was so utterly a countryman for nine-tenths of his life, and so utterly a priest for the rest. His very sturdiness and breeziness made his reverence the more evident and pathetic: he read the Mass rapidly, in a low voice, harshened by shouting in the open air over his sports, made his gestures abruptly, and yet did the whole with an extraordinary attention. After the communion, when he turned for the wine and water, his face, as so often with rude folk in a great emotion, browned as it was with wind and sun, seemed lighted from within; he seemed etherealized, yet with his virility all alive in him. A phrase, wholly inapplicable in its first sense, came irresistibly to the younger priest's mind as he waited on him. "When the strong man, armed, keepeth his house, his goods are in peace."

Robin heard the third Mass, said by Mr. Ludlam, from a corner near the door; and this one, too, was a fresh experience. The former priest had resembled a strong man subdued by grace; the second, a weak man ennobled by it. Mr. Ludlam was a delicate soul, smiling often, as has been said, and speaking little—"a mild man," said the countryfolk. Yet, at the altar there was no weakness in him; he was as a keen, sharp blade, fitted as a heavy knife cannot be, for fine and peculiar work. His father had been a yeoman, as had the other's; yet there must have been some unusual strain of blood in him, so deft and gentle he was—more at his ease here at God's Table than at the table of any man.... So he, too, finished his Mass, and began to unvest....

Then, with a noise as brutal as a blasphemy, there came a thunder of footsteps on the stairs; and a man burst into the room, with glaring eyes and rough gestures.

"There is a company of men coming up from the valley," he cried; "and another over the moor.... And it is my lord Shrewsbury's livery."

III

IN an instant all was in confusion; and the peace had fled. Mr. John was gone; and his voice could be heard on the open stairs outside speaking rapidly in sharp, low whispers to the men gathered beneath; and, meanwhile, three or four servants, two men and a couple of maids, previously drilled in their duties, were at the altar, on which Mr. Ludlam had but that moment laid down his amice. The three priests stood together waiting, fearing to hinder or to add to the bustle. A low wailing rose from outside the door; and Robin looked from it to see if there were anything he could do. But it was only a little country servant crouching on the tiny landing that united the two sets of stairs from the court, with her apron over her head: she must have been in the partitioned west end of the chapel to hear the Mass. He said a word to her; and the next instant was pushed aside, as a man tore by bearing a great bundle of stuffs—vestments and the altar cloths. When he turned again, the chapel was become a common room once more: the chest stood bare, with a great bowl of flowers on it; the candlesticks were gone; and the maid was sweeping up the herbs.

"Come, gentlemen," said a sharp voice at the door, "there is no time to lose."

He went out with the two others behind, and followed Mr. John downstairs. Already the party of servants was dispersed to their stations; two or three to keep the doors, no doubt, and the rest back to kitchen work and the like, to give the impression that all was as usual.

The four went straight down into the hall, to find it empty, except for one man who stood by the fireplace. But a surprising change had taken place here. Instead of the solemn panelling, with the carved shield that covered the wall over the hearth, there was a great doorway opened, through which showed, not the bricks of the chimney-breast, but a black space large enough to admit a man.

"See here," said Mr. John, "there is room for two here, but no more. There is room for a third in another little chamber upstairs that is nearly joined on to this: but it is not so good. Now, gentlemen—"

"This is the safer of the two?" asked Robin abruptly.

"I think it to be so. Make haste, gentlemen."

Robin wheeled on the others. He said that there was no time to argue in.

"See!" he said. "I have not yet been taken at all. Mr. Garlick has been taken; and Mr. Ludlam has had a warning. There is no question that you must be here."

"I utterly refuse—" began Garlick.

Robin went to the door in three strides, and was out of it. He closed the door behind him and ran upstairs. As he reached the head his eye caught a glint of sunlight on some metal far up on the moor beyond the belt of trees. He did not turn his head again; he went straight in and waited.

Presently he heard steps coming up, and Mr. John appeared smiling and out of breath.

"I have them in," he said, "by promising that there was no great difference after all; and that there was no time. Now, sir—"And he went towards the wall at which, long ago, Mr. Owen had worked so hard.

"And yourself, sir?" asked Robin, as once more an innocent piece of panelling moved outwards under Mr. John's hand.

"I'll see to that; but not until you are in—"

"But—"

The old man's face blazed suddenly up.

"Obey me, if you please. I am the master here. I tell you I have a very good place."

There was no more to be said. Robin advanced to the opening, and sat down to slide himself in. It was a little door about two feet square, with a hole beneath it.

"Drop gently, Mr. Alban," whispered the voice in his ear. "The altar vessels are at the bottom, with the crucifix, on some soft stuff.... That is it. Slide in and let yourself slip. There is some food and drink there, too."

Robin did so. The floor of the little chamber was about five feet down, and he could feel woodwork on all three sides of him.

"When the door is closed," said the voice from the daylight, "push a pair of bolts on right and left till they go home. Tap upon the shutter when it is done."

The light vanished, and Robin was aware of a faint smell of smoke. Then he remembered that he had noticed a newly lit fire on the hearth of the hall.... He found the bolts, pushed them, and tapped lightly three times. He heard a hand push on the shutter to see that all was secure, and then footsteps go away over the floor on a level with his chin.

Then he remembered that he must be in the same chamber with his two fellow-priests, separated from them by the flooring on which he stood. He rapped gently with his foot twice. Two soft taps came back. Silence followed.

IV

HE was in complete and utter darkness. There was not a crack anywhere in the woodwork (so perfect had been the young carpenter's handiwork) by which even a glimmer of light could enter. A while ago he had been in the early morning sunlight; now he might be in the grave.

For a while his emotions and his thoughts raced one another, tumbling in inextricable confusion; and they were all emotions and thoughts of the present: intense little visions of the men closing round the house, cutting off escape from the valley on the one side and from the wild upland country on the other; questions as to where Mr. John would hide himself; minute sensible impressions of the smoky flavour of the air, the unplaned woodwork, the soft stuffs beneath his feet. Then they began to extend themselves wider, all with that rapid unjarring swiftness: he foresaw the bursting in of his stronghold; the footsteps within three inches of his head; the crash as the board was kicked in: then the capture; the ride to Derby, bound on a horse; the gaol; the questioning; the faces of my lord Shrewsbury and the magistrates...and the end....

There were moments when the sweat ran down his face, when he bit his lips in agony, and nearly moaned aloud. There were others in which he abandoned himself to Christ crucified; placed himself in Everlasting Hands that were mighty enough to pluck him not only out of this snare, but from the very hands that would hold him so soon; Hands that could lift him from the rack and scaffold and set him a free man among his hills again: yet that had not done so with a score of others whom he knew. He thought of these, and of the girl who had done so much to save them all, who was now saved herself by sickness, a mile or two away, from these hideous straits. Then he dragged out Mr. Maine's beads and began to recite the "Mysteries."

THERE broke in suddenly the first exterior sign that the hunters were on them—a muffled hammering far beneath his feet. There were pauses; then voices carried up from the archway nearly beneath through the hollowed walls; then hammering again; but all was heard as through wool. Even while he followed the sounds, he understood why my lord Shrewsbury had made this assault so suddenly, after months of peace.... He perceived the hand of Thomas FitzHerbert, too, in the precision with which the attack had been made, and the certain information he must have given that priests would be in Padley that morning.

There were noises that he could not interpret—vague tramplings from a direction which he could not tell; voices that shouted; the sound of metal on stone.

He did interpret rightly, however, the sudden tumult as the gate was unbarred at last, and the shrill screaming of a woman as the company poured through into the house; the clamour of voices from beneath as the hall below was filled with men; the battering that began almost immediately; and, finally, the rush of shod feet up the outside staircases, one of which led straight into the chapel itself. Then, indeed, his heart seemed to spring upwards into his throat, and to beat there, as loud as knocking, so loud that it appeared to him that all the house must hear it.

Yet it was still some minutes before the climax came to him. He was still standing there, listening to voices talking, it seemed, almost in his ears, yet whose words he could not hear; the vibration of feet that shook the solid joist against which he had leaned his head, with closed eyes; the brush of a cloak once, like a whisper, against the very panel that shut him in.

The climax came in a sudden thump of a pike foot within a yard of his head, so imminent, that for an instant he thought it was at his own panel. There followed a splintering sound of a pike-head in the same place. He understood. They were sounding on the woodwork and piercing all that rang hollow.... His turn, then, would come immediately.

Talking voices followed the crash; then silence; then the vibration of feet once more. The strain grew unbearable; his fingers twisted tight in his rosary, lifted themselves once or twice from the floor edge on which they were gripped, to tear back the bolts and declare himself. It seemed to him in those instants a thousand times better to come out of his own will, rather than to be poked and dragged from his hole like a badger. In the very midst of such imaginings there came a thumping blow within three inches of his face, and then silence. He leaned back desperately to avoid the pike-thrust that must follow, with his eyes screwed tight and his lips mumbling. He waited...and then, as he waited, he drew an irrepressible hissing breath of terror, for beneath the soft padding under his feet he could feel movements; blow follow blow, from the same direction, and last a great clamour of voices all shouting together.

Feet ran across the floor on which his hands were gripped again, and down the stairs. He perceived two things: the chapel was empty again, and the priests below had been found.

V

HE could follow every step of the drama after that, for he appeared to himself now as a mere witness, without personal part in it.

First, there were voices below him, so clear and close that he could distinguish the intonation, and who it was that spoke, though the words were inaudible.

It was Mr. Garlick who first spoke—a sentence of a dozen words, it might be, consenting, no doubt, to come out without being dragged; congratulating, perhaps (as the manner was), the searchers on their success. A murmur of answer came back, and then one sharp, peevish voice by itself. Again Mr. Garlick spoke, and there followed the shuffling of movements for a long while; and then, so far as the little chamber was concerned, empty silence. But from the hall rose up a steady murmur of talk once more....

Again Robin's heart leaped in him, for there came the rattle of a pike-end immediately below his feet. They were searching the little chamber beneath, from the level of the hall, to see if it were empty. The pike was presently withdrawn.

For a long while the talking went on. So far as the rest of the house was concerned, the hidden man could tell nothing, or whether Mr. John were taken, or whether the search were given up. He could not even fix his mind on the point; he was constructing for himself, furiously and intently, the scene he imagined in the hall below; he thought he saw the two priests barred in behind the high table; my lord Shrewsbury in the one great chair in the midst of the room; Mr. Columbell, perhaps, or Mr. John Manners talking in his ear; the men on guard over the priests and beside the door; and another, maybe, standing by the hearth.

He was so intent on this that he thought of little else; though still, on a strange background of another consciousness, moved scenes and ideas such as he had had at the beginning. And he was torn from this contemplation with the suddenness of a blow, by a voice speaking, it seemed, within a foot of his head.

"Well, we have those rats, at any rate."

(He perceived instantly what had happened. The men were back again in the chapel, and he had not heard them come. He supposed that he could hear the words now because of the breaking of the panel next to his own.)

"Ralph said he was sure of the other one, too," said a second voice.

"Which was that one?"

"The fellow that was at Fotheringay."

(Robin clenched his teeth like iron.)

"Well, he is not here."

There was silence.

"I have sounded that side," said the first voice sharply.

"Well, but—"

"I tell you I have sounded it. There is no time to be lost. My lord—"

"Hark!" said the second voice. "There is my lord's man—"

There followed a movement of feet towards the door, as it seemed to the priest.

He could hear the first man grumbling to himself, and beating listlessly on the walls somewhere. Then a voice called something unintelligible from the direction of the stairs; the beating ceased, and footsteps went across the floor again into silence.

VI

HE was dazed and blinded by the light when, after infinite hours, he drew the bolts and slid the panel open.

He had lost all idea of time utterly: he did not know whether he should find that night had come, or that the next day had dawned. He had waited there, period after period; he marked one of them by eating food that had no taste and drinking liquid that stung his throat but did not affect his palate; he had marked another by saying compline to himself in a whisper.

At a later period he had heard the horses being brought round the house; heard plainly the jingle of the bits and a sneeze or two. This had been followed by long interminable talking, muffled and indistinguishable, that came up to him from some unknown direction. Voices changed curiously in loudness and articulation as the speakers moved about.

At a later period a loud trampling had begun again, plainly from the hall: he had interpreted this to mean that the prisoners were being removed out of doors; and he had been confirmed in this by hearing immediately afterwards again the stamping of horses and the creaking of leather.

Again there had been a pause, broken suddenly by loud women's wailing. And at last the noise of horses moving off; the noise grew less; a man ran suddenly through the archway and out again, and, little by little, complete silence once more.

Yet he had not dared to move. It was the custom, he knew,

sometimes to leave three or four men on guard for a day or two after such an assault, in the hope of starving out any hidden fugitives that might still be left. So he waited again—period after period; he dozed a little for weariness, propped against the narrow walls of his hiding-hole; woke; felt again for food and found he had eaten it all… dozed again.

Then he had started up suddenly, for without any further warning there had come a tiny indeterminate tapping against his panel. He held his breath and listened. It came again. Then fearlessly he drew back the bolts, slid the panel open and shut his eyes, dazzled by the light.

He crawled out at last, spent and dusty. There was looking at him only the little red-eyed maid whom he had tried to comfort at some far-off hour in his life. Her face was all contorted with weeping, and she had a great smear of dust across it.

"What time is it?" he said.

"It…it is after two o'clock," she whispered.

"They have all gone?"

She nodded, speechless.

"Whom have they taken?"

"Mr. FitzHerbert…the priests…the servants."

"Mr. FitzHerbert? They found him, then?"

She stared at him with the dull incapacity to understand why he did not know all that she had seen.

"Where did they find him?" he repeated sharply. "The master…he opened the door to them himself." Her face writhed itself again into grotesque lines, and she broke out into shrill wailing and weeping.

CHAPTER IV

I

MARJORIE was still in bed when the news was brought by her friend. She did not move or speak when Mistress Alice said shortly that Mr. FitzHerbert had been taken with ten of his servants and two priests.

"You understand, my dear. They have ridden away to Derby, all of them together. But they may come back here suddenly."

Marjorie nodded.

"Mr. Garlick and Mr. Ludlam were in the chimney-hole of the hall," whispered Mistress Alice, glancing fearfully behind her.

Marjorie lay back again on her pillows.

"And what of Mr. Alban?" she asked.

"Mr. Alban was upstairs. They missed him. He is coming here after dark, the maid says."

AN hour after supper-time the priest came quietly upstairs to the parlour. He showed no signs of his experience, except perhaps by a certain brightness in his eyes and an extreme self-repression of manner. Marjorie was up to meet him, and had in her hands a paper. She hardly spoke a single expression of relief at his safety. She was as quiet and business-like as ever.

"You must lie here tonight," she said. "Janet has your room ready. At one o'clock in the morning you must ride: here is a map of your journey. They may come back suddenly. At the place I have marked here with red there is a shepherd's hut; you cannot miss it if you follow the track I have marked. There will be meat and drink there. At night the shepherd will come from the westwards; he is called David, and you may trust him. You must lie there two weeks at least."

"I must have news of the other priests," he said.

Marjorie bowed her head.

"I will send a letter to you by Dick Sampson at the end of two weeks. Until that I can promise nothing. They may have spies round the house by this time tomorrow, or even earlier. And I will send in that letter any news I can get from Derby."

"How shall I find my way?" asked Robin.

"Until it is light you will be on ground that you know." She flushed slightly. "Do you remember the hawking, that time after Christmas? It is all across that ground. When daylight comes you can follow this map." She named one or two landmarks, pointing to them on the map.

"You must have no lantern."

They talked a few minutes longer as to the way he must go and the provision that would be ready for him. He must take no Mass requisites with him. David had made that a condition. Then Robin suddenly changed the subject.

"Had my father any hand in this affair at Padley?"

"I am certain he had not."

"They will execute Mr. Garlick and Mr. Ludlam, will they not?"

She bowed her head in assent.

"The Summer Assizes open on the eighteenth," she said, "There is no doubt as to how all will go."

Robin rose.

"It is time I were in bed," he said, "if I must ride at one."

The two women knelt for his blessing.

At one o'clock Marjorie heard the horse brought round. She stepped softly to the window, knowing herself to be invisible, and peeped out.

All was as she had ordered. There was no light of any kind: she could make out but dimly in the summer darkness the two figures of horse and groom. As she looked, a third figure appeared beneath; but there was no word spoken that she could hear. This third figure mounted. She caught her breath as she heard the horse scurry a little with freshness, since every sound seemed full of peril. Then the mounted figure faded one way into the dark, and the groom another.

II

It was two weeks to the day that Robin received his letter. He had never before been so long in utter solitude; for the visits of David did not break it; and, for other men, he saw none except a hog-herd or two in the distance once or twice. The shepherd came but once a day, carrying a great jug and a parcel of food, and set them down without the hut; he seemed to avoid even looking within; but merely took the empty jug of the day before and went away again. He was an old, bent man, with a face like a limestone cliff, grey and weather-beaten; he lived half the year up here in the wild Peak country, caring for a few sheep, and going down to the village not more than once or twice a week. There was a little spring welling up in a hollow not fifty yards away from the hut, which itself stood in a deep, natural rift among the high hills, so that men might search for it a lifetime and not come across it.

Robin's daily round was very simple. He had leave to make a fire by day, but he must extinguish it at night lest its glow should be seen, so he began his morning by mixing a little oatmeal, and then preparing his dinner. About noon, so near as he could judge by the sun, he dined; sometimes off a partridge or rabbit; on Fridays off half a dozen tiny trout; and set aside part of the cold food for supper; he had one good loaf of nearly black bread every day, and the single jug of small beer.

The greater part of the day he spent within the hut, for safety's sake, sleeping a little, and thinking a good deal. He had no books with him; even his breviary had been forbidden, since David, as a shrewd man, had made conditions, first that he should not have to speak with any refugee, second, that if the man were a priest he should have nothing about him that could prove him to be so. Mr. Maine's beads, only, had been permitted, on condition that they were hidden always beneath a stone outside the hut.

After nightfall Robin went out to attend to his horse that was tethered in the next ravine, over a crag; to shift his peg and bring him a good armful of cut grass and a bucket of water. (The saddle and bridle were hidden beneath a couple of great stones that leaned together not far away.) After doing what was necessary for his horse, he went to draw water for himself; and then took his exercise, avoiding carefully, according to instructions, every possible skyline. And it was then, for the most part, that he did his clear thinking.... He tried to fancy himself in a fortnight's retreat, such as he had had at Rheims before his reception of orders.

III

THE evening of the twenty-fifth of July closed in stormy; and Robin, in an old cloak he had found placed in the hut for his own use, made haste to attend to what was necessary, and hurried back as quickly as he could. He sat a while, listening to the thresh of the rain and the cry of the wind; for up here in the high land the full storm broke on him. (The hut was wattled of osiers and clay, and kept out the wet tolerably well.)

He could see nothing from the door of his hut except the dim outline of the nearer crag thirty or forty yards off; and he went presently to bed.

He awoke suddenly, wide awake—as is easy for a man who is sleeping in continual expectation of an alarm—at the flash of light in his eyes. But he was at once reassured by Dick's voice.

"I have come, sir; and I have brought the mistress' letter."

Robin sat up and took the packet. He saw now that the man carried a little lantern with a slide over it that allowed only a thin funnel of light to escape that could be shut off in an instant.

"All well, Dick? I did not hear you coming."

"The storm's too loud, sir."

"All well?"

"Mistress Manners thinks you had best stay here a week longer, sir."

"And...and the news?"

"It is all in the letter, sir."

Robin looked for the inscription, but there was none. Then he broke the two seals, opened the paper and began to read. For the next five minutes there was no sound, except the thresh of the rain and the cry of the wind. The letter ran as follows:

"Three more have glorified God today by a good confession—Mr. Garlick, Mr. Ludlam, and Mr. Simpson. That is the summary. The tale in detail has been brought to me today by an eye-witness.

"The trial went as all thought it would. There was never the least question of it; for not only were the two priests taken with signs of their calling upon them, but both of them had been in the hands of the magistrates before. There was no shrinking nor fear showed of any kind. But the chief marvel was that these two priests met with Mr. Simpson in the gaol; they put them together in one room, I think, hoping that Mr. Simpson would prevail upon them to do as he had promised to do; but, by the grace of God, it was all the other way, and it was they who prevailed upon Mr. Simpson to confess himself again openly as a Catholic. This greatly enraged my lord Shrewsbury and the rest; so that there was less hope than ever of any respite, and sentence was passed upon them all together, Mr. Simpson showing, at the reading of it, as much courage as any. This was all done two days ago at the Assizes; and it was today that the sentence was carried out.

"They were all three drawn on hurdles together to the open space by St. Mary's Bridge, where all was prepared, with gallows and cauldron and butchering block; and a great company went after them. I have not heard that they spoke much on the way, except that a friend of Mr. Garlick's cried out to him to remember that they had often shot off together on the moors; to which Mr. Garlick made answer merrily that it was true; but that 'I am now to shoot off such a shot as I never shot in all my life.' He was merry at the trial, too, I hear; and said that 'he was not come to seduce men, but rather to induce them to the Catholic religion, that to this end he had come to the country, and for this that he would work so long as he lived.' And this he did on the scaffold, speaking to the crowd about him of the salvation of their souls, and casting papers, which he had written in prison, in proof of the Catholic faith.

"Mr. Garlick went up the ladder first, kissing and embracing it as the instrument of his death, and to encourage Mr. Simpson, as it was thought, since some said he showed signs of timorousness again when he came to the place. But he showed none when his turn came, but rather exhibited the same courage as them both, Mr. Ludlam stood by smiling while all was done; and smiling still when his turn came. His last words were, *Venite benedicti Dei*; and this he said, seeming to see a vision of angels come to bear his soul away.

"They were cut down, all three of them, before they were dead; and the butchery done on them according to sentence; yet none of them cried out or made the least sound; and their heads and quarters were set up immediately afterwards on poles in diverse places of Derby; some of them above the house that stands on the bridge and others on the bridge itself. But these, I hear, will not be there long.

"So these three have kept the faith and finished their course with joy. *Laus Deo*. Mr. John is in ward, for harbouring of the priests; but nothing has been done to him yet.

"As for your reverence, I am of opinion that you had best wait another week where you are. There has been a man or two seen hereabouts whom none knew, as well as at Padley. It has been certified, too, that Mr. Thomas was at the root of it all, that he gave the information that Mr. John and at least a priest or two would be at Padley at that time, though no man knows how he knew it, unless through servants' talk; and since Mr. Thomas knows your reverence, it will be better to be hid for a little longer. So, if you will, in a week from now, I will send Dick once again to tell you if all be well. I look for no letter back for this since you have nothing to write with in the hut, as I know; but Dick will tell me how you do; as well as anything you may choose to say to him.

"I ask your reverence's blessing again. I do not forget your reverence in my poor prayers."

AND so it ended, without signature—for safety's sake.

An hour later, with the first coming of the dawn, the storm ceased. (It was the same storm, if he had only known it, that had blown upon the Spanish Fleet at sea and driven it towards destruction. But of this he knew nothing.) He had not slept since Dick had gone, but had lain on his back on the turfed and blanketed bed in the corner, his hands clasped behind his head, thinking, thinking, and re-thinking all that he had read just now. He had known it must happen; but there seemed to him all the difference in the world between an event and its mere certainty. It had been two of the men whom he had seen say Mass after himself—the ruddy-faced, breezy countryman, yet anointed with the sealing oil, and the gentle, studious, smiling man who had been no less vigorous than his friend....

But there was one thing he had not known, and that, the recovery of the faint heart which they had inspirited. And then, in an instant he remembered how he had seen the three, years ago, against the sunset, as he rode with Anthony....

His mind was full of the strange memory as he came out at last, when the black darkness began to fade to grey, and the noise of the rain on the roof had ceased, and the wind had fallen.

It was a view of extraordinary solemnity that he looked on, as he stood leaning against the rough door-post. The night was still stronger than day; overhead it was as black as ever, and stars shone in it through the dissolving clouds that were passing at last. But, immediately over the grim, serrated edge of the crag that faced him to the east, a faint and tender light was beginning to burn, so faint that as yet it seemed an absence of black rather than as of a colour itself; and in the midst of it, like a crumb of diamond, shone a single dying star. The air was cold and fresh and marvellously scented, after the rain, with the clean smell of strong turf and rushes. It was as different from the peace he had had at Padley as water is different from wine; yet it was peace, too, a confident and expectant peace that precedes the battle, rather than the rest which follows it....

CHAPTER V

I

IT was the sixth night after Dick Sampson had come back with news of Mr. Alban; and he had already received instructions as to how he was to go twenty-four hours later. He was to walk, as before, starting after dark, not carrying a letter this time, after all, in spite of the news that he might have taken with him; for the priest would be back before morning and could hear it all then at his ease.

Every possible cause of alarm had gone; and Marjorie, for the first time for three weeks, felt very nearly as content as a year ago. Not one more doubtful visitor had appeared anywhere; and now she thought herself mistaken even about those solitary figures she had suspected before. After all, they had only been a couple of men, whose faces her servants did not know, who had gone past on the track beneath the house; one mounted, and the other on foot.

There had been something of a reaction, too, in Derby. The deaths of the three priests had made an impression; there was no doubt of that. Mr. Biddell had written her a letter on the point, saying that the blood of those martyrs might well be the peace, if it might not be the seed, of the Church in the district. Men openly said in the taverns, he reported, that it was hard that any should die for religion merely; politics were one matter and religion another. Yet the deaths had dismayed the simple Catholics, too, for the present; and at Hathersage church, scarcely ten miles away, above two hundred came to the Protestant sermon preached before my lord Shrewsbury on the first Sunday after.

The news of the Armada, too, had distracted men's minds wonderfully in another direction. News had come in already, she was informed, of an engagement or two in the English Channel, all in favour of its defenders. More than that was not known. But the beacons had blazed; and the marketplace of Derby had echoed with the tramp of the train-bands; and it was not likely that at such a time the attention of the magistrates would be given to anything else.

So her plans were laid. Mr. Alban was to come here for three or four days; be provided with a complete change of clothes (all of which she had ready); shave off his beard; and then set out again for the border. He had best go to Staffordshire, she thought; for a month or two, before beginning once more in his own county.

SHE went to bed that night, happy enough, in spite of the cause, which she loved so much, seeming to fail everywhere. It was true that, under this last catastrophe, great numbers had succumbed; but she hoped that this would be but for a time. Let but a few more priests come from Rheims to join the company that had lost so heavily, and all would be well again. So she said to herself: she did not allow even in her own soul that the security of her friend and the thought that he would be with her in a day or two, had any great part in her satisfaction.

She awoke suddenly. At the moment she did not know what time it was or how long she had slept; but it was still dark and deathly still. Yet she could have sworn that she had heard her name called. The rushlight was burned out; but in the summer night she could still make out the outline of Mistress Alice's bed. Yet all was still there, except for the gentle breathing: it could not have been she who had called out in her sleep, or she would surely show some signs of restlessness.

She sat up listening; but there was not a sound. She lay down again; and the strange fancy seized her that it had been her mother's voice that she had heard.... It was in this room that her mother had died.... Again she sat up and looked round. All was quiet as before: the tall press at the foot of her bed glimmered here and there with lines and points of starlight.

Then, as again she began to lie down, there came the signal for which her heart was expectant, though her mind knew nothing of its coming. It was a clear rap, as of a pebble against the glass.

She was up and out of bed in a moment, and was peering out under the thick arch of the little window. And a figure stood there, bending, it seemed, for another pebble; in the very place where she had seen it, she thought, nearly three weeks ago, standing ready to mount a horse.

Then she was at Alice's bedside.

"Alice," she whispered. "Alice! Wake up.... There is someone come. You must come with me. I do not know—" Her voice faltered: she knew that she knew, and fear clutched her by the throat.

The porter was fast asleep, and did not move, as carrying a rush-light she went past the buttery with her friend behind her saying no word. The bolts were well oiled, and came back with scarcely a sound. Then as the door swung slowly back a figure slipped in.

"Yes," he said, "it is I.... I think I am followed.... I have but come—"

"Come in quickly," she said, and closed and bolted the door once more.

II

It was a horrible delight to sit, wrapped in her cloak with the hood over her head, listening to his story in the hall, and to know that it was to her house that he had come for safety. It was horrible to her that he needed it—so horrible that every shred of interior peace had left her; she was composed only in her speech, and it was a strange delight that he had come so simply. He sat there; she could see his outline and the pallor of his face under his hat, and his voice was perfectly resolute and quiet. This was his tale.

"Twice this afternoon," he said, "I saw a man against the sky, opposite my hut. It was the same man both times; he was not a shepherd or a farmer's man. The night before, when David came, he did not speak to me; but for the first time he put his head in at the hut-door when he brought the food and made gestures that I could not understand. I looked at him and shook my head, but he would say nothing, and I remembered the bond and said nothing myself. All that he would do was to shut his eyes and wave his hands. Then this last night he brought no food at all.

"I was uneasy at the sight of the man, too, in the afternoon. I think he thought that I was asleep; for when I saw him for the first time I was lying down and looking at the crag opposite. And I saw him raise himself on his hands against the sky, as if he had been lying flat on his face in the heather. I looked at him for a while, and then I flung my hand out of bed suddenly, and he was gone in a whisk. I went to the door after a time, stretching myself as if I were just awakened, and there was no sign of him.

"About an hour before sunset I was watching again, and I saw, on a sudden, a covey of birds rise suddenly about two hundred yards away to the north of the hut—that is, by the way that I should have to go down to the valleys again. They rose as if they were frightened. I kept my eyes on the place, and presently I saw a man's hat moving very slowly. It was the movement of a man crawling on his hands, drawing his legs after him.

"Then I waited for David to come, but he did not come, and I determined then to make my way down here as well as I could after dark. If there were any fellows after me, I should have a better chance of escape than if I stayed in the hut, I thought, until they could fetch up the rest; and, if not, I could lose nothing by coming a day too soon."

"But—" began the girl eagerly.

"Wait," said Robin quietly. "That is not all. I made very poor way on foot (for I thought it better to come quietly than on a horse), and I went round about again and again in the precipitous ground so that, if there were any after me, they could not tell which way I meant to go. For about two hours I heard and saw nothing of any man, and I began to think I was a fool for all my pains. So I sat down a good while and rested, and even thought that I would go back again. But just as I was about to get up again I heard a stone fall a great way behind me: it was on some rocky ground about two hundred yards away. The night was quite still, and I could hear the stone very plainly.... It was I that crawled then, further down the hill, and it was then that I saw once more a man's head move against the stars.

"I went straight on then, as quietly as I could. I made sure that it was but one that was after me, and that he would not try to take me by himself, and I saw no more of him till I came down near Padley—"

"Near Padley? Why—"

"I meant to go there first," said the priest, "and lie there till morning, But as I came down the hill I heard the steps of him again a great way off. So I turned sharp into a little broken ground that lies there, and hid myself among the rocks—"

Mistress Alice lifted her hand suddenly.

"Hark!" she whispered.

Then as the three sat motionless, there came, distinct and clear, from a little distance down the hill, the noise of two or three horses walking over stony ground.

III

For one deathly instant the two sat looking each into the other's white face—since even the priest changed colour at the sound. (While they had talked the dawn had begun to glimmer, and the windows showed grey and ghostly on the thin morning mist.) Then they rose together. Marjorie was the first to speak.

"You must come upstairs at once," she said. "All is ready there, as you know."

The priest's lips moved without speaking. Then he said suddenly:

"I had best be off the back way; that is, if it is what I think—"

"The house will be surrounded."

"But you will have harboured me—"

Marjorie's lips opened in a smile.

"I have done that in any case," she said. She caught up the candle and blew it out, as she went towards the door.

"Come quickly," she said.

At the door Janet met them. Her old face was all distraught with fear. She had that moment run downstairs again on hearing the noise. Marjorie silenced her by a gesture....

The young carpenter had done his work excellently, and Marjorie had taken care that there had been no neglect since the work had been done. Yet so short was the time since the hearing of the horses' feet, that as the girl slipped out of the press again after drawing back the secret door, there came the loud knocking beneath, for which they had waited with such agony.

"Quick!" she said....

From within, as she waited, came the priest's whisper.

"Is this to be pushed—?"

"Yes; yes."

There was the sound of sliding wood and a little snap. Then she closed the doors of the press again.

IV

Mr. Audrey outside grew indignant, and the more so since he was unhappy.

He had had the message from my lord Shrewsbury that a magistrate of her Grace should show more zeal; and, along with this, had come a private intimation that it was suspected that Mr. Audrey had at least once warned the recusants of an approaching attack. It would be as well, then, if he would manifest a little activity....

But it appeared to him the worst luck in the world that the hunt should lead him to Mistress Manners' door.

It was late in the afternoon that the informer had made his appearance at Matstead, thirsty and dishevelled, with the news that a man thought to be a Popish priest was in hiding on the moors; that he was being kept under observation by another informer; and that it was to be suspected that he was the man who had been missed at Padley when my lord had taken Garlick and Ludlam. If it were the man, it would be the priest known by the name of Alban—the fellow whom my lord's man had so much distrusted at Fotheringay, and whom he had seen again in Derby a while later. Next, if it were this man, he would almost certainly make for Padley if he were disturbed.

Mr. Audrey had bitten his nails a while as he listened to this, and then had suddenly consented. The plan suggested was simple enough.

One little troop should ride to Padley, gathering reinforcements on the way, and another on foot should set out for the shepherd's hut. Then, if the priest should be gone, this second party should come on towards Padley immediately and join forces with the riders.

All this had been done, and the mounted company, led by the magistrate himself, had come up from the valley in time to see the signalling from the heights (contrived by the showing of lights now and again), which indicated that the priest was moving in the direction that had been expected, and that one man at least was on his track. They had waited there, in the valley, till the intermittent signals had reached the level ground and ceased, and had then ridden up cautiously in time to meet the informer's companion, and to learn that the fugitive had doubled suddenly back towards Booth's Edge. There they had waited then, till the dawn was imminent, and, with it, there came the party on foot, as had been arranged; then, all together, numbering about twenty-five men, they had pushed on in the direction of Mistress Manners' house.

As the house came into view, more than ever Mr. Audrey reproached his evil luck. Certainly there still were two or three chances to one that no priest would be taken at all; since, first, the man might not be a priest, and next, he might have passed the manor and plunged back again into the hills. But it was not very pleasant work, this rousing of a house inhabited by a woman for whom the magistrate had very far from unkindly feelings, and on such an errand.... So the informers marvelled at the venom with which Mr. Audrey occasionally whispered at them in the dark.

He grew a little warm and impatient when no answer came to the knocking. He said such play-acting was absurd. Why did not the man come out courageously and deny that he was a priest? He would have a far better excuse for letting him go.

"Knock again," he cried.

And again the thunder rang through the archway, and the summons in the Queen's name to open. Then at last a light shone beneath the door. (It was brightening rapidly towards the dawn here in the open air, but within it would still be dark.) Then a voice grumbled within.

"Who is there?"

"Man," bellowed the magistrate, "open the door and have done with it. I tell you I am a magistrate!"

There was silence. Then the voice came again.

"How do I know that you are?"

Mr. Audrey slipped off his horse, scrambled to the door, set his hands on his knees and his mouth to the keyhole.

"Open the door, you fool, in the Queen's name.... I am Mr. Audrey, of Matstead."

Again came the pause. The magistrate was in the act of turning to bid his men beat the door in, when once more the voice came.

"I'll tell the mistress, sir.... She's a-bed."

His discomfort grew on him as he waited, staring out at the fast yellowing sky. He turned to his men.

"Now, men," he said, glaring like a judge, "no violence here, unless I give the order. No breaking of aught in the house. The lady here is a friend of mine; and—"

The great bolts shot back suddenly; he turned as the door opened; and there, pale as milk, with eyes that seemed a-fire, Marjorie's face was looking at him; she was wrapped in her long cloak and her hood was drawn over her head.

He saluted her.

"Mistress Manners," he said, "I am sorry to incommode you in this way. But a couple of fellows tell me that a man has come this way, whom they think to be a priest. I am a magistrate, mistress, and—"

He stopped, confounded by her face. Her whole soul was in her eyes, crying to him some message that he could not understand.... He looked at her.... Then he began again:

"It is no will of mine, mistress, beyond my duty. But I hold her Grace's commission—"

She swept back again, motioning him to enter. He was astonished at his own discomfort, but he followed, and his men pressed close after; and he noticed, even in that twilight, that a look of despair, went over the girl's face, sharp as pain, as she saw them.

"You have come to search my house, sir?" she asked. Her voice was as colourless as her features.

"My commission, mistress, compels me—"

Then he noticed that the doors into the hall had been pushed open, and that she was moving towards them. And he thought he understood.

"Stand back, men," he barked, so fiercely that they recoiled. "This lady shall speak with me first."

He passed up the hall after her. He was as unhappy as possible. He wondered what she could have to say to him; she must surely understand that no pleading could turn him; he must do his duty. Yet he would certainly do this with as little offence as he could.

"Mistress Manners—" he began.

Then she turned on him again. They were at the further end of the hall, and could speak low without being overheard.

"You must begone again," she whispered. "Oh! you must begone again. You do not understand; you—"

Her eyes still burned with that terrible eloquence; it was as the face of one on the rack.

"Mistress, I cannot begone again. I must do my duty. But I promise you—"

She was close to him, staring into his face; he could feel the heat of her breath on his face.

"You must begone at once," she whispered, still in that voice of agony. He saw her begin to sway on her feet and her eyes turn glassy. He caught her as she swayed. "Here! you women!" he cried.

V

He took particular pains to do as little damage as possible. First he went through the out-houses, himself with a pike testing the haystacks, where he was sure that no man could be hidden.

As he passed, a little later, the inner door into the buttery passage, he could hear the beating of hands on the hall-door. He went on quickly to the kitchen, hating himself, yet determined to get all done quickly, and drove the kitchen-maid, who was crouching by the unlighted fire, out behind him, sending a man with her to bestow her in the hall. She wailed as she went by him, but it was unintelligible, and he was in no mood for listening.

"Take her in," he said; "but let no one out, nor a message, till all is done."

Then at last he went upstairs, still with his little bodyguard of four, of whom one was the man who had followed the fugitive down from the hills.

He began with the little rooms over the hall: a bedstead stood in one; in another was a table all piled with linen; a third had its floor covered with early autumn fruit, ready for preserving. He struck on a panel or two as he went, for form's sake.

As he came out again he turned savagely on the informer.

"It is damned nonsense," he said; "the fellow's not here at all. I told you he'd have gone back to the hills."

The man looked up at him with a furtive kind of sneer in his face; he, too, was angry enough; the loss of the priest meant the loss of the heavy reward.

"We have not searched a room rightly yet, sir," he snarled. "There are a hundred places—"

"Not searched! You villain! Why, what would you have?"

"It's not the manner I've done it before, sir. A pike-thrust here, and a blow there—"

"I tell you I will not have the house injured! Mistress Manners—"

"Very good, sir. Your honour is the magistrate...I am not."

The old man's temper boiled over. They were passing at that instant a half-open door, and within he could see a bare little parlour, with linen presses against the walls. It would not hide a cat.

"Do your search, then!" he cried. "Here, then, and I will watch you! But you shall pay for any wanton damage, I tell you."

The man shrugged his shoulders.

"What is the use, then—" he began.

"Bah! search, then, as you will. I will pay."

They were opposite the old picture. Beneath it there showed a crack in the wainscoting....

"If it please your honour we will break in this panel" came the smooth, sneering voice that he loathed.

He could scarcely refuse leave. Besides, the woodwork was flawed in any case—he would pay for a new panel himself.

"There is nothing there!" he said doubtfully.

"Oh, no, sir," said the man with a peculiar look. "It is but to make a show—"

The old man's brows came down angrily. Then he nodded; and, leaning against the window, watched them.

One of his own men came forward with a hammer and chisel. He placed the chisel at the edge of the cracked panel, where the informer directed, and struck a blow or two. There was the unmistakable dull sound of wood against stone—not an echo of resonance. The old man smiled grimly to himself. The man must be a fool if he thought there could be any hole there!...Well, he would let them do what they would here; and then forbid any further damage.... He wondered if the priest really were in the house or no.

The two men had their heads together now, eyeing the crack they had made.... Then the informer said something in a low voice that the old man could not hear; and the other, handing him the chisel and hammer, went out of the room, beckoning to one of the two others that stood waiting at the door.

"Well?" sneered the old man. "Have you caught your bird?"

"Not yet, sir."

He could hear the steps of the others in the next room; and then silence.

"What are they doing there?" he asked suddenly.

"Nothing, sir.... I just bade a man wait on that side."

The man was once more inserting the chisel in the top of the wainscoting; then he presently began to drive it down with the hammer as if to detach it from the wall.

Suddenly he stopped; and at the same instant the old man heard some faint, muffled noise, as of footsteps moving either in the wall or beyond it.

"What is that?"

The man said nothing; he appeared to be listening.

"What is that?" demanded the other again, with a strange uneasiness at his heart. Was it possible, after all! Then the man dropped his chisel and hammer and darted out and vanished. A sudden noise of voices and tramplings broke out somewhere out of sight.

"God's blood!" roared the old man in anger and dismay. "I believe they have the poor devil!"

He ran out, two steps down the passage and in again at the door of the next room. It was a bedroom, with two beds side by side: a great press with open doors stood between the hearth and the window; and, in the midst of the floor, five men struggled and swayed together. The fifth was a bearded young man, well dressed; but he could not see his face.

Then they had him tight; his hands were twisted behind his back; an arm was flung round his neck; and another man, crouching, had his legs embraced. He cried out once or twice.... The old man turned sick...a great rush of blood seemed to be hammering in his ears and dilating his eyes.... He ran forward, tearing at the arm that was choking the prisoner's throat, and screaming he knew not what.

And it was then that he knew for certain that this was his son.

CHAPTER VI

I

ROBIN drew a long breath as the door closed behind him. Then he went forward to the table, and sat on it, swinging his feet, and looking carefully and curiously round the room, so far as the darkness would allow him; his eyes had had scarcely time yet to become accustomed to the change from the brilliant sunshine outside to the gloom of the prison. It was his first experience of prison, and, for the present, he was more interested than subdued by it.

He had not said one word to his father. The shock was complete and unexpected. He had seen the old man stagger back and sink on the bed. Then he had been hurried from the room and downstairs. As the party came into the buttery entrance, there had been a great clamour; the man on guard at the hall doors had run forward; the doors had opened suddenly and Marjorie had come out, with a surge of faces behind her. But to her, too, he had said nothing; he had tried to smile; he was still faint and sick from the fight upstairs. But he had been pushed out into the air, where he saw the horses waiting, and round the corner of the house into an out-building, and there he had had time to recover.

He was led out again presently, and set on a horse. And while a man attached one foot to the other by a cord beneath the horse's belly, he looked like a child at the arched doorway of the house; at a patch of lichen that was beginning to spread above the lintel; at the open window of the room above.

He vaguely desired to speak with Marjorie again; he even asked the man who was tying his feet whether he might do so; but he got no answer. A group of men watched him from the door, and he noticed that they were silent. He wondered if it were the tying of his feet in which they were so much absorbed.

Little by little, as they rode, this oppression began to lift. Half a dozen times he determined to speak with the man who rode beside him and held his horse by a leading rein; and each time he did not speak. Neither did any man speak to him. Another man rode behind; and a dozen or so went on foot. He could hear them talking together in low voices.

He was finally roused by his companion's speaking. He had noticed the man look at him now and again strangely and not unkindly.

"Is it true that you are a son of Mr. Audrey, sir?"

He was on the point of saying "Yes," when his mind seemed to come back to him as clear as an awakening from sleep. He understood that he must not identify himself if he could help it. He had been told at Rheims that silence was best in such matters.

"Mr. Audrey?" he said. "The magistrate?"

The man nodded. He did not seem an unkindly personage at all. Then he smiled.

"Well, well," he said. "Less said—"

He broke off and began to whistle. Then he interrupted himself once more.

"He was still in his fit," he said, "when we came away. Mistress Manners was with him."

Intelligence was flowing back in Robin's brain like a tide. It seemed to him that he perceived things with an extraordinary clearness and rapidity. He understood he must show no dismay or horror of any kind; he must carry himself easily and detachedly.

"In a fit, was he?"

The other nodded.

"I am arrested on his warrant, then? And on what charge?"

The man laughed outright.

"That's too good," he said. "Why, we have a bundle of popery on the horse behind! It was all in the hiding-hole!"

"I am supposed to be a priest, then?" said Robin, with admirable disdain.

Again the man laughed.

"They will have some trouble in proving that," said Robin viciously. They ate as they rode, and reached Derby in the afternoon.

At the very outskirts the peculiar nature of this cavalcade was observed; and by the time that they came within sight of the market-square a considerable mob was hustling along on all sides. There were a few cries raised. Robin could not distinguish the words, but it seemed to him as if some were raised for him as well as against him. He kept his head somewhat down; he thought it better to risk no complications that might arise should he be recognised.

As they drew nearer the marketplace the progress became yet slower, for the crowd seemed suddenly and abnormally swelled. There was a great shouting of voices, too, in front, and the smell of burning came distinctly on the breeze. The man riding beside Robin turned his head and called out; and in answer one of the others riding behind pushed his horse up level with the other two, so that the prisoner had a guard on either side. A few steps further, and another order was issued, followed by the pressing up of the men that went on foot so as to form a complete square about the three riders.

Robin put a question, but the men gave him no answer. He could see that they were preoccupied and anxious. Then, as step by step they made their way forward and gained the corner of the marketplace, he saw the reason of these precautions; for the whole square was one pack of heads, except where, somewhere in the midst, a great bonfire blazed in the sunlight. The noise, too, was deafening; drums were beating, horns blowing, men shouting aloud. From window after window leaned heads, and, as the party advanced yet further, they came suddenly in view of a scaffold hung with gray carpets and ribbons, on which a civil dignitary, in some official dress, was gesticulating.

It was useless to ask a question; not a word could have been heard unless it were shouted aloud; and presently the din redoubled, for out of sight, round some corner, guns were suddenly shot off one after another; and the cheering grew shrill and piercing in contrast.

As they came out at last, without attracting any great attention, into the more open space at the entrance of Friar's Gate, Robin turned again and asked what the matter was. It was plainly not himself, as he had at first almost believed.

The man turned an exultant face to him.

"It's the Spanish fleet!" he said. "There's not a ship of it left, they say."

When they halted at the gate of the prison there was another pause, while the cord that tied his feet was cut, and he was helped from his horse, as he was stiff and constrained from the long ride under such circumstances. He heard a roar of interest and abuse, and, perhaps, a little sympathy, from the part of the crowd that had followed, as the gate closed behind him.

II

As his eyes became better accustomed to the dark, he began to see what kind of a place it was in which he found himself. It was a square little room on the ground floor, with a single, heavily-barred window, against which the dirt had collected in such quantities as to exclude almost all light. The floor was beaten earth, damp and uneven; the walls were built of stones and timber, and were dripping with moisture; there was a table and a stool in the centre of the room, and a dark heap in the corner. He examined this presently, and found it to be rotting hay covered with some kind of rug. The whole place smelled hideously foul.

From far away outside came still the noise of cheering, heard as through wool, and the sharp reports of the cannon they were still firing. The Armada seemed very remote from him, here in ward. Its destruction affected him now hardly at all, except for the worse, since an anti-Catholic reaction might very well follow.... He set himself, with scarcely an effort, to contemplate more personal matters.

He was astonished that his purse had not been taken from him. He had been searched rapidly just now, in an outer passage, by a couple of men, one of whom he understood to be his gaoler; and a knife and a chain and his rosary had been taken from him. But the purse had been put back again.... He remembered presently that the possession of money made a considerable difference to a prisoner's comfort; but he determined to do as little as he was obliged in this way. He might need the money more urgently later.

By the time that he had gone carefully round his prison-walls, even reaching up to the window and testing the bars, pushing as noiselessly as he could against the door, pacing the distances in every direction—he had, at the same time, once more arranged and rehearsed every piece of evidence that he possessed, and formed a number of resolutions.

It was perfectly clear by now that his father had been wholly ignorant of the identity of the man he was after. The horror in the gasping face that he had seen so close to his own, above the strangling arm, set that beyond a doubt; the news of the fit into which his father had fallen confirmed it.

Next, he had been right in believing himself watched in the shepherd's hut, and followed down from it. This hiding of his in the hills, the discovery of him in the hiding-hole, together with the vestments—these two things were the heaviest pieces of testimony against him. More remote testimony might be brought forward from his earlier adventures—his presence at Fotheringay, his recognition by my lord's man. But these were, in themselves, indifferent.

His resolutions were few and simple.

He would make no demand to see anyone; since he knew that whatever was possible would be done for him by Marjorie. He would deny nothing and assert very little if he were brought before the magistrates. Finally, he would observe the hours of prayer so far as he could. He had no books with him of any kind. But he could pray God for fortitude.

CHAPTER VII

I

THERE was a vast crowd in the marketplace at Michaelmas to see the judges come—partly because there was always excitement at the visible majesty of the law; partly because the tale of one at least of the prisoners had roused interest. It was a dramatic tale: he was first a seminary priest and a Derbyshire man (many remembered him riding as a little lad beside his father); he was, next, a runaway to Rheims for religion's sake, when his father conformed; third, he had been taken in the house of Mistress Manners, to whom, report said, he had once been betrothed; last, he had been taken by his father himself. All this furnished matter for a quantity of conversation in the taverns; and it was freely discussed by the sentimental whether or no, if the priest yielded and conformed, he would yet find Mistress Manners willing to wed him.

There was a deal of loyal cheering as the procession went by; for these splendid personages on horseback stood to the mob for the power that had repelled the enemies of England; and her Grace's name was received with enthusiasm. Behind the judges and their escort came a cavalcade of riders—gentlemen, grooms, servants, and agents of all sorts. But not a Derby man noticed or recognised a thin gentleman who rode modestly in the midst, with a couple of personal servants on either side of him. It was not until the visitors had separated to the various houses and inns where they were to be lodged, and the mob was dispersing home again, that it began to be rumoured everywhere that Mr. Topcliffe was come again to Derby on a special mission.

THE tidings came to Marjorie as she leaned back in her chair in Mr. Biddell's parlour and listened to the last shoutings.

She had been in town now three days.

Ever since the capture she had been under guard in her own house till three days ago. Four men had been billeted upon her, not, indeed, by the orders of Mr. Audrey, since Mr. Audrey was in no condition to control affairs any longer, but by the direction of Mr. Columbell, who had himself ridden out to take charge at Booth's Edge, when the news of the arrest had come, with the prisoner himself, to the city. It was he, too, who had seen to the removal of Mr. Audrey a week later, when he had recovered from the weakness caused by the fit sufficiently to travel as far as Derby; for it was thought better that the magistrate who had effected the capture should be accessible to the examining magistrates. It was, of course, lamentable, said Mr. Columbell, that father and son should have been brought into such relations, and he would do all that he could to relieve Mr. Audrey from any painful task in which they could do without him. But her Grace's business must be done, and he had had special messages from my lord Shrewsbury himself that the prisoner must be dealt with sternly. It was believed, wrote my lord, that Mr. Alban, as he called himself, had a good deal more against him than the mere fact of being a seminary priest: it was thought that he had been involved in the Babington plot, and had at least once had access to the Queen of the Scots since the fortunate failure of the conspiracy.

All this, then, Marjorie knew from Mr. Biddell, who seemed always to know everything; but it was not until the evening on which the judges arrived that she learned the last and extreme measures that would be taken to establish these suspicions. She had ridden openly to Derby so soon as the news came from there that for the present she might be set at liberty.

The lawyer came into the darkening room as the square outside began to grow quiet, and Marjorie opened her eyes to see who it was.

He said nothing at first, but sat down close beside her. He knew she must be told, but he hated the telling. He carried a little paper in his hand. He would begin with that little bit of good news first, he said to himself.

"Well, mistress," he said, "I have the order at last. We are to see him tonight. It is 'for Mr. Biddell and a friend.'"

She sat up, and a little vitality came back to her face; for a moment she almost looked as she had looked in the early summer.

"Tonight?" she said. "And when—"

"He will not be brought before my lords for three or four days yet. There is a number of cases to come before his. It will give us those two or three days, at least, to prepare our case."

He lifted his eyes to hers. There was still enough light from the windows for him to see her eyes, and that there was a spark in them that had not been there just now. And it was for him to extinguish it.... He gripped his courage.

"I have had worse news than all," he said.

Her lips moved, and a vibration went over her face. Her eyes blinked, as at a sudden light.

"Yes?"

He put his hand tenderly on her arm.

"You must be courageous," he said. "It is the worst news that ever came to me. It concerns one who is come from London today, and rode in with my lords."

She could not speak, but her great eyes entreated him to finish her misery.

"Yes," he said, still pressing his hand on to her arm. "Yes; it is Mr. Topcliffe who is come."

He felt the soft muscles harden like steel.... There was no sound except the voices talking in the square and the noise of footsteps across the pavements. He could not look at her.

Then he heard her draw a long breath and breathe it out again, and her taut muscles relaxed.

"We...we are all in Christ's hands," she said.... "We must tell him."

II

It appeared to the girl as if she were moving on a kind of set stage, with every movement and incident designed beforehand, in a play that was itself a kind of destiny—above all, when she went at last into Robin's cell and saw him standing there, and found it to be that, in which so long ago she had talked with Mr. Thomas FitzHerbert....

The great realities were closing round her, as irresistible as wheels and bars.

First, it was she who had first turned her friend's mind to the life of a priest. Had she submitted to natural causes, she would have been his wife nine years ago; they would have been harassed no doubt and troubled, but no more. It was she again who had encouraged his return to Derbyshire. If it had not been for that, and for the efforts she had made to do what she thought good work for God, he might have been sent elsewhere. It was in her house that he had been taken, and in the very place she had designed for his safety. If she had but sent him on, as he wished, back to the hills again, he might never have been taken at all. She felt even as if she were responsible for the manner of his taking, and for the horror that it had been his father who had accomplished it; if she had said more, or less, in the hall on that dark morning; if she had not swooned; if she had said bravely: "It is your son, sir, who is here," all might have been saved. And now it was Topcliffe who was come—(and she knew all that this signified)—the very man at whose mere bodily presence she had sickened in the court of the Tower. And, last, it was she who had to tell Robin of this.

Even as she waited, with Mr. Biddell behind her, as the gaoler fumbled with the keys, she was aware that the last breath of resentment had been drawn.... It was, indeed, a monstrous power that had so dealt with her.... It was none other than the will of God, plain at last.

She knelt down for the priest's blessing, without speaking, as the door closed, and Mr. Biddell knelt behind her. Then she rose, and went forward to the stool and sat upon it.

He was hardly changed at all. He looked a little white and drawn in the wavering light of the flambeau; but his clothes were orderly and clean, and his eyes as bright and resolute as ever.

"It is a great happiness to see you," he said, smiling, and then no more compliments.

"And what of my father?" he added instantly.

She told him. Mr. Audrey was in Derby, still sick from his fit. He was in Mr. Columbell's house. She had not seen him.

"Robin," she said (and she used the old name, utterly unknowing that she did so), "we must speak with Mr. Biddell presently about your case. But there is a word or two I have to say first. We can have two hours here, if you wish it."

Robin put his hands behind him on to the table and jumped lightly, so that he sat on it, facing her.

"If you will not sit on the table, Mr. Biddell, I fear there is only that block of wood."

He pointed to a block of a tree set on end. It served him, laid flat, as a pillow. The lawyer went across to it.

"The judges, I hear, are come tonight," said the priest.

She bowed.

"Yes; but your case will not be up for three or four days yet."

"Why, then, I shall have time—"

She lifted her hand sharply a little to check him.

"You will not have much time," she said, and paused again. A sharp contraction came and went in the muscles of her throat. It was as if a hand gripped her there, relaxed, and gripped again. She put up her own hand desperately to tear at her collar.

"Why, but—" began the priest.

She could bear it no more. His resolute cheerfulness, his frank astonishment, were like knives to her. She gave one cry.

"Topcliffe is come... Topcliffe!..." she cried. Then she flung her arm across the table and dropped her face on it.

It was quite quiet after she had spoken. The priest did not stir from where he sat a couple of feet away; only the swinging of his feet ceased. She drove down her convulsions; they rose again; she drove them down once more. Then the tears surged up, her whole being relaxed, and she felt a hand on her shoulder.

"Marjorie," said the grave voice, as steady as it had ever been, "Marjorie. This is what we looked for, is it not?...Topcliffe is come, is he? Well, let him come. He or another. It is for this that we have all looked since the beginning. Christ His Grace is strong enough, is it not? It has been strong enough for many, at least; and He will not surely take it from me who need it so much...." (He spoke in pauses, but his voice never faltered.) "I have prayed for that grace ever since I have been here.... He has given me great peace in this place.... I think He will give it me to the end.... You must pray, my...my child; you must not cry like that."

She lifted her agonized face for a moment, then she let it fall again. It seemed as if he knew the very thoughts of her.

"This all seems very perfect to me," he went on. "It was yourself who first turned me to this life, and you knew surely what you did. I knew, at least, all the while, I think; and I have never ceased to thank God. And it was through your hands that the letter came to me to go to Fotheringay. And it was in your house that I was taken.... And it was Mr. Maine's beads that they found on me when they searched me here—the pair of beads you gave me."

Again she stared at him, blind and bewildered.

He went on steadily:

"And now it is you again who bring me the first news of my passion. It is yourself, first and last, under God, that have brought me all these graces and crosses. And I thank you with all my heart.... But you must pray for me to the end, and after it, too."

CHAPTER VIII

I

"Water," said a sharp voice, pricking through the enormous thickness of the bloodshot dark that had come down on him. There followed a sound of floods; then a sense of sudden coolness, and he opened his eyes once more, and became aware of unbearable pain in arms and feet. Again the whirling dark, striped with blood colour, fell on him like a blanket; again the sound of waters falling and the sense of coolness, and again he opened his eyes.

For a minute or two it was all that he could do to hold himself in consciousness. It appeared to him a necessity to do so. He could see a smoke-stained roof of beams and rafters, and on these he fixed his eyes, thinking that he could hold himself so, as by thin, wiry threads of sight, from falling again into the pit where all was black or blood-colour. The pain was appalling, but he thought he had gripped it at last, and could hold it so, like a wrestler.

As the pain began to resolve itself into throbs and stabs, from the continuous strain in which at first it had shown itself—a strain that was like a shrill horn blowing, or a blaze of bluish light—he began to see more, and to understand a little. There were four or five faces looking down on him: one was the face of a man he had seen somewhere in an inn... it was at Fotheringay; it was my lord Shrewsbury's man. Another was a lean face; a black hat came and went behind it; the lips were drawn in a sort of smile, so that he could see the teeth.... Then he perceived next that he himself was lying in a kind of shallow trough of wood upon the floor. He could see his bare feet raised a little and tied with cords.

Then, one by one, these sights fitted themselves into one another and made sense. He remembered that he was in Derby gaol—not in his own cell; that the lean face was of a man called Topcliffe; that a physician was there as well as the others; that they had been questioning him on various points, and that some of these points he had answered, while others he had not, and must not. Some of them concerned her Grace of the Scots.... These he had answered. Then, again, association came back....

"As thy arms, O Christ..." he whispered.

"Now then," came, the sharp voice in his ear, so close, and harsh as to distress him. "These questions again.... Were there any other places besides at Padley and Booth's Edge, in the parish of Hathersage, where you said Mass?"

"...O Christ, were extended on the Cross—" began the tortured man dreamily. "Ah-h-h!"

It was a scream, whispered rather than shrieked, that was torn from him by the sharpness of the agony. His body had lifted from the floor without will of his own, twisting a little; and what seemed as strings of fiery pain had shot upwards from his feet and downwards from his wrists as the roller was suddenly jerked again. He hung there perhaps ten or fifteen seconds, conscious only of the blinding pain—questions, questioners, roof, and faces all gone and drowned again in a whirling tumult of darkness and red streaks. The sweat poured again suddenly from his whole body.... Then again he sank relaxed upon the floor, and the pulses beat in his head, and he thought that Marjorie and her mother and his own father were all looking at him....

He heard presently the same voice talking:

"—and answer the questions that are put to you.... Now then, we will begin the others, if it please you better.... In what month was it that you first became privy to the plot against her Grace?"

"Wait!" whispered the priest. "Wait, and I will answer that." He understood that there was a trap here. The question had been framed differently last time. But his mind was all a-whirl; and he feared he might answer wrongly if he could not collect himself. He still wondered why so many friends of his were in the room—even Father Campion...

He drew a breath again presently, and tried to speak; but his voice broke like a shattered trumpet, and he could not command it.... He must whisper.

"It was in August, I think.... I think it was August, two years ago."

"August...you mean May or April."

"No; it was August.... At least, all that I know of the plot was when...when—" His thoughts became confused again; it was like strings of wool, he thought, twisted violently together; a strand snapped now and again. He made a violent effort and caught an end as it was slipping away. "It was in August, I think; the day that Mr. Babington fled, that he wrote to me; and sent me—" He paused: he became aware that here, too, lurked a trap if he were to say he had seen Mary; he would surely be asked what he had seen her for, and his priesthood might be so proved against him.... He could not remember whether that had been proved; and so...would Father Campion advise him perhaps whether...

The voice jarred again, and startled him into a flash of coherence. He thought he saw a way out.

"Well?" snapped the voice. "Sent you? ...Sent you whither?"

"Sent me to Chartley; where I saw her Grace...her Grace of the Scots; and... 'As thy arms, O Christ...'"

"Now then; now then! ...So you saw her Grace? And what was that for?"

"I saw her Grace...and...and told her what Mr. Babington had told me."

"What was that, then?"

"That...that he was her servant till death; and...and a thousand if he had them. And so, 'As thy arms, O—'"

"Water," barked the voice.

Again came the rush as of cataracts; and a sensation of drowning. There followed an instant's glow of life; and then the intolerable pain came back; and the heavy, red-streaked darkness....

II

He found himself, after some period, lying more easily. He could not move hand or foot. His body only appeared to live. From his shoulders to his thighs he was alive; the rest was nothing. But he opened his eyes and saw that his arms were laid by his sides; and that he was no longer in the wooden trough. He wondered at his hands; he wondered even if they were his... they were of an unusual colour and bigness; and there was something like a tight-fitting bracelet round each wrist. Then he perceived that he was shirtless and hoseless; and that the bracelets were not bracelets, but rings of swollen flesh. But there was no longer any pain or even sensation in them; and he was aware that his mouth glowed as if he had drunk ardent spirits.

He was considering all this, slowly, like a child contemplating a new toy. Then there came something between him and the light; he saw a couple of faces eyeing him. Then the voice began again, at first confused and buzzing, then articulate; and he remembered.

"Now, then," said the voice, "you have had but a taste of it...." The phrase repeated itself like the catch of a song.... When he regained his attention, the sentence had moved on.

"...these questions. I will put them to you again from the beginning. You will give your answer to each. And if my lord is not satisfied, we must try again."

"My lord!" thought the priest. He rolled his eyes round a little further. And he saw a little table floating somewhere in the dark; a candle burned on it; and a melancholy face with dreamy eyes was brightly illuminated.... That was my lord Shrewsbury, he considered....

"... in what month that you first became privy to the plot against her Grace?"

Sense was coming back to him again now. He remembered what he had said just now.

"It was in August," he whispered, "in August, I think; two years ago. Mr. Babington wrote to me of it."

"And you went to the Queen of the Scots, you say?"

"Yes."

"And what did you there?"

"I gave the message."

"What was that?"

"...That Mr. Babington was her servant always; that he regretted nothing, save that he had failed. He begged her to pray for his soul, and for all that had been with him in the enterprise."

It appeared to him that he was astonishingly voluble, all at once. He reflected that he must be careful.

"And what did she say to that?"

"She declared herself guiltless of the plot...that she knew nothing of it; and that—"

"Now then; now then. You expect my lord to believe that?"

"I do not know.... But it was what was said."

"And you profess that you knew nothing of the plot till then?"

"I knew nothing of it till then," whispered the priest steadily.

"But—"

(A face suddenly blotted out more of the light.)

"Yes?"

"Anthony—I mean Mr. Babington—had spoken to me a great while before—in... in some village inn.... I forget where. It was when I was a lad. He asked whether I would join in some enterprise. He did not say what it was.... But I thought it to be against the Queen of England.... And I would not."

He closed his eyes again. There had begun a slow heat of pain in ankles and wrists, not wholly unbearable, and a warmth began to spread in his body. A great shudder or two shook him. The voice said something he could not hear. Then a metal rim was pressed to his mouth; and a stream of something at once icy and fiery ran into his mouth and out at the corners. He swallowed once or twice; and his senses came back.

"You do not expect us to believe all that!" came the voice.

"It is the truth, for all that," murmured the priest.

The next question came sudden as a shot fired.

"You were at Fotheringay?"

"Yes."

"In what house?"

"I was in the inn—the 'New Inn,' I think it is."

"And you spoke with her Grace again?"

"No; I could not get at her. But—"

"Well?"

"I was in the court of the castle when her Grace was executed."

There was a murmur of voices. He thought that someone had moved over to the table where my lord sat; but he could not move his eyes again, the labour was too great.

"Who was with you in the inn—as your friend, I mean?"

"A...a young man was with me. His name was Merton. He is in France, I think."

"And he knew you to be a priest?" came the voice without an instant's hesitation.

"Why—" Then he stopped short, just in time.

"Well?"

"How should he think that?" asked Robin.

There was a laugh somewhere. Then the voice went on, almost good-humouredly:

"Mr. Alban, what is the use of this fencing? You were taken in a hiding-hole with the very vestments at your feet. We know you to be a priest. We are not seeking to entrap you in that, for there is no need. But there are other matters altogether which we must have from you. You have been made priest beyond the seas, in Rheims—"

"I swear to you that I was not," whispered Robin instantly and eagerly, thinking he saw a loophole.

"Well, then, at Châlons, or Douay: it matters not where. That is not our affair today. All that will be dealt with before my lords at the Assizes. But what we must have from you now is your answer to some other questions."

"Assuming me to be a priest?"

"Mr. Alban, I will talk no more on that point. I tell you we know it. But we must have answers on other points. I will come back to

Merton presently. These are the questions. I will read them through to you. Then we will deal with them one by one."

There was the rustle of a paper. An extraordinary desire for sleep came down on the priest; it was only by twitching his head a little, and causing himself acute shoots of pain in his neck that he could keep himself awake. He knew that he must not let his attention wander again. He remembered clearly now that Father Campion was dead, and that Marjorie could not have been here just now.... He must take great care not to become so much confused again.

"THE first question," read the voice slowly, "is, whether you have said Mass in other places beside Padley and the manor at Booth's Edge. We know that you must have done so; but we must have the names of the places, and of the parties present, so far as you can remember them.

"The second question is, the names of all those other priests with whom you have spoken in England, since you came from Rheims; and the names of all other students, not yet priests, or scarcely, whom you knew at Rheims, and who are for England.

"The third question is, the names of all those whom you know to be friends of Mr. John FitzHerbert, Mr. Bassett, and Mr. Fenton—not being priests, but Papists.

"These three questions will do as a beginning. When you have answered these, there is a number more. Now, sir."

The last two words were rapped out sharply. Robin opened his eyes.

"As to the first two questions," he whispered. "These assume that I am a priest myself. Yet that is what you have to prove against me. The third question concerns...concerns my loyalty to my friends. But I will tell you—"

"Yes?" The voice was sharp and eager.

"I will tell you the names of two friends of each of those gentlemen you have named."

A pen suddenly scratched on paper. He could not see who held it.

"Yes?" said the voice again.

"Well, sir. The names of two of the friends of Mr. FitzHerbert are Mr. Bassett and Mr. Fenton. The names—"

"Bah!"

"You are playing with us—"

"The names," murmured the priest slowly, "of two of Mr. Fenton's friends are Mr. FitzHerbert and—"

A face, upside-down, thrust itself suddenly almost into his. He could feel the hot breath on his forehead.

"See here, Mr. Alban. You are fooling us. Do you think this is a Christmas game? I tell you it is not yet three o'clock. There are three hours more yet—"

A smooth, sad voice interrupted. The reversed face vanished.

"You have threatened the prisoner," it said, "but you have not yet told him the alternative."

"No, my lord.... Yes, my lord. Listen, Mr. Alban. My lord here says that if you will answer these questions he will use his influence on your behalf. Your life is forfeited, as you know very well. There is not a dog's chance for you. Yet, if you will but answer these three questions—and no more:—(No more, my lord?)—Yes; these three questions and no more, my lord will use his influence for you. He can promise nothing, he says, but that; but my lord's influence—well, we need say no more on that point. If you refuse to answer, on the other hand, there are yet three hours more today; there is all tomorrow, and the next day. And, after that, your case will be before my lords at the Assizes. You have had but a taste of what we can do.... And then, sir, my lord does not wish to be harsh...."

There was a pause.

Robin was counting up the hours. It was three o'clock now. Then he had been on the rack, with intervals, since nine o'clock. That was six hours. There was but half that again for today. Then would come the night. He need not consider further than that.... But he must guard his tongue. It might speak, in spite—

"Well, Mr. Alban?"

He opened his eyes.

"Well, sir?"

"Which is it to be?"

The priest smiled and closed his eyes again. If he could but fix his attention on the mere pain, he thought, and refuse utterly to consider the way of escape, he might be able to keep his unruly tongue in check.

"You will not, then?"

"No."

The appalling pain ran through him again like fiery snakes of iron—from wrist to shoulders, from ankles to thighs, as the hands seized him and lifted him....

There was a moment or two of relief as he sank down once more into the trough of torture. He could feel that his feet were being handled, but it appeared as if nothing touched his flesh. He gave a great sighing moan as his arms were drawn back over his head; and the sweat poured again from all over his body.

Then, as the cords tightened:

"As thy arms, O Christ, were extended..." he whispered.

CHAPTER IX

I

A great murmuring crowd filled every flat spot of ground and pavement and parapet. They stood even on the balustrade of St. Mary's Bridge; there were fringes of them against the sky on the edges of roofs a quarter of a mile away. No flat surface was to be seen anywhere except on the broad reach of the river, and near the head of the bridge, in the circular space, ringed by steel caps and pike-points, where the gallows and ladder rose. Close beside them a column of black smoke rose heavily into the morning air, bellying away into the clear air. A continual steady low murmur of talking went up continually.

There had been no hanging within the memory of any that had roused such interest. Derbyshire men had been hung often enough; a criminal usually had a dozen friends at least in the crowd to whom he shouted from the ladder. Seminary priests had been executed often enough now to have destroyed the novelty of it for the mob; why, three had been done to death here little more than two months ago in this very place. They gave no sport, certainly; they died too quietly; and what peculiar interest there was in it lay in the contemplation of the fact that it was for religion that they died. Gentlemen, too, had been hanged here now and then—polished persons, dressed in their best, who took off their outer clothes carefully, and in one or two cases had handed them to a servant; gentlemen with whom the sheriff shook hands before the end, who eyed the mob imperturbably or affected even not to be aware of the presence of the vulgar. But this hanging was sublime.

First, he was a Derbyshire man, a seminary priest and a gentleman—three points. Yet this was no more than the groundwork of his surpassing interest. For, next, he had been racked beyond belief. It was for three days before his sentence that Mr. Topcliffe himself had dealt with him. Of course, young Mr. Audrey had not been on the rack for the whole of every day. But he had been in the rack-house eight or nine hours on the first day, four the second, and six or seven the third. And he had not answered one single question differently from the manner in which he had answered it before ever he had been on the rack at all. (There was a dim sense of pride with regard to this in many Derbyshire minds. A Derbyshire man, it appeared, was more than a match for even a Londoner and a sworn servant of her Grace.) It was said that Mr. Audrey would have to be helped up the ladder, even though he had not been racked for a whole week since his sentence.

Next, the trial itself had been full of interest. A Papist priest was, of course, fair game. But this Papisher had hit back and given sport. He had flatly refused to be caught, though the questions were swift and subtle enough to catch any clerk. Certainly he had not denied that he was a priest; but he had said that that was what the Crown must prove: he was not there as a witness, he had said, but as a prisoner; he had even entreated them to respect their own legal dignities! But there had been a number of things against him, and even if none of these had been proved, still, the mere sum of them was enough; there could be no smoke without fire, said the proverb-quoters. It was alleged that he had been privy to the plot against the Queen (the plot of young Mr. Babington, who had sold his house down there a week or two only before his arrest); he had denied this, but he had allowed that he had spoken with her Grace immediately after the plot; and this was a highly suspicious circumstance: if he allowed so much as this, the rest might be safely presumed. Again, it was said that he had had part in attempts to free the Queen of the Scots, even from Fotheringay itself; and had been in the castle court with a number of armed servants, at the very time of her execution. Again, if he allowed that he had been present, even though he denied the armed servants, the rest might be presumed. Finally, since he was a priest, and had seen her Grace at a time when there was no chaplain allowed to her, it was certain that he must have ministered their Popish superstitions to her, and this was neither denied nor affirmed: he had said to this that they had yet to prove him a priest at all. The very spectacle of the trial, too, had been remarkable; for, first, there was the extraordinary appearance of the prisoner, bent double like an old man, with the face of a dead one, though he could not be above thirty years old at the very most; and then there was the unusual number of magistrates present in court besides the judges, and my lord Shrewsbury himself, who had presided at the racking. It was one of my lord's men, too, that had helped to identify the prisoner.

But the supreme interest lay in even more startling circumstances: in the history of Mistress Manners, who was present through the trial with Mr. Biddell the lawyer, and who had obtained at least two interviews with the prisoner, one before the torture and the other after sentence. It was in Mistress Manners' house at Booth's Edge that the priest had been taken; and it was freely rumoured that although Mr. Audrey had once been betrothed to her, yet that she had released and sent him herself to Rheims, and all to end like this. And yet she could bear to come and see him again; and, it was said, would be present somewhere in the crowd even at his death.

Finally, the tale of how the priest had been taken by his own father—old Mr. Audrey of Matstead—him that was now lying sick in Mr. Columbell's house—this put the crown on all the rest. A hundred rumours flew this way and that: one said that the old man had known nothing of his son's presence in the country, but had thought him to be still in foreign parts. Another, that he knew him to be in England, but not that he was in the county; a third, that he knew very well who it was in the house he went to search, and had searched it and taken him on purpose to set his own loyalty beyond question. Opinions differed as to the propriety of such an action....

So then the great crowd of heads—men from all the countryside, from farms and far-off cottages and the wild hills, mingling with the townsfolk—this crowd, broken up into levels and patches by river and houses and lanes, moved to and fro in the October sunshine, and sent up, with the column of smoke that eddied out from beneath the bubbling tar-cauldron by the gallows, a continual murmur of talking, like the sound of slow-moving wheels of great carts.

II

HE felt dazed and blind, yet with a kind of lightness too as he came out of the gaol-gate into that packed mass of faces, held back by guards from the open space where the horse and the hurdle waited. A dozen persons or so were within the guards; he knew several of them by sight; two or three were magistrates; another was an officer; two were ministers with their Bibles.

It is hard to say whether he were afraid. Fear was there, indeed— he knew well enough that in his case, at any rate, the execution would be done as the law ordered; that he would be cut down before he had time to die, and that the butchery would be done on him while he would still be conscious of it. Death, too, was fearful, in any case.... Yet there were so many other things to occupy him—there was the exhilarating knowledge that he was to die for his faith and nothing else; for they had offered him his life if he would go to church; and they had proved nothing as to any complicity of his in any plot, and how could they, since there was none? There was the pain of his tormented body to occupy him; a pain that had passed from the acute localized agonies of snapped sinews and wrenched joints into one vast physical misery that soaked his whole body as in a flood; a pain that never ceased; of which he dreamed darkly, as a hungry man dreams of food which he cannot eat, to which he awoke again twenty times a night as to a companion nearer to him than the thoughts with which he attempted to distract himself. This pain, at least, would have an end presently. Again, there was an intermittent curiosity as to how and what would befall his flying soul when the butchery was done. "To sup in Heaven" was a phrase used by one of his predecessors on the threshold of death.... For what did that stand? ...And at other times there had been no curiosity, but an acquiescence in old childish images. Heaven at such times appeared to him as a summer garden, with pavilions, and running water and the song of birds…a garden where he would lie at ease at last from his torn body and that feverish mind, which was all that his pain had left to him; where Mary went, gracious and motherly, with her virgins about her; where the Crucified Lamb of God would talk with him as a man talks with his friend, and allow him to lie at the Pierced Feet…where the glory of God rested like eternal sunlight on all that was there; on the River of Life, and the wood of the trees that are for the healing of all hurts.

And, last of all, there was a confused medley of more human thoughts that concerned persons other than himself. He could not remember all the persons clearly; their names and their faces came and went. Marjorie, his father, Mr. John FitzHerbert and Mr. Anthony, who had been allowed to come and see him; Dick Sampson, who had come in with Marjorie the second time and had kissed his hands. One thing at least he remembered clearly as he stood here, and that was how he had bidden Mistress Manners, even now, not to go overseas and become a nun, as she had wished, but rather to continue her work in Derbyshire, if she could.

So then he stood, bent double on two sticks, blinking and peering out at the faces, wondering whether it was a roar of anger or welcome or compassion that had broken out at his apparition, and smiling— smiling piteously, not of deliberation, but because the muscles of his mouth so moved, and he could not contract them again.

He understood presently that he was to lie down on the hurdle, with his head to the horses' heels.

This was a great business, to be undertaken with care. He gave his two sticks to a man, and took his arm. Then he kneeled, clinging to the arm as a child to a swimmer's in a rough sea, and sank gently down. But he could not straighten his legs, so they allowed him to lie half sideways, and tied him so. It was amazingly uncomfortable, and, before he was settled, twice the sweat suddenly poured from his face as he found some new channel of pain in his body.…

An order or two were issued in a loud, shouting voice; there was a great confusion and scuffling, and the crack of a whip. Then, with a jerk that tore his whole being, he was flicked from his place; the pain swelled and swelled till there seemed no more room for it in all God's world; and he closed his eyes so as not to see the house-roofs and the faces, and the sky whirl about in that mad jigging dance....

After that he knew very little of the journey. For the most part his eyes were tight closed; he sobbed aloud half a dozen times as the hurdle lifted and dropped over rough places in the road. Two or three times he opened his eyes to see what the sounds signified, especially a loud, bellowing voice almost in his ear that cried texts of Scripture at him.

"*We have but one Mediator between God and man, the Man Christ Jesus....*"

"*We then, being justified by faith... For if by the works of the Law we are justified....*"

He opened his eyes wide at that, and there was the face of one of the ministers bobbing against the sky, flushed and breathless, yet indomitable, bawling aloud as he trotted along to keep pace with the horse.

Then he closed his eyes again. He knew that he, too, could bandy texts if that were what was required. Perhaps, if he were a better man and more mortified, he might be able to do so as the martyrs sometimes had done. But he could not...he would have a word to say presently perhaps, if it were permitted; but not now. His pain occupied him; he had to deal with that and keep back, if he could, those sobs that were wrenched from him now and again. He had made but a poor beginning in his journey, he thought; he must die more decently than that.

The end came unexpectedly, just when he thought he had gained his self-control again, so as to make no sound at any rate, the hurdle stopped. He clenched his teeth to meet the dreadful wrench with which it would move again; but it did not. Instead, there was a man down by him, untying his bonds. He lay quite still when they were undone; he did not know which limb to move first, and he dreaded to move any.

"Now then," said the voice, with a touch of compassion, he thought. He set his teeth, gripped the arm and raised himself—first to his knees, then to his feet, where he stood swaying. An indescribable roar ascended steadily on all sides; but he could see little of the crowd as yet. He was standing in a cleared space, held by guards. A couple of dozen persons stood here; three or four on horseback; and one of these he thought to be my lord Shrewsbury, but he was not sure, since his head was against the glare of the sun. He turned a little, still holding to the man's arm, and not knowing what to do, and saw a ladder behind him; he raised his eyes and saw that its head rested against the cross-beam of a single gallows, that a rope hung from this beam, and that a figure sitting astride of this cross-beam was busy with this rope. The shock of the sight cooled and nerved him; rather, it drew his attention all from himself.... He looked over again, and behind the gallows was a column of heavy smoke going up, and in the midst of the smoke a cauldron hung on a tripod. Beside the cauldron was a great stump of wood, with a chopper and a knife lying upon it.... He drew one long steady breath, expelled it again, and turned back to my lord Shrewsbury. As he turned, he saw him make a sign, and felt himself grasped from behind.

III

He reached at last with his hands the rung of the ladder on which the executioner's foot rested, hearing, as he went painfully up, the roar of voices wax to an incredible volume. It was impossible for any to speak so that he could hear, but he saw the hands above him in eloquent gesture, and understood that he was to turn round. He did so cautiously, grasping the man's foot, and so rested, half sitting on a rung, and holding it as well as he could with his two hands. Then he felt a rope pass round his wrists, drawing them closer together.... As he turned, the roar of voices died to a murmur; the murmur died to silence, and he understood and remembered. It was now the time to speak.... He gathered for the last time all his forces together. With the sudden silence, clearness came back to his mind, and he remembered word for word the little speech he had rehearsed so often during the last week. He had learned it by heart, fearful lest God should give him no words if he trusted to the moment, lest God should not see fit to give him even that interior consolation which was denied to so many of the saints—yet without which he could not speak from the heart. He had been right, he knew now: there was no religious consolation; he felt none of that strange heart-shaking ecstasy that had transfigured other deaths like his; he had none of the ready wit that Campion had showed. He saw nothing but the clear October sky above him, cut by the roofs fringed with heads (a skein of birds passed slowly over it as he raised his eyes); and, beneath, that irreckonable pavement of heads, motionless now as a cornfield in a still evening, one glimpse of the river—the river, he remembered even at this instant, that came down from Hathersage and Padley and his old home. But there was no open vision, such as he had half hoped to see, no unimaginable glories looming slowly through the veils in which God hides Himself on earth, no radiant face smiling into his own—only this arena of watching human faces turned up to his, waiting for his last sermon.... He thought he saw faces that he knew, though he lost them again as his eyes swept on—Mr. Barton, the old minister of Matstead; Dick; Mr. Bassett.... Their faces looked terrified.... However, this was not his affair now.

As he was about to speak he felt hands about his neck, and then the touch of a rope passed across his face. For an indescribable instant a terror seized on him; he closed his eyes and set his teeth. The spasm passed, and so soon as the hands were withdrawn again, he began:

"Good people"—(at the sound of his voice, high and broken, the silence became absolute. A thin crowing of a cock from far off in the country came like a thread and ceased)—"Good people: I die here as a Catholic man, for my priesthood, which I now confess before all the world." (A stir of heads and movements below distracted him. But he went on at once.) "There have been alleged against me crimes in which I had neither act nor part, against the life of her Grace and the peace of her dominions."

"Pray for her Grace," rang out a sharp voice below him.

"I will do so presently.... It is for that that I am said to die, in that

I took part in plots of which I knew nothing till all was done. Yet I was offered my life, if I would but conform and go to church; so you see very well—"

A storm of confused voices interrupted him. He could distinguish no sentence, so he waited till they ceased again.

"So you see very well," he cried, "for what it is that I die. It is for the Catholic faith—"

"Beat the drums! beat the drums!" cried a voice. There began a drumming; but a howl like a beast's surged up from the whole crowd. When it died again the drum was silent. He glanced down at my lord Shrewsbury and saw him whispering with an officer. Then he continued:

"It is for the Catholic faith, then, that I die—that which was once the faith of all England—and which, I pray, may be one day its faith again. In that have I lived, and in that will I die. And I pray God, further, that all who hear me today may have grace to take it as I do—as the true Christian religion (and none other)—revealed by our Saviour Christ."

The crowd was wholly quiet again now. My lord had finished his whispering, and was looking up. But the priest had made his little sermon, and thought that he had best pray aloud before his strength failed him. His knees were already shaking violently under him, and the sweat was pouring again from his face, not so much from the effort of his speech as from the pain which that effort caused him. It seemed that there was not one nerve in his body that was not in pain.

"I ask all Catholics, then, that hear me to join with me in prayer.... First, for Christ's Catholic Church throughout the world, for her peace and furtherance.... Next, for our England, for the conversion of all her children; and, above all, for her Grace, my Queen and yours, that God will bless and save her in this world, and her soul eternally in the next. For these and all other such matters I will beg all Catholics to join with me and to say the Our Father; and when I am in my agony to say yet another for my soul."

"*Our Father...*"

From the whole packed space the prayer rose up, in great and heavy waves of sound. There were cries of mockery three or four times, but each was suddenly cut off.... The waves of sound rolled round and ceased, and the silence was profound. The priest opened his eyes; closed them again. Then with a loud voice he began to cry:

"O Christ, as thine arms were extended—"

He stopped again, shaken even from that intense point of concentration to which he was forcing himself by the amazing sound that met his ears. He had heard, at the close of the *Our Father*, a noise which he could not interpret: but no more had happened. But now the whole world seemed screaming and swaying: he heard the trample of horses beneath him—voices in loud expostulation.

He opened his eyes; the clamour died again at the same instant.... For a moment his eyes wandered over the heads and up to the sky, to see if some vision.... Then he looked down....

Against the ladder on which he stood, a man's figure was writhing and embracing the rungs kneeling on the ground. He was strangely dressed, in some sort of a loose gown, in a tight silk night-cap, and his feet were bare. The man's head was dropped, and the priest could not see his face. He looked beyond for some explanation, and there stood, all alone, a girl in a hooded cloak, who raised her great eyes to his. As he looked down again the man's head had fallen back, and the face was staring up at him, so distorted with speechless entreaty, that even he, at first, did not recognise it....

Then he saw it to be his father, and understood enough, at least, to act as a priest for the last time.

He smiled a little, leaned his own head forward as from a cross, and spoke....

"*Te absolvo a peccatis tuis, in nomine Patris et Filii et Spiritus Sancti....*"

IV

HE only awoke once again, after the strangling and the darkness had passed. He could see nothing, nor hear, except a heavy murmuring noise, not unpleasant. But there was one last pain now into which all others had passed, keen and cold like water, and it was about his heart.

"O Christ—" he whispered, and so died.

CLUNY MEDIA

Designed by Fiona Cecile Clarke, the CLUNY MEDIA *logo depicts a monk at work in the scriptorium, with a cat sitting at his feet.*

The monk represents our mission to emulate the invaluable contributions of the monks of Cluny in preserving the libraries of the West, our strivings to know and love the truth.

The cat at the monk's feet is Pangur Bán, from the eponymous Irish poem of the 9th century. The anonymous poet compares his scholarly pursuit of truth with the cat's happy hunting of mice. The depiction of Pangur Bán is an homage to the work of the monks of Irish monasteries and a sign of the joy we at Cluny take in our trade.

"Messe ocus Pangur Bán,
cechtar nathar fria saindan:
bíth a menmasam fri seilgg,
mu memna céin im saincheirdd."